THIS TIME SAMANTHA WASN'T SO STARTLED BY SLOAN'S KISS

She melted into it slowly, balancing her hands against his solid chest and shoulders as he pulled her closer. The touch of his lips still had the ability to send her head spinning.

"Oh, God, don't," she whispered against his mouth when he came up for air, but she wasn't heeding her plea any more than he was.

Sloan Talbott wanted her. It was impossible to believe, but she could feel it in the way his hands clasped her waist beneath her coat, the way they pulled her closer, touching her, holding her. Samantha tasted it on his mouth, in the desperate heat of his kiss. His body couldn't lie.

Sloan convinced her, but Samantha was thoroughly shaken by the knowledge. She was feeling sensations that she'd never felt before, sensations that she knew weren't proper. She knew what was happening. She just didn't know how to stop it.

Denim and Lace

Patricia Rice

A TOPAZ BOOK

TOPAZ
Published by the Penguin Group
Penguin Books USA Inc., 375 Hudson Street,
New York, New York 10014, U.S.A.
Penguin Books Ltd, 27 Wrights Lane,
London W8 5TZ, England
Penguin Books Australia Ltd, Ringwood,
Victoria, Australia
Penguin Books Canada Ltd, 10 Alcorn Avenue,
Toronto, Ontario, Canada M4V 3B2
Penguin Books (N.Z.) Ltd, 182–190 Wairau Road,
Auckland 10, New Zealand

Penguin Books Ltd, Registered Offices:
Harmondsworth, Middlesex, England

First published by Topaz, an imprint of Dutton Signet,
a division of Penguin Books USA Inc.

First Printing, July, 1996
10 9 8 7 6 5 4 3 2 1

Chapter One

Sierra Mountains
October 1868

"**I** may have to kill him."

The words were horrifying, even though said in the most thoughtful tones a soft, feminine Tennessee accent could produce.

The wagon lurched over a rock, and the speaker hauled on the reins while her companion grabbed her bonnet and held on to the rough wooden seat.

The October air was pleasantly mild for this high in the Sierras, but the occupants of the wagon weren't aware of that. Too tired to admire the occasional flutter of a golden leaf as it blew by on the breeze, they had their eyes set on the swirl of gray smoke coming from just over the next hill. Two thousand miles they had come, and the end was near.

"You can't kill him, Samantha. They'd put you in jail and hang you, and then we would all starve. What would that solve?"

Sam smiled a trifle grimly. Leave it to Harriet to see things in a practical perspective. Her younger sister had the bright blue eyes and golden curls of a china doll, but she had the brain of a first-class merchant. If anything, Harriet's looks were her downfall. Had she been as homely as Samantha, she could have started her own mercantile store, and no one would have thought twice about it. As it was, men only laughed at her when she tried to persuade them she was more than qualified to run a store.

On the other hand, Sam was just as plain as they came, but she didn't have a penchant for sitting in a musty old store, counting pennies. She wanted to work the land, and she watched the plant life around her with more than just a casual interest. Her father had promised that the valley he had found would be temperate enough for good crops despite its location. He'd said the soil was rich and the water plentiful, a veritable treasure trove better than any gold or silver a man could want. Sam knew her father well enough to have her doubts, and those doubts grew by leaps and bounds at the sight of rocky soil and towering evergreens, but it was much too late to go back now.

"What am I supposed to do when I meet the man?" Sam returned to the subject, casting aside her concerns for the future for the worries of the present. "Ask him politely what he did to our father? Smile and tell him we haven't heard from our father since he threw him out of town? Demand he find Daddy or we'll call the law? From what I understand, this character is the law here."

Harriet gave Sam's drawn face a worried look. Two thousand miles had taken their toll on her sister. As the eldest, Sam had always been their father's favorite, the son he'd never had. She'd imitated everything her father had done since she was little more than a toddler, and she resembled him in more ways than anyone else in the family. She had always adopted a boy's attire and preferred the occupations of males to females, but after two thousand miles of acting as man of the family, Sam was actually beginning to look like a man. Her hands were callused from days hauling on the reins of recalcitrant oxen. Her always slender figure had slimmed to wiriness from riding her horse in search of game. No hat brim could keep the pounding sun from setting freckles running rampant across her nose and cheeks. And she'd cropped her hair short for ease of care. The red curls were growing out now, but they were the only real evidence that she might be other than a half-grown boy. That, and her voice. Samantha's sultry tones could be a trifle disconcerting coming from a redheaded tomboy wearing pants.

"Maybe someone has shot him already," Harriet said decisively. "A man like that is bound to be shot sooner or later. Then we can just find Daddy and tell him to come back."

Samantha sighed. She loved her father dearly, but she knew better than anyone that her father wouldn't be content to settle in a valley and raise crops and chickens. He had a wandering mind that kept him flitting from one project to another, always forsaking them as soon as the challenge was solved rather than carrying it through to riches. He might come back to visit if they settled here, but he would never stay. At least now they would be close enough for him to visit.

"There it is! There it is!" Twelve-year-old Jack galloped his pony ahead of the two wagons, sending up swirls of dust in his wake.

The dust worried Sam, too, but she tried not to think about this evidence of lack of rain as she gazed eagerly at the scattering of buildings in the road ahead. She sighed with relief that they were more than the shacks and tents she had seen in the mining towns. Good solid adobe had been used in the construction of these buildings, a certain sign of permanence. Her father hadn't been dreaming when he had chosen this town.

Jack galloped away, and Sam bit her lip in displeasure. Her Uncle William was supposed to have acted as head of the family when they joined the wagon train. A widower with a young son to raise, he had thought it a good idea to join his brother in California rather than suffer the aftermath of a war he'd never believed in. But William had died of cholera long before the wagons had reached the plains, and Jack had run wild ever since.

Conscious of Harriet's excitement and the eagerness of her mother and Harriet's twin, Bernadette, in the wagon behind them, Sam urged the weary beasts to a faster pace. As if sensing the end to this journey, they plodded obediently onward.

They had left the rest of the wagon train behind some days ago, following the directions from Emmanuel Neely's letter. This had to be their new home. If nothing else, their father gave excellent directions. He'd said the old Spanish mission town would be easy to find. He'd bought the deed to their house from the Spanish grandee who owned the original land grant after the church left. The description of their new home would have been sufficient to draw them out here without all the other factors that had induced their move.

The sun settled low on the horizon as they rattled down the hill. The wagons threw up clouds of dust, but the little town appeared serene and golden in the dying light. The hotel and trading post looked just as Emmanuel had described it: the lower half of adobe and shaded by a gallery on the wooden second floor. As Emmanuel had said, the town still looked like an old mission plaza. The hotel formed one side of the square. Stables, a blacksmith shop, and a harness-maker's establishment formed most of another side. Instead of a church, however, the third side held a lovely old home with sprawling porches and glass windows and trees forcing their way through the desolate dust of the front yard. That would be their home.

Nearly faint with relief that her father had actually found them decent accommodations, Sam took her time examining the rest of the town. She couldn't tell if the rest of the buildings on the plaza contained shops or residences, but most of them seemed solidly built with tile roofs and adobe foundations. A few wooden shacks were scattered in the streets off the plaza, but this was definitely not a mining town. She had seen enough of them as they had come over the mountains. Her father had written colorful letters describing some of the activities of the miners. Her gently bred mother had nearly expired at the words. She would have never survived in those crude surroundings.

As it was, Sam's father had been ominously silent on the subject of their new neighbors, except for that last letter mentioning his confrontation with Sloan Talbott. The man had to be a menace, even if her father's description hadn't confirmed it. Greedy, stingy, mean-tempered, and violent—Sloan Talbott didn't sound like the kind of acquaintance one looked forward to. But he was the only inhabitant of the town they knew anything about. He was the man Sam thought she might have to kill.

As the wagons rode slowly into the deserted plaza in a curtain of dust, a few people wandered into the daylight from cavernous, dark doorways to examine the novelty. After a sharp whistle or two, more came out to observe the sight.

Sam itched uneasily, watching the watchers from the

corners of her eyes. Every last filthy one of them was male.

Hideously conscious that they were four women and a boy, Sam donned her most menacing expression and shifted her gun belt forward where it could be seen. Pulling her hat over her face, she prayed that they thought she was a man. Seeing her in a loose checkered shirt and a leather vest, they shouldn't be able to tell much else—for the moment. She found the rifle at her foot and eased it closer.

Sam clenched her teeth at the sound of whistles and shouts. Bernadette must have her bonnet off. She cast a quick glance at Harriet, but as usual, the practical twin was examining their new home with an experienced eye and wasn't in the least aware of the attention they attracted. It must be nice to be so accustomed to attention that one could ignore it. Scowling, Sam looked for Jack as she halted the oxen in the shade of the town's only trees.

He was nowhere to be seen, but his pony was tied to the porch post. Men already sauntered across the plaza before the second wagon came to a halt. Grabbing her rifle, Sam jumped down and started back to her mother's wagon. If Harriet would step to it, she could be off the far side of the wagon and into the house before the men reached her. Sam's goal was to reach her mother and Bernadette before every man jack in town had them surrounded.

Cautious enough to see the danger, Alice Neely had already pulled her long skirts around her to climb from the wagon. Bernadette, however—despite her mother's warning—was dreamily admiring the shaded porch of their new home, as completely unaware of her swarming admirers as her twin.

"I'll get her in the house, Sam," Alice said, hurrying toward the lead oxen. "But there isn't any way we can keep them out. We're going to need their help to unload the wagons. Distract them with hard work and offers of payment, and I'll see what I can do."

Sam wasn't certain if the approaching men were the equivalent of man-eating Zulus or not, but her protective instincts were the same. At least back in Tennessee she had known the scores of admirers haunting their front room in hopes of some sight of the twins, and she had known their weaknesses well enough to keep them off balance. Ever since the Neelys had set out for California, however, it had been a constant battle. There had been women with the wagon train, but none of them quite like the twins. And once they all reached California, there seemed a dearth of females in every town they passed. Miners waved bags of gold at them in hopes of drawing the twins' attention. Less scrupulous men had crept up at night and tried to carry them off. Sam had every right to be wary of this crowd of breeches-wearing rattlers coming at them now.

Sam glared at the crowd and held her rifle across her chest. They stared back with all the interest of curious puppies. What appeared to be the town drunk still had his whiskey bottle in hand as he politely ran his palm over his vest to clean it off before offering it for a handshake. He was short and wiry and had a hank of sandy hair hanging over his face—and a gun belt slung dangerously over his narrow hips.

Sam ignored him and turned her glare and her rifle to the next man who dared get too close. He towered over her with a grim expression to match her own, but she detected an odd gleam of satisfaction in his eyes as he stared back.

"Sloan ain't going to like this one bit," he announced without preamble, before adding, "welcome to Talbott." He might have added more, but a swift inspection of the red-haired creature confronting him left him doubting the proper form of address.

Before Sam could reply, another man staggered forward, this one elderly, stooped, and squat, but with the distinctive long tresses of an Indian. A face weathered to the brown wrinkles of a walnut shell stared back at her, and Sam found herself eye-to-eye with the wisdom and pain of the ages. He grunted something noncommittal before heading toward her cattle.

Sam didn't like Indians around her cattle. She had gained enough experience in this trip to know that Indians and cattle had a tendency to depart in the same direction, and that direction wasn't her own.

She turned to call a halt, when an ominous rumble began at the rear of the house and migrated forward until the entire town shook with the impact of an explosion that sent a spiral of smoke and dirt straight up into the air.

"Jefferson Neely!" Samantha screamed, before sprinting in the direction of the house and the billowing smoke.

Chapter Two

The tall man who had greeted them grabbed a shovel and ran after Samantha. The others scattered in search of equivalent tools as the first flash of fire shot into the air. Sam nearly fell in the dust as she slid around the back corner of the house, but righted herself in time to see bits of flaming paper fly upward, threatening the wooden porch of their new home.

"Jefferson Neely!" she screamed again as she discovered her cousin just where she expected him to be—right at the center of trouble.

A blackened ring of smoke circled his face around his spectacles, but he didn't look the least deterred by the chaos around him. Not until Samantha grabbed his earlobe and jerked him backward out of danger did he look in the least repentant.

The tall man shoveled a mound of dust on the already dying flames. Other men ran to join him, waving pickaxes and shovels of every degree of repair. The noticeable absence of water to douse the flames made Sam's heart plunge a little further. What had they got themselves into now?

Refusing to give in to her fears, Sam jerked her cousin around to face her. "What in blue blazes did you think you were doing?"

"Owww! Sam, let go of me! I didn't do nothing." Jack wiped at his chubby face with the back of his dirty sleeve. "I just wanted to celebrate with fireworks like Dad did last Fourth of July."

Samantha tried to harden her heart as she grabbed his shirt collar and shook him, but she heard the cry behind the defensiveness, and she couldn't give him the punishment he deserved. He had probably been saving that gun-powder all across the country to use as a celebration when they finally arrived. That would be just like something his father would have done. And not knowing how to do it properly, but experimenting anyway, would be just like his uncle. The Neelys were known for their curiosity, but never for their caution.

"He needs a man to tan his hide," the tall man offered as he wiped sweat from his brow and came forward. "Dr. Cal Ramsey, at your service, ma'am." He held out his hand in introduction.

Samantha sighed. Her disguise had worked for as long as it had taken her to open her mouth. Praying this was a man she could trust, she took the offered hand and shook it. "Samantha Neely, sir, and this is my cousin, Jack."

The others were already crowding around, offering names, making welcoming noises, and looking her over as if she were a prized heifer. When men even took to looking at her, she knew they were desperate. She tried not to glance at the house where her mother had kept the twins hidden, despite the excitement. She had the uneasy feeling that this town wasn't going to have a lot of women to call on for help.

"We didn't mean to stir up such excitement upon arrival, gentlemen." Sam leapt into a lull in the conversation. At the sound of her voice, they all fell silent. Unnerved by this rapt attention, she tried to politely send them away. "We thank you, but it's getting late, and we need to unpack. If there's any of you who could lend a hand unloading some of our things, we'd be happy to pay."

She had scarcely got all the words out of her mouth before several of the younger men peeled off from the crowd and loped toward the wagons. A voice from the remaining crowd cried out, "Do you cook, ma'am?"

Flustered by their continued stares, Samantha resorted to a spurt of temper. "Of course I cook. Do I look helpless?"

Ramsey stepped in to smooth ruffled feathers. "He means we don't really need to be paid to help, but there isn't a one of us who wouldn't appreciate a home-cooked meal."

Oh, Lord. Sam's heart fell to her stomach as she glanced nervously toward the house. They all meant to help. Her mother would die of exhaustion just trying to keep the twins away from them. Drawing a deep breath, she tried again. "Well, we'd be mighty glad to oblige, but our supplies are a little low . . ."

That statement wasn't even out of her mouth before men were yelling, "I've got chickens!" "There's flour at the trading post!" "I've been saving those tinned peaches!" And before she could comment, they were off and running.

It looked like the payment for unloading two wagons was to feed the entire town.

"I don't think you ought to go out there just yet, Samantha," Alice Neely protested as she made biscuits from some of the supplies left over from the prior night's meal. "They all seem friendly enough, but you don't know what will happen if you go out there alone."

Sam knew her mother's real worries without her saying them aloud. Emmanuel Neely's enthusiastic letters had come to a grinding halt the day he left this place. Chances were very good that he never left here alive. If someone in this town had killed him, would that someone hold the same grudge against the entire Neely family?

It didn't seem likely, but death came so easily out here that it seemed safest to hide from it. Samantha felt the ache of her father's absence, but he had been gone from as much of her life as he had been in it, so she could hide the ache well. She wasn't the dreamer that her father was. She was a provider, and she meant to provide.

"I'll take a gun belt and a rifle. It isn't likely anyone will bother me. And I suspect it's too early yet for any of them to be up and about. I'll be back before they have time to besiege the house, I promise."

Alice smiled faintly. "Dr. Ramsey seemed like a gentleman. He seemed quite smitten with you."

Uneasy with the thought that someone had been watching her when she hadn't known it, Sam shifted from foot to foot, waiting to make her escape. "He doesn't look like any doctor I've ever met."

"Men are different out here. We'll get used to it, I'm sure."

Men were the same everywhere, and she would never get used to it, but Samantha nodded obediently and made her escape. Men and thoughts of men made her uncomfortable, but she would feel fine once she was in the saddle with a rifle in her hand. She didn't have to think about men and their sly looks and knowing touches when she was wandering the woods in the early dawn. She could pretend the only living things on God's earth were the birds singing in the trees and the rabbits she meant to have for supper.

The sun took a long time rising over the mountains, but Sam was content to weave her mount through needle-strewn paths and smell the air. This was her idea of heaven, and she hesitated to disturb it with an explosion of gunfire. Maybe she could meet some Indians who would teach her to use bows and arrows. Somehow, that seemed a much more civilized manner of hunting in these pristine woods.

So lost in her thoughts was she that she almost didn't see the shadow darting from tree to tree near the clearing ahead. When she did take notice, she narrowed her eyes. No animal she knew moved with such furtive clumsiness. It had to be a man.

Gripping her rifle carefully, Sam eased her horse off the path and closer to the clearing. Whatever the man watched was in that direction. Perhaps he'd found a pond and ducks. She hadn't had roast duck in a long while. Mouth watering at the thought, she climbed down and tied the horse to a tree, then hid behind a massive evergreen at the clearing's edge.

Disappointment at not finding a pond almost distracted her from the scene unfolding before her. She knew the other hunter was poised and ready to strike just beyond that other stand of trees. But the only animal to be seen was a horse with a saddle on its back, taking water from a meager stream. These mountains had too much game for any sane man to want to eat horse.

She was a second too late in realizing another man stood on the far side of that horse. Screaming a warning, Sam aimed her rifle in the direction of the furtive shadow, but her target fired first.

The horse whinnied in terror, rising up on its hind legs, and crashing down again. Sam sent a bullet winging toward the hidden assailant before he could fire again. The man at the stream got off one shot before he staggered backward, but his attacker had already disappeared. To Sam's horror she could see the man at the stream drop to his knees and lose his grip on his gun while his horse reared and kicked over him.

Without thinking, she flew into the open clearing. The horse was wild-eyed and prancing too near to the place where the man had gone down. Snorting through red-edged nostrils, it towered over her, tossing its tangled mane. A bigger, meaner-looking stallion she'd never encountered, and it didn't appear to be half-broke. A horse like that could trample a man and never know the difference.

Catching the horse's reins, Sam stood back, murmuring the soothing words she had learned at her father's knee. She was no stranger to horses. Her father had raised some of the best horses in the country before he decided he'd done his job and needed something new to do. The stallion jerked in fear, trying to free itself, but she gentled it with words and touches until it stood shivering but still.

Then she looked for the wounded man.

He was on his knees and struggling to rise, but blood seeped through his fingers from the wound in his shoulder. He was the biggest man she'd ever had the misfortune to come across, or perhaps just the idea of being this close and needing to help him exaggerated his size. Whatever it was, it made her heart squeeze into her throat and block her breathing as she crouched down beside him.

"Put your arm around me. We've got to get you into the saddle."

Eyes of icy gray and muddied with pain turned to study her with contempt. Her eyes were almost on a level with his when she kneeled beside him, giving some indication of her height. But she was slender, no bigger than a gangly youth, and his expression conveyed his opinion of her offer. "I'll manage. Just go back to where you came from."

Shocked at his rudeness, Sam thought she really ought to do just that. Perhaps she ought to shove him over and make him work a little harder just for the meanness of it. But it wasn't in her nature to ignore the injured or hurt the helpless. Smiling unpleasantly, she grabbed the handkerchief he was pulling from his pocket and applied it firmly to the wound.

"I can see why they took a shot at you. Hold that tight so it doesn't bleed so much." Without asking, she grabbed his good arm and hauled it around her shoulders to help him stand.

He was heavy; there was no getting around that. She staggered as his weight shifted to her shoulders when they stood up. She thought he might be deliberately giving her all his weight until she glanced up to see his eyes closed against the pain. He couldn't bend his wounded arm to hold the cloth to it, and blood poured down the sleeve of his dark shirt.

The amount of blood made her waver, but the cynical flicker of his eyelids as she hesitated straightened Sam's spine. "I can't get you into that saddle. Is there any place close I can take you until I can get help?"

He gave her a wary look. Even wearing her usual checkered shirt and vest, it was evident up close that she wasn't a boy. Sam waited as he took in this fact and nodded slowly. She breathed a sigh of relief that he no longer rejected her help.

"Cabin up the path. I can make it."

Sure, and hell had tulips, but Sam didn't mouth that sentiment out loud. Wishing she'd had the sense to bind the wound before she'd lifted him, she moved her feet in the direction indicated. Tending the wounded had always been her mother's job. She didn't have much experience at it.

Concentrating on the task ahead, neither of them spoke as they staggered up the dusty path into the pine woods. If the gunman was still around, they would make splendid targets, but he had obviously run at the first sign of a wit-

ness. That was *one* thing in her favor, Sam counted as she
shuffled along with the stranger's heavy weight across her
shoulders. She couldn't think of any others to count right
off hand. Not crumpling to the ground might make
number two.

Muttering to herself in this manner, she managed to
distance herself enough from the task to reach the cabin.
It wasn't more than a collection of split logs, but it offered shelter of sorts. It hadn't seemed quite humane to
leave the man lying on the ground while she went for
help.

He collapsed on a low-lying pallet strung to the walls.
He'd closed his eyes again, and the dark shock of curls
falling across his forehead made his skin seem pale.
Nervously, Sam pulled the handkerchief from his dangling hand and tried to apply it to the gaping hole in his
shoulder, but blood had matted the shirt and his skin, and
she couldn't be certain what she was doing.

"I've got to get help. I don't know what to do." She
didn't even have a petticoat to rip up and use for bandages. What did men use when caught unprepared? Their
shirts. Flushing at that thought, she glanced around helplessly for likely clothes.

"Get my shirt off. Use the clean side to wrap it." His
words were more a moan than a order, but the effect was
the same.

Setting her teeth, Sam ripped at the buttons of his shirt,
surprised at the expensive black cambric beneath her fingers, but distracted by the amount of man revealed when
the buttons popped open.

Her father was the only man she'd ever seen partially
undressed, and this man looked nothing like her father.
Dark hair curled on a broad chest that appeared made of
steel for all that it was tanned a burnished brown. A ripple of pain moved through the muscles beneath her hand
as she pulled at the shirt, and she nearly jerked her hand
away in fear.

This would work a whole lot better if she could close
her eyes. Taking a deep breath, she peeled the shirt off his
good arm. If she could only tear it off his back, it might
be easy, but this was good cloth and not easily torn.

"You're going to have to sit up. I can't get this off you otherwise."

He didn't waste breath on words, but used his good arm to prop himself up, allowing her to pull the shirt around him. When it reached the matted blood on his shoulder, he cursed, and Sam halted.

Dropping back to the pallet, he opened his eyes and gave her a look of disgust, then grabbed the shirt from her hands. With a single rip he tore the shirt from the wound and off his other arm.

"There's a knife in my boot. Cut the shirt in half and wrap it tight around my shoulder. That should stop the bleeding."

If it wasn't obvious that he was fighting unconsciousness, Sam would have told him what he could do with his knife. She didn't take orders easily, and she certainly didn't take them from men who looked at her as if she were little more than a mindless lump of lead. But he apparently knew what he was doing, and she didn't, so she took his words and applied them to action.

He grunted with pain when she had to move him to get the shirt around his shoulder, but he clenched his teeth and kept silent as she tied the shirt and pulled it as tightly as she could manage around the padding of his handkerchief.

"That'll do. Ride back and get Injun Joe. Give him a pot of coffee before he comes up here. He'll take care of the rest."

Sam looked doubtful. It was obvious the stranger was about to pass out from pain and loss of blood. What he needed was a doctor and not an Indian medicine man. "Injun Joe? The old Indian? He doesn't look like he can ride. Why don't I get Dr. Ramsey?"

The man grimaced. "Ramsey won't come. The old Indian is Chief Coyote." He pronounced the word Ki-oat. "Coyote can tell you where to find Joe."

Sam wasn't going to argue with a man in the process of bleeding to death. Without a word she ran out of the cabin and toward the horses waiting in the clearing below.

Her patient lay breathing heavily into the silence the patter of her departing feet left behind. He didn't know who the hell she was or what kind of woman wore pants, but he would remember that anxious look in stunning blue eyes for the rest of his days. It had been a long time since anyone had looked at him with anything resembling concern, and he knew full well that those eyes would never look the same at him again once she reached town.

As the pain came to claim him, he savored the picture of riotous red curls and young breasts pressed against thin gingham. Maybe they were making women different these days. He'd have to live to find out.

Chapter Three

"The only man likely to be out there at this time of day is Sloan Talbott. What did he look like?"

She had obviously woke the doctor from a hangover. His face was unshaven, and he wore only a wool undershirt over a pair of pants he had hastily donned and hadn't fastened. He rubbed at eyes bleary from lack of sleep and shoved a hank of hair out of his face. Samantha strived to keep her patience. "He's bigger than you, with dark, curly hair. What does that matter? He's going to bleed to death unless someone helps him." She tried not to think about the hated name the doctor had mentioned. She couldn't hate a man who was very likely dying. She couldn't even think straight with the urgency of the situation.

"That's Talbott. Let him die. The world will be a better place." Without further explanation, Ramsey shut the door in her face.

Samantha stared at the closed door with incredulity. People didn't behave like that where she came from. She pounded on the door futilely for a full minute before giving in to the realization that he wasn't coming back.

She could haul him out of there at gunpoint, but the journey here hadn't hardened her to that extent. A man held at gunpoint wasn't likely to be very helpful in any case.

Sloan Talbott. Damn, but she should have known. Mean, hateful, wretched excuse for a human being that he obviously was, she still couldn't let him just die like that. If she meant to kill him, she wanted him to know why.

Furious, scared, Sam ran across the plaza to her mother. She didn't even know where to find Chief Coyote or Injun Joe, and neither one of them seemed likely candidates for healing.

A few minutes later, she was staring at her mother with equal incredulity. "Me? You want me to go back there? What am I going to do?"

"Whatever is necessary. I'll give you some supplies and send Jefferson out to find your Indian or whatever. If he needs to have coffee poured into him, it's going to be a while before he can get up there. It doesn't sound like the man can last that long."

"But you know how to do these things. I don't. Let me find Chief Coyote while you go tend to him."

"I don't know where he is, and you know I don't ride. This is the only way. Get a basket while I get some bandages."

Lord God in Heaven please help and guide her because she was going to need every ounce of strength and patience she possessed to go back up there again. Samantha prayed with every terse instruction and new medicine added to the basket. She might tend a lame horse or help birth a new calf, but she had never tended to a human being before, and particularly not one as big and mean and ornery as this one. She would rather face the gunman in the woods than her patient.

But within minutes she was riding out with her basket of supplies tied to the saddle and her rifle in her hand. She would take great pleasure in shooting at anyone who might interfere in hopes that it might be the sneaking bastard who had gotten her into this mess. And if she didn't find the bastard, she just might shoot the man in the cabin and put him out of his misery.

He had looked at her as if she were lower than a worm in an apple. He had talked to her as though she were a bumbling idiot. He hadn't shown the slightest iota of gratitude for her aid. From what she understood, he ought to be grateful that she had even bothered to try and warn him. She could have just let the gunman kill him.

Muttering to herself, Sam battened down her courage until she was angry enough to face the miserable wretch when she reached the cabin. The prospect of opening the door and finding him dead was a trifle daunting, but she would never know by standing outside.

Kicking open the door with her foot and keeping her hands firmly on her rifle and basket of supplies, she carefully scanned the interior before entering. The room was too small to hide anyone. Propping a boot stand against the door to hold it open and give her light, she approached the bed.

He looked to be asleep. A beard heavier than the doctor's shaded his jaw. She could see now that his hair was more brown than black, but it was curlier and shaggier than her own. She grinned at that. She hated her curls, but at least women were supposed to have curls. She bet he took a lot of ribbing for his.

The bleeding seemed to have stopped, but her mother had said it would start again when she removed the bandage. It seemed to her it would make sense to leave the bandage on instead of disturbing it, but there was more than likely dirt in the wound, and it had to be cleaned. She glanced nervously at his back. Her mother had said she ought to find a hole behind his shoulder where the bullet came out, and if she didn't, the bullet would have to be removed. She didn't see a second hole, but the shirt might cover it.

She tried to unwrap the makeshift bandage as gently as possible, but when she pulled it away, he groaned and opened his eyes.

"Where's Injun Joe?" Pain laced his words, but they came out as cantankerous as he intended.

"Jack's gone to look for him. I didn't think it wise to leave this untended until he could get here."

That was unarguable. Grimacing, he lay back against the bed. "You can't cut the bullet out. Just douse it with alcohol and tie it back again."

One thing you didn't say to a Neely was "can't." The last time Sam had heard that word, she'd tied and roped a cow faster than the half-wit who had said she couldn't. And heaven only knew, their house had been littered with the inventions her father had created when he'd been told things like he couldn't pump hot water into a sink or churn butter without hands. No Neely turned down a challenge.

"You want to drink this before I use it?" Samantha handed him the full bottle of whiskey with one hand while producing a scalpel from her basket with the other.

Sloan looked at the scalpel, up at the red-haired madwoman, then reached for the bottle. He drained a goodly portion of the liquid in a few gulps and handed it back to her.

"Do you know what you're doing?"

"Nope." Cheerfully, Sam stuck the scalpel into the whiskey bottle and swished the instrument around as her mother had told her to do. She was beginning to enjoy this game now that she knew him as the man who had driven her father out of town.

He looked obligingly furious at her good humor, but saved his breath for important things. "Have you got anything in there to pack the wound? You'll not see a blamed thing when I'm bleeding like a stuck pig."

He'd downed a quarter of a bottle of good Kentucky bourbon, and his words weren't even slurred. That ought to tell her something about what kind of man this was. Her daddy didn't approve of drinking, and she was inclined to believe he was right, but this man could use some pickling to soften him.

She found the cotton batting her mother had said to use and showed it to him. Her patient nodded approvingly.

Under Talbott's directions, Sam slowly cut into the wound and packed it. She rather thought patients ought to be screaming with pain rather than giving orders to their doctors, but Talbott wasn't screaming, and he seemed to know what to do when she certainly didn't. Not only did she not know what to do, she was terrified from the moment she set scalpel to skin. Sam considered screaming for him.

She tried to tell herself that cutting through flesh wasn't any different than skinning a squirrel, but that didn't relieve her nausea when she felt the first squirt of blood. Squirrels were at least dead before she skinned them. And they didn't have arms like steel bands to wrap around her to hold her steady. And they didn't clench their teeth and keep back groans of agony while directing their skinning.

She was ready to weep before the scalpel finally disturbed something hard, and Talbott finally screamed and blacked out on her. After that, the tears ran freely down her cheeks while she pried the bullet loose. Blood ran everywhere. She could scarcely see to tell what she was doing. But she could feel the damned bullet and knew it had to come out. She was a Neely. She could do it.

Remembering just in time to douse the tweezers with alcohol, she entered the wound one more time, grasped the bullet, and jerked.

It wasn't any worse than pulling a splinter, after all. That didn't stop the tears running down her face. She brushed them off on her shirtsleeve and wished she could remember what her mother and Talbott had said about cleaning and packing the wound. There was more blood here than she'd ever seen out of a hog at butchering time.

The even rise and fall of his chest gave her some comfort. She kind of liked the looks of his bare chest. It was rounded and hard where it was broadest, not like the flat chests of the men she knew. And his stomach rippled with ridges like a washboard. She thought that odd, but she couldn't help following the whorls of hair to his navel. It gave her something to think about while she worked.

She tried not to think much beyond that. The arm he had gripped her with had fallen when he passed out, and she didn't have its strength to rely on anymore. She'd always thought of her father as strong, but she could see that she didn't know anything about such things after experiencing Talbott's grip. Once he got hold of her, she'd never get free until he was ready to let her go. She didn't think any of her tricks would force him to release a hold. He was a walking steel trap.

Not walking at the moment, of course. That relieved some of her anxieties, but produced others. She had the bleeding stopped and the wound cleaned and bandaged, but he was still unconscious and Injun Joe hadn't appeared. What did she do now?

She waited. She watched the rise and fall of his chest a little while. That began to make her feel itchy, and she ran out to the stream and brought back water to wash herself. His eyes remained closed, but he was jerking nervously. She bathed his forehead, and he relaxed again.

He had a massive jaw beneath the cover of his beard. She could imagine him biting her finger off with one click of his teeth. His nose had been broken at some point. There was a slight hump where it had healed crookedly. Heavy dark eyebrows accentuated a face that wasn't made to look pleasant. But in sleep, he looked relatively serene. She found a small nick beside his mouth and smiled. Had he given up shaving because of that?

To her relief, she heard the sound of a horse coming up the path. Picking up her rifle, she stood back from the doorway and glanced outside.

The drunken gunslinger from yesterday rode up the road, his back painfully straight as he tried to remain upright. He'd cleaned up pretty good. Even his hair looked as if it had been dunked and combed back. It was apparent that he was in as much pain as her patient, however, only not for the same reasons.

As he drew abreast of the cabin, the gunman made an attempt at a gallant bow and nearly fell from the horse. With a shrug, he slid down and watched her rifle through reddened eyes. He hadn't shaved in days either. Men away from women apparently didn't bother with such niceties, Sam observed. His sandy beard and thinning long hair were laced with gray, but she had no clue to his age as he spoke.

"My good woman, I could shoot that weapon from your fingers before you knew what happened. Would you kindly turn it away?"

Samantha nearly laughed, but something in his eyes kept her from doing so. She politely turned the rifle toward the floor. Injun Joe wasn't any taller than she, and he was more wiry than broad. She could knock him flat if she wanted. It was a good thing for him that she didn't want to.

"Do I address you as Mr. Joe?"

He relaxed, and a wry smile almost made him handsome as he replied, "Just Joe will be more than adequate.

Your mother is a fine woman. Coffee like hers has to be made in heaven."

Well then, he was at least partially sober. Samantha stepped aside and beckoned him to enter. "I've removed the bullet and patched him up, but he's out like a light."

"I am not. You can go now."

The voice seemed to belch from the bowels of hell. Samantha scowled and contemplated kicking his bed, but she'd been brought up better than that. She must be getting used to his wretched behavior, for she only replied, "I'm gone, Your Highness. Don't bother to thank me."

And she was out the door before he could do so—or not, which was more likely.

After the woman left, Sloan heard Joe's disapproving silence and attacked first. "What in hell is a woman doing in town? Can't I leave the place for a few days without it erupting in chaos?"

"Ain't just one woman, but four of them, lookers every one. The one that just left is the plainest of the lot." Joe's practiced grammar slipped immediately into the vernacular with the absence of the female.

Sloan bit back a groan. If that virago who had just left was the plainest, then the others had to be more beautiful than mortals were allowed. Such things weren't possible. Joe must have been drunk when he saw them. Joe was always drunk.

"She's not plain," was the only reply he made.

"She's got freckles all over her face." Enjoying himself for a change, Joe pulled up a chair and didn't bother removing his medicinal whiskey from his pocket.

"I didn't notice. What's her name?"

Joe might be a drunk, but he wasn't a fool. He gave the simple answer. "Sam. That hair of hers is redder than a sunset."

Sam. Sloan studied that briefly. It gave him something to do besides notice the pain. "Samantha," he finally decided. "No man would name his daughter Sam. And her hair isn't red. It's richer than that. Too much gold for auburn, though. Wonder what women call it?"

"Red." Grinning hugely, Joe propped his feet on the

bed and leaned his chair back. "Want me to drive them off?"

"I'll help you, just as soon as I'm back on my feet."

That wasn't what he wanted to hear. Joe gave the bed a vicious kick and reached for his whiskey, ignoring Sloan's wince of pain. "I don't know why I stay with you. I could go to San Francisco where there's a world of women."

"Because I pay you, that's why."

And as if that were the final word on any subject, Sloan closed his eyes and firmly refused to be drawn out again.

Chapter Four

"**Y**ou took the bullet out all by yourself?" Jack's eyes went wide as saucers behind his wire-framed glasses as he gazed at his taciturn cousin. As female cousins went, she wasn't half bad, but he wished she were a boy.

"Yeah." Sam brushed a stray curl from her face and continued to clean her rifle. It had been nearly twenty-four hours since she had left that monster in his cabin, and she hadn't heard a word. It didn't sit well with her to leave a job undone. But he had ordered her out. She couldn't go where she wasn't wanted.

Jack munched on a licorice stick. "The men down at the saloon say he's a real bear. They're taking bets on if he'll die and when."

Sam shot her young cousin a sharp look. "What were you doing at the saloon?"

He shrugged innocently. "All the men hang out at the saloon. It's great. They're going to teach me to play billiards."

Oh, Lord, give her strength. They had come to a town with nothing but men, and every man jack of them was a bad example. Drunks and gamblers and billiard players. No wonder there wasn't a church in town. What in the world had possessed her father to buy this property?

"Don't any of these men have anything better to do than hang around the saloon all day?" she asked grumpily, snapping the rifle back together again.

"They only hang out there at night, when there's nothing to do. A lot of them work for Talbott. He owns the lumber mill and the smithy and the hotel and everything. He's got a logging operation and a mine back up the mountain somewhere. And he has cattle and sheep and hogs. Some of the others do, too. They work." Jack defended his newfound friends vehemently.

Sure they did. That's why they had time to hang around the front porch and wait for the twins to come out. That's why there was always one of them at the door, wanting to know if they could help out around the house. They worked all right. At whatever they wanted to, whenever they got around to it. Men were like that.

She threw a look over her shoulder as her mother came out the back door, drying her hands on her apron. They both glanced at the cloudless blue sky, but said nothing. The rain barrels were empty, and the only well appeared to be the one in the plaza. They needed Emmanuel to invent a pump or dig a well or do a rain dance. Running water was a luxury they had grown accustomed to.

"I reckon you'd better go check on your patient, Samantha." Alice sat down in a cane chair and picked up a potato from the basket one of the men had left the night before. She produced a paring knife from her apron pocket and began to peel.

Samantha had no real inclination to join her in peeling potatoes, but she wasn't inclined to visiting the sick, either—especially not grumpy bears. "He told me to go away. And it probably isn't proper for me to call on a man like that."

"He's had time to turn up feverish, and I doubt that Joe stayed up all night drinking coffee. I think the proprieties can be waived in this case. A man's life is at stake."

From the sounds of it, the man's life wasn't worth much, but Sam knew that tone of voice. There wasn't much point in arguing with her mother when she sounded like that.

"I'll take Jack with me, keep him out of trouble. What am I supposed to do if he's feverish?"

Half an hour later, she and Jack were riding out of town with a basket of nourishing broths and medicines. Alice Neely should have been a physician. She had a need to heal and a talent for doing so that men like Dr. Ramsey would never possess. Unfortunately, Alice Neely was a woman and society expected her to stay home and take care of a family. It had never even occurred to her that she could do anything else.

But it had occurred to Sam. A lot of things had occurred to Sam that she should never have pursued further. But looking and acting like a man had given her a different perspective on life than most women, and she wouldn't ever be as malleable as the twins or her mother. She had made that vow a dozen years ago when she had been told she couldn't attend the horse sales and the accompanying races because she was a girl. She had attended, all right, and her horse had brought a fat purse after she'd sneaked in as a jockey and ran it to first place. Her father had never told her she couldn't after that, but other men weren't quite so understanding.

At twenty-four, she faced the fact that she would never marry. She wasn't particularly concerned. With a father who wandered, she had a ready-made family to look after. She liked being her own boss. That men still treated her as a helpless female frustrated her, but she had learned how to deal with it, often with a humor that turned the tables. Being cut out of male activities made her angriest because she was helpless to do anything about it. She couldn't go where she wasn't wanted, and it had become obvious a long time ago that they didn't want her.

Not being able to join the men after dinner to discuss politics wasn't quite the same as being told to get out of a man's cabin, but the distinction was a nicety that eluded Sam. If men didn't want her, she didn't need them. She was perfectly fine on her own. She rather thought the man in the cabin had the same idea. But her mother's word was law, and she would obey.

Injun Joe's horse was still tethered in the lean-to outside the cabin. That meant he either managed to get along with the curmudgeon all night or had passed out drunk. Sam wasn't reassured by either possibility. Anybody who could get along with a mean-tempered bear wasn't quite right in the head.

Knocking, she received no answer. That didn't bode well. Easing the door open, she allowed light to penetrate the dark interior. No sound greeted her. Taking a deep breath, she pushed the door wide and stepped inside. A knife whizzed past her head and thumped loudly into the wooden door frame.

Sam froze, then turned an outraged look to the unrepentant man upon the bed. "You knew I was out there. There was no call for that."

Talbott gave her an icy glare. "You weren't invited."

Even Jack hesitated to enter at this reception. He stood behind Sam and peered around her warily. Too furious to care, Sam grabbed the knife hilt and jerked it out of the frame. Brandishing it in one hand and clenching her basket in the other, she approached the bed. She could see Injun Joe wiping sleep from his blurred eyes in the corner, but the empty bottle beside his pallet said all that was necessary. He wasn't going to interfere.

"A Neely doesn't leave a job undone. If you're feverish, you've got to have medicine. And if you're not, you've got to have food. And in either case, the wound needs tending. You're going to have to get better before I can kill you proper."

The name "Neely" brought a flicker of something to his eyes, but it was gone in an instant when Sam dug the knife into the bandage around Talbott's shoulder and cut through it with a single swipe. He yelped as she tore it loose, but held his tongue as she examined the wound for any signs of infection.

"You might live. I daresay there's a number of people around these parts who won't thank me for it." Sam reached for a fresh bottle of liquor to use on the wound.

She still wore her low-crowned straw hat as if she meant to leave at any moment, but the burnished curls that escaped around her cheeks and forehead and nape glistened in the sunlight coming through the door. Sloan watched with grudging fascination—until he became aware that her top shirt button had come undone.

That was even better. He could surreptitiously watch for the motion that would give him a glance at her bare breast, because he knew damned good and well she didn't wear anything beneath that coarse cotton. The way the material clung to her told him that.

He held his breath as she applied the alcohol and cleaned the wound. She was doing a fine job. He didn't

need to instruct her. If he could just get her to shift a little
more to the right . . .

A shot shattered the silence of the close confines of the
cabin. Sam shrieked and jumped backward and almost
lost her grip on the bottle. Sloan grabbed for the pistol
hidden beneath his blanket. Injun Joe just looked green
and staggered to the doorway to empty the contents of his
stomach in the yard.

That reaction brought Sam to her senses. Grimly
swinging in the direction of her young cousin, she caught
him blowing smoke from the barrel of his father's Colt.
"Jefferson Jackson Neely, I'm going to shove that thing
down your throat if you *ever* pull a fool trick like that
again!"

"There was a whopper of a rat sneaking in under that
log. I was just getting rid of him for you." Defiantly, Jack
holstered the gun and crossed his arms over his chest in
a gesture vaguely reminiscent of his father when he was
up to something. "Besides, that bastard was trying to look
down your shirt."

Sam gasped, turned beet red, and swung back to glare
at her unabashed patient. For once, she was speechless.

Sloan appreciated that fact. He had half a mind to grin
at her astonished expression, but he merely shrugged his
uninjured shoulder and met her gaze coolly. "A man can't
help seeing what's right before his eyes."

She would have to kill him. That's all there was to it.
But first she meant to horsewhip him through the middle
of town. Something of that thought must have appeared in
her expression. Sloan grabbed the bandage from her hand
and gestured at the door.

"There's the way out. Joe will put this on for me."

"Oh, no, you're not going to get off that easy." Sam
wasn't normally a mean-spirited person, but she had just
discovered she possessed a weapon that she could wield
against this man without fear of retribution. He was helpless and hated it. And she meant to rub it in. "You're going to lie right there and let me fix that bandage, and then
you're going to finish every bit of this broth my mother
made if I have to shove it down your throat. I said I'd
look after you, and I mean to keep my word."

Fastening every button on her shirt until it was closed tight around the collar, Sam smiled widely at his scowl and set about her task.

Injun Joe leaned against the door frame and watched this performance with dazed awareness. No man ever stood up to Sloan Talbott. No God-respecting woman ever came into his vicinity more than once. That skinny woman was asking for disaster. But when Talbott just lay there and let her do her damage, Joe shrugged and turned a watery glare on the boy scouring the cabin for more targets.

"Come here, boy. We've got water to fetch." He staggered out without waiting to see if his orders were followed.

Jack gave his cousin a quick glance, decided she was still engaged in a battle of wills with Talbott, and gladly took the excuse to escape.

"I want meat. I don't want any of that stinkin' broth." With the bandage tied, Sloan shoved his way to a sitting position, concealing the agony it cost him. The rough cabin wall was the only support he could find, and he leaned against it, safely putting himself out of the madwoman's reach unless she meant to crawl up on the bed to get him.

Sam liked him better flat on his back. When he sat like that, the bronzed bands of muscle on his chest and the bulge of his biceps reminded her that he was half naked. She ought to be grateful that he still wore his trousers.

"You'll have the broth or I'll pour it on you," she purred sweetly. Continuing in a syrupy drawl, she added, "I shot those squirrels myself. They're a might tough for eatin', maybe, but they make a fine broth."

The shock of that deliberately sultry voice shot right through Sloan. He had been so busy admiring her curls and trying to get a look at her chest that he hadn't really listened. Besides, she'd been harping and nagging and yelling, and even if it came out as sweet as syrup, it wasn't the same as this tone. She did this on purpose. He would swear to it.

He gave her a suspicious glare, but she only smiled innocently, her bright blue eyes a reminder of the anxiety he had seen there earlier. He held out his good arm. "Give it to me. I'll feed myself."

"The last time I did that for Jack, he threw the bowl at me. Now you wouldn't be thinkin' of doin' that, would you now?"

He had, but if Jack were that criminal demon in here earlier, he wouldn't be lowered to the same level. Sloan smiled unpleasantly. "Now do I look like the sort of man who would do something like that? I've got better plans for you."

Her mother had tied the lid to the bowl with a towel so the broth wouldn't slosh too much. Sam had managed to get it unfastened, but the temptation was more than she could stand. Letting the towel and the lid slip from her hands, she splashed some of the still warm liquid across his bare belly.

Sloan yowled and reached to knock the bowl from her hands, but the pain in his shoulder jerked him back again. Clenching the bandage, he glared at her. "You're enjoying this, aren't you?"

"Evidently, so are you, or you wouldn't continue to behave like a wet cat just to annoy me. I didn't come here for the fun of it, you realize. I have better things to do with my time."

"Like what? Punching cattle?" Sloan gave her denims a disdainful look as he reached for the bowl she handed him.

"Like finding enough meat to salt away to keep my family from going hungry all winter." Sam handed him the bowl and spoon and stepped out of throwing range.

He had some difficulty balancing the bowl with his bad arm and eating with his left hand, but he managed it. He threw her a veiled look that held a hint of triumph. After a few awkward spoonfuls, however, he gave up and drank directly from the bowl.

He was unbathed, unshaven, and his hair was a disgraceful tangle, but he still managed to make the act of sipping broth from a bowl a matter of elegance. She couldn't imagine him cleaned up, but she could see him sipping tea from a porcelain cup without disgracing himself. Sloan Talbott was a dangerous man in more ways than one.

He gave her another glance when he drained the bowl. "You'll not have time to salt anything until you get down out of the mountain. I'd recommend you start moving on before the snow flies."

Maliciously, she contemplated leaving the biscuits and ham in the basket and having them for lunch. But he still had some funny idea that he was in charge here. She meant to disillusion him.

Producing the covered pan of mouth-watering biscuits, Sam held it in her palm, took the lid off, and helped herself. Daintily wiping the corner of her mouth while he glared at her, she waited until the bite was completely chewed before deigning to reply.

"We're not going anywhere, Mr. Talbott. The house is ours and we intend to stay." She donned an expression of concern as his brows pulled together in a black line of fury. "You look a bit peevish, sir. I do believe the excess of exercise has been bad for you. I'll just put these away for another time. Why don't you lie down and get some rest?"

Covering the pan, she started to return it to the basket. A hairy hand wrapped around her wrist with a band of steel.

"I'm feeling just fine. It's you who look a little pale. Let me relieve you of that burden." Sloan grabbed the pan from her hands at the cost of another shooting pain of agony that didn't stop at his shoulder, but swept right through his middle until he had to bite his lip to keep from screaming. It was worth every ounce of pain to see her astonishment at his maneuver as he sat back against the wall again, this time with the pan of biscuits in his lap.

"You underestimate me, Miss Neely," he continued conversationally. "I'll be back in town tomorrow. If you're not gone by then, I'll help you pack. I don't allow women in my town. I won't let you wait around to find out why."

Sam wanted to slap that self-satisfied expression off his face, but she had to remember he was an injured man.

She would take care of him soon enough. She had just the whip she meant to use.

"You underestimate a Neely, Mr. Talbott," she answered serenely. "If we condescend to lend you our presence, you won't have anything to say about it."

She swept out as if she wore satins and lace and feathers in her hair.

Sloan stared after her, sure he was hallucinating. She was no more than a ragtag redheaded tomboy with a voice like honey and a tongue of vinegar. The sudden departure of light when she left the room just meant the sun had gone behind a cloud.

Any more of that voice of hers, and she would have him believing in witches.

Chapter Five

"They're living where?" The words were more a shout of incredulity than a question as Sloan glared at his drunken bodyguard.

Joe shrugged and grabbed a rein before the movement could throw him off his horse. "In that big house on the plaza that's been empty since we got here. I thought maybe you meant to save it for your bride."

"Bride? Are you out of your ever-lovin' . . ." The string of epithets that followed was not entirely coherent, but covered Joe's present incapacity and ranged to his ancestors before diverting to the castigation of women as a whole.

Joe didn't look impressed. "They moved in two whole wagon loads of things and dismantled the canvas rigging. They're here to stay."

"Over my dead body." Giving a wince as his body reminded him that time might be sooner than expected, Sloan urged his stallion to a faster pace. He couldn't leave the damn place for two minutes without trouble starting.

"Does that mean I need to sober up and start doing my duty?" Joe studied the half-empty bottle in his hand with regret.

"Against a bunch of women? You think I can't handle a bunch of women on my own? Maybe that rotgut finally got to your brain."

Not in the least insulted, Joe took another gulp and tucked the bottle back into his saddlebag. "If you could handle women, you wouldn't mind them moving in. Nope. I reckon it's time I dried out for a spell. You're going to need me."

Sloan snorted. "Suit yourself." Then urging his mount to a gallop that strained his shoulder to the limits, he raced into town. Those women would be out of town before sunset.

"Those women" were doing laundry in the back yard with the help of every man in town. Vats of water bubbled over a giant fire from which barrels of sudsy water and rinsing pans were constantly replenished by a stream of male water carriers. Sheets already flapped in the brisk breeze off the mountain while more men struggled to hang ropes for the rest of the loads. From the mounds of laundry left, it was apparent that this joint effort was instigated by shared needs. The women needed someone to do the heavy work, and the men needed their laundry done.

Within the discreet shade of the sagging wagon shed, one of the twins washed female undergarments and hung them out of sight of hungry male eyes. The wind through the cracks would have to dry the delicate linens without the help of the sun. Although she kept her back to the activity outside, preventing anyone from seeing through the open door, more than one man strained his eyes to see around her. Whispers ran rampant as the men speculated on the silks and laces that might now be adorning the old shed walls. It had been a long time since any of them had seen silks and laces.

The other twin stayed out of sight in the kitchen, stirring up smells that had mouths watering before the sun even reached its zenith. A basket of apples had appeared on the porch one morning, and the scent of baking pie could be distinctly discerned from the savory odor of stewing meat.

It was into this scene that Sloan rode. He'd stopped at the hotel to wash and change and rest a spell, until his shoulder stopped throbbing, but he wanted to give the women plenty of time to start packing. If the wagons were packed by nightfall, they could move out in the morning.

The sight of laundry flapping in the breeze and men

swarming across the yard warned that his task might not
be so easily accomplished as he had hoped.

Avoiding the activity in the back, Sloan stalked through
the front door without knocking. The house had been
empty for as long as he had known it, a haven for dust
and spiders and rodents. The sight of it newly swept clean
and decorated with shaded lamps and velvet-covered
chairs did nothing to improve his humor.

Entering the kitchen, where he hoped to find the
woman of the house, he startled a vision in green dimity
and a starched apron. A golden halo of curls around an
angelic face was caught at the nape in a ribbon before
cascading down her back. She took one look at Sloan and
screamed so loud he feared the adobe would shake loose
from the rafters.

The scream shook him slightly. Women didn't generally scream when he came in sight, especially since he'd
taken care to shave and clean up. But as she backed up
against the far door, Sloan began to enjoy the position. He
crossed his arms over his chest and glared as viciously as
he could manage.

"Mama! Samantha!" The screams echoed out the windows and through the room as she held her ladle out like
a weapon. "Keep away from me!"

Sloan leaned against the door frame and growled maliciously, "What are you going to do, shoot me with stew?"

She was pretty in her confusion, but he liked the next
sight that appeared better.

Samantha came racing through the doorway, rifle in
hand, red curls bouncing, freckled nose pink from heat
and exertion. She wasn't confused, she was furious, and it
took only one glimpse of him for her to turn the rifle in
his direction.

Sloan didn't shift his position. He didn't doubt that she
knew how to use that thing; he was just confident she
wouldn't. Women were like that. But the crowd of men
forming behind her was another matter entirely. They all
owed him, but he wouldn't count on calling in their debts
right now.

"What in hell do you think you're doing to my sister?"
Sam stepped in front of Bernadette, blocking her from

Sloan, but not from the crowd of men behind them. She wanted to swear out loud. She wanted to tell Bernie to check to see if their mother had gone to protect Harriet. And she wanted to slap the man before her silly. Unable to do everything at once, she settled for aiming the rifle at his crotch.

"Put that blamed thing down before you hurt someone," he answered crossly. "That make has a hair trigger, and I've done nothing to sing soprano for. If that screaming banshee is your sister, I just startled her a mite."

Sam moved the rifle a fraction so it aimed closer to the wall behind him. "Where I come from, people knock before entering."

"Where I come from, people don't have to knock at their own doors. This is my house, and you're all trespassing."

Sam heard Bernie's gasp behind her. The men remained silent, but she knew they'd heard. They'd probably known all along. That didn't change the facts. "If this is the town of Talbott, and this is the Alvarez hacienda on the plaza, you're lying, and I want you out of here now, *Mister* Talbott. We have the deed in our possession."

He didn't know what the hell the Alvarez hacienda might be, but Sloan knew what he owned and what he didn't. Straightening, he stepped closer to the termagant with the big mouth. She really did have a big mouth, he noticed. Full, generous lips spread across a face as delicately made as some of his mother's finest porcelain. Somehow, the incongruous combination worked with this woman.

"And I own the land grant for this entire side of the mountain. Whatever you have is a worthless piece of paper. This is my town, my mountain, and women aren't welcome here. I'll give you until sundown tomorrow to get out."

The men outside were murmuring angrily. Samantha felt a sinking sensation in her stomach that she had known before, but she wasn't about to let anyone else know it. Her father didn't always spend a lot of time on details. He believed the best of everyone. Sometimes it worked; sometimes it didn't. She had a sneaking suspicion this was one of those times that it hadn't, but she couldn't let anyone else know that. They had come two thousand miles to settle in this home. She wasn't going to let a mean-spirited, ill-tempered bully of a man send them out into the cold world, homeless. She wouldn't think about his claim to the entire side of the mountain. Maybe her valley wasn't on his part of the mountain.

"I don't know anything about land grants, Mr. Talbott. I just know we have the deed to this house. I'll hold my deed up to your grant in court anytime. You just tell us where to find the judge."

She had him there. So far he'd been judge, sheriff, and town council all in one, but even with Sloan's lack of legal knowledge, he knew that a judge couldn't rule on his own case. He wouldn't let that deter him, however.

He smiled unpleasantly. "The nearest judge is probably down in Sacramento. You're free to go look for him if you like. But in the meantime, I'm moving all this crap out into the street. I'd recommend that you take it with you."

"You and who else, Talbott?" Ramsey shoved his way in from the back porch. He hadn't been one of those helping with the laundry, but he'd sensed the change in the mood of the crowd from his office. He'd come in time to hear this last.

Sloan gave the doctor a look of contempt. "If need be, I'll do it alone. I'm not asking for any help from anybody."

Deciding it was time to see what the fuss was all about, Mrs. Neely hurried through the path the doctor had made, confident that Harriet was safe with Jack for the moment. Bernadette ran to her side as soon as she entered, and she gave the girl a hug as she examined the tall man standing off an entire town. She didn't need to see the sling around his arm to know who he was.

"Mr. Talbott! We finally get a chance to meet. Come in, sit down. You really aren't well enough to be on your feet already." She pulled out a kitchen chair and shoved it in his direction, then glided toward the stew pot hanging over the fire. Even after a morning over laundry tubs, she appeared cool and crisp. Tendrils of hair curled about her face, and she didn't wear the usual number of petticoats, but to men who hadn't seen real ladies in years, she appeared the epitome of all the proper females they had left behind.

Talbott hesitated a moment too long. Before he could object, the woman was handing him a bowl of stew and pushing him down into the chair. He could have let her drop the stew. He could have shoved her back. But he had never in his life treated a woman like that, and he wasn't prepared to start with this one. He sat.

Samantha stared in amazement as her mother bustled about, fussing over napkins and biscuits and jam and sending someone out to bring back whatever Talbott favored from the saloon. Sam had threatened the man with a rifle, and he had laughed. Her mother had done nothing but hand him food, and he crumpled. There was a lesson in this, but it wasn't one she was prepared to learn.

Stalking out, carrying her rifle with her, Sam left the two of them to fight it out. A few of the men followed to help her with the remaining laundry, but most lingered on the porch where her mother and Bernadette were apparently in the first stages of feeding the masses.

Injun Joe waited at the big vat, staring into the swirling water of clothes with a blank expression. When Sam approached, he looked up and asked without curiosity, "Did he scare you off yet?"

Now that he was cleaned up and partially sober, Sam could guess his age to be about the same as her father's. A scattering of gray threaded through his sandy hair, but his eyes seemed older. She could tell he didn't have an ounce of Indian in him, but she'd wager he'd lived a hard life longer than she'd been on this earth. She answered him with a degree of respect she hadn't shown Talbott.

"I daresay mother will scare him off first. What does he have against women?"

Joe didn't smile. "If there were a whole town full of them, he probably wouldn't care one way or another. But there aren't enough of you to go around, and that's going to cause trouble. I thought your father was brighter than that."

"You know my father? Do you know where he went?" Sam couldn't keep the eagerness from her voice.

Joe's face instantly closed. "Met him, if his name's Neely. Don't know anything else."

He walked off in the direction of the hotel tavern.

Samantha wanted to throw something at him. Frustration practically steamed out her ears, and men were at the bottom of it. She was going to have to do something or crack under the pressure. She'd give anything if Sloan Talbott would just walk out of that house right now. She'd have him down on the ground faster than he knew what hit him.

Unable to unleash her frustration in violence, she sauntered over to the shed and Harriet.

Harriet had long since finished her laundering and was engaged in an energetic game of poker with Jack that involved some rather complicated twists that Samantha didn't wish to question. When Jack won the round with a handful of unrelated cards and had to stand on his hands for reward, Samantha gave into their laughter and forgot about Talbott. Temporarily.

Sloan hadn't forgotten about her. While the determined Alice Neely bombarded him with food and the ethereally lovely Bernadette fluttered around him with graciousness, he concentrated his thoughts on the redheaded witch with the rifle. She had left him in this menagerie, knowing full well he wouldn't be able to escape without insulting her family and infuriating the entire population. The other damned idiots around here might not know what these women were doing, but he wasn't blind. One way or another the women would have to go.

Tomorrow he would figure out how to get rid of them.

Chapter Six

Tomorrow came and brought with it the first of the winter rains. Sloan sat on the gallery above the tavern, smoking a cheroot and contemplating the gray downpour rapidly turning the streets to running rivers of mud. It was not the most auspicious day to turn a passel of women into the cold.

But the notion of allowing the women to stay trapped all winter in this town full of men bored from lack of anything constructive to do did not sit well with him. It might serve the women right, but despite all appearances, he wasn't a vindictive man. For their own good, he had to get them out of here.

Matters might have been a little safer had he allowed the usual whores to take up residence, but he'd turned them all back down the mountain at gunpoint. Since his wife had made it clear that he couldn't differentiate between ladies and whores, he'd decided ten years ago that he could do without the entire female gender. Nothing he'd seen since had changed his mind any.

The men wouldn't appreciate his turning the women away, but they despised him anyway. A man didn't get where he wanted to go by being liked. He got there by getting things done. For the last ten years Sloan had been getting things done, and he was coming to like it. There were times when he still wished things could have been different, but he could live with them the way they were. He didn't need those women disrupting what he'd built here. That's all women were good for—causing trouble. He'd had his fair share of trouble, and he didn't need any more of their kind of grief.

"You're no good at sneaking anymore, Joe," he called

over his shoulder to the man coming lightly up the stairs behind him. "Just keep your shooting arm straight."

"You weren't this much of a bastard when you first came out here." Joe leaned against the wooden railing and crossed his arms over his chest as he stared at his employer. "Women must make you mean."

"Women will make any man mean, given time. That's not what I called you up here for. Have you been keeping an eye out for strangers like I asked?"

Joe gave him a look of disgust. "I may be a drunk, but I'm not blind. There ain't been anybody through here that you don't know about."

"If that's the truth, then it's someone here who shot me." Sloan threw the cheroot stub into the muddy stream flowing beneath the gallery.

"I can understand that. The men want those women to stay, and some of them might get nasty enough to take exception if you throw them out. That's just on top of the usual run of things. Ramsey hates your guts on general principles. The miners think you don't pay them their fair share. Graham is still sore 'cause you broke his head in that last fight. The list goes on, as if I had to tell you."

"Guess you and Coyote are the only ones around here that haven't got a grievance against me. It's nice to be loved." Sloan propped his boots on the railing and didn't look in the least concerned. "But they've all hated me before and never taken shots at me. If the women are the only new arrivals, then it must be related to them."

"You don't think one of them did it, do you?" Joe's usual taciturn expression faded almost to incredulity.

"That redheaded witch might have if she'd known who I was; she might yet. But no, they didn't know anything about me then; I'd just about swear to that. How long had they been in town before I knew about it?"

"They came in the evening before you got shot. We helped them unload, and they didn't once mention your name. Neither did anyone else that I know of."

"Well, the redhead was out with a rifle first thing the next morning, but that doesn't mean anything. If she hadn't yelled, I wouldn't be here now."

"I daresay she's regretting it." Joe glanced over his

shoulder at the house across the plaza. "Don't see anybody preparing to move."

"They can't stay here. You know that." Without saying
more, Sloan swung his boots down and stood up. The
topic was no longer under discussion.

Making his way down the covered outside stairs overlooking the kitchen courtyard behind the hotel, Sloan
spied a shadow of movement near the garden wall and
halted. He had learned caution in his first days out here,
and he had cultivated it with a passion ever since. Moving
shadows where there should be none were meant for in-
vestigation.

Figuring if he could see only shadows, they couldn't
see him any better, he hurried down the stairs and into his
office on the left. From there he strode through the hotel
lobby, the smoking parlor, the dining room, and turned
right into the corridor leading to the kitchen. Not that one
could call it much of a kitchen. The last cook had heard
about a mountain made of silver and went in search of it.
The only cooking that got done here now was what Coyote did, and that didn't need a stove.

Sloan refused to think about the steamy potatoes and
tender meat he'd eaten at the Neelys the day before. He'd
survived on roasted squirrels before. He didn't need good
cooking now. If he did, he'd find a new cook. There were
bound to be a few around 'Frisco the next time he went
there.

The movement he had seen had been just around the
corner of the storage shed on the far side of the kitchen.
Moving cautiously now, Sloan peered through the narrow
apertures of the kitchen corridor and tried to see into the
rain-drenched courtyard. He couldn't imagine anyone lingering for long in that downpour. Seeing nothing, he
crossed to the kitchen door and listened carefully to the
sounds from the other side.

He could hear the noise of metal scraping against
stone. Someone was definitely out there.

Releasing his arm from the sling, Sloan pulled the
knife from his boot with his good hand and held his gun
in the other. He wouldn't let whoever was out to get him
catch him napping this time.

He kicked the door open and caught the shadow of movement long enough to pinpoint his target. With a grin of enjoyment, he flung the knife with enough strength and accuracy to pin his victim to the wall by the tail of his shirt.

Jack screamed and held his hands up against the wall. "Don't shoot me! Don't shoot me. I didn't hurt nothin'. Honest!"

Glancing down at the hole in the earthen floor that was rapidly filling with water, Sloan was of another opinion about that. He glared at the terrified twelve-year-old and pointed at the damage. "You call that nothing? What in hell did you think you were doing?"

Jack snapped his mouth shut and didn't answer.

Sloan stepped closer. "You'd better answer me, boy, or you'll go back to your mama with one ear missing." The fact that his knife was in the wall beside the boy didn't seem to detract from his threat. The boy turned refreshingly pale beneath his tan.

"She ain't my mama. She's my aunt. And Sam will come and get you if you hurt me. Don't think she won't."

"And don't think I won't be waiting for her." Aware that the scar at the side of his mouth gave him a rather menacing smile, Sloan smiled.

Jack tore at the knife hilt in his eagerness to escape.

Sloan slapped his boot on the shirttail, holding the boy to the wall as he jerked the knife from its resting place and palmed it. "Are you going to tell me what you were doing, or do you want to choose which ear you want to lose?"

"Digging. Sir." Jack visibly gulped at the sight of the knife.

"I can see that." Sloan kept his voice placid. The kid was likely to faint if he terrorized him anymore. "Why were you digging?"

Rebellion flickered in the boy's eyes, but the knife's forward movement quenched it. "They said you have buckets of gold hidden in here. That spot was soft."

Sloan almost chuckled. Almost. The boy had thought to become wealthy by digging in the easiest spot. That was typical of some of these dunderheads that came to make their fortunes in California. The boy was young yet. He would learn.

"If I had buckets of gold I wouldn't keep them where every damn man in this town could get at them. Do I look like a fool, boy? There isn't any gold here. The only gold that's to be had in these parts is buried so deep in these mountains you'd have to turn them inside out to find it. That's why the gold-seekers have moved on." He took his foot down and released the boy. "Now fill that hole back up and pound it down good before the place washes away."

"You've got a mine. I heard them say so." Free now, Jack was defiant once more.

"It's a quicksilver mine. You'd better start listening a little more closely and not go off half-cocked. Now get busy." Sloan gestured at the shovel.

Jack scowled, but did as told. He had little choice. Sloan stood right there until he'd finished.

"He did what?" Scandalized, every female in the house turned to stare at Jack as he ran into the house, soaked to the bone and covered with mud and late for lunch. His excuse was a solid one.

"He pinned me to the wall with his knife! A great big nasty old one with a bone handle and everything. I bet there was even blood still on it!"

Sam had seen the knife in question. It did have a bone handle, but it was small enough to fit in a boot. Still, the man didn't have any cause to terrify a little boy like that, not to mention endangering his life if that knife had gone wrong.

"What were you doing over there anyway?" she asked suspiciously.

Jack squirmed and reached for the heated towel Harriet handed him. His mutters were lost in the thickness of the cloth.

Samantha grabbed his collar with one hand and the towel with the other. Separating them, she repeated, "What were you doing over there?"

He gave Sam a defiant glance. "Looking for gold."

With a look of disgust, she handed him the towel and started for the door. "I'll be back in a little while."

"Samantha Neely, you can't go over there like that! I'm certain Mr. Talbott had his reasons," Alice called after her.

Sure he did, Sam muttered to herself as she grabbed her rifle and pulled a weather slicker over her head. He hated children as well as women. He probably hated everybody. Well, when she was through with him, he could hate all he wanted, but he would damned well leave all Neelys alone.

The road was a funnel of mud running from the mountain. Sam glared at it as if it had been personally created to annoy her. Then taking a deep breath, she stepped out into the mud and rain and started across the plaza toward the hotel.

She had reached the other side of the dead grass and weeds that represented the square and was about to plunge into the muddy street in front of the hotel and trading post when the lobby door opened and a man came flying across the porch, sliding on the wet stairs before landing on his bottom in the mud.

"Get your horse and get out now!" A menacingly tall but familiar figure filled the doorway, hands on hips as he glared at his victim in the street.

"I'll pay you as soon as I find that silver!" The figure in the mud propped himself up on his elbows and pleaded. "I've paid you before, haven't I?"

"Donner, if you haven't got it through your head yet, you're not ever going to get it through your head. You got to make money before you spend it. Now get out of here and find a real job." Sloan was about to turn back into the lobby when a drenched figure in a loose slicker came out of the downpour to help Donner up and to glare at Sloan as if he were a demon straight from hell. He lingered just to hear the sound of her voice.

"You can't throw a man out into the streets on a day like this. He could catch pneumonia. What kind of bas . . ." She amended her epithet hastily, "beast are you?"

Sloan hooked his thumbs in his pockets. "It's likely to

be snowing by nightfall. I was doing him a favor by doing it early."

"It's not as if your damned hotel is full of paying customers," Donner said angrily, getting up and trying to brush off the mud. "It's not hurting you any to let me stay."

"Just looking at your ugly face pains me," Sloan retorted. "You can be off the mountain by nightfall. Charm some silly woman down in the valley into taking you in."

"I'm going to get you for this, Talbott." Shaking off Samantha's helping hand, he started for the stables.

Up to her knees in mud with rain drenching every uncovered inch of her trousers, Sam caught the young man's arm. "If you can't find another place to stay, we've got a shed out back. There's no stove, but you can probably keep a fire going. It's dry, anyway."

"Thank you, ma'am." There was nothing ugly about the young man, who lifted his hat and gave her a short bow. He had a wide brow and a nice smile as he acknowledged her offer. "It's good to know there's still some decency in this world." He turned and gave a final glare to Talbott before stalking off.

Still warm and dry under the shelter of the overhanging gallery, Sloan leaned against the door frame and contemplated the drowned rat standing in the street. "Did you have more heartwarming words to say, Miss Neely?"

"You enjoy being a bastard, don't you? You like terrorizing little children and kicking a man when he's down. You're enjoying watching me stand here in the pouring rain and mud while you're all warm and dry up there on the porch. A decent man would have invited me in to get dry by now. But you're not a decent man, at all, are you?"

The question was obviously rhetorical. Sloan watched cautiously as she marched up the steps, dripping a trail of wet and mud across the planks. "I'd be happy to help you take off your wet clothes," he murmured sympathetically.

She was too angry to get any angrier at his suggestive phrase. Doffing her dripping slicker, Sam threw it in his face, slammed her heel behind his knees to throw him off balance, and shoved him in the direction of the street. Sloan grabbed a post before he could fall, but his sore shoulder protested the treatment. Before he could unwrap the slicker and grab for her, she shoved him from behind. This time, he went down.

He didn't go down easily or get very far, but he was using his hands to push himself out of the mud when Sam stepped daintily over him. "We'll discuss children and knives when you're in better shape, *Mister* Talbott," she murmured softly as she passed by.

Sloan contemplated grabbing her ankle and giving a good jerk, but his shoulder wasn't going to allow that just yet. As he pushed himself up and watched her sassy rear end swing across the plaza, he had a good mind what he would do when he got the chance. And Miss Tennessee Samantha wasn't going to like it one little bit.

Chapter Seven

"The kid's staying over in their wagon shed. Ramsey gave him an old stove to keep warm, and he's sleeping in one of the wagon beds to stay off the ground. He's sitting there now, carving firewood into totem poles." Joe threw himself into one of the wooden rockers lining the second-story gallery, propped his boots on the railing, and glared contentedly at the mud wallow of the street. If he wasn't drunk, he preferred to look at the world through a glare.

Sloan shifted his sore shoulder as he leaned against a post. "Totem poles?"

The question was an idle one, and Injun Joe didn't dignify it with an answer. His employer's thoughts had obviously strayed elsewhere. Since the objects of his malevolence were even now scrubbing the mud off their wide front porch, he didn't have to wonder what Sloan was thinking. Joe sighed and admired the sight of a gingham bow wrapped directly over a delightfully rounded derriere bent in cheerful labor. It was like watching Christmas packages at work.

And the man beside him wanted to get rid of them. Joe shook his head in disbelief. Employer or not, Sloan Talbott was purely demented.

Without a word Sloan straightened and disappeared down the corridor toward his private quarters. When Joe saw him next, he was emerging from the saloon, wearing frock coat, tie, and ruffled shirt. Joe immediately counted the women on the porch across the street. Three. There were only three of them. And the one missing was the one who counted.

Damn, he muttered to himself, glancing casually up

and down the street—not that he could go warn the termagant even if he saw her, but somebody ought to.

Across the street Sloan came to a halt before the eldest Neely. He should have addressed the mother from the beginning. He waited for her to stand up and acknowledge his presence before making his bows. She wiped her hands on her apron and regarded him thoughtfully as he did so.

"Mr. Talbott." She nodded in recognition. "The weather has improved, hasn't it? Would you care for a cup of coffee?"

"No, ma'am, this will take but a minute. I think there has been some misunderstanding on the part of you and your daughters, and I would like to correct it, if I might. As much as I appreciate the care you are taking of this property, the matter remains that it is mine and not yours. I believe under the circumstances that you would do better to continue on down the mountain for the winter. You could be in Sacramento in a day or two, or take a boat on to 'Frisco. Up here isn't any place for decent women."

"Decent women make their own places, Mr. Talbott," she answered calmly. She turned to the twins, who now watched with varying degrees of concern and wariness. "Go on in and start the coffee brewing, girls. I promised Mr. Donner a bite of lunch before he sets out. You might check on the roast."

When they were gone, she turned back to Talbott. "Mr. Donner is a charming young man, but I fear he is a bit of a dreamer. Someone needs to look after him."

"He's a lazy no-account, and if you start housing all the layabouts in this town, you'll go broke feeding them. There's men a-plenty who will take advantage of any sign of weakness."

"That may be your experience, Mr. Talbott, because you look through eyes blinded by bitterness. Try removing those blinders sometime. Mr. Donner is a very talented young man. He's just not a miner."

Sloan was about to take objection to this assessment when he realized what the woman was doing. She was stalling. And he was letting her. Before his astonishment faded, he had already realized it was too late. Samantha strode out the front door, rifle in hand.

Sloan gave the woman in front of him a wry look. She'd sent the twins after their sister as surely as his name wasn't Talbott, but he'd been too blinded by his respect for a decent woman to recognize the ploy. He'd been out of civilization too long if he'd forgotten the wiles of a woman. He deserved the comeuppance.

"Well, Mr. Talbott, come to nail little boys to the wall again today? Or have you devised new and more inventive methods of amusing yourself? Perhaps you'd like to scalp the twins or shove my mother into the street?"

Strangling was the pleasure he had in mind, Sloan decided as he turned to face this attack. He wanted his hands around that long, slender neck. He wanted to watch that mop of red hair tumble around her face when he shook her senseless. His glance fell to her open-necked white shirt, and he felt his mouth dry. He could see a hint of lace behind the linen, and his mind immediately drew an image of firm breasts pushing unfettered at that scrap of lace. He almost swallowed his tongue before he recovered his senses.

He returned his gaze to her face and reminded himself of Joe's words that she was plain. She had freckles. Her mouth was too wide for her face. But her lips were moist and rosy . . .

"I've given you and your mother ample warning, Miss Neely." He forced his voice to its most formidable, refusing to take up her sassy challenge. He'd terrorized men twice her size. It was time he applied his full strength instead of pussyfooting around. "If your wagons aren't loaded and ready to go by tomorrow morning, I'll have my men over here loading them for you. I want you out of here."

Samantha didn't cock the rifle; she merely moved it into a more threatening position. "Good luck, Mr. Talbott. No doubt you'll be able to find a few men willing to take money to throw us out, but you'll have to do it over the bodies of everyone else in town. I hate to see it come to a shoot-out, but I'll do whatever it takes to protect what's ours. This house is ours."

"It damn well is not!" He was losing his temper. He knew better than to lose his temper. Sloan took a deep breath and tried to find a reasonable solution. Hell, he didn't want to shoot at women. He hated women, distrusted them thoroughly, but he recognized their physical helplessness. Unfortunately, this redheaded brat didn't. She thought she was his equal.

"It damn well is too!" she yelled at him.

That was when the brilliance of the idea came to him. Sloan's smile took on a sinister aspect as he regarded her rifle thoughtfully. "Want to bet?" he asked casually.

That stopped her in her tracks. She looked at him as if he were crazed. Perhaps he was. But Sloan had gotten where he was by knowing how to manipulate people and situations. He knew damned well he'd have a war on his hands if he tried a physical show of strength against these women. Perhaps there was a better way.

She watched him warily. "What are you talking about?"

He gave her rifle a meaningful look. "You don't want a battle over this any more than I do. Someone might get hurt. So let's settle this like men, just between us."

Mrs. Neely gave an irate hiss. "Mr. Talbott! Samantha is a young lady. It's unfortunate that she dresses as she does—"

Sloan cut her off with the wave of his hand, keeping an eye on Sam. "How good are you with that thing?" His nod indicated the weapon in her hands. He recognized the make. An old Sharps—it was known for its deadly accuracy, but the single-shot action and primer cartridges had seen their day.

As she caught the drift of his thoughts, Sam began to smile. "Damned good, Mr. Talbott. Are you ready to get beat by a woman?"

"The idea of even competing with a woman is reprehensible enough, Miss Neely, but if that is the only way I can get you peacefully out of my town, I'll do it." He hated taking advantage of a woman, but it was for their own damn good that he did this. With malice aforethought, he added, "I'll have Joe set up the targets. The first to knock them all down is the winner. I win, you leave town tomorrow. You win, you can stay the winter."

"Oh, how very generous of you," Samantha snarled. "The whole entire winter. I'm overwhelmed." When he scowled at her sarcasm, she suddenly smiled. "Obviously my reputation precedes me, and you fear losing, so you're hedging the bet. Well, I'll excuse you this time. By spring my father will have returned, and we'll prove that this place is ours. I can afford to be magnanimous."

The sudden spread of that wide smile left Sloan momentarily paralyzed, but her words jolted him into speech quickly enough. He gave her a look of disgust, then started down the stairs to the street. "Remember that when you're climbing back in that wagon in the morning," he called over his shoulder.

Samantha smiled serenely as he strode across the muddy plaza. The promised snow hadn't come, and the sun today took the chill from the air. It was a perfect day for hog killing.

"Sam, do you know what you're doing?" Mrs. Neely inquired anxiously behind her. "You don't know anything about this man. What if he cheats? You've given our word we'll leave. Where will we go?"

Samantha smoothed the long bore of her rifle. "Don't worry, Mama. Sloan Talbott is too arrogant to lower himself to cheating, but he'll take every advantage he can. Arrogance doesn't pay in the long run. It leads to underestimating one's opponents."

Still smiling, she returned to the house to clean her weapon and find her ammunition pouch.

By the time Injun Joe had the duplicate targets set up on the edge of town, word of the challenge had spread rapidly. Men came riding in from the hills to watch the show. Doc Ramsey found himself a ringside seat and declared himself judge. Even Chief Coyote took an interest, positioning himself on an empty whiskey barrel beside the splintered trunk of a dead pine. A crowd had begun to form before either of the participants made an appearance.

Samantha tried to persuade her mother and sisters to stay behind, away from the unruly crowd of men, but they refused. She knew better than to argue with her mother. The twins pulled on matching poke bonnets that successfully concealed most of their faces. Their long woolen shawls might hide their figures with some degree of success, but Sam didn't think that mattered any to those women-hungry men out there. She gave a sigh of exasperation and prayed she wouldn't have another battle on her hands before she could end this one with Talbott.

But her mother's dignified carriage and the modest appearance of the twins served to keep the crowd respectful when they appeared. Amos Donner acted as escort for Mrs. Neely, giving her his arm to lean on. Sam kept a lookout for Jack, but he'd disappeared earlier that morning. She didn't think he would miss this spectacle, but she wanted to make certain he didn't have any of his little "surprises" in store for her.

She breathed a sigh of relief when she found him talking with a group of the idlers from the saloon. She wished there were other boys his age around here so he didn't have to hang around with that crowd, but at least he was where she could keep an eye on him. Her relief lasted long enough to see an exchange of money. He was taking bets on the outcome of this shoot-out.

Tapping her mother's arm and nodding in Jack's direction, Samantha left her to deal with the rascal. She had better things to do.

She found Sloan leaning nonchalantly against a fence rail, his rifle laid to one side as if of little importance while he gossiped with his companions. He was taller than any man here, and the blinding white of his shirt front emphasized his dissimilarity from the working men around him. Wearing clothes that needed professional laundering was just one of the ways he displayed his arrogance, Samantha noted with irritation. Leaving that magnificent rifle lying about as if it were nothing was another.

She felt her stomach grip uncomfortably as she took careful note of his weapon. Among his many interests, her father counted weaponry one of the more fascinating. He avidly kept up with all the latest developments and corresponded regularly with men like Smith and Wesson and lesser known inventors like himself. At one time or another he'd possessed prototypes of almost every gun on the market. Samantha recognized this one all too well. Her father had declared it one of the best he'd ever seen: a Henry repeating rifle.

Well, she'd known Talbott would take advantage where he could. She wished she had her father's Spencer, but wishing wouldn't get her out of this predicament. Only quick thinking and good shooting would.

She ambled up to the men at the fence rail as if she hadn't a worry in the world. Nodding to a few of the familiar faces, she turned directly to Talbott and indicated the targets with a gesture. "Either you haven't got much confidence in your abilities, or you're planning on making this easy for me, aren't you?"

She hit Sloan right between the eyes with that one, she could tell. Another man might have turned purple with the insult, but she had to give Talbott credit for control. His eyes merely narrowed a fraction, and his jaw muscle contracted as he regarded her as if she were a particularly venomous insect.

"By all means, Miss Neely, have Joe adjust the targets to your specifications. Never let it be said that I denied a lady."

She was conscious of all eyes upon her and did no more than nod agreement. She'd got what she wanted. There was no sense in antagonizing the man completely. Some men might get reckless when angry. She suspected this man would only get even.

Joe looked surprised and started to protest when Samantha directed the targets be moved back another hundred feet. But one look at her face and his employer's stifled that notion. Grudgingly, he hauled the wooden crates farther from the crowd. Someone else carried the bottles that would be the targets.

As Joe set the last bottle on the last crate, the crowd grew quiet. Samantha was conscious of her family standing near Doc Ramsey and Donner. Those were her allies, the ones who counted on her to win today. She couldn't afford to lose. They had nowhere else on earth to go.

If she had other supporters in the crowd, she couldn't tell. All these men worked for Talbott some way or another. They couldn't openly defy him. But she suspected most of them had an interest in keeping the women around town. They wouldn't be men if they didn't. She wondered what that made Talbott.

A mechanical man, she decided, as her antagonist approached from the right. His face could have been molded from steel. He moved with the grace and precision of fine machinery. Lord, if she didn't know better, she'd say her father had invented this mechanical man to specifications guaranteed to tempt any woman alive. Broad shoulders tapered to narrow hips and long, powerful legs. Beneath that fancy coat she knew he had muscles that rippled with a strength even his hard-working miners couldn't possess. She suspected if she aimed a bullet through his chest it would pass right through without making any contact with his nonexistent heart.

She just prayed that Talbott didn't shoot like a mechanical man. Her only advantage was in the range and accuracy of her old Sharps rifle, and the fact that her father had adapted it to take the new metallic cartridges. Talbott wouldn't know about that. He would be thinking she'd have to prime the gun after every shot, taking seconds off her time. The bastard. Even with her little surprise, she couldn't beat the quickness of a repeating rifle. She'd just have to win on her greater accuracy—unless, of course, he was a better shot.

Feeling nervousness finally stealing over her insides, Samantha held out her hand to her opponent. "May the better woman win," she said without a smile.

Gravely, he took her hand, and she felt a shiver go up her arm at the touch. She saw a flicker of something, surprise perhaps, behind Talbott's eyes as if he felt it, too, but then his expression was as blank as before. He dropped her hand and made a polite bow. "Ramsey will give the starting signal."

At the crack of the judge's whip, both competitors began firing. Samantha ignored her opponent, concentrating

on felling a target with every shot. With the need to reload everytime, she couldn't afford to miss even one. But
she seldom ever did. She was placing her money on
Talbott missing. It was her only hope.

She could hear the shrill screams of the twins over the
explosion of cheers from the rest of the crowd as she took
out the third bottle in a row. Maybe it would be better to
take her sisters out of this place and back to civilization.
Maybe she was doing the wrong thing by keeping them
here. But it was too late to consider any alternatives now.
She was primed to win. She had to win. She had to shake
the conceit out of the man beside her, make him stand up
and take notice.

He was calmly emptying his repeating rifle. He had
eight shots before he had to reload. There were eight targets. He'd done that on purpose, the arrogant bastard.
Samantha jammed a new cartridge in her weapon,
knocked down the fourth bottle, and loaded again. She
was quick, and she was good. She knew that for a fact.
She just didn't know how good Talbott was.

She heard a roar from the crowd, but couldn't take the
time to see what it was about. Talbott was still firing, so
he hadn't won yet. He must have missed a bottle. She
splintered the fifth bottle. Three more to go.

Beside her, Talbott stopped to reload, and Sam's heart
began to sing. He'd missed! He'd missed a target! She
jammed another cartridge into the breech, fired, repeated,
and took out the sixth and seventh bottles. One more to
go. She loaded again just as Talbott lifted his rifle beside
her to take his final target.

The crowd shrieked and yelled and jumped up and
down as both bottles shattered at the same time. All the
targets were down. Gritting her teeth at this defeat, Sam
reloaded her rifle. Gun smoke drifted across the field
when she finally turned to the man lowering his fancy repeating weapon.

He just looked down at her for a minute. She thought
maybe he saw her heart pounding against her chest. He
was so damned tall, even taller than she, and not many
men could claim that. He was broad and hard and could
probably break her in half if he tried. He looked like he

would like to try. But he was dressed in the formal garb of a gentleman, and she prayed he would behave like one.

"You are very good, Miss Neely." The voice rumbled grudgingly up from his chest.

She was terrified he would suggest another match. Her father had given her the modified Sharp when he'd grown dissatisfied with the cartridges occasionally jamming instead of expelling. It didn't make much difference when hunting, but if the gun barrel got heated, the problem developed more frequently. Her gun barrel was heated now.

Sam said nothing that would antagonize Talbott. She was too terrified to say anything at all.

He seemed to accept her silence as reply enough. He removed the rifle from her hands and examined the modification that had allowed her to fire so much more quickly than he had expected. He raised an eyebrow and asked, "Your father's invention, I suppose?"

Sam nodded. Carefully, she glanced at his rifle. "He kept the Spencer for himself. Personally, I think the Winchester is going to be a better rifle now that they've got the kinks worked out of the ammunition."

For just a moment a smile hovered around the corners of Talbott's mouth. It disappeared instantly, but there was no anger in his voice when he replied, only a certain degree of respect. "Your father should have stayed back East to aid in that quest. A rifle that shoots fifteen rounds is a formidable weapon. I think we've reached a draw, Miss Neely."

Verbally as well as physically, Sam thought. He knew as much about rifles as she did. She nodded and became aware that the crowd had grown silent, waiting.

As if realizing this, Talbott raised his voice so it could be heard easily. "I'll concede defeat when a woman can match me to a draw. You and your family are free to stay the winter, Miss Neely, but I beg you to reconsider. This is not the kind of place where you'll be comfortable."

She wanted to kick him in the shins for the insult to her gender, while the crowd roared its approval of his decision. But she managed a syrupy smile as she answered, "Oh, we'll be comfortable, Mr. Talbott. You're the one who will squirm before it's over."

His look as she walked away wasn't a pleasant one.

Chapter Eight

From her window on the east end of the house, Samantha could see the majestic rise of the mountains they had crossed to reach this place. In the weeks since they had been here, she'd heard all sorts of stories about the treacheries and magnificence of those mountains. Even if only half the stories were true, they were worth exploring. She wanted to see the giant trees and the waterfalls that practically fell from the heavens. But most of all, she wanted to see her valley.

None of the men seemed to know about the valley her father had described, the valley to which she held title. Her father had said it had running water even in summer, that the grass was greener than Tennessee, and the weather perfect for every kind of crop. Of course, he had recommended horses and grain, but Sam had heard they grew grapes and peaches farther down the mountain in the flatlands below. She wondered if her valley would support fruit.

Not if it was much farther up than where she stood now, she decided as she watched the clouds covering the peaks. It was snowing up there. Besides apples, she couldn't think of too many fruits she could grow in snow.

It had always been her dream to have a farm of her own. Left to herself, she would need only a one-room cabin, but she wanted a huge barn, one large enough to house any variety of animal. She could support herself easily once she had that. She'd been saving her money for as long as she could remember. She had enough to make a good start.

But the dream didn't seem as clear as she remembered. She had always imagined herself alone in that cabin, but she shied away from that thought lately. She'd always known her sisters would grow up and get married and her mother would follow her father, so alone was the only way she could be. But she wasn't at all sure that was what she wanted any longer.

She didn't think about it too much. She knew the valley was out there somewhere, waiting for her. She would find it one of these days. Right now, too many other things needed doing. She certainly didn't have time to consider who might share a valley with her.

With the use of some of Emmanuel Neely's tools, Donner had built a washstand for Samantha's bedroom, and she admired his handiwork as she bent over it to splash her face. Donner might be a lousy miner, but he had a natural talent with wood. This stand might not be the expensive mahogany of her mother's stand, but he'd made the knotty pine shine just as handsomely. If this had been a civilized town, he could make a living at wood-working.

She heard a door slam as Jack erupted into the house. Her cousin never calmly walked. He ran, leapt, jumped, and occasionally, erupted. Just exploded all over the place. She wondered what had caused his excitement this time.

She wandered into the hall just in time to hear his words carry from the front parlor.

"There's a wagon train coming over the pass! Bradshaw saw it. Says they're up to their ears in snow already and they'll never make it. He says we ought to send out a rescue party."

"And what does Mr. Talbott have to say about that?"

Samantha entered the parlor in time to hear her mother's inquiry. She could have answered it without Jack's help. She trusted her cousin wouldn't repeat the language Sloan Talbott no doubt had used.

Talbott had pretty much stayed out of their way these last few weeks. He'd taken some of his quicksilver and cattle down the mountain to sell, so he hadn't even been around much of the time. And when he was here, he stayed over at the hotel. Still, she always knew when he stood on that gallery, smoking his cheroots. She could feel his gaze bore holes through her no matter where she went.

"Talbott said if anybody went out there, they'd have to lead the train down the mountain instead of back here. He said anybody fool enough to cross the mountains this late was too stupid to be of any use here."

Samantha laughed silently at Sloan's assessment of the wagon train's inhabitants. He probably wasn't too far wrong. She hadn't been overly impressed by the caliber of some of the people with whom they had traveled. But there would be women in those wagons—and children. It would be good to have someone besides men around.

She reached for her boots and began pulling them on. Alice Neely gave her a hard look.

"Where do you think you're going, Samantha Susan?"

She jerked the knee-high leather on. "Out to find us some new neighbors. Is Doc Ramsey going with the rescue party, Jack?"

Jack made a scornful grimace. "Nah, he's in his cups again. But you'd better hurry if you're goin'. Bradshaw and the others about have their mules ready."

"Go find some snowshoes for me, then. I can be over there in a few minutes." Sam pulled down the rabbit coat she'd made for herself last winter. It shed like heck, but it was warmer than the thin wool mantles her sisters wore.

"Samantha Neely, you are not going out there in that weather with those men. It's too dangerous. You don't know the territory as they do." Alice paced the room as her daughter continued preparing herself for the outdoors.

There was some truth in what her mother said, but Samantha had more imperative reasons for going than staying. She gave her mother a direct look. "If I don't go, Bradshaw will lead those wagons out of the mountains instead of back here. They'll be days longer on the trail. There could be sick and injured. Do you think they ought to suffer for Talbott's selfishness?"

That appealed to her mother's nurturing tendencies. Alice Neely immediately stopped pacing and considered the thought. "The snow will most likely be down here by this afternoon. They'll have to battle it all the way down the mountain. Someone could get hurt." She hesitated. "Mr. Talbott isn't going to like it. There's really no place for anyone else to stay here."

"Mr. Talbott will have to open up his hotel until they can make other arrangements. It's not as if he were full to brimming with guests." Wrapping a knitted scarf around her neck and head, Samantha started for the door.

Jack brought both pairs of snowshoes before she got farther than the plaza. Her father had showed her how to use the large, netlike contraptions to hunt in the mountains in winter. Walking on top of snow was a good deal easier than sloshing knee-deep in it. She would be able to keep up with the men easily.

She frowned as she realized Jack had wrapped himself in his heaviest coat and scarf. "You can't go. You've got to stay with Mother and the twins."

"There ain't nobody here to bother them. You're the one needs lookin' after," he announced calmly.

That was a crock of manure, but she didn't have time to argue with the brat now. The mules and the men were already heading out of town.

Some of them cheered when she hurried to join them. Others looked at her a trifle sullenly, but Sam didn't care. If there were women and children out there, she meant to bring them back. Right at this moment she couldn't tell whether she did it for the benefit of the women on the wagon train, her family, or to spite Sloan Talbott. It was all one and the same to her.

When they reached the snow line and she and Jack stopped to tie on their snowshoes, some of the men hooted and none of them waited. They sang a different tune when the two of them caught up easily and passed on ahead while the men worked to smash a trail through drifts.

"Hey, reckon Donner could make me a pair of them when we get back?" Bradshaw yelled after them. "They'd sure be handy for settin' traps."

Her coat was too bulky to shrug. Samantha held up her hands in indifference. "Ask Donner. Maybe aspen works as well as willow, I don't know."

"What we need is skis," someone else yelled back.

"That's what Thomson calls them things he crosses the mountains with. We could put the wagons on those things and slide them down the hills."

"My uncle made some of those," Jack yelled back. "They didn't work very well in Tennessee."

Sam pushed on ahead, leaving the men to exchange their stories. She hadn't realized how eager she was for female companionship until she found herself hurrying ahead. The burden of constantly watching over her mother and her sisters had become heavier than she knew. With other women in town, she wouldn't have to constantly monitor her family's movements. If she thought about it at all, she would have to admit that Sloan Talbott was partially right. A town full of men and four women was not the best place to live. But it was the only place they had, and she would make the best of it.

The trek up the mountain through the snow grew worse as the day went on. They were walking through clouds by noon. Sam had to slow up and let some of the men more familiar with the landmarks take the lead. Any trace of a path was lost in the solid white blanket forming beneath their feet. She wished for something warmer on her legs and vowed to make deerskin trousers out of the next deer she took.

Heavy gray clouds prevented any sign of the sun even when the sheets of snow opened enough to let them see the sky, but Samantha surmised the late November sun was well on its way down by the time they found the wagon train. The settlers had apparently given up for the day, not even trying to circle the wagons in such uncertain terrain. Some of the inhabitants had cleared open spaces and attempted to keep fires going, but they saw only a few dark figures near the wagons. Those few began to shout when the mule party loomed into view.

Now that she could see where she was going, Samantha hurried ahead of the others, Jack following close behind. They must have appeared relatively harmless because the posted guards only watched them, rifles idly at their sides. Before she could even call a greeting, a woman climbed out of a wagon, carrying a child in her arms.

Afterward, Samantha realized she should have known

better. She had seen enough women with sick children come to her mother's door to know the signs. But just knowing they had arrived in time to keep these people from freezing to death made her too joyous to pay attention to details. She waved her arms in greeting and watched as more people poured from the wagons, cheering.

Women wept, children cried in excitement, and weary men waited in silence as the mule train came down the hill. Until Sam spoke, none knew her as female, but the instant she opened her mouth, she found herself surrounded by women.

"Is there a doctor?" several asked. "We need a doctor. How far is it to town?" The questions flew fast and furious from there.

Sam heard Bradshaw explaining they'd have to wait until dawn to guide them down the mountain. It didn't take her mother's doctoring instincts for Sam to know that could be too late for the fevered infant the first terrified woman had come out holding. And apparently there were others in the wagons, others too ill or injured to come out on their own. Stepping awkwardly in her snowshoes, she came up beside Bradshaw.

She knew this man as one of Talbott's mine foremen. He was a burly man with an uncertain disposition. He was one of the few men in town who hadn't welcomed their arrival with open arms. More than any of the others, he would follow Talbott's orders. Somehow, she had to change his mind.

"There's sickness here," she told him when he glanced down at her with irritation. "That baby won't last through the night. We've got to get them back to Dr. Ramsey."

He scowled. "Talbott says we're to take them down the mountain. He doesn't want any women and children around. He sure as hell won't want sick ones."

"You want them to die?" Sam demanded. "You want their deaths on your conscience? Take the others down the mountain if you have to, but we've got to get the sick ones out of here tonight."

A small cluster of people began to form around them, and Bradshaw raised his head to glare at them. The men from the wagon train had already heard the word "doctor" and were nodding in agreement with Sam. Some were already ordering their wives to wrap up the children and prepare them to be carried out. The men from the mule train glanced worriedly back and forth from Bradshaw to Sam.

"They're like to die going back anyway," Bradshaw protested. "It's gonna be full dark soon, and the snow ain't stopped yet."

"We've got lanterns," one of the men yelled.

"There could be wolves and hungry grizzlies out there," Bradshaw countered.

Sam gave him a look of contempt. "I'll shoot them if you can't." She turned to the group of men from town. "Is there anybody here willing to lead us back?"

Injun Joe sauntered out with a disgusted expression. "Come on, get them together, and let's get going. I know the way."

One by one the owners of the mules broke away from the crowd to help women and children onto the animals' backs. Sam wanted to hug the cantankerous Injun Joe, but his expression kept her well away. She knew he did this against his best interests, and he would no doubt be sorry for it in the morning, but for once in his life, he was doing the right thing.

The long trek back was made easier because they went downhill with the snow and wind at their backs. Even then, many of the children wept from the cold. The woman holding the sick infant just sat silently astride the mule, clinging to the mound of blankets that didn't make a sound. Samantha walked by her side when she could, reassuring her that there was a doctor and warmth ahead. She wasn't certain the woman even knew she was there, but she had to say something. The grief emanating from the young mother was that strong.

Some of the women still had strength enough to ask questions, but they grew silent, too, as they began to understand they weren't heading for civilization. Only the thought of the doctor ahead kept them moving. They didn't seem aware that they could freeze to death in the bitter cold of the wagons if they stayed behind.

Again, Sloan was right. These people shouldn't be out here. Sam didn't know who they were or where they were going, but they had no business out here in the wilderness without even the rudiments of knowledge of how to survive. People that foolish couldn't be much of an asset to a community, but they shouldn't be condemned to die for their ignorance.

It was in utter exhaustion that the small band of travelers entered the town late that night. Alice Neely was one of the first to run out to greet them. She found Sam and Jack among the arrivals, gave them hugs, and moved unerringly to the woman with the infant.

Sam could see Talbott's cheroot appear on the gallery above them. She didn't think he would be coming down to welcome the new arrivals. Even Injun Joe seemed to have disappeared now that they had reached town. People and mules milled uncertainly about the plaza. Without wagons or tents, they had no place to go. Even though the snow was lighter here, it was still too cold to camp out without shelter. Sam gave a sigh of exasperation. Someone had to take charge.

"Mama, we'd better get the sick ones into the hotel. There's too many of them to take to the house. Maybe some of the men can move the billiard tables out of the way so we can set up pallets in the saloon."

Alice Neely nodded immediate agreement and began leading her first few patients toward the hotel. She spoke to several other of the women as she walked, and a small train of people followed her. Sam turned to one of the miners who had admired her snowshoes and asked him to gather up some of the men to move the tables. He glanced up at the cheroot burning on the gallery, looked at Sam, shrugged, and went to do as told.

It was a showdown all over again.

Chapter Nine

Kneeling beside the child lying lifelessly on the floor, Ramsey took one look, cursed, stood up, and came toward the two women waiting near the door. On the floor all across the room slept exhausted mothers, groaning patients, and a few weeping children.

"Smallpox," he muttered in disgust. "Unless you've had vaccinations, you'd better get the hell out of here."

"We've been vaccinated," Alice Neely replied calmly. "My husband insisted on it when the children were young. Where should we start?"

Ramsey glanced at Samantha. She looked to be dropping in her tracks, but she didn't murmur a word of protest as her mother apparently signed her up for nursing duty. "Talbott will be in here raising hell before long. You'd better get on home until the shouting is done."

Samantha was too tired to argue. She merely picked up a water pitcher someone had carried in and went to the closest patient moaning and tossing with the fever stage of the disease. As she poured the boy a cup of water, Alice Neely turned questioningly to the doctor for orders.

Ramsey shrugged. "There's not much we can do. I'll bleed them. You try to keep them cool. That shouldn't be too difficult. It's already cold as hell in here."

He stomped off before Alice Neely could protest. Samantha saw her mother glancing worriedly at the doctor and knew the problem. Her mother didn't believe in bleeding a patient, and her father had called all physicians who used leeches and lancets quacks. But it was the accepted method of treatment for fevers, and Ramsey was a doctor with medical training. They weren't.

While Ramsey started on the far end of the room with

his blood-letting equipment, Samantha and Alice worked their way from the other side with cooling water and soothing words. They had only the one bowl and pitcher between them. Mothers with children tore off petticoats to make rags to dip in the bowl to wipe sweating foreheads. Some of the women were ready to succumb to the fever themselves. Only one of the men had admitted to feeling ill, and he tossed now with as much pain as fever.

Alice gestured in his direction as she whispered to Samantha, "The disease has already erupted. We need unguents."

Ramsey hadn't said anything about the soothing unguents needed to prevent the pustules from erupting and corroding. Sam bit her bottom lip and debated the problem. "I'll ask him. Jack's still outside. If Ramsey doesn't have anything, Jack can go over and wake Bernie. She'll know where to find your medicines."

They had left the twins sleeping, knowing by morning they would need someone to relieve them long enough to get rest. Sam knew she ought to turn over her duties to Bernie as it was. She was too tired to move. But she kept waiting for Talbott to come down. She wanted to be there when he had the audacity to try to throw them out. She was thoroughly surprised that he wasn't here already.

She grimaced as she watched Ramsey use his lancet to slice the skin of a young girl. She looked around for his bottle of alcohol to dip the knife in, but he just laid the instrument in the bowl with the blood he was draining.

Frowning, Sam started to comment when her instinct warned someone had entered the door behind her. Not just someone. Talbott. He was like a malevolent force emanating vibrations of sheer anger. She scarcely had time to turn and confirm her instinct before Talbott grabbed Ramsey's coat collar, jerked backward, and sent the physician sprawling across the wooden floor.

He smashed his boot on Ramsey's wrist when the doctor reached for his bloody knife. He grabbed the doctor's black bag and flung it violently into the empty fireplace. When Ramsey struggled to right himself, Talbott grabbed his collar again, pulled him up, and sent him flying again with a powerful blow to the stomach. This time, the doctor stayed down.

Talbott bent over, grabbed the bloody bowl, and shoved it at Samantha. "Get this damn thing out of here. Bring me clean water, pitchers of it. Bring me whiskey from the bar. We'll need clean cups for each patient in here."

Astonished, but not about to argue, Samantha asked hastily, "Unguents? Some of the pustules are erupting. If you haven't got any, mother has some at the house."

Sloan stood and really looked at her for the first time since entering. Her eyes were wide, pupils dilated with fear, but she didn't budge an inch when he towered over her. Exhaustion drew her skin tight across delicate cheekbones and shadowed her eyes. Her hair still had diamonds of snow clinging to it, but she had discarded her bulky coat to work more quickly. One of the women tending her child wore the rabbit fur now. Sloan cursed softly, thoroughly, and without compunction as she cringed from his tirade.

"Send that damned hellion for the unguent. Get one of your sisters over here to help, and get yourself to bed before we have to treat you, too."

Sam blinked, nodded, and disappeared from view. Sloan doubted if she was obeying his orders, or at least the ones with which she disagreed. He didn't have time to correct that. Ramsey was trying to rise and sneak out. He turned and kicked the man in the posterior just for good measure.

"Go near that whiskey bottle for anything but medicinal purposes and I'll cut your head open with it. When she brings the water, add a dollop of whiskey to each cup and feed it to the ones still awake. We've got to keep liquids down them."

Sloan knew that the woman at the far end of the room was staring at him, but he was beyond caring. He meant to kill Joe when he found him, but he couldn't do anything else tonight but tend to these blasted people he hadn't wanted here in the first place.

He had known letting women on his mountain meant trouble. He'd known it, and still he'd let them stay. He was going to pay for that mistake a thousand times over, he could tell already.

Sloan knelt beside a weeping woman rocking a silent infant. Pain and anguish rocketed through him as if it had never left. He wanted to scream with it, to shout and weep and vent the savage fury boiling in him as he gazed at the dying child. Those lifeless eyes were in a face probably no older than Aaron's had been. The image of that blood-shattered body came instantly to mind with just the name, and Sloan almost bent double in agony.

He wouldn't think about it. He wouldn't think of anything. There wasn't anything he could do. Children died all the time. He couldn't stop it. He couldn't save his own son. How could he save anyone else's? Hell, he had killed his own son. Wouldn't that send these good women screaming if they knew it?

Sloan felt more than heard Samantha's presence behind him. He took the pitcher of water and cup she handed him and sent her for a spoon. It wouldn't do much good to try to get water down an infant, but it would give the mother something to do, make her feel less helpless. Maybe the fever would break. Maybe it wouldn't. It was in God's hands now, not his own.

He didn't believe in God, but it was easier to blame some invisible being rather than himself. He'd blamed himself for months and years, railed at fate, cursed every god in the firmament. He didn't care any longer. He just did what he had to do.

As he worked his way around the room, dispensing cool water mixed with whiskey, rubbing unguent on skin so racked with pain that his patients screamed with the agony of his touch, Sloan realized Samantha was the shadow behind him handing him the cream, the pitcher, the rags he needed before he asked for them. He scowled, finished what he was doing, and turned quickly enough to catch her before she could dodge out of his sight again.

He didn't lay a hand on her. He gave himself credit for that much control. He merely pointed at the door and said, "Out."

She set her lips, seemed ready to argue, but apparently seeing something in his face she didn't like, she spun on her heel and left. Sloan turned to see Alice Neely watching him. He ignored her and went back to work, but he had the feeling he had just done something that met with her approval.

He didn't need any woman's approval. He didn't need a hotel full of smallpox patients either. Hell, he didn't need anything or anyone at all, but he was stuck with them. All he could do for the moment was get these fool people well again and send them on their way down the mountain.

Sloan was sleeping in one of the chairs from the saloon when Samantha and Harriet arrived near noon. He heard the women whispering instructions and reassurances to each other, and he wondered why he'd bothered coming down at all. These Neely women had everything under control. He might as well go back to bed with a bottle of good bourbon as Ramsey had done earlier.

He opened one eye and found the strange woman still rocking her infant. She was probably doing it out of sheer inertia by now. And they said women were the weaker sex. He grunted and opened the other eye. Weak, hell. They were stronger than oxen when they put their minds to it. He should know.

Sloan staggered from the chair, ignoring the beautiful twin gaping at him. Samantha already knelt beside the woman and infant. He'd sent her home once. Why the hell didn't she have the sense to stay there? There wasn't a blamed thing anyone could do here but watch people die.

He groaned inwardly as both women looked up to him with hope in their eyes. There wasn't any hope. There wasn't a single damned thing he could do about it. He took the infant from the woman's arms, examined the tiny, limp body, looked under blue eyelids, felt the fever raging, and shook his head. He put the child into Samantha's arms and pointed the terrified mother to an empty pallet. With luck, he might save the woman.

Hugging the infant to her breast, Samantha watched Sloan Talbott step over sleeping forms, test clammy brows, and lift weak heads for drinks. The infant in her arms didn't stir, but she made reassuring noises to the anxious mother fighting sleep beside her. The woman eventually gave up and fell into exhausted slumber. Sam clung more tightly to the infant. His breathing was ragged, and his diaper was still dry. She knew that wasn't a good sign.

She wasn't any good at nursing. She made a point to stay out of sickrooms. With her mother and the twins around to tend the ill, her services had never really been needed. But this time, she couldn't stay away.

Sloan came back and showed her how to persuade little sips of water down the baby's lifeless throat. She sponged the child with cool water as he suggested, finding the little pustules breaking out on delicate skin. She could feel her heart bleeding as the small body in her hands writhed with the pain of her touch. The cool water soothed him again, but she didn't think it was sleep that he fell into.

Sloan had ordered a quarantine of the saloon and its inhabitants, allowing in only those who could show proof that they'd been vaccinated. That included very few of the newcomers. Now that they'd found safety for their families, the men dropped like flies in the streets, leaving Sloan's men to carry them into the impromptu hospital.

Alice Neely returned with Harriet and some of the men that had been approved for admittance. They carried buckets of hot oatmeal and platters of biscuits for the healthy, a cold thin gruel for the sick. Samantha nibbled on a biscuit while trying to get the gruel down the infant's throat. Sloan seemed to inhale a bowl of oatmeal between one patient and the next.

Sam calculated they reached the height of the epidemic late that afternoon when almost the entire wagon train filled the saloon and spilled over into the lobby and down the hall. She prayed the rest of the town had either been vaccinated or stayed away, because she didn't think she would have enough strength to go through this again if the disease returned a few days from now in people newly exposed to it.

Sloan had gone out and found Ramsey and held him at gunpoint until the doctor had returned to nursing the newest patients. Samantha shook her head in weary confusion as she watched her nemesis work his way around the room, patient by patient. Sloan cursed. With two days' growth of beard, he looked like hell warmed over. He smelled of whiskey as much as Ramsey did. But he wasn't drunk, he washed his hands between every patient, and he spoke reassuringly and confidently to every man, woman, and child he tended. He was an enigma, a contradiction, a puzzle to solve as she rocked the infant and watched.

By the time the infant died that evening, the child's mother was too ill to notice. Tears of grief and weariness slipped down Samantha's cheeks as the tiny body in her arms hiccupped, gasped, and stopped breathing. She kept rocking back and forth, not knowing what else to do, unable to grasp her helplessness against the finality of death.

Something in her attitude must have changed because Sloan appeared beside her before she could even accept what had happened. He leaned over, touched his hand to the child's nonexistent pulse, spit a vivid curse, and walked away. Sam listened in exhausted amazement as he kept on walking through the doorway, down the hall, and up the stairs. A door crashed somewhere overhead as he reached his room. Then there was silence.

Her mother hurried over to relieve Sam of the burden. One of the less ill women from the wagon train joined her. Between them, they had the situation well in hand. Samantha was left with nothing to do but stare at the ceiling overhead where another outbreak of curses had erupted, accompanied by the crash of something breakable. More crashes followed. At this rate, there wouldn't be a single piece of glass left in the hotel.

She had no right to go to him. Sloan Talbott was an impossible man with hidden hurts festering behind that cruel facade of his. He wasn't her responsibility.

But he had stepped in where he didn't have to and helped when he didn't want to. For that, he deserved some modicum of compassion. Samantha went in search of Injun Joe.

The gunfighter was bleary-eyed with drink, but he staggered immediately to his feet when Sam told him what had happened. She watched to make certain he headed in the right direction, then dragged her feet back across the plaza toward home to get some rest.

Chief Coyote sat cross-legged on her front porch, smoking a long-stemmed pipe. Sam stopped some distance from him and waved him away. "Keep away from me, Chief," she called. "I might be contagious."

He gazed at her from dark eyes sunk behind masses of wrinkles. "I not die when people did," he informed her calmly. "I watch, see if white people die like my people."

She didn't want to get into that one. She didn't want to imagine sitting there day after day, watching one person after another dying until an entire tribe was wiped out, just as this wagon train of people might do. Death was something she had always accepted, but she had never watched an infant die before he even had a chance to live.

Catching her breath on a sob, Sam marched past the old Indian, leaving him to his deathwatch. Maybe he was right to hope they would all die. White people had probably brought the disease that killed his friends and family. But she had no stomach for retribution. She only wanted to go to bed and cry.

Coyote nodded his head as he heard the muffled sobs through the pane of weak glass behind him. He watched without expression as someone carried the tiny body wrapped in linen out of the hotel, and one of the men camped in the plaza began to wail his grief.

White babies died just as red ones did. The powerful medicine of Sloan Talbott couldn't stop death.

Chapter Ten

"**G**et the hell out of my sight, Ramsey!" The cry carried clearly through the windows of the hotel and into the street where Samantha stood.

Arms loaded with fresh blankets, she turned to the wiry figure lounging against the porch post. "Sometime I would like explained to me why the town saloon-keeper tends the sick while the doctor spends his time with the whiskey. I know men are queer creatures, but this goes a little beyond queer."

Injun Joe gave a laconic shrug as Ramsey came flying through the hotel doors headfirst, whiskey bottle still clutched in his arms. "Makes as much sense as a woman wearing pants, I reckon," was his only response.

Giving the gunslinger an ugly look, Sam stepped over Ramsey's recumbent body and into the hotel. She was beginning to accept things like bodies lying in the street and Indians on her porch. She wondered if her father had realized what kind of life he had led the gentle women of his family into. Back in Tennessee they'd had a comfortable farmhouse, a civilized town to visit, and neighbors who could be counted on. The women were ladies, the men were gentlemen, and if anyone stepped outside the boundaries, the community as a whole dealt with them. In this blasted town there were a hundred different entities and no whole, and certainly not a gentleman to be found anywhere.

"I told you to get your ass out of here before I kick it out!"

The shout came from the saloon. Samantha held her blankets in front of her and stepped out of range, waiting for the next body to be heaved through the doorway. Talbott was on a real roll this morning.

"Take your infernal Bible and shove it—" The imprecation was cut short by a woman's soft warning.

The preacher who had arrived with the wagon train stumbled into the hall, shaking his head as he passed Samantha without seeing her. He clutched his Bible much as Ramsey clutched his bottle, hurrying to avoid his predecessor's fate. Glowering, Samantha marched into the makeshift hospital room to confront the human grizzly bear rapidly emptying it of its ambulatory inhabitants.

"Clear out, Talbott, and get some sleep before you murder the rest of us." She threw the blankets down on a chair and, hands on hips, faced the big man in the room's center—the man everyone was trying to avoid.

If he looked like hell a few days ago, he looked three times worse today. His dark curly hair was matted against his bare neck; his collar had wilted and disappeared long before. A week's growth of dark beard made him as hairy as any grizzly she could imagine, and the red, bleary eyes that stared out at her from behind that bush made her wince. His normally pristine white shirt was covered in soot and various human excretions. He'd rolled the sleeves back and tore open the neck to reveal a red flannel undervest that Sam thought rivaled his eyes for color. She grimaced when he turned his malignant stare on her.

He stepped over a body sleeping on a pallet and parked himself directly in front of her. "Maybe I should practice with you," he growled. "This is all your damned fault in the first place."

Oh, that was good. That was rich. Samantha drew herself up straight to face him and just barely resisted spitting in his eye. All her fault! As if she were God to visit pestilence upon the face of the earth. Just to spite one Sloan Talbott, no doubt.

"You're good, Talbott, I'll grant you that. First a drunk, then a preacher, and now a mere female. Why don't you heave me through the door like Ramsey? Show your masculine prowess. Prove you're bigger than all of us." She held up her arms to show she wasn't resisting.

"I *am* bigger than all of you," he roared. "And if you

don't get the hell out of my sight, I'll heave you anywhere I like!"

He was looking for a fight. He was looking for someone to kill. Sam understood that instantly. His fists were
clenched in fury. Sloan Talbott was a volcano just waiting
to erupt. If another man stood here now, Sloan would
splatter him against the wall and not look back. But
something in his background kept him from hitting a
woman. She understood that, too.

And she grinned. She held up her fists as men did and
swung at him. "Make me, big boy!"

He caught her swing in one hand and shoved her backward. "I'll turn you over my knee and tan your hide if
you don't know what's good for you."

"Bet you can't catch me!" She kicked his shin and
darted out of his reach, keeping well within distance of
the door to safety.

He roared. He grabbed for her. She dodged his arm and
ducked under it, running for the door, still crying, "Bet
you can't catch me!"

He was off after her faster than a hound on a possum
trail. Injun Joe jumped out of the way as they flew out the
door and into the street, Samantha half a dozen paces in
the lead. Her trousers gave her the kind of stride she
never would have had if she'd worn feminine finery, and
Sloan regaled her with a string of vitriolic phrases ex-
pressing his opinions on her attire as she darted between
the tents and wagons that had gradually found their way
down the mountain from the snow-filled pass.

Men scattered as the two of them raced across the frozen plaza, down the wooden porch of the hacienda,
around the wagon shed, and back again toward the empty
blacksmith shop. Sam was laughing, her face red with the
wind as she threw taunts over her shoulder. What could
be seen of Sloan's face was red, but whether with wind or
fury no one could say. Whenever he began gaining on her,
Sam threw her agile legs into a leap over some obstruction Sloan had to race around and took off again in a
different direction.

Injun Joe finally put a halt to the madness by the simple expedient of sticking his boot out just as Sloan passed

by. Sloan hit the boot running, went reeling head over heels, and landed facedown in an ice-coated puddle in the street. He shoved himself up, spluttering, but before he could raise himself enough to murder anyone, Joe put his boot on Sloan's neck and shoved him down again.

"Reckon you'll kill yourself if you keep that up," he drawled as Sloan went down again.

Finding herself suddenly uncontested, Sam swung around and shouted a protest. "Hey, that's unfair! I was winning this fine without your help." She stalked up and kicked Joe's boot out of the way.

"Ain't no winning a contest with no beginning and no end," Joe replied dourly. "If you're gonna kill each other, at least do it with rules."

"I'm not going to kill her. I'm going to shove her into a dress and tie her there until she learns to act like a female," Sloan growled, pulling himself up from the street.

"Don't you like my pretty trousers?" Sam taunted, holding out her denim-covered legs for inspection. "At least they're cleaner than yours. You look like something a wildcat wouldn't touch."

"Then the wildcat's got more sense than you," Joe admonished with disgust. He turned back to a surly Sloan. "You wanna race, do it fair and square. First one to the dead pine wins." He pulled a Colt from his holster and raised it in the air.

"Wait a minute." Sloan halted him, glaring down at the irritating female panting almost as hard as he. He bet she didn't wear anything more than a man's undershirt under that flimsy cloth. He could see every curve and valley. That thought gave him the perfect vengeance. "I'm not running anywhere unless I get something out of it. If I can't tan her hide, I want some other reward."

"For losing? Not on your life, Talbott."

"If I win, you've got to wear dresses." He practically stood nose-to-nose with her.

Sam laughed. "If I win, *you've* got to wear dresses!"

They had gathered a crowd by now. The men hooted over this riposte. Money quickly began exchanging hands. Faces appeared at the hotel windows to see what the noise was about. Sloan's glare and Sam's laughter explained little. Joe raising his gun and the two combatants toeing the line someone had drawn in the mud spoke volumes.

The shot exploded in the chilly air. Both contestants took off with long, loping strides, easily keeping abreast. Sam's legs weren't as long as Sloan's, but she was lighter and more agile. She could leap over fallen tree limbs and icy puddles while Sloan had to slow to keep from falling on them.

But with a clear field and a straight shot, Sloan's greater strength and stamina had all the advantages. As soon as they cleared the debris of town, he was off and running, leaving the cheers and roar of the crowd behind. Samantha came in a very poor second.

He waited for her at the pine stump, arms crossed triumphantly over his chest. Sam really wanted to punch him now. She'd instigated this for his own good. He ought to be thanking her instead of looking so damned smug. She had probably been better off when he was exploding with fury. She didn't like the look in his eyes one little bit.

"I hope you have a nice selection of gowns, Miss Neely," he taunted as she stopped in front of him.

"It won't make any difference, Talbott. I can still beat you hands down, wearing a dress, if I want to." Sam shoved her hands in her pockets and glared. She was wishing she'd clarified this wager a little better.

"Just like you beat me now, huh? Well, what are you waiting for? Start with a green one. I bet you look real good in green."

"I bet I do, too, but you'll never know. I'll wait until you fall asleep before I come out. You can't stay awake forever."

Behind the beard Sloan's grin was slow and nasty. Sam preferred it when he didn't try to smile. She gulped and took a step backward.

"I can't sleep forever, either," he reminded her. "You promised to wear dresses if I won. I didn't mean one dress. I didn't mean for a few hours. You've got to wear dresses just like any female. Dresses, not trousers. All the time."

Furious, Sam clenched her hands on her hips. "Now wait one cotton-pickin' minute! If you think I'm going to go around hauling skirts and crinolines when I try to hunt—"

"You'll have to give up hunting then, won't you? And fighting. And otherwise behaving like an undisciplined brat. Get your sisters to teach you how to act. You'll catch on in a few hundred years or so."

He stalked off, leaving Samantha to stand flabbergasted and red-faced behind him. A few hundred years or so? She was going to kill him. She would have to. He couldn't insult a Neely like that.

He could and he had. Sulkily, Sam followed Sloan's path back to town. Men were cheering and pounding the wretch on the back as he headed back to the hotel, hopefully to sleep. She'd just done them all a favor by letting him work out his temper, and they didn't even appreciate it. Instead, they whistled and yelled when she walked across the plaza to the house. Maybe it was time she found that valley. She really didn't like people all that much.

But she was a Neely, and she honored her bets. She came out again a little while later wearing one of her mother's old dresses over her shirt and denims. No one had specified what she had to wear under the dress, and the skirt was too short on her to wear petticoats with nothing under them.

A few men hooted as she crossed the plaza, but with Talbott out of the way, the contest wasn't as interesting. They went back to what they were doing while Samantha went back to work.

Her mother and sister looked at her questioningly, but gossip about the race had already made its way into the sickroom. They went on about their business and left Sam to hers. Talbott, thankfully, had finally gone to his room to rest.

Some of the women had recovered enough to help. One of these came to join Samantha now. Handing her a water pitcher, she began to talk idly. It took Sam a few minutes before she realized the direction the conversation was taking.

"Don't you think a town like this could use a school-teacher? I haven't seen many children around, but perhaps some of the men could use some learning?"

The woman was pretty, blond, and well-rounded. Sam didn't think school-teaching was exactly what she had in mind. She scowled and poured another cup of water and held it to her patient's mouth. "There aren't *any* children here at all, except my cousin. Talbott owns this town. He won't pay a teacher to stay and teach his men."

The woman's eyes strayed to the door leading upstairs. "He's rather a forceful man, isn't he?"

Sam snorted. "That's a polite way of putting it. Where were you people headed?" It was time to change the subject.

"We were going to start our own community, one where everybody lived by the Scriptures. Reverend Hayes agreed to lead the flock to the promised land, but it doesn't look very promising to me. I thought we were going where the sun always shines and we would never be cold."

Sam shrugged and moved with her to the next patient. "I hear it's like that down in the valley. You just haven't gone far enough."

"I think I've gone about as far as I want to with this bunch," she announced through tightened lips. "My sister is the one who belongs to the good reverend's flock, not me. I just came because it sounded like a better life than the old one, but I'm tired of being preached at."

The woman didn't have to clarify. Sam had seen it all before. Pretty women couldn't help but flirt. Men couldn't help but flirt back. Two thousand miles with the same limited number of people produced a bad set of circumstances for flirting, especially if most of the men were married. A town full of single men was just what the schoolteacher needed.

"There's no place to stay here," Sam reminded her. "You could take a room in the hotel if Talbott would let you, but he hates women."

"Hates women?" The teacher looked surprised. "He didn't look like a man who hates women to me. Women are the only people in this room he treats with respect."

"Yeah, well, that's the queer thing about Talbott. If he doesn't know what else to do with you, he treats you respectfully and hopes you'll go away."

The woman's laughter was annoyingly cheerful. "He obviously knows what to do with you. Are you his sister?"

It was really one insult too many for this day. Sam contemplated dumping the contents of the pitcher over the woman's head, but she refused to lower herself to Sloan's level and take her irritation out on the innocent. She managed a tight smile and replied, "No, I'm the hate of his life," and walked away.

She had wanted to bring women into this community, dadgum it. Why in hell was she discouraging the first one to show an interest? It was quite contrary of her. She would have to make a point of talking to all the women. Wouldn't it serve Talbott right if an entire religious community decided to settle right here?

By the time she worked her way around the room, she had talked to everyone including a butcher, a baker, and a candlestick maker, she was certain. A carpenter was interested, but he'd lost his wife on the journey. A couple of the younger men were interested in the mines. The farming families meant to move on. A few unattached females were wavering in the face of a town full of single men. Only two widows had children, but that would be a start.

Sam was feeling a little more confident by the time she left the hotel that evening. What could Talbott do if the wagon train moved on and left some folks behind? He couldn't make women and children walk down the mountain. She didn't think he would even try. She was beginning to think Sloan Talbott was more bark than bite. Besides, it would serve the surly bastard right.

Outside, Injun Joe leaned against the porch post as if he'd never moved all day. He gave Samantha's attire a cursory look, grunted, and lifted his bottle to his lips. Wiping his mouth off with his sleeve, he commented, "You'll not win in that getup."

She had already noticed that Joe's grammar slipped with his level of drunkenness. She was amazed that

Talbott put up with this town full of sots. She didn't think he was given to drinking much himself. She wasn't certain why anyone would hire a drunken gunfighter, either, but Joe was kind in his own odd way.

She gave him a questioning look. "Win?"

Joe gave her a look of disgust. "You don't know nothin' about nothin', do you? You didn't even see him lookin' at that pretty little scrap of lace you were wearin' under your clothes. Hell, give a man a sight of a little lace, and he comes grovelin'. And what do you do when you have the opportunity to bring him to his knees? You wear trousers under that getup. He's got you beat hands down now. He's got you coverin' up that sassy little rear he's been droolin' over, and you make it easy for him by coverin' up your legs. Sometimes, I think you ain't got no sense a'tall."

He staggered back into the hotel then, leaving Samantha to stare after him in sheer astonishment.

Was he talking about Sloan Talbott? Drooling? Over her?

The man had obviously pickled his brain.

Chapter Eleven

Samantha watched the activity in the plaza outside her window. It was past dawn, and the settlers were making coffee over their fires. Already a few of the wagons had gone down into the valley, looking for a better place to stay. The ones remaining were the ones who still had sick in the hotel. If somebody didn't do something soon, the entire train would go, leaving them back where they started—four women against a town of men.

Sloan Talbott had been less than encouraging to the few tentative offers the settlers had made, she knew. The blacksmith had admired the empty smithy, and he was a married man with two children. One of the men who had already been down to the valley and back was talking about setting up a general store inside the derelict trading post. These were civilized people, people accustomed to buying and selling, who wanted barbers and woodworkers and schoolteachers, not the riffraff Talbott fostered. These were the kind of people who would make a town.

And no one was making any effort to persuade them to stay.

As Sam watched, Sloan stepped out on the gallery to gaze sourly at the plaza full of wagons and people milling in his muddy front yard. He had shaved his beard and donned full dress garb again, as if his gentlemanly clothes were a suit of armor to ward off evil. She wondered whom he got to starch and iron that little frill on his shirt. She frowned when she caught the schoolteacher gazing up at him. No doubt a woman like that would gladly perform those little services for him, among others.

Joe's words of the previous evening came back to her. They had never really left her mind. They'd woven their way in and out of her sleep all night. Give a man a sight of a little lace, he'd said. He'd said she had a sassy little rear. What was a "sassy little rear," and how did one know if she had one? She wasn't used to thinking of herself as the kind of woman men liked to look at. The twins were the ones men liked. Joe had to be more drunk than she thought.

But if she had to wear a dress to show she honored the bet, why shouldn't she experiment a little? Talbott hadn't shown much interest in the twins. He wasn't even looking at the schoolteacher now, although the woman was doing everything within her power to attract his attention. Sam couldn't imagine him being interested in a tall skinny woman like herself if he wasn't interested in the twins or the schoolteacher, but she didn't have to whistle and "yahoo" to get his attention. She could kick his shins just as well in skirts as in pants.

And if she could distract him once she got his attention, maybe she could persuade him into considering letting these people stay. The idea was as far-fetched as they came, but it couldn't hurt any to try.

Bernadette made a sleepy protest when Sam dragged her out of bed, but once she understood that her older sister actually meant to dress herself up in female regalia, she became demonstratively cooperative. The women of the Neely family had been trying to get Sam into dresses for years.

"We'll have to start with your Sunday gown until we can let the hem out of one of ours," Bernie decided as she scanned Sam's limited wardrobe. "Our crinolines will be too short, too, but that won't matter so much. You'd never keep them out of the mud otherwise. You'll need stockings. Let me find some stockings."

She went sailing off to the room she shared with Harriet, leaving Sam to gaze with dismay at the array of feminine finery lined up across her bed.

The frilly chemises and drawers were her own. Just because she wore denim didn't mean she didn't like lace. It just meant that denim was more practical for her everyday chores. She didn't know who would chop the wood and hunt for meat while she wore this gear, but a wager was a wager.

By the time she had on chemise and drawers and stockings and the old-fashioned petticoat she preferred to crinoline and hoops, Samantha was immensely grateful to her father for forbidding corsets. The twins had occasionally raised complaints that their waists were unfashionably wide without them, but her father had merely recited the dire maladies that would occur should they choose to squash their internal organs into sausages. That had shut up all further complaints until they needed reminding again. Sam had never given a thought to the size of her waist.

She gave it a thought now as she pulled the taffeta over her head. The gown would have to be green, she grumbled, but it was the only dress even remotely likely to fit. As Bernadette pulled the hooks at the back, Samantha took a deep breath and prayed it would close. She hadn't worn it since well before they'd left Tennessee.

The waist wasn't a problem. She'd apparently lost weight in the months of traveling. But now that Bernie fastened it, Sam remembered why she hadn't worn it much even back home. She had outgrown the bodice years ago and never bothered to replace it. She took another deep breath and let her sister fasten the top hook. When she breathed out again, she thought she now knew how a sausage felt.

Bernadette looked skeptically at the way the gathered material pulled taut across Samantha's breasts. The neckline was high, and Samantha had chosen a bodice design which hid her well beneath loose folds of cloth falling from her shoulders and gathering at her waist much as if she were garbed in a shawl, but it wasn't enough. Beneath those loose folds Sam's breasts strained at the slick material.

Both women gave sighs of resignation as they confronted the mirror in their mother's room. Sam would never be a fashionable lady. They could brush her bright red curls into rough ringlets over her ears if they pulled and pinned and prayed and made secure knots in the ribbons. The three rows of taffeta flounces on the skirt disguised some of her height and slenderness. The gathered bodice gave some credence to womanly curves. But they both knew the moment she moved it would be like looking at a man walking in woman's clothes.

"It will have to do, Bernie. You'd need a magic wand to do better. Maybe when Talbott sees me in this, he'll order me back to pants." Sam didn't really believe that. She figured he was more likely to enjoy how ridiculous she looked and make her suffer. But she had to try.

She figured her mission would be more successful if she could be one of those petite misses with shiny curls peeping out from beneath a demure little hat covered in ruffles and lace, but she had to make do with what she was given—and that was precious little. Lifting up her rustling skirt and petticoat, Sam strode out of the house and toward the hotel.

Men came out of the wagons to stare. By the time she crossed the plaza, they were pouring out of every nook and cranny in town. She'd think they'd never seen a woman before, but the town currently crawled with them. Somehow, this was all Sloan's fault. She would make him pay one day, just see if she didn't.

The epidemic had dwindled until all the patients once more filled just the saloon. Ramsey was working with one of the patients now, but Sloan wasn't anywhere in sight. Alice Neely gave her oldest daughter's attire a speculative look, but she was too tired to question. Sam sent her mother back to the house to rest.

Clara, the schoolteacher, arrived to lend a hand. She so obviously looked for Sloan that Sam had to grit her teeth. If she ever caught herself being that obvious, she was going to burn this dress and to hell with the wager. She threw herself into her chores with more efficiency and ignored the comings and goings from the sickroom.

Having decided a little talk with the wagon master would persuade his unwanted visitors to move on, Sloan was on his way outside when he halted to inspect the sickroom. He'd threatened Ramsey with banishment from the saloon if he didn't stay sober and help with the sick. The disease was reaching the last stages of its course now, and there wasn't anything anyone could do but ease the pain. They didn't need Sloan in there for that. But he couldn't help stopping, just to see how they fared.

His gaze instantly took notice of the tall figure in emerald silk taffeta. Silk wasn't a material frequently employed in hospital rooms. The full petticoat and large flounces were ridiculously useless in a room packed solid with pallets with scarce inches to spare between. The other women had worn old cottons and let them drag on the floor rather than wear their crinolines in here. This woman obviously had more curves than brains he noted as she bent to examine a patient, giving him a fine view of a slender waist and well-turned ankles encased in silk stockings.

When she straightened and turned around, Sloan employed himself admiring the anterior view. The full skirt belled out from a tiny waist, making it impossible to guess the actual curve of her hips, but he had no trouble determining the fullness of her breasts beneath that thin material. She wasn't overdeveloped, but she certainly wasn't shy in that department either. She knew how to make the best of her assets, he'd give her that.

He let his gaze drift upward to determine if there was any more worth watching. He felt as if he'd been socked in his midriff when a pair of emerald fires finally turned and focused on him. Samantha!

It wasn't possible. His gaze hastily slid downward, checking off the rounded breasts, the tiny waist, the flounced skirt—full feminine attributes. His gaze returned to her face. Samantha's flashing eyes still regarded him as if he were a male dog who had just used her leg as a watering post. Nobody else ever looked at him like that.

He grinned. He would no doubt crack his face after so much disuse, but he grinned. He couldn't help it. The long, tall tomboy in skirts. Sloan stepped into the room and walked around her to admire the sight. She stood stiffly for his inspection, and he could see ire in the rigidness of her spine. No soft woman this, despite the disguise. She was going to kill him. And he was going to enjoy every minute of it.

"Well, you clean up pretty good for a kid," he admitted with a chuckle.

"I'm not a kid. I'll have you know I'm twenty-four and as close to an old maid as you'll ever meet."

He tried not to laugh outright. Old maid! Mermaid, maybe, rising from a sea of green froth, but there was nothing old about her. Probably nothing maid about her either, but that was a technicality he didn't care to entertain. He pulled experimentally at the wide loose sleeves.

"Going to be hard not to get tangled in a gun with these." He kicked aside a few acres of skirt and petticoat as he returned to stand in front of her again. "Haven't you got anything more suitable for working in here? You'll smother the patients."

If looks could kill, he'd have died twice over by now, Sloan surmised, but that didn't stop him from admiring the front of her bodice again. He'd seen some of what she disguised under all that silk, but somehow it looked even more enticing when wrapped up like a Christmas package. He wanted to untie the bow.

"I've got pants," she informed him flatly. "You want me to be practical, I'll wear pants."

Sloan couldn't believe he heard himself chuckling. He couldn't remember a time when he'd ever felt better. He had the little termagant trussed up like a turkey, and he liked it that way. He held out his arm, and when she didn't respond as required, he grabbed her hand and curled her fingers around his elbow.

"I'm sure you'll figure out how to be practical and keep our wager once you apply your mind to it. Let's go visiting, shall we?"

Samantha decided killing wasn't good enough for him. Instant death was too easy. He needed to suffer first. He needed to suffer for a long, long time. She was certain she would think of any number of suitable tortures just as soon as she got away from him. Right now, walking at his side and holding his arm like this, she couldn't think of anything but a desire for death—hers or his, whichever came first.

Injun Joe wasn't at his post, but plenty of other people hung around to watch as Sloan Talbott escorted the fancified tomboy into the street. Sam tried not to cringe as men hooted or stared. She knew they would have done the same if Sloan had been the one to lose the wager. Everybody liked a good joke, and she was a big one without a doubt.

Clara came scurrying after her, smiling and saying what a lovely couple they made. Sam rolled her eyes when the schoolteacher quickly turned her attention to Sloan. Beside her, she heard one of the men snicker, but Sloan seemed quite intent on listening to the woman's breathless chatter.

"A school, Miss Whitaker? You think my men would like a school? How original of you. Have you discussed it with them?"

Samantha hid her smile. Sloan might be listening, but she knew sarcasm when she heard it. If the pretty Miss Whitaker didn't watch out, he'd slice her to ribbons with his vicious tongue. Not that the schoolteacher was likely to notice right away. He was so quick, so incisive, that she would probably just fall apart in a dozen pieces before she knew she'd been injured. Samantha tugged Sloan's arm and nodded in the direction of the young blacksmith. "You need to meet Thomas Craycraft. The hotel needs iron door hinges instead of those rotting leather ones. He says he can make them in no time."

Sloan scowled and walked away from the schoolteacher without a word of parting, heading directly for the well-muscled young man Samantha had pointed out. Accustomed to Sloan's tempers, Sam merely hurried to keep up with him.

Noting Sloan's direction, the young man stepped out to greet him. "Mornin', Mr. Talbott. My wife and I've been admiring this place you've got here. That's a right nice smithy sitting there unused. Mind if I ask how much you'd charge in rent? I've brought my own equipment so I could get into business right away. I reckon I could pay you something up front if you want."

At the mention of the word "wife," Sloan stiffened, but Samantha noted the anger seemed to go out of him. Sloan Talbott was a very odd man. She'd never understand him if she lived to be a hundred, but then, she didn't have to. All she needed to do was understand him enough to persuade him to keep a few of these people.

"Mr. Craycraft, I'll consider the offer, but I'll tell you right here and now, this isn't any place for a woman. I could use a good smithy, I'll admit, but the Neely ladies will be gone come spring, and there won't be anyone to keep your wife company."

The young man looked surprised, but didn't appear ready to question Talbott's assertion. Samantha scowled, pinched the wretched man through his suit coat, and spoke for herself. "We're not planning on going anywhere come spring, Mr. Craycraft. That's just a notion Mr. Talbott's got in his head. We'd be purely delighted to see another woman around town."

Sloan jerked her away, leaving the man staring after them in confusion. "You're leaving in the spring," he growled low in her ear as he made a steady path for his next target. "The bet was only good for the winter."

"The bet has nothing to do with it at all, Mr. Talbott, as I told you at the time. That house is ours, and we're staying." Sam pulled her arm away and sashayed ahead of him. One thing she could say for petticoat and taffeta: They crackled and rustled quite nicely when she was mad.

Sloan caught up with her and grabbed her arm before she could approach the Bible-toting preacher. "Go home and put something practical on while I get these people out of here. You're needed back in the sickroom, not out here."

She gave him a sassy look. "This is the only dress I own, Mr. High-and-Mighty Talbott. And I've decided I like wearing it. Why don't you go terrify the preacher some more while I talk to Mr. Smith. He wants to open a general store."

"*I* own the general store," he informed her furiously, keeping a grip on her arm as she lifted her skirt and started across the plaza.

"What general store, Mr. Talbott? That miserable hole in the wall covered with dust and rat droppings? That's not a general store. That's a disgrace."

"I'll hire someone to clean it up, but I'll be damned if I let you bring in competition."

"Hire Harriet and I'll agree, but you've got to put her

in charge. She knows twenty times what you do about what people want to buy." Samantha halted abruptly, startling even herself with this new notion.

Talbott stared at her as if she were crazed, but the idea was positively perfect, and she beamed up at him.

"Harriet? That wouldn't be one of the twins, would it?" he asked cautiously.

"See? You won't even have to allow another woman into town. She's just one of us. She can make you more money in one day than you're making now in two weeks."

He frowned. "What would a woman know about what men want? This isn't high society here. They'd walk all over a little thing like that."

"Not while they're bending over backward trying to sweeten her up. But you'll still need to hire Mr. Smith to bring up the supplies she orders. You're going to need different stock than what you're carrying now once these women start moving in."

Enraged, he dropped her arm and glared at her. "There are no women moving in."

"The blacksmith's wife," she reminded him.

"One."

"Clara's the blacksmith's sister-in-law." She smiled sweetly.

"Damn it to hell, I'm not having *any more women in this town!*"

From behind him Reverend Hayes approached nervously. "Perhaps this isn't the best time, Mr. Talbott, but I was wondering . . . Do you think we might have use of your empty kitchen for a chapel?"

Samantha thought Sloan's eyes just might bulge from his head. His veins certainly turned a nice shade of blue as he swung to glare at the preacher. All in all, she thought the preacher came off fairly easy when Sloan merely roared, "You can take your hell and damnation to perdition for all I care!" and stalked off.

That sounded like a yes to her.

Chapter Twelve

"What we need is a restaurant." Alice Neely stabbed a needle through the blue alpaca hem she was adjusting for her oldest daughter.

"Your cooking is just fine. Why would we need to eat out?" Samantha murmured absently as she studied the intricacies of the bodice interior she was supposed to take in.

"I mean, *I* need to start a restaurant. It's not quite right for the men to keep bringing me supplies in hopes I'll cook them something. And we could use a little extra cash around here. Even if Harriet gives us a bit of a discount at the store, supplies are expensive. And I don't see much hope of farming come spring."

Samantha blinked her eyes and looked up at her mother. Alice Neely had worked every day of her life, but she had never worked for money. Straits must be getting pretty dire, indeed. "Don't you think Daddy will have found us by then?"

Alice hid the worried look in her eyes by bending to bite off the piece of thread she was using. She knotted the end and reached for the spool without looking at any of the girls watching her. "It's a big state. He could be anywhere. He never was much for farming, anyway."

This commonplace knowledge reassured the twins, but not Samantha. Her father liked writing letters. He wrote pages of commentary even when he didn't know how he would mail it. They should have heard from him by now.

"The valley is bound to be out there somewhere. We'll farm it when the weather turns. We'll just have to hire someone to do the plowing." She said this as much to reassure herself as her mother.

Alice nodded uncertainly. "I suppose. But we could still use the cash. If we can just put enough on credit to get started, we can earn it back quickly, I imagine. These men are all starved for good cooking."

Samantha made an unintelligible noise as she jabbed her needle into the material. "The schoolteacher certainly isn't going to give them that. Even Joe couldn't eat that pie she made for Talbott."

Harriet giggled in her corner. "Joe brought it in and tried to sell it by the piece, but even the preacher knew better than to touch it when he found out where it came from. Seems she near burned down the wagon train when she tried to cook over a fire."

"Girls, gossip isn't polite," Alice admonished. "I want to know if any of you have objections to the restaurant. We'll have to set up tables in the parlor, so you better think about it hard."

"Where will we entertain our callers?" Bernadette inquired, frowning as she looked around the long front room they were currently using.

"Callers? What callers? Talbott has ordered his men to stay clear of us upon penalty of dismissal. We're not likely to have callers. We're not likely to have customers when it comes down to it." Samantha grimaced at her snarled thread as she tried to untangle it.

"There's still some of the men from the wagon train, and people like Doc Ramsey that he can't dismiss. And the others won't stay behind once they hear about the food. They'll come." Alice said this with complete assurance in her culinary abilities.

"I'm willing to agree just to see Talbott's face when he finds out what's going on, but there's one minor matter to overcome. There isn't any way he's going to let me out of this wager to wear pants again so I can hunt. What will we do for meat?" Giving up on the bodice, Sam sat back and looked to her mother for a suggestion.

Alice Neely had apparently thought this through thoroughly. "We'll pay someone to bring in meat. It would be nice if Mr. Talbott would sell us some of his stock, but Bradshaw actually offered to have someone go down and buy a cow if I could cook it. It's cold enough out there now to keep it frozen until spring. We'll do just fine."

"You'll have to charge exorbitant prices. Donner will have to build us more tables." Samantha played devil's advocate, but in truth, she wanted to dance with delight. Talbott had been more than surly these last few weeks. He'd been downright cantankerous. He practically growled every time she came near him. She'd like to think it was the silk and the laces her family decorated her in for their amusement, but she suspected pure frustration at not getting his own way ate at him. He now had seven women and four children in his precious town. Not only did he have the four Neelys and Jack, the blacksmith's wife and her sister and their two children, but one of the widows and her youngest from the wagon train had decided to rent a hotel room for the winter rather than try to find a house in the valley. Sam figured the widow planned on marrying the first man who asked rather than go house hunting, but Talbott had been denied any say in the matter. The widow had wept herself into hysteria when Talbott tried to turn her out, and the men had threatened to quit if he didn't let her stay.

She could almost feel sorry for the man if she didn't hate him so much. Sloan still wouldn't say a word about her father. He wouldn't admit to knowing about the valley. And he wouldn't give up on these damned dresses. He'd caught her once going up a tree after a kitten with her skirt tucked up in her sash and nearly laughed himself silly. She would make him pay for that yet.

Opening a restaurant was a good start.

"They're doing *what*?" Sloan swung on his heel and skewered his right-hand man with a black glare.

Seemingly oblivious that he ought to be falling down dead, Joe twirled his gun and sighted it at some object out the window. "Opening a restaurant. I've got a personal invitation to opening night. They promised to make me peach pie from those canned peaches Miss Harriet had shipped in last week."

"They can't open a restaurant," Sloan said flatly.

"That's my property. I didn't give them permission to open anything."

Joe shrugged, twirled his gun again, and holstered it. "Don't see anything wrong with eating a decent meal for a change."

"If I wanted decent meals, I'd hire a cook! Next thing we know, people will think this is a real hotel. They'll be coming up the mountain, looking for rooms and planning on eating at a fancy restaurant." Sloan stalked restlessly up and down the floor of his room. He was bored. He needed to go to 'Frisco and find a woman. He needed to do something before he started losing his mind. He was imagining Samantha Neely serving peach pie to a passel of miners, and he wanted to shove all their faces in it.

"This *is* a hotel," Joe answered laconically, taking a seat on a wooden chair and propping his boots on the bed. "Used to be people up here all the time on the way over the pass to the silver mines. You could make a mint of money just off those idiots who come here wanting to climb the peaks now."

That wasn't worth the effort of an answer. Sloan slammed out of the room and headed for his office. He'd come out here to the wilds of the Sierras for a reason. He had bought this mountain and kept it off the beaten path for a reason. He avoided people for a reason. He might occasionally forget why he kept on living, but he damned well knew why he was out here. Because he detested people. He detested civilization. And he particularly detested lying, conniving, thieving women.

And now he remembered why he detested women. They manipulated things. They manipulated people. Hell, they manipulated every man who crossed their paths. He refused to be one of the manipulated anymore. He'd sworn off that kind of existence ten years ago.

A few minutes later, he discovered he had donned his Colts and was loading his rifle. He shrugged. He didn't need an arsenal to scare away a few women, but it wouldn't hurt to keep the men out of his way. It was going to be a damned long winter if he didn't do something soon.

As he went outside, Sloan noted the lanterns hanging

festively from the porch rafters outside the hacienda.
More light poured through the windows. Despite the fact
that the unrelenting western sun would rot right through
the fabric, the women had hung wine-colored velvet on
those front windows, just as if they still lived back East.
It did give the room a certain cozy familiarity as he strode
in, but the sight of nearly a dozen tables crowded end to
end did not.

The room was packed with diners. Men waited on the
parlor sofas pushed up against the walls. Real china and
silver sparkled on the tables. Each table had a candle, although the candleholders were a little mismatched. Some
of the tables were covered with fine linen. Others had little more than hastily hemmed fabric gathered from the
never-ending store of surprises the Neelys had hauled in
here. Other settlers might strew half their possessions
across the countryside, getting here. The enterprising
Neelys had apparently picked up everything everyone
else had left behind.

Sloan was still chewing on this knowledge when
Samantha swept into the room, carrying a tray filled with
dishes. It wasn't the tray he noticed first. It was the dress.
Those damned dresses were driving him to distraction.
She never looked quite normal in one, probably because
they were always made for somebody else. But she always managed to startle him in some new and different
way. This time, she had gone out of her way to drive him
nuts.

She was wearing the same thing as one of the twins.
On the twin, the modest blue merino and ruffled apron
looked perfectly normal. On Samantha, the hem came
nearly half a foot from the ground, and he could clearly
see her ankles in their scuffed boots. He caught himself
straining for a glimpse of stocking, wondering what kind
she wore or if she wore any. The gown swirled just barely
above the top of her half boot. He knew he could tell if
he just watched closely . . .

Sloan suddenly realized the room had fallen silent. He
glanced up and found the whole damned place staring at
him, including Samantha. As he pictured the sight he
must make wearing Colts and carrying a rifle, standing in

the doorway trying to look under a woman's clothes, he ground his teeth together. The woman was driving him insane.

As he shoved his way past the tables toward Sam, she blithely continued serving her customer. She had the tray emptied by the time he grabbed her elbow and jerked her away from Ramsey's table. The good doctor was practically grinning, but said nothing as Sloan steered his waitress out of hearing.

"What in hell are you doing in that getup? Practicing for the role of saloon girl?"

Sam raised her auburn eyebrows. "It's a dress. You told me to wear dresses, remember? I know it doesn't fit very well, because it's Bernie's. Mother insisted that the twins have matching uniforms to wait on tables, but Bernie was a bit . . ." She hesitated over the description of her sister's female complaint. "Bernie isn't feeling well. So I'm taking her place." Realizing she owed him no explanation, she glared back at him. "Now unhand me. I've got work to do."

"You damned well do not. I'm shutting this place down. You can tell all your customers this is their last meal. I'm going back to talk to your mother."

Samantha deliberately blocked his path. "I wouldn't do that if I were you. Mother's up to her ears in feathers at the moment."

"Feathers?" Sloan wasn't certain he heard right. He had just noticed that Sam hadn't bothered fastening the top two tiny buttons of her bodice. The gown was too high-necked for it to make much difference, but he kept staring at the rest of that row of buttons. He was in the habit of ignoring her admonitions, but this one about feathers struck him as slightly incongruous. Maybe his eyesight was affecting his hearing.

"Feathers. Jack was supposed to have plucked the chickens this afternoon, but some of your cronies at the billiard parlor distracted him. You really don't want to see my mother when she's up to her ears in chicken feathers."

"Hey, Talbott! We were here first. Get in line like the rest of us. We're waiting for our suppers," a voice called from across the room.

Samantha made a small noise and escaped Sloan's grasp, hurrying back toward the kitchen. Not about to be thwarted by chicken feathers, Sloan followed close on her trail. Her strides were long, but her hips swayed quite satisfactorily, he noted. She really was a female, just a rather unusual one.

Walking from the candlelit ambiance of the parlor into the chicken-strewn chaos of the kitchen set him momentarily aback. Samantha disappeared somewhere into the hellish interior of steaming pots and smoking stove before he could see where she went.

"Here, throw this out the back door." Someone shoved a dishpan full of dirty water into Sloan's hands. He stared at it incredulously, looked around for somewhere to unload it, and came to the conclusion that the back door was the only safe place. Boiling pots or chopping knives covered every other surface.

As he wended his way across a feather-strewn floor, between nearly a half dozen swaying skirts, Sloan kept his eye out for Samantha. He noted her position chopping chickens at a cutting board in the corner. Satisfied he knew where to find her, he hauled the water out the back door, heaved it off the porch, and returned to the chaotic kitchen.

Alice Neely was stirring something in a skillet, testing the contents of a pot, and ordering her nephew to get the broom moving before she took it to his rear end. Sloan didn't think it diplomatic to try talking to an angry woman wielding a skillet, and he turned in search of Samantha. She wasn't where he'd left her.

Cursing, he stalked through the room toward the parlor where she no doubt showed her ankles to half the men in town again. He ought to be thanking her. The saloon would be packed tonight with men too horny to sleep. Didn't the female have any idea at all of what she did to them?

The schoolteacher sidled in front of him before he could reach the kitchen door. Wiping her hands on her apron, she smiled up at him. "I could make up a plate for you back here, Mr. Talbott. We're having chicken and dumplings. They're quite delicious."

Lord, he didn't know how long it had been since he'd had chicken and dumplings. He didn't spend much time thinking about what he couldn't have, but his stomach told him he really needed a decent meal. His head told him he had to get Samantha the hell out of that dining room.

Sloan made a cursory nod and pushed past the schoolteacher. He practically crashed into Samantha out in the hall as she hurried back with another empty tray.

"Good, there you are." She thrust the empty tray at the schoolteacher standing in the doorway and spoke to Sloan at the same time. "Mr. Smith has a seat at his table, and he says he wants to talk to you. He thinks he's found another outlet for your lumber."

Before he knew what hit him, Sloan found himself sitting at the table with the merchant, discussing board footage, while Samantha placed the most heavenly plate of chicken and dumplings in front of him that he'd ever seen. Sipping at a glass of wine, he forgot about throwing the women out and concentrated on calculating the profits of the deal Smith was talking about.

Sloan had eaten everything set before him and hammered out the deal by the time he realized the room was beginning to empty. The blacksmith's wife and one of the twins cleared tables. Smith stood and settled the bill with Alice Neely. Sloan searched the room for Samantha.

She wasn't there. He had a bone to pick with that brat. He was still irritated that she'd suckered him into eating in the damned place instead of shutting it down. But the food in his stomach kept him from being too volatile on that subject. He had another subject on his mind now.

He shoved past empty tables and into the hall leading to the kitchen. He could hear women's voices back there. He didn't want another encounter with the damned schoolteacher and her cow eyes, but maybe she'd get the message this time.

He threw open the kitchen door, found Samantha at the washbasin, and pushed the schoolteacher out of his path as he entered. Everyone else had sense enough to stay out of his way as he crossed the room. Even Sam looked resigned as she saw him coming. She was drying her hands on a towel by the time Sloan grabbed her arm and hauled her toward the rear door.

"Mr. Talbott, you have been away from civilization entirely too long if you think this is the way a gentleman treats women," she scolded as the door slammed behind them.

He ignored the complaint. "I'll wager you that my saloon is pack-jammed full of men right now, Miss Neely, drinking themselves under the table even though it's a work night."

"Your saloon is always pack-jammed full of drunks, Mr. Talbott. I fail to see what business that is of ours." Samantha backed up closer to the wall and away from his menacing proximity.

"You really don't understand at all, do you?" Sloan braced his arms on either side of her head, trapping her there. "Men are perfectly content to live together when there aren't any women around. But just give them a sight of swinging hips and a glimpse of female ankles, and they go insane. They'll be killing each other before this is all over, and you'll be to blame, Miss Neely."

"That is the most patently ridiculous thing you have ever said, Mr. Talbott, and you've said many. The men understand our rules. If one of them so much as makes an inappropriate comment, the others have our permission to throw him out. They'll behave, sir, if they value a good meal. And I believe they do."

She was staring up at him through eyes wide with anger and not an ounce of fear. She had her hair pulled back in some kind of knot behind her head, emphasizing the high curve of her cheekbones. Three of those little buttons at her neck were open now, and she didn't have any idea what he was talking about. Sloan really didn't think he had any choice. He was either going to kill or kiss her.

He kissed her.

Chapter Thirteen

Completely taken by shock, Sam did nothing more than dig her fingers into the wall when Sloan Talbott bent his head and put his mouth against hers. She couldn't remember if anyone had ever dared try to do such a thing to her before. She didn't try to think of anything at all. She just tried to stay upright.

It was freezing out here, but his mouth was hot. She could feel heat emanating from the rest of him, too, but only his lips touched her. Some subconscious urge wished for more, but she was having difficulty enough dealing with just this one contact. He didn't let go or move away, and her lips seemed to melt under the pressure.

Sloan slanted his head to taste a little more. Sam felt certain he meant to devour her as he had the chicken and dumplings earlier. But oddly enough, she found herself responding. Her lips tentatively returned the kiss, and she felt strange tinglings in her middle when his demands became more forceful. He was practically pressing against her, and he seemed to demand more than she knew how to give.

His tongue traced the line of her mouth, and she shivered. He nibbled at her bottom lip, and she gasped. Then his tongue dipped inside her mouth, and she grasped his shirt front for support.

She couldn't stand. She was going to melt right here on the porch. She felt his breath inside hers, tasted the chicken and the wine on his tongue, felt the heat of him filling her. She had no experience at this, knew no response to make. Only instinct kept her clinging to his shirt front as she allowed this invasion.

He caught her shoulders and pulled her to him until she

was pressed up and down against him and could feel the
hard metal of his buckles pushing into her belly and the
buttons of his vest squeezing against her breasts. She was
going to expire right here and now. He was going to suck
the breath from her and kill her. And she was going to die
with the pleasure of it.

The porch door slammed, and they jumped apart so fast
that Sam nearly fell. Sloan cursed, glowering at the
midget, who interrupted by heaving a pan of dishwater
over the rail. With one last look at Sam, Sloan stalked off.

Jack propped the empty pan on the rail and looked in
his cousin's direction. "That wasn't Talbott out here, was
it?"

"It was the devil himself. Didn't you see his tail
twitching?" Irritated with herself, irritated with Jack, Sam
grabbed the kitchen door.

"You don't have to be so grumpy. I just asked 'cause
someone was in here looking for him. Seems there's a
fight over at the saloon, and they need him to stop it."

That's just what she needed to hear. It was a damned
good thing they hadn't got around to naming the terms of
the wager. The good Lord only knew what he'd demand
in payment for this one. She thought maybe he had already claimed it.

When she entered the kitchen, her mother merely
handed her a pot to scrub and said, "That man has a short
fuse. You'd better stick to kitchen detail in the future."

Leave it to her mother to understate the obvious. Still
rubbing her mouth thoughtfully an hour later when she
retired to bed, Sam curled up beneath the covers and tried
to pretend nothing out of the ordinary had happened. But
she had little enough experience lying to others. She had
great difficulty lying to herself.

Sloan Talbott had kissed her. He hadn't *just* kissed her.
She'd had other men and boys smear their mouths across
hers before. There was absolutely no comparison. Sloan
had done things to her mouth that made her feel him right
down to her knees. To her toes, even. He'd done things no
man had ever done, things that ought to have been disgusting, things that would have been disgusting had any
other man tried them.

The really horrific, terrifying part about it all was that she had *liked* what Sloan had done to her.

And the part that made her whimper and bury her head under the pillow was that she wanted him to do it again.

Sloan slid his Colt back into his holster and watched wearily as Joe marched two more of the brawlers into the cold night air. A little snow would bring them to their senses fast enough, but he wouldn't get much work out of them in the morning. There'd be more bumped heads and cut fingers in the mines and mill tomorrow than they'd had the past month, and it was all the fault of those damned women.

He would have to do something about it, but he didn't know what. Maybe he ought to import a wagon load of whores from 'Frisco. That ought to serve a dual purpose by sending the good women screaming out of town and satiating the hungers they left behind. He just didn't know what he'd do with a saloon full of whores after everything settled back down. Besides, those paid women were diseased more often than not. It was one of the reasons he hadn't availed himself of the opportunity when he was down there. He knew too damned much about venereal disease to play fast and loose with it just for a few minutes' fling.

But abstinence created equal dangers, as he was discovering. He couldn't believe what he'd done tonight.

Climbing the stairs to his room, Sloan wished he could kick himself all the way up. He'd bet about now that Sam would gladly do the favor for him. She was probably washing her mouth out with lye soap. He couldn't blame her. Maybe he'd made his point, but it wasn't well done of him. He'd played the part of cad for so long it had apparently become second nature.

He was going to pay the price with another sleepless night. He threw open his bedroom door and started to cross the floor to the window. Only instinct told him he wasn't alone, and he swung just in time to see the shadow separating itself from the wall.

Sloan dodged and felt the gun butt meant for his head slam into the shoulder that was still weak from the last attack. He groaned and bent over with the pain, but not enough for the intruder to get the advantage. Sloan shoved his elbow backward viciously, connecting with some soft part of his attacker's anatomy. The man yipped and pulled back, but a second later the light from the hall caught on a gleam of silver. Sloan just had time to fall to the floor and roll away before the intruder brought the knife down where he had just stood.

Sloan kicked upward rapidly, but his attacker had apparently realized he'd lost the advantage of surprise. He was gone before Sloan could get to his feet and chase him.

He tried. He ran to the hall and looked down the stairs, but he saw no one. He tried the door to the gallery, but if the intruder had left that way, he'd already disappeared over the rail or down the outside stairs. Sloan ran down and checked the downstairs lobby, noted who was left in the saloon, and went outside to investigate the street. Other than the few late-night drunks in the saloon, there was no one out of the ordinary.

Joe materialized out of the shadows. "Looking for someone?"

"A man with a knife for my back. Seen him?"

Joe gave a pithy curse, then glanced at the shadows of his employer's face. Sloan looked more tired than angry. That was odd for a man who carried a wagon load of anger with him on a good day. Joe pulled his gun from his holster and checked the horses up and down the street. "I'll take a look around, but those same nags have been there this past hour or more."

"I didn't hear anything. I'd venture to say he's on foot."

They both knew what that meant: The man who wanted Sloan dead lived somewhere nearby. Joe grunted and stalked off to examine the nearest alley. Sloan returned inside.

In the chaos of these last two months since the women arrived, he'd almost forgotten his attacker. He'd better not be so careless again. There were too many strangers around these days.

He wanted to blame this, too, on the women, but he

couldn't pinpoint the connection. The first attack had come the morning after they arrived, but Sam had been the one to save him. The person who had jumped him just now couldn't have been female. Even Sam didn't have that kind of strength. And heaven only knows, someone would have noticed if a woman had gone up and down those stairs.

But the coincidence of their arrival and the first attack bothered him. And tonight he'd been distracted by the opening of the restaurant and Sam's kiss. Surely no one could have known . . .

Disgusted with the wayward path of his thoughts, Sloan flung his hat at the dresser and pulled off his coat. No one was going to kill him for kissing Sam except Sam herself.

But he would have to cut his own throat if he didn't stop thinking about repeating that pleasure. Hell, if he needed a woman, he had the widow and the schoolteacher just waiting to welcome him with open arms. He didn't need to take on a hellion who would no doubt part his hair for him if he so much as tried it again.

She was driving him to distraction, Sloan decided for the hundredth time as he crossed his boots on the rail and glared down at the plaza. Just when he needed to concentrate most, she was out there in that ridiculous crinoline with the December wind blowing it back and forth, giving him tantalizing glimpses of ruffles and lace. He'd figured Sam to wear pants under all that nonsense. He couldn't believe she owned ruffles and lace. And ribbons. He thought he'd caught a glimpse of a blue ribbon holding up her stocking.

Every other woman in town had sense enough to stay inside on a day like this, but not Sam. He'd not seen her wearing the hoops before. He wondered what possessed her to wear them now. He ought to be wondering which of his men attempted to kill him.

He caught the sound of her voice carrying on the wind. "Jack! Jefferson Neely! Where are you?"

Sloan rolled his eyes and returned his boots to the floor. He'd seen the little devil slipping behind the hotel into the walled courtyard again. He'd let him go, figuring he couldn't dig up much in this frozen ground, but Samantha wasn't likely to find him there. The brat ought to be in school, but the new schoolteacher didn't seem much interested in teaching, probably because nobody had offered to pay her.

Somebody needed to keep an eye on one Jefferson Neely. So far the little devil had managed—among other things—to get one of the mules drunk enough to break down his stall in some experiment on the effects of alcohol, which also involved a couple of chickens, an alley cat, and a stray dog. He'd set fire to a hay bale, playing with a magnifying glass, shot out the store windows while attempting to turn a derringer into a revolver, and nearly cut his hand off trying to throw a knife as he'd seen Sloan do. Jefferson Neely was a storm just looking for port.

Sloan caught up with Samantha just as she rounded the corner by the saloon. She'd been careful to avoid him lately, but she couldn't very well get around him now in this narrow alley while wearing that ridiculous cage. He tipped his hat back and studied the monstrosity a moment before turning quizzically to her.

"Did you think you could fly like a kite in that thing, maybe?"

"If I could, I would. Have you seen Jack?" She shoved a tumbling curl out of her face with a gesture of irritation. "He's supposed to help peel potatoes."

"Well, can't rightly blame the boy for hiding then. That's women's work." Sloan crossed his arms over his chest, anticipating the fireworks to follow.

She just gave him a look of scorn and began backing out of the alley. "Fine. Don't help me. I'll look elsewhere. Good day, Mr. Talbott."

He didn't want to let her go. He was damned bored, and she was more entertainment than he'd had in years. "Somebody's going to have to make that boy mind, or he's going to grow up to be a criminal, Miss Neely," he called after her.

She'd reached the corner, but she turned to yell back, "Just look at what fine examples of manhood he has to emulate, Mr. Talbott. If we're lucky, he'll grow up to be just like you, and all he'll do is terrorize women and drive men to drink."

He grinned. She was the only damned woman in the world who could make him laugh, and she was dead serious. He followed her out of the alley, caught the sway of her hoop, and jammed his boot down on her skirt before it could swing up and hit him in the face. She came to a sudden halt at the tug on her waist.

"I've got a little bargain for you."

She swung around as much as she could with his foot holding her in place. "I'm not interested in your little bargains, Mr. Talbott. I can't even do you a favor without having you throw it in my face. Let me go, sir."

"You'll like this one, Sam. I'll get the boy to peel the potatoes and mind his manners for the rest of the week."

She watched him suspiciously. "In return for what?"

He looked her up and down, from the velvet jacket with its big bow in back, to her flower-trimmed bonnet, to the wide expanse of alpaca spreading over her hoop. She almost looked the part of a lady. She very definitely looked the part of a woman. And it was driving him crazy. Here was his chance to put a stop to it while saving face. For once, he was willing to lose a bet.

"In return for a kiss," he answered cheerfully, knowing full well he didn't have a chance of making that misbegotten son of trouble behave.

Her look of scorn said she knew it, too. "And if you can't make him behave?"

Sloan shrugged. "You can go back to wearing pants."

She positively beamed. If she could have gotten to him through all that wiring, she might even have hugged him. As it was, she nodded eager agreement and held out her hand. "It's a deal, Mr. Talbott."

She wasn't wearing gloves. Well, he couldn't expect someone like Sam to pick up all the ladylike habits right away. He crushed her cold fingers between his and shook on it. She had a strong grip, but her hand was slender and practically engulfed in his. It felt good there. He dropped it as soon as he realized that.

"I'll haul him to your kitchen in a couple of minutes."

Sloan pushed his hat down and strode back down the alley.

The creative little beggar was lying flat on top of the grape arbor and focusing what appeared to be a pair of binoculars on one of the hotel rooms. Sloan was willing to wager the bank that the room belonged to the merry widow. He would have to ask Sam how old this little monster was. If he was old enough to look for naked women, he was old enough for more trouble than the wager was worth. Or maybe he could be bribed.

Slipping beneath the arbor, Sloan pulled out his knife and cut through a couple of the ancient vines. They were practically the only thing holding the old latticework up. Once they were loosened, he hooked his fingers around a rotten slat and pulled.

The entire center of the arbor came crashing down, Jack with it. The boy lay stunned, looking up as Sloan towered over him.

"Looks like it's back to potato peeling for you," Sloan said casually, prodding him with his boot.

Watching him warily, Jack started disentangling himself from shredded vine and broken lattice. "I coulda broke my neck," he mumbled.

"You could have broken your neck and lain here for days if I hadn't been here," Sloan said unremorsefully. "The widow could have come to the window and seen you and screamed her head off, and half the town could have come out and shot you down. We're going to have to reach some agreement here."

"Agreement?" Jack brushed slivers of torn vine from his coat, not looking at Sloan anymore. His cheeks had reddened, not necessarily from the cold.

"Yeah. You're going to have to start doing what your aunt and cousins tell you to do."

"That ain't an agreement. That's slavery." Brushing off the back of his pants, Jack stood up. Rebellion was back in the thrust of his chin.

"Look, we can do this one of two ways." Sloan pulled a vine out of the neck of the kid's coat. "You can do what you're told, or I'll blister your behind." Jack gave him a defiant look in response to that. "Or you can do what you're told, and when I'm satisfied you're behaving, I'll give you a book I've got full of naked women."

His eyes lit like lanterns. "A whole book full of them? What kind of book is that?"

An anatomy book, but Sloan didn't tell him that. He was guaranteed a few days of peace, then Jack would slip up, and that would be that. With satisfaction, he replied, "A *really* good book, if you get my drift. Now go peel those potatoes."

By the end of the week Sam would be back in pants and life would return to seminormal again. In the meantime, Sloan had a killer to catch.

Chapter Fourteen

"Aren't you supposed to be somewhere else?" Sloan asked absently when The Nuisance materialized inside his office, casually scanning the shelves of books. He had shut himself in here to do the monthly accounts, but he'd found himself making lists of the men who'd been in the saloon the night he'd been attacked, lists of men who were in town that night, lists of men who might hate him enough to kill him. The lists were depressingly long.

He looked up and scowled at Jack. The boy had occupied his shadow all week long. He'd ignored him at first, then tried to put him to use. When he'd caught him sampling the whiskey they were supposed to inventory, Sloan had sent him back to his aunt. He could understand why she hadn't kept him around very long.

"They're making pies and told me to get lost." Jack didn't even turn around. He was methodically searching each shelf with his eyes.

Sloan could guess what he was looking for, and he stifled his grin. Until the Neelys came along, he'd been able to scare a full-grown man with a glare. Now, he couldn't even scare a half-pint with a glare and a growl. It made it a little difficult to be convincing around his men. They might jump when he barked, but then they would catch sight of The Nuisance sitting at his feet and decide maybe he wasn't so dangerous after all. He was going to have to shoot someone just to prove his point if this kept up.

"Nice to see you've learned how to obey," Sloan answered sarcastically. He got up from his desk and threw a sheaf of papers on a table. "Here, make yourself useful.

Practice your math along with obedience and add these up for me."

"That's hard work!" Jack protested as he looked at the long columns of numbers.

"Good. It'll give you something to do for a while." Sloan slammed out of his office.

The widow was complaining she didn't have enough wood for the stove in her room. He felt more like chopping wood than adding numbers. Besides, everyone knew he spent the end of the month in his office. If they came looking for him, he wouldn't be there, and they wouldn't know where to find him. He wasn't in the mood for talking to anybody.

He didn't like the idea of someone trying to kill him. He hadn't gotten where he was in ten years by being Mr. Nice, but he'd always considered himself fair. Men didn't have to work for him. They could go elsewhere. He knew he was a harsh taskmaster, but he paid well. What would anyone have to benefit from killing him?

That question left him smashing wood into tiny splinters. Only one person in this world would have benefitted from his death, and she'd already taken everything he'd once owned, including his name. Melinda didn't even know where he was now and certainly had no reason to care. He couldn't imagine how she could think she could get anything else out of him even if she knew where to find him. And he'd made certain she couldn't.

So that left someone right here. Doc Ramsey hated his guts on general principles, but did he hate him enough to kill him? He'd been here when Sloan arrived. He'd been sopping up whiskey ever since, when he wasn't butchering his patients. He wasn't dependent on Sloan in any way, so he would derive nothing but drunken satisfaction if Sloan should die. That didn't sound like enough to kill. Besides, Ramsey couldn't shoot a grizzly at point blank.

He could narrow the list down to men who knew how to shoot and use a knife, but that didn't eliminate many. A man had to know how to use weapons if he meant to survive out here. Even that fool Donner knew how to wield a knife—he used one in his woodworking. Hell,

Sloan wagered even Sam knew how to use a knife, and she certainly knew how to use a rifle.

It just didn't make good sense. If he died, the mine and the mill and the hotel would close for lack of anyone to operate them. Everyone would be out of a job. It had to be vengeance. Some idiot had gone around the bend and decided to exact retribution for some imaginary wrong.

Deciding that didn't make him feel any better, Sloan splintered the last log and gathered a load to carry up to the widow. He didn't want to run a damned hotel. Hell, if he had paying guests, he'd have to hire maids and clerks and whatnot. That blamed well wasn't worth the effort. He may have come a long way from what he'd been trained to do, but he wasn't ready to go that far yet.

Dumping the load of wood at the widow's door and getting the hell out before she could pounce on him, he headed for the general store. There was something else he didn't want to do. He'd kept some stores at the trading post so his men could have supplies, but he wasn't a shopkeeper. Still, now that the store was running full-time, he supposed he couldn't neglect it. He had a damned lot of money invested in that inventory Sam's little sister had insisted on.

When he swung the door open, he found both twins inside. He assumed the one behind the counter was Harriet because it was Harriet who minded the store. Beyond that, he couldn't tell one from the other.

"I thought you were baking pies," he said abruptly, shoving past a table full of cloth and aiming for the till. He didn't mean to sound curt. He just hadn't expected to find them here.

"They're all ready to go in the oven. Mama can handle that. Is there something you needed, Mr. Talbott?" Harriet stepped out of the way as he opened the cash drawer.

"Proof I'm not going broke financing all these gew-gaws. Where are the books?"

Harriet slid a ledger from beneath the counter. "It's all right here. Most of it's in credit, though. You'll have to take the sums out of the men's pay on the first of the month."

"Credit!" Sloan glared at her. To his gratification, she cringed a little. The twins looked like plaster saints. It made him feel guilty as hell to terrify them, but it felt good to know he could still terrify someone. "Who in hell told you that you could give them credit? You don't even know how much they make. They could run up bills higher than their paychecks and take off before the first."

Harriet straightened her shoulders and tightened her mouth in a manner vaguely reminiscent of her older sister. "You can't run a store without credit. People expect it. And I had Mr. Injun Joe tell me how much each man makes, and I only let them charge up to half of that. I figure the other half gets spent over at the saloon."

Damn! He really was out of touch if women had gotten this smart since he'd been around them last. He knew some of them were good in the kitchen, a few of them were good in bed, but he'd never had much use for them outside of that. If she was that smart, she was probably robbing him blind.

Sloan picked up the ledger and started for the door. "I'll bring this back when I'm through with it."

"I've got a daily journal to go with it, Mr. Talbott," she called after him. "Would you like that too?"

He didn't even know what a journal was, but that didn't matter. He held out his hand and the second twin ran to carry it to him. He was beginning to think he should have shot Emmanuel Neely the first day he'd set foot in this town. Then these women would never have shown up on his doorstep, and he could have gone on living in peace and ignorance. Now he would have to be a bookkeeper.

To add insult to injury, he saw Samantha running across the plaza toward him as he stepped outside the store. She was probably coming to protect her little sisters from the big bad wolf, except she wasn't carrying a rifle. She didn't carry a rifle much these days. She had her hands full of petticoats instead.

Sloan derived a certain sense of satisfaction from that even if he preferred the idea of getting her back into pants again. He was just waiting for Jack to embroil himself in a major pot of trouble before conceding defeat. Surprisingly, the week was almost up, and the kid had remained remarkably obedient, relatively speaking, of course. Still, it couldn't last much longer. It had better not last much longer. He was enjoying watching for those slender ankles entirely too much.

"Mr. Talbott, do you know where Jack is? There's smoke coming from behind the hotel, and he has an affinity for fires. I didn't know if you were burning . . ."

She grabbed her skirt and ran after him when Sloan took off at a long lope toward the hotel. He hadn't left any fires burning. He was used to the cold.

He turned around and shoved Sam toward the street when she started to follow him down the alley. "Stay here. Those damned petticoats will go up in flames if there's any fire back there. Go find Joe if you have to do anything."

He trusted her to do as told, although he couldn't have said why if he'd troubled to ask himself. He didn't.

The alley separated the sprawling hotel from Ramsey's adobe shack. The livery was on the far side. Behind them all was the courtyard some efficient Spaniard had built for his kitchen gardens and vinery. The gardens had long since died, and he used the yard for little more than equipment storage, but there was lumber everywhere. The back stairs were wood. Firewood filled one corner. The men had stored lumber for repairs in no certain order wherever they found an opening. The whole yard would go up in flames before it started on the hotel and livery. That would take about five minutes, and they had no water pump.

It wasn't the yard that was on fire. It was the hotel. Sloan cursed and grabbed an axe and a bucket of dirt as smoke rolled out of his office window. He'd left the kid in there.

He smashed through the window frame, and flames instantly flashed through the gush of fresh air. He heaved the bucket of dirt on them, but it only made the smoke thicker.

Making a muffler of his coat, Sloan ran around to the back entrance. Smoke seeped along the high ceilings of the hall, but there wasn't any flame yet. He blessed the foot-thick walls and raced for the office door. It was open.

Fire danced along his bookshelves and crept toward his carpet, but he didn't see any sign of Jack. As a matter of fact, it looked very much like the fire had come from above. Heavy timber rafters supported the wooden floor directly overhead. The rafters were still in place, but fire still licked through the gaping holes between them.

He was aware of running footsteps coming through the front hall. Sloan hoped they had buckets of water, but he didn't linger to find out. The unmistakable shouts of a young boy came from somewhere overhead.

He raced up the stairs, only to lose himself in thick clouds of smoke. Dropping to the floor, he crawled cautiously in the direction of the shouts. The fire must have started in the rooms above the office and not the hall because the floor here was still intact.

He could hear Jack's shouts coming from the front, from the direction of his own rooms. He should have gone up by the gallery stairs. His room was the only one with access to the back stairs. All the other front rooms led to the gallery. Why in hell didn't Jack go out the front?

As if in answer, a beam engulfed in flame crackled and crashed across the only other exit.

Sam watched in horror as another billow of smoke erupted from an upstairs window. Men poured in from all directions, carrying shovels and buckets, but she didn't see any hope. Flames danced across the timbers supporting the tile roof. Ice-covered rain barrels were being rolled into line. Someone systematically chopped through the ice while others filled their buckets when the water was uncovered, but they couldn't possibly work fast enough.

She heard a wagon full of empty barrels race out of town toward the nearest stream, but it wouldn't be enough. They might save the town, but they would never save the hotel. Did anyone know where Sloan was?

She'd told Joe, and he'd gone running toward the back,

but she hadn't seen him in a while either. Men were on the gallery, pouring water through windows and doors, but smoke still continued to billow around them.

That's when she heard Jack's cry and knew beyond a shadow of doubt where Sloan had gone.

Without a sliver of compunction, Sam ripped the fastenings holding her skirt to her bodice, shoved the mass of petticoats to the ground, and stepped over the puddle of material in just her drawers and top. She couldn't climb into that building wearing a walking firetrap.

She heard her mother and the twins screaming in protest as she ran down the alley, but sometimes she just had to ignore what was right and do what had to be done. Men wouldn't listen to her if she gave them orders, and none of them were doing what needed to be done.

The entrances through the gallery were obviously inaccessible. She checked the back and found Injun Joe and some of the others working back there. It looked as if they had much of the fire out in the office, but the back stairs were gone. That left only one alternative, one none of the men had considered, lunkheads that they were.

She didn't hear Jack anymore. She couldn't see Sloan anywhere. That meant both of them were still in there. She knew beyond a shadow of doubt if either of them were safe, they would be right in the midst of the fire fighting. They weren't. That meant they had to be trapped upstairs.

She found the old ladder just where she'd seen it last, in the alley. It didn't look particularly stable and probably wouldn't hold a grown man for more than a few minutes, but it might hold her if she moved fast.

She slammed the ladder against the side of the building and started scrambling up before anyone knew what she was about. She could hear Doc Ramsey below her yelling curses, but that was typical. Some of the others came running, but it was too late to stop her. She felt the ladder steady from someone holding the bottom. She gave him a mental thank you as she grabbed the window frame and shoved it up.

The room looked like a sitting room of some sort, but

the smoke filling it prevented her from seeing much. As she threw her leg over the sill, a sliver of flame licked at the top of the door. She was operating on sheer energy without thought of fear, but the crackle of fire gave her cause for hesitation.

"Thank God!" The voice came from close by, and Samantha nearly jumped out of her skin.

Before she could turn to investigate the source, Sloan had materialized beside her. Through the dim light she could tell he was carrying someone, and she very much feared it was Jack.

"Damn!" he muttered as he recognized her. Then noting her eccentric garb, he cursed a little more pithily and jerked his head at the window. "Get out of here. Tell one of those dolts to send someone up to get the kid. I've got to go back and find the widow."

Sam was already back to the window ledge. "They've already got her and her kid out. The ladder won't hold anyone else. I'll go partway down, and you'll have to hand Jack out to me. Then pray the ladder holds together enough so you can follow." Samantha coughed as she hurried to put her words into action.

She didn't give him a lot of choice. Most of the fire may have been doused, but the smoke made it impossible to breathe. The window was their only escape. Sam let herself partway down the ladder and waited for Sloan to hand Jack over the sill. She caught the boy around the waist and wobbled unsteadily, clutching Jack and the ladder and hanging on until one of the men below understood.

Ramsey grabbed a box, stood it on end, and reached high enough to grab Jack out of her hands. Sighing with relief, Sam rushed down the ladder and clenched her fingers into fists as Sloan lowered himself out the window.

The ladder broke apart before he climbed halfway down. Feeling it give, he jumped clear, falling backward, and slamming his sore shoulder into the building behind him. But he was on his feet and following the men carrying Jack out of the alley before anyone could offer a hand.

Sam raced after them. The sight of Jack's lifeless face

released all the fears she had ignored earlier. She was literally shaking in her shoes by the time she rounded the corner just in time to see Sloan grab Jack from Ramsey and throw the boy on the ground.

Chapter Fifteen

By the time Sam caught up with them, Sloan had Jack sprawled in the frozen street, and he was bent over him, breathing into his mouth. Somewhere in the background the widow screamed for attention, and men still ran up and down with buckets of water, but Sam's concentration was entirely on Sloan and Jack. One of the twins brought her a blanket, and Sam wrapped it around herself without conscious thought.

Sloan pushed on Jack's chest, forcing smoke out of his lungs, then breathing into his mouth again. Jack didn't move at all. That frightened Sam more than anything. A Jack who didn't move was either sleeping or dead.

She grabbed her mother's hand when she found herself next to her. Alice Neely's grip was so tight it hurt, but Sam scarcely noticed. She clung to her mother as Sloan worked.

He was such a big man, he had to be crushing Jack's chest, but he seemed to wield his size with gentleness. There was no questioning the intensity of his concentration as he pushed and blew, pushed and blew. He didn't even curse. For Sloan not to curse under pressure meant he had closed everything else out. He was putting all of himself into saving a boy he didn't even like.

Samantha didn't think these things through as she watched the man she hated working over her lifeless cousin. She just knew she didn't hate him anymore. She couldn't hate a man who worked so desperately to save a child, who had obviously risked his life to save that child. The callous, angry man everyone saw from day to day wasn't the same man here right now. He might return any minute, but she had seen past the barrier he presented to the world.

Tears rolled down Sam's cheeks by the time Jack stirred. She held her breath and prayed frantically until Jack thrashed against the pressure of Sloan's hands. Then she dropped to her knees beside her cousin and hugged him, while her mother went to Sloan. Sam couldn't bring herself to look at Sloan. There was something too fragile between them right now. It would shatter if she looked too closely.

Kneeling in the street, Sloan swayed slightly as Sam took charge of her cousin. He wasn't thinking anything, feeling anything. A cool hand examined the painful burns on his hands and arms, but he hadn't noticed the injuries until she touched them. He merely watched as the boy breathed on his own, coughed, and tried to wiggle from the hands of the men picking him up. He was alive. He'd made the boy live.

It didn't make up for the one who had died. He would never replace the one who had died. But it helped in some inexplicable way. Sloan let the Neely woman salve his hands and tried to breathe fresh air into his own lungs.

By the time his thinking was restored, Sloan's hands hurt like hell, his shoulder hurt worse, but the fire was out. He gazed up at the smoke-blackened walls of his home, shrugged, and followed the Neely women across to the house where they had taken Jack and the others hurt in the fire.

It wasn't the scene of chaos he'd anticipated. The twins had obviously learned from their mother. They had their patients seated and sipping at coffee as if they were guests. The men were all too eager to ignore their pains while watching the women work. The widow wasn't quite so docile. As soon as Sloan walked in, she hurried to his side. She didn't seem harmed beyond disheveled hair and a ruined gown, and Sloan shoved her aside.

"All my things were back there, Mr. Talbott," she cried as he strode past. "What am I going to do?"

"Do without." The fool that he had once been many years ago would have held her hand and sympathized, but that man had died. The man he was now didn't care about

anything else but killing whoever had set that fire—
because he knew it had been set. There wasn't any other
reason in the world to explain it. The firewood he'd left
for the widow had been moved to provide kindling for the
flames.

Sloan made mental notes of who was present and who
wasn't as he strode through the front parlor and sought
the back bedrooms where Sam would have taken her
cousin. It was just one more list to add to his collection,
but one of these days, something was going to click.

Sam didn't evince any surprise when he walked in. She
still wore little more than a blanket. Sloan was conscious
enough to note that fully now. Jack was sitting up in bed,
hacking, trying to swallow some concoction she offered
him.

At Sloan's appearance Sam merely stood up and gestured toward the pitcher. "You'd better drink some of
that, too. Mama said it will help."

He hadn't noticed, but he was parched. He poured a
glass and winced as his shoulder refused to move with
him. Before he realized he'd done it, Sam was tugging
him into a chair.

"You've hurt that shoulder again. Get your shirt off.
I'll call Mama to come look at it."

He sat, but he shrugged off her offer. "I don't need
nursing." He turned to examine Jack. He took a sip of the
liquid, grimaced, and set the glass aside. Jack watched
him warily. Sloan noted the size of his pupils, took his
scrawny wrist and checked his pulse, put his head to the
boy's chest and listened to his breathing. Jack writhed beneath these ministrations, but didn't make a vocal protest.

Straightening, Sloan sipped at the liquid again. "You'll
live," he concluded. "Now tell me what happened."

He knew Sam was staring at him in astonishment, but
he didn't intend to explain. His first goal was to find the
man who had tried to kill him, and in the process had
nearly killed three others. Sloan figured shortly he'd start
remembering the sight of Sam crawling through the window in nothing more than a shirtwaist and pantalets, but
he'd had ten years of experience in pushing away those

kind of thoughts. His formidable concentration was one of his best assets.

Jack coughed, tried to drink from his glass, and coughed some more. Sam planted herself between the bed and Sloan.

"Let him alone for now. He won't be going anywhere. You need to have that shoulder looked at, and Jack needs to rest. You can ask your questions when you're both feeling better."

He wasn't used to interference. Sloan glared at the slender wraith in his way. She'd forgotten what she wore or wasn't wearing. The blanket gaped revealingly, presenting him with the fascinating sight of lace-trimmed drawers and a chemise dangling daintily beneath a sprigged muslin bodice. Buttons marched up the nicely curved front of her bodice, and he momentarily considered unfastening them to explore the undertrimmings.

When he realized what he was doing, he growled, stood up, and shoved Samantha toward the door. "You win. Go get some pants on before one of my men discovers you're actually a female."

Her eyes widened into astounding blue pools. Then she glanced down at herself, turned red, and practically ran out of the room.

Satisfied, Sloan sat himself back beside the bed. Jack still watched him warily, but he no longer cared. The tightening in his groin drove away any remembrance of other pain. He'd like to damn Samantha to hell, or take her to bed and drive himself into her. He didn't care which. It wasn't a mood made for concentration.

"Tell me what happened," he said curtly, just to divert his attention from the woman who had run out.

"I smelled smoke." Jack coughed and took a sip of his drink.

Sloan leaned wearily back in his chair and eyed his recalcitrant patient. "And?" he prompted.

Jack shrugged in embarrassment. "I went to see where it came from. I thought maybe someone needed rescuing."

Sloan rolled his eyes heavenward. Pure Neely. He would have to strangle the whole damned family to prevent the contagion from spreading. With a sigh of resignation, he returned his gaze to the bed. "And of course, it never occurred to you to run for help instead."

Jack's jaw clenched and he turned away. "That's not what my dad would have done."

Of course, it wasn't. His dad was probably just like Emmanuel Neely—nuts. But the boy must have idolized him, and Sloan couldn't help but feel a pang of something he'd rather not categorize as he watched the boy struggle with the pain of his loss. He'd loved his dad. Children didn't know any better.

In a softer voice Sloan said, "I understand. It's okay. You ran upstairs to see if you could warn anyone. What did you see?"

The boy took a deep breath and choked on the cough that came out. Sloan was instantly at his side, holding him up, applying pressure to his chest, helping him breathe. The kid was too young and small to rescue himself. He was a helpless bag of bones and blubber. Sloan held him carefully, and when he breathed again, made no objection when Jack turned into his arms and cried.

Sam had to take that moment to walk in on them. She had changed into a man's shirt and vest and a pair of denims that did nothing to disguise the curve of her hips or the trim size of her waist. Sloan decided he was too old and set in his ways for this. He leaned back against the headboard and closed his eyes. The boy huddled against him, obviously unaware of his cousin's appearance.

Sloan jerked his head in the direction of the door. Sam's eyes narrowed suspiciously. She took a good look at her cousin and satisfied herself that he was taken care of before obeying his unspoken order. Sloan heard her walking out. He didn't dare open his eyes again until she was gone.

"All right. What did you see when you got upstairs?" He hated being relentless, but there was a killer loose in this town, and he had to find him.

Jack sniffled and shrugged manfully. "Smoke was coming from your room. I thought maybe you were in there, so I opened the door. Fire shot out everywhere, and I yelled. Then I tried to get down to Widow Black's. A timber came down and I couldn't get past it. I don't remember too much after that."

"When you were down in my office, did you see anyone? Outside the window, going down the hall, anything?"

Jack finally straightened up and stared at him. "You think someone started it?"

Sloan stared back. "You got a better idea?"

Jack's eyes widened much as his cousin's had earlier. "It wasn't me!"

"Never said it was. But there wasn't anything in my room to catch fire by itself."

"Maybe it started in the widow's stove and went down the hall?"

It wasn't likely from what he'd seen, but Sloan didn't try to explain that. He'd go back over there himself in a little while and explore. "I'll look into it. You get some rest, and if you remember anything, you send for me. That was a brave thing you did, trying to rescue the widow. Next time, try to get a little help first. It's always better to do these things in pairs."

"I'll remember that," the boy answered solemnly, but his freckled face nearly beamed with the praise.

Such a little thing, a word of praise, but it could turn a man around. Sloan tried not to feel it as Jack gazed at him with pride, then closed his eyes to rest as ordered. He didn't want the boy looking at him like that. He didn't want anyone looking at him like that. He preferred to be despised and feared.

He strode out of the Neely house as if the hounds of hell were on his heels.

Sam watched him go, but didn't go after him. Sloan Talbott was a big man. He could look after himself.

Sam watched from her window as men scrambled up and down the side of the hotel, repairing the roof supports, installing new floors, checking the gallery for damage. She didn't know where Sloan Talbott had spent these chilly nights, but he apparently had no intention of taking shelter there much longer. Except for the singe marks around some of the windows, the hotel would be in better shape than before.

She turned away from the window. It was January, and they still hadn't heard from her father. She wanted to go down the mountain to the nearest town, but her mother wouldn't hear of it. If she could just get down there and question a few people, she might turn up some clue. Few people forgot a man like Emmanuel Neely.

But she couldn't take one of the twins with her, and her mother insisted it wouldn't be proper to take any of the men, and riding out alone would be the height of foolishness. It would have been different if she'd been a man, but she wasn't.

That fact had been a major disappointment to everyone in her life. Sam knew her father had dreamed of boys to follow in his footsteps. He'd had a boy's name ready for each and every one of them. He'd named her for his father, Samuel. Harriet and Bernadette had been named for his uncles, Harold and Bernard. She'd always wondered what he would have named a fourth girl if nature had so blessed him. He didn't have any more uncles. Would he have tried to name one after her mother's father next? Aloysius was a hard one to feminize.

Despite his disappointment, her father had loved them in his own way. He'd made them dolls that moved and doll dishes that didn't break. But dolls and playing house had never interested Sam. She'd wanted to go where her father went and do what her father did. And he'd indulged her as he'd indulged all the women of his house.

She couldn't believe he would disappear without warning. He would never have left her wondering. She knew it as surely as she knew her own name. He was out there somewhere, waiting for her to come for him—if he hadn't met with a fatal accident.

Even then, Sam expected he would have carried enough documentation on him so that someone would have written to notify them of his death. People just didn't ignore Emmanuel Neely. They wouldn't ignore his body either—unless he'd been deliberately murdered and hidden from view.

She didn't like to think about that. The only person she knew who might be capable of such treachery was a man who had kissed her nearly senseless and showed kindness to a little boy he had no reason to like. When she'd first arrived, she'd thought Sloan Talbott capable of murder. She wasn't sure of that any longer.

Without anywhere else to go, she wandered across the street toward all the activity. She didn't actually go looking for him, but Sloan was hard to miss. He was directing the placement of lumber in the courtyard behind the hotel. Jack sat near his feet, carefully measuring off lengths and marking them for Injun Joe to saw.

Sloan glanced at her as she entered the walled garden, then looked away again to one of the men installing wooden riders for the rear staircase. "What do you want?" he asked brusquely.

"I thought maybe I could help." Sam shoved her hands into her pants pockets. For some reason, she felt nearly as awkward wearing pants now as she had when she wore skirts.

"Why don't you go shoot a squirrel?"

He still wasn't looking at her. Sam scowled. "Why? We've got more beef and pork than we had back home."

"Then go knit a scarf or something."

He was deliberately dismissing her. She wanted to kick his shins to get his attention. "I can't knit. I'm tired of sitting around. I want to help. Is that a grape arbor over there?"

At that completely irrelevant question, Sloan glanced back at her. She was looking at the arbor and not at him and missed his expression. "What does it look like?" he asked irritably.

"It ought to be pruned. I experimented with grapes back home, but I never found a variety that grew well there. Do you get many grapes?"

"How the hell do I know? I'm not a gardener."

"I am," she answered softly, wistfully. "Daddy said he'd bought me the finest valley in the country for my garden, but no one can tell me where it is. Do you mind if I take a look at your vines?"

She walked off, not waiting for a reply. Sloan watched her go without saying a word. The emptiness ringing from that husky, sultry voice of hers struck corresponding chords in a part of him that he hadn't thought existed any longer. His insides lurched as he watched the natural sway of her hips as she strode away. It wasn't just the way she looked in denims that made him ache.

The lady was as lonely and bored as he was—unfulfilled, looking for something that wasn't there. Maybe he could show her where to find what they were both missing.

Chapter Sixteen

S loan let the thought of Sam dangle in the back of his mind while he worked on the hotel. She made him itchy, and he didn't have time for itchy. He had work that needed to be done and a killer to find.

But he couldn't concentrate. All of his life he had been able to call on his formidable concentration to accomplish his goals. But now, when his life could be at stake, he found himself watching for a pair of denim-covered legs swinging from the grape arbor or the sound of a sultry voice calling Jack to dinner.

The blamed woman had adopted his grape arbor. She spent hours every day gazing up at the ancient woody vines, snipping carefully, unwinding yards of cuttings from the crumbling slats. He could hear her actually talking to the blamed things. Crooning was maybe a better word. The sound sent shivers straight up his back, or more accurately, right to his loins.

When he hollered for Joe to carry a load of newly cut lumber up to the second floor and discovered the old goat was in the arbor instead of where he should be, Sloan exploded. Stalking across the yard, scattering workers left and right, he came up behind his right-hand man and shouted in his ear, "What the hell do you think you're doing?"

Joe jumped and nearly dropped the pruning shears he held. Recovering, he handed the shears through the vines to the feminine hand reaching down for them. "She's going to kill herself working up there."

"That's not your concern. I'm going to kill you if you don't get back to work."

By this time, Sam had stuck her head down through the

broken slats of the arbor to see what the yelling was about. As Joe walked off, muttering angrily, she lowered herself through the vines to the ground.

She was wearing a fringed buckskin jacket over a faded blue work shirt open enough at the neck to reveal shadows and curves Sloan didn't want to see. Irritated, he growled, "Get the hell out of my life!"

"I'm not in your life; I'm in your arbor." She propped the pruning shears on her hip like a rifle and gazed back at him as if she were in her proper place and he was the one who courted madness.

Something in Sloan snapped. He had dragged himself through his own murky hell for ten years now, trudging through an abyss in hopes of seeing daylight somewhere ahead. Just when he thought he was making a little progress, somebody tried to kill him. He'd been shot at, almost knifed, and burned out of his own home. His nerves were a ragged edge. These women frayed them to threads of exquisite pain. And now he couldn't see any farther than a pair of long legs in denims and high-heeled boots. Something had to give.

He didn't think it was his mind that snapped, but anything was possible where these Neely women were concerned. "If you don't get out of my sight and stay out of my sight, I'm coming after you with a whip," he warned her.

Sam tilted her head and regarded him quizzically. "Is that what you told my father to drive him out of here? He's a peace-loving man. He doesn't like provoking fights."

Sloan reached for his hat and curled his fingers around the brim to keep from curling them around her throat. "Your father had my men up in the hills roping mustangs and breaking their damned necks! He's lucky I didn't throttle him. And if you don't get out of my sight, I'm going to throttle you."

"Roping mustangs!" She brightened at this new piece of information. "Then he must have been meaning to stock the valley with horses. Do the mustangs have good bloodlines? I've heard about the Spanish breeds. Are they close? Could I find them on my own?"

This wasn't going as he had hoped. She stood there with blue eyes sparkling, red hair curling from beneath her hat brim in a riot of sunshine, looking like some kind of sprite in work clothes, and all Sloan could think about was the softness of the skin lurking behind rough fabrics. She was supposed to cringe, and he was supposed to furiously drive her out of here. Instead, he eyed the curve of her breast and wondered what would happen if he put his hand around it.

That was the proverbial straw. If he couldn't even concentrate long enough to throw one feeble female out of his yard, he was going to have to take drastic action. He didn't even have to think about what that action ought to be. He knew it instantly, had known it for some time. He needed a woman. And since this was the woman driving him to distraction, it seemed reasonable to take his needs out on her. They would both be better for it later; she just didn't know it yet. All he had to do was bring her around to his way of thinking.

"How the hell do I know anything about mustangs or what your father planned? Why don't you just go after him and ask?"

That startled her out of her complacence. She stared up at him, and Sloan had to keep himself from checking to see if he'd just sprouted wings. She had the most extraordinary way of looking at a man, as if he were larger than life. It wasn't precisely the reaction he wanted. He'd meant to irritate her into agreeing with him.

"You know where he went?" she asked breathlessly.

Sloan shrugged. "Ariposa would be my guess. It's the next logical step. He planned on going to the coast just to say he'd been, but he wanted to explore the mountains. He meant to hire a team to take him back through the giant forest."

"Why are you telling me all this now?" A dozen other questions danced on Sam's tongue, but something in Sloan's eyes made hot flames lick along her skin. He made her feel all squirmy inside, and she didn't like it a bit. He knew something, but he meant to make her pay to find out. She could see it coming.

"Because I want you out of my hair, out of my town,

out of my life. I want you gone. If the only way to do it is to find your father, then we'll go find your father."

Joy surged through Sam's veins. Here was her chance at last! She didn't like the way Sloan put it. She didn't want to give up their house or her valley, but once they found her father, he would straighten out those matters. But she knew Sloan well enough to know he wasn't doing this out of the generosity of his heart. He might react unexpectedly in moments of tragedy or emergency, but that didn't drive him now. She narrowed her eyes and regarded him warily.

"What are you expecting in return?" she demanded.

He studied her carefully. "I'll take you down to Ariposa. I haven't got time to go any farther than that. You can ask around all you want, but he won't be there. I'll have to hire someone to track him."

Samantha shivered at the gravelly tone of Sloan's voice as he said that. He said things she wanted to hear, but he didn't tell her what strings were attached. Sloan Talbott was a complicated man, but above all, he was just that—a man. Men didn't think as she did. They had ulterior motives behind everything they said or did. That Sloan Talbott was sounding reasonable was enough to make her afraid.

She should be afraid of his larger size, his powerful frame, his icy eyes, his cold expression. He could make a grown man squirm with a look. But his physical aspect didn't scare her. Actually, once she got past his intimidating stance, she found him physically appealing in a way that she found few men. She wished she were the kind of woman men liked to kiss, but apparently that one time had been an aberration. Sloan hadn't made any further attempts to corner her, as much as she would have liked to kiss him again. No, she wasn't afraid of Sloan physically. She was afraid of that formidably devious mind of his.

Sighing, she prodded for the "if, and, or but" behind his promises. "It costs money to hire trackers. Why would you do that?"

"You aren't going to like it." He crossed his arms over his chest and watched the impatience in her face.

"I already know that. I never mistook you for a generous man." She imitated his stance, wishing it were a rifle in her hands instead of pruning shears.

"I want a night in your bed," he said bluntly, insolently, watching for the flare of outrage.

Her eyes widened to saucers. She didn't even have the grace to redden or look away in embarrassment. She merely looked incredulous. "My bed? Why?"

"Assuming you know the usual reasons and that you're questioning my choice and not what I mean to do there, I want a woman and you're convenient. Beyond that, I figure you're not the marrying kind. You dress like a man, act like a man, try to be a man, so you probably think like a man in wanting to avoid the limitations of marriage. A man takes sex where he can find it and walks away afterward without all the clinging sentimentality of a female. That's what I want. If that's what you want, we'll go down to Ariposa and ask about your father. With any luck, when we find him, you and your family will get the hell out of my life."

Stunned, Sam froze where she was, staring into the icy pools of Sloan's eyes. Her thoughts whirled in dizzying circles, but she would never make any sense of them while he stood there. He was challenging her, that she understood. Just as he had challenged her to a shoot-out and a foot race, he was setting her up now. It was her own fool fault if she fell for it.

"I'll take it under consideration," she answered stiffly. Then whirling around, she walked away, oblivious to the stares of men as she crossed the yard without a word.

Refusing to think any further about it, Sloan returned to his work, satisfied he had done everything possible to relieve the current impossible state of affairs.

Ignoring her mother's questioning looks and Jack's pestering questions, Samantha donned her rabbit coat, found her rifle, and set out for the woods. She always thought better surrounded by nature. She needed to be outdoors and away from people.

That was why she needed her valley. She wasn't like her mother and the twins. She didn't need people around her. She wasn't a social person. She liked the feel of sinking her hands deep in dirt, planting the twigs that would become an orchard. She liked sitting in a field of sweet grass, listening to the birds sing, watching the colts romp. She liked standing in a crystalline snowbank and admiring the myriad tracks of little animals across a field. She felt alive out here and stifled inside.

If she could find her father, he would tell her where to find the valley. He would know if it was better for their family to stay here where they weren't wanted or if they should go somewhere else. He could solve so many problems that she didn't feel capable of dealing with. He couldn't solve the problem that bothered her now.

Sloan Talbott wanted to go to bed with her.

That was truly the most insane thing Sam had ever heard of in her life, so insane that she thought possibly she had dreamed it. She didn't mean to go back and ask to make sure though. She had to make the decision first, then she would check to see if he really meant it. She wouldn't make a fool of herself over nothing.

The snow wasn't that deep this far down the mountain. She trudged along rabbit paths, trying to lose herself between the trees, being careful to avoid the sudden dropoffs that snow could hide. She could do all that by instinct, after years of walking through Tennessee mountains. The problem of Sloan Talbott required more than instinct.

He thought she acted like a man. He probably hadn't meant that to be flattering, but she accepted the idea for what it was worth. She knew she didn't behave much like a woman ought to. Harriet could add figures and run a store like a man, but she always behaved like a lady. Sam simply didn't have the patience for petticoats and sidesaddles and demure smiles. She said what she thought, did what was necessary, and despised having to wait for a man to do it for her if she could do it herself. If that made her like a man, then so be it.

But she wasn't a man. She was a woman. She felt the same things other women felt when an attractive man looked at her. Sloan could make her feel all shivery inside with just one glance. His kiss had practically melted her knees. She wanted to feel what a woman felt when a man takes her in his arms. She wanted to feel desired.

The idea was practically laughable. What man would desire a female wearing denims, one with hair the color of carrots and a face as plain as a barn door? Even here, where the men were desperate for women, she attracted only a few stares and whistles. No man really approached her for anything more. Of course, they might be afraid she would pull a gun on them if they did, and they were probably right. The only man in town who interested her was Sloan Talbott.

She didn't know why that was so. He was irascible and infuriating. Why couldn't a gentle man like Donner attract her? She could almost imagine a peaceful life with a man like Donner. He could lose himself in his woodworking while she nurtured her fields and animals. They would never be rich, but they could be happy. Content, maybe. Bored, most likely.

Donner was boring. Sloan was not. Sloan was the least boring man she'd ever had the misfortune to encounter. She alternately wanted to hit him or kiss him. She certainly never could live with him. But he didn't ask that. He'd made that perfectly obvious.

Sam knew what he wanted. She hadn't grown up on a farm without learning a few things. Her sisters might hide in the house when it came time to breed the mares, but she'd stood right there watching it happen. It was a horrifying and magnificent sight. She knew men weren't stallions, but she figured once aroused they were probably just as mindless. She just couldn't place Sloan anywhere in that mental image. She couldn't imagine him aroused, she couldn't imagine him aroused by her, and she couldn't imagine him mindless.

But why else would he have made that obscene proposal? If he was trying to drive her screaming from the mountain, he had picked the wrong Neely. She wasn't squeamish about what happened between men and women. It was a perfectly natural part of life.

Maybe he thought she found him so revolting that she would reject him out of hand, and then he would spring some other evil plan on her. That would be typical of him, but she didn't think he was that obtuse. He had to know she was attracted to him. Any woman would be attracted to him. He had to know that.

He actually thought she would consider the notion. That was the only conclusion she could draw. And the horrible part was, he was right. She desperately wanted her father back. She would do almost anything to find him. And she didn't find Sloan's proposal completely unattractive. She had always known she was destined to spend her life as a spinster. She was nearly twenty-five years old, and no man had ever been interested in her. Why shouldn't she explore this one chance to know what it was like to be a woman?

The fact that she actually considered Sloan's proposal appalled her morally, but in no other way.

Sam stopped in her tracks and rested her rifle butt in the snow as she realized how far along she had come in her thinking. She could see the tracks of a deer ahead of her, but her mind wasn't on the deer.

Behind her, evergreen branches rustled. She swirled, raising her rifle at the same time.

"Don't shoot." Sloan stepped calmly around the tree, holding his hands up to indicate he was weaponless. "I just came to tilt the odds in my favor."

Before Samantha could grasp what he meant, he set her rifle aside and pulled her into his arms.

Chapter Seventeen

This time Sam wasn't so startled by Sloan's kiss. She melted into it slowly, balancing her hands against his solid chest and shoulders as he pulled her closer. The touch of his lips still had the ability to send her head spinning, but the heat seeping through her was strong, pinning her feet to the ground, pinning the rest of her to Sloan.

"Oh, God, don't," she whispered against his mouth when he came up for air, but she wasn't heeding her own plea any more than he was. Headily, she met the thrust of his tongue with her own, and tasted his groan with the same pleasure with which it was emitted.

Sloan Talbott wanted her. It was impossible to believe, but she could feel it in the way his hands clasped her waist beneath the coat, the way they spread over her hips and bottom and pulled her closer, touching her, holding her, making her feel him. She tasted it on his mouth, in the desperate heat of his kiss. His body couldn't lie.

He convinced her, but the knowledge thoroughly shook her. When he nudged her hat away and kissed behind her ear, Sam buried her face in his wide shoulder and clung for dear life. He crushed her against him and held her tight, advancing his cause with a trail of kisses down the curve of her neck. She felt sensations she'd never felt before, sensations she knew weren't proper, sensations that would lead to her ruin. She wasn't ignorant; she knew what was happening. She just didn't know how to stop it.

"Sloan, don't," she protested when his hands roamed upward, deliberately zeroing in on the places aching for his touch.

"Don't?" he murmured against her ear, his thumbs rubbing temptingly at the lower curve of her breasts. "Don't stop, do you mean?"

He knew it wasn't. He was being deliberately provocative. She ought to kick him or stamp on his toes or something, but she merely leaned into Sloan's embrace, sighing in pleasure when his fingers finally moved a fraction of an inch higher. One thumb caressed a nipple hidden beneath layers of clothing, and just that one touch shot straight through to her loins as if the two places were connected by telegraph wires.

"Not here, not like this." Those were words she could mean. She might not want him to stop, but she didn't want him to take her out here, in a snowbank. She didn't want to be mounted like a mare. That thought gave her sufficient strength to shove him away.

Sloan looked down at her through eyes that were first heated, then vaguely amused. He hadn't shaved, and the heavy stubble of his beard made him look the part of highway robber or worse. She ought to punch that cursed square jaw of his. Instead, she traced her fingers down the harsh bristle of his face.

"Then you'll go with me?" he demanded.

There wasn't an ounce of tenderness in his expression. His gaze was as relentless and demanding as his words. If she said no, she had no doubt that he would proceed to kiss her off her feet again, and seduce her until he reduced her to a quivering mass of jelly. Sam had half a notion to say no just to have him try.

That thought bent her lips into a tiny smile. Her mouth felt swollen where he'd kissed her, but she caught the sudden hunger in his eyes when he looked at her there. That made her feel a bit better. She didn't want to be just a convenient female. She wanted to be one that he had to have.

"I hate it when a woman looks at me that way," he growled. "I feel like a particularly tasty slice of toast and jam."

Sam laughed. She couldn't help it. He growled like a surly bear denied his portion of honey, but he complained about how she looked at him! He frowned at her laughter and let her go, crossing his arms over his chest and waiting impatiently for her to recover and be sensible.

She wasn't much inclined to be sensible, never had been, not in the way most people meant it. It wasn't sensible for a woman to want to be treated like a man, although it made perfect sense to Sam. She just had a warped view of the world. He would have to get used to it.

"You look more like a porcupine than toast and jam," she informed him. "And you've made my mouth all sore. Is it red? How am I going to go home if my face is all scraped from your whiskers?"

His frown became more quizzical than angry. He continued keeping his distance, but he examined her face thoughtfully before replying. "It will fade in a few minutes. Your mother will just think you were out in the cold too long."

Sam slid her hands under her coat, unconsciously covering herself. "Why do you look at me like that?"

"Well-l-l . . ." he drawled the word so long she had some doubt that he would answer. "You're a hard one to place. One of your sisters would have smacked me in the jaw if I'd done to them what I did to you. The Widow Black would have smiled like a cat with cream and moved in for more. Your schoolteacher would have been screaming for marriage. That's what a man usually expects when he makes his move. I should have known you wouldn't do what's expected, but I expected a rifle in my belly before I expected to be laughed at."

Sam shrugged uncomfortably. "I wasn't exactly laughing at you." She squirreled her face up and corrected herself. "Maybe I was. I mean, what am I supposed to do when you're kissing me one minute and growling at me the next? Are you going to bark and bite my leg if I try to walk away?"

A shadow of a grin flitted along Sloan's lips. "Possibly. I could think of worse things to bite than your leg. I can think of better ones, too."

She wasn't going to get into that. He was looking at her as if she were his next meal again. She turned aside and started for the path toward town. "What did you come up here for?"

"To keep you from talking yourself out of it. I thought you might need a little reminder of what you'd be missing." He fell into step beside her.

"Gad, you're a conceited oaf," she said without rancor. "Is this the way you talk to all your ladies, or am I the only one treated to your bluntness?"

Sloan remained unruffled. "I haven't bothered with ladies in years. They're not worth the trouble. Most of the women I've known since I've been out here are blunter than I am. The odds are pretty much in their favor, and they know it. If I wasted time pussyfooting around, they'd be off with another man before I could get what I wanted."

"How romantic." Sam heard the sarcasm in her voice and winced. She didn't have a romantic bone in her body, but his calculated method of pursuit set her teeth on edge. No doubt she was just one among many he had set his sights on. She didn't have to wonder how many he'd won. His cavalier attitude showed he was accustomed to getting what he wanted.

He gave her a sharp glance. "I'm not looking for romance."

She lifted her chin and kept her gaze on the road ahead. "I know what you're looking for. The word isn't a pretty one."

He stayed silent longer than was good for either of them. Finally, he just shrugged. "We both get what we want. That's the basis our society is built on."

Sam gave an inelegant snort. "You must be pretty desperate if I'm what you want. Why not one of the twins? Or the widow. She probably wouldn't cost you anything."

"The twins would faint if I laid a hand to them. The widow wouldn't be satisfied with just one night. You know all that as well as I do. What you're looking for is pretty words. I haven't got any. I need a woman, and you've got the appropriate requirements. You want your father found and I've got the means. Fair trade."

"You're disgusting." She said it with feeling. He *was* disgusting. The fact that she actually considered his proposal was equally disgusting. He was right, and that irritated her even more. She wanted him to tell her that she was more intriguing than any woman he'd ever met. She wanted to think herself the only woman he desired. That was a lot of bull. He'd stated the situation clearly. He just hadn't added that she wanted him as much as he did her. She wondered if that was out of politeness or ignorance. Since he was seldom polite, she had to believe he just didn't realize how she felt.

"My mother won't let me go anywhere with you." She avoided the touchy subject, turning it to a more pertinent one.

"You're what? Twenty-five? You can go anywhere you want. You just don't want to risk her disapproval."

Sam grimaced. "All right, I don't want to risk her disapproval. I want to find my father, but I don't want to lose my mother in return."

"I'll talk to her."

She waited for him to say more, but he seemed to think that was all there was to it. He'd talk to her, and everything would be fine. Lord, but the man was a conceited ass. She almost hoped her mother would throw him out on his face. Almost. The rest of her was growing excited about finding her father and terrified over an experience she'd never thought to face.

When Sam didn't ask any more questions, Sloan said nothing else. They strolled back into town in silence. They certainly didn't resemble a courting couple, nor could they be compared to good friends out hunting together. There was absolutely nothing between them but this insane bargain they forged together. Sam tried to force herself to see the impracticalities of it, but she couldn't get past Sloan's physical presence. As long as he was there, she wanted to feel his kisses. She wanted to feel a great deal more than that. The thought made her blush.

He happened to glance down at the same time as the pink suffused her cheeks. His lips turned up in the corners with a whimsical grin at this display of her innocence. At her age, he didn't figure she was completely innocent, but she certainly wasn't as experienced as the widow. The war would have changed a lot of things for women in the South. He wondered just precisely what went through her head right now, but he was better off not knowing. The less he knew about her, the more impersonal he could keep this.

"You won't need to worry about any unwanted results from this, you know. I'm experienced at preventing conception."

The pink turned a deeper shade of rose, but she nodded curtly. "If we go soon, it will be the best time of the month. My father read a medical tract on the subject, and he and my mother have experimented with the precepts. They didn't plan twins, but they planned the distance between our births."

Sloan made a mental blasphemous curse. Was there anything Neely hadn't experimented with? Did he share all his experiments with his eccentric daughter? He could almost wager her father hadn't explained this particular experiment to the twins.

"Fine. Will tomorrow be too soon?"

She cast him a sideways glance. "One night, and only after you've set someone on my father's trail?"

"Let's say twenty-four hours. It's been a long time for me." Sloan said that steadily, as if the notion didn't send his blood racing and his heart pounding. He was ready to drag her off right now.

The red was rapidly receding from her cheeks. She looked pale as she nodded agreement. "Twenty-four hours. I didn't think it possible, but if you say so . . ."

"I say so." He caught her elbow as they reached the porch to the hacienda. "Go play with your arbor. I'm going to have a talk with your mother."

Sam didn't want to leave. She wanted to hear what he could possibly say to her mother to persuade her to let one of her daughters wander off for who-knew-how-long with a man. At sight of the irritated tic in Sloan's jaw muscle, she set her lips and marched off.

Sloan let himself in the front door. Since the Neelys had turned the parlor into a restaurant, people came and went as they needed. He found a couple of his men in there now, consuming bowls of soup as if they'd never seen the like before. He felt his stomach rumble with hunger and conceded a decent meal wouldn't be amiss. But he had business to attend to first.

He crossed the room and went down the hall to the kitchen. The woman inside looked up with impatience, then shoved a straying strand of hair from her brow as she recognized him.

Sloan didn't bother with the preliminaries. "Sam and I are going down to Ariposa tomorrow to look for her father."

Alice Neely gave him a hard look that encompassed his unshaven face, his muddy boots, and the general disarray of his unpressed clothes. He hadn't bothered changing into anything appropriate when he'd left his work in the yard. She made him feel every social transgression before she answered.

"Does Sam know this?"

He almost laughed at her tone. She didn't trust him any more than her daughter did. He merely made a curt nod. "We're agreed."

Her lips pressed together in a thin line of disapproval, but she merely replied, "You're both grown people. I can't stop you."

He'd forgotten what it was like to have a mother who could make him feel two inches small with just a look. Alice Neely conveyed a whole book more than just that in her tone. If he harmed one hair on her daughter's head, she would no doubt stomp his face in. But she would never know what Samantha didn't tell, so he wouldn't lose sleep over it.

"I'll bring her back as soon as we find out something."

"I'm sure you will," she said dryly. "Just make certain you're around in another nine months to deal with any consequences."

"There won't be any consequences. You raised your daughters right." Right for him, anyway.

As if she could read his mind, she shook her head. "I raised them to know their own minds. You'd best know yours."

With that, she turned back to the pot she was stirring, effectively dismissing him.

Deciding he wasn't hungry anymore, Sloan left the hacienda. Alice Neely's parting words tolled like harbingers of doom. He'd best know his own mind. Of course he knew his own mind. He wanted a clean, decent woman who came without any strings attached. He'd been too long without releasing his baser urges. Once he'd satisfied those urges and got rid of his obsession with a long-legged female in denims, he could get something done.

In the meantime, he'd better make a few preparations for his journey out of the mountains. This might be just his chance to trap a killer.

Chapter Eighteen

"**D**on't let anyone see you leave town. Follow us at a discreet distance. Give him time to think he's safe." Sloan slung his saddlebags over his horse and bent to check the girth straps.

Joe polished his gun and looked irritated. "I've been doing this a hell of a lot longer than you, son. I just don't like your taking the woman with you. That complicates things."

Sloan straightened the saddle blanket and double-checked the supplies in his bags again. "Women always complicate things. That's their place in life. I'll make sure she takes her rifle along."

Joe grunted his opinion of that, but didn't offer it aloud. Sloan obviously had his mind on other things.

Sam glared at the mirror in irritation and settled the problem of her unruly hair by pulling a hat over it. Her mother came in, took one look at her attire, and swept the hat from her head.

"You can't go into town looking like that, Samantha Susan. Go put a dress on now, before you shame us all."

Sam glanced down at her very best shirt and trousers and shook her head. "This will have to do. I'm not riding down a mountain in a dress. Besides, I don't have a side-saddle."

Her mother bit her bottom lip and busied herself searching through the wardrobe. "If the gown is long enough, you won't need a sidesaddle. Just wear your high boots. At least you'll look halfway decent when you get to town. I don't know what your father is going to say as it is. This is entirely improper."

Sam turned and caught her mother hiding her head in the wardrobe. She felt a tug of something uncomfortable—not precisely guilt, but something akin to it. She was a tremendous disappointment to both her parents, she knew. She could never be the son her father wanted, and never be the kind of lady her mother thought she ought to be. And now she was about to do something so reprehensible that she couldn't even say it to herself and certainly not to her mother. Her mother was trying hard not to weep at her unladylike tendencies, at what she must perceive to be her failure to raise her daughter properly, and Sam wasn't making it any easier for her.

She came up behind her mother and gave her a hug. "It's a long way into town. Why don't I take a dress and keep it in my bag until we're almost there? Then I can put it on before I ride into town and it will look good as new."

Her mother nodded and pulled out a gown Samantha had shoved to the back. "Maybe you better take two gowns, dear. You don't know how long you'll be gone."

Sam carefully folded the gowns, refraining from reminding her mother that she wouldn't have any petticoats to go under them. She could just see herself riding down the mountain, pulling a cartload of crinolines if she wasn't careful. "We won't be gone but a few days, depending on the weather. Sloan says he won't go any farther than Ariposa."

Tears rimmed her mother's eyes when she turned to meet Sam's gaze, but she only nodded a silent agreement. A person would think she was going off to be married and never coming back the way her mother carried on.

Uneasily, hoping Sloan hadn't said something unconscionable, Sam checked her image in the mirror once more. There wasn't anything she could do to make herself beautiful. She would just have to settle for clean and neat. Deciding she'd accomplished that much, she set her hat at an angle, kissed her mother's cheek, and picked up her saddlebags. It was much easier to walk out if she just thought of herself as going to find her father. What happened along the way was irrelevant.

Sloan was already leading their horses out of the stable.

She'd brought one of her father's carefully bred stallions out here, and the animal tossed its mane restlessly in the sunlight. It hadn't received anywhere near the exercise it should have these last weeks. Sam just hoped Sloan was ready for a race down the mountain. Gallant wouldn't be in a mood for walking.

She fed the horse an apple and soothed it with words while Sloan adjusted her gear. His breath frosted in the dawn air as he worked, and Sam couldn't help watching him. He moved with precision and efficiency, checking every detail with admirable thoroughness. While her mind wandered to the beauty of frost-trimmed branches, the sensual heat of the animals in their care, the excitement of knowing they would soon be alone together, he seemed concerned only with the security of their gear and the weight of their supplies.

While her mind wandered, Sam also noted the way Sloan's hat sat down over his eyes, the way his lambskin coat stretched over his shoulders, and the powerful bulge of his thighs as he bent to check beneath her horse. She'd never noticed these things in a man before, and they made her stomach roil nervously. For the first time, she recognized the immense distance between them. Sloan was probably ten years older than herself or more, and from the looks of him, he'd packed those years with experiences she would never know. She'd led a relatively sheltered life until she'd come out here. She had no idea what kind of life Sloan had led. For all she knew, he could be a convicted murderer.

She was absolutely, completely, utterly out of her mind. By the time she reached this conclusion, Sloan was done with his inspection and waited impatiently for her to mount.

When she just stared at him, he grumbled, "You want a lift?"

She hadn't needed help mounting a horse since she was knee high to a grasshopper. She gave him a disdainful look, placed her toe in the stirrup, and swung up gracefully. If she couldn't do much of anything else, she could ride a horse with style.

It gave her considerable pleasure to see the admiration

flickering briefly in Sloan's eyes as he watched. She might not be beautiful, but she had one or two other assets.

She hauled on Gallant's reins as he wheeled impatiently. She saw Doc Ramsey watching through bleary eyes from his windows. The blacksmith was already lighting his fires for the day, and he stopped to wave. A few of the millworkers headed out for the mill, and they halted to watch as Sloan mounted his horse. Sam turned her mount to wave farewell to her mother and the twins, then set Gallant to the road. She saw no point in reining him in forever.

She heard Sloan galloping behind her. She imagined he was swearing at her for not waiting for him to lead the way, but only one road led out of here, and she didn't have any difficulty following it. If he thought he was gaining some submissive female, he might as well learn the truth right up front.

The town had been built at the top of an open slope, and it was safe enough to let the animals have their heads as they raced across the field. Sloan's animal soon passed her by, but Sam didn't care. She hadn't actually been racing so much as enjoying the wind in her hair. He'd know it if she decided to race him.

But if they had a long journey ahead, it was better to pace their mounts. She fell into a trot when Sloan did. The path narrowed up ahead anyway.

They had nothing in common to talk about. Sam wasn't much at small talk in the best of situations, and she wouldn't classify this as one of her better social occasions. Sloan didn't seem prepared to help her out any. He'd barely grunted more than a brief acknowledgment of her presence.

"Where you from originally?" she finally asked, just because she thought something ought to be said.

He didn't even look at her. "Boston."

Boston. He might as well have said London, England. She knew absolutely nothing about Boston, except it was probably a pretty fancy place compared to Spring Creek, Tennessee.

"How long have you been out here?"

"Long enough."

She had an apple in her saddlebags. Maybe if she threw it at his head he'd pay attention. Shooting him seemed a little drastic. "Are you always this voluble or do I just bring it out?" she asked sarcastically.

Sloan swung his head long enough to take note of her expression, then returned his concentration to the road ahead. "You've got a damned annoying mouth on you, you know that, don't you?"

She wouldn't waste the apple. A good rock would suffice. Sam's lips turned up in a malicious smile, and she began to whistle. She couldn't whistle worth a tinker's damn. It should be interesting to see how long it took to break down his taciturnity.

She could see Sloan's shoulders hunch in irritation as they threaded their horses through a mound of boulders. He tried to ride farther ahead, but she kept her horse right on the tail of his. She whistled a little louder and admired the cascade of pines down the mountainside. Patches of snow filled the shaded areas between, but the sun was doing its best to melt it off everywhere else.

"Will you stop that damned caterwauling?" he finally snarled.

"Woke up on the wrong side of the bed, did we?" she asked, undisturbed. "I can see we're destined to have a lovely time of it. I suppose you're of the 'slam, bam' school without even the 'thank you, ma'am,' after."

He turned and glared at her. "What the hell are you talking about?"

Sam shrugged. "Artistic perceptions. Do you read, Mr. Talbott?"

Mouth tightening in a grim line, Sloan slowed his horse until she rode beside him. "You're going to irritate me until I talk, aren't you?"

"How very perceptive of you. You may choose the topic if you prefer." Samantha attempted to maintain her pose of insouciance, but Sloan was even more impressively powerful on horseback than on foot. She almost regretted attracting his attention.

"Since I don't suppose you know anything about the

market prices of lumber or demand for quicksilver, we're more or less committed to personal topics, aren't we?"

The man could be articulate when he wanted to, she noted grudgingly. "It seems that way. I don't suppose you know much about farming or breeding horses or anything like that."

"Not a thing." He gave her a quick glance. "If you've really got your heart set on farming, you'd do much better down in the valley. The climate and soil have to be better."

Sam grinned at this obvious ploy. "Maybe so, but land costs money. I've got enough to buy a little lumber, some seed and grafts and things, but not enough to buy land. My father must have decided the land he bought up the mountain was a better deal for his money. I've got to take what he gives me."

"He can't give you what doesn't belong to him. I own this side of the mountain. I don't know where in hell he thinks he's bought a farm, but if it's anywhere on this side, it's mine."

"We can't very well argue the point until we find him, can we?"

"Have you got a deed?"

Samantha squirmed in her saddle and stared straight ahead. "It wouldn't be very wise of me to admit it if I did, would it? You might try some reprehensible means to separate me from it."

He gave a snort of exasperation. "I don't have to separate you from it. If the land's not on my side of the mountain, I don't need the blamed thing. If it is on my side, the deed's invalid. I just asked because deeds generally contain the coordinates of the land. It would help to figure out where your farm is if I could see the deed."

She considered that for a moment. "There's a description," she admitted. "It's not a very scientific description. It mentions rock walls and a boulder shaped like a hatchet and things like that. My father included what he thought were the approximate coordinates, but he didn't have adequate equipment with him and I can't read surveyor's reports. I've been looking around and haven't found anything to meet the description yet. I just thought I'd wait until spring and explore a little farther afield."

"When we get back, give me the descriptions. Maybe I can make something of them. But I'm warning you, there are a lot of spurious deeds floating around out here. The Mexicans were lax about property lines and keeping records and so forth. A lot of them have been selling these crazy deeds that mean nothing in any court of law. Your father may have fallen victim to one of those bandits."

Sam stiffened her shoulders. "My father is an extremely intelligent man and an excellent judge of character. He wouldn't waste his time or money on anything any less than legitimate."

"He tried to tell me what we're calling Mt. Whitney isn't the highest peak," he warned her. "He also preached that the Indians were the actual owners of the land, and we ought to negotiate with them instead of the Spaniards."

"I don't know anything about Mt. Whitney, but he's probably right about the Indians. We had the same trouble back in Tennessee, and I must say the United States government has never acted honorably in their behalf. I daresay the same sort of things happened out here, only the Spanish were probably the first to walk all over the Indian hunting grounds."

"Indians don't own property," Sloan explained impatiently. "They don't understand the concept. Hell, the Spanish had a hard enough time with the concept of ownership. They just figured there was enough land out here for everybody, and they all went their happy way. We live in a modern world now. We know things can't be done that way. That's why we have deeds and surveys and courts of law to back up a man's claim to ownership. The Indians never established ownership in any legal manner."

She sent him a sharp look. "Fine, Mr. Lawyer. And I suppose if the Chinese sail over here and take over the country and decide all the land belongs to the government and not to individuals, you'll say that's the modern way and agree to it."

She stuck her nose up in the air when he gave her that exasperated, male what-are-we-going-to-do-with-the-dumb-female look.

"The Chinese aren't going to take over the country," was his stoic response.

"I bet the Indians said the same thing," she muttered under her breath.

"I heard that. They fought and lost. Conquerors always have their choice of land. History speaks for itself."

"William the Conqueror preferred his soldiers to marry into Saxon families and claim property that way. It was much more effective than ripping noble families out of their homes and sending them out to foment trouble."

Sam thought she noticed a look of interest on his face, but she refused to turn and look at him squarely. It was scarcely a triumph when a man finally discovered she had brains.

"I'll go find an Indian princess and marry her, if that makes you happy."

She was trying to come up with an appropriately sarcastic reply when the sound of gunfire split the chilly morning air.

Sam dropped to the side of her horse, clinging to its neck, and raced for the cover of the nearest rocky overhang.

Chapter Nineteen

Even though he'd been listening for it, the gunfire startled Sloan. He'd become entirely too engrossed in conversation with Little Miss Spitfire. When he saw her drop to the side of her horse, his heart literally caught in his throat, and he chased her down the trail.

His heart was already beating faster than normal by the time Sam reined the damned stallion in beneath an overhang and slid to the ground, pulling her rifle from the scabbard in the same motion. Sloan had a brief fantasy of being gunned down by a half-pint female before realizing she was doing precisely what he would have done: taking cover and bringing out her weapons before scouting the danger.

If the shot had been meant for him, the killer had lost his opportunity. Colt in hand, Sloan slid to the ground and found a niche behind a boulder. The shelter Sam had chosen was perfect for covering the path they'd left behind them. Anyone coming down it would be spotted instantly. It was a pity he couldn't say the same for anyone coming up it.

"Stay down," he hissed when Sam peered over her shelter. "If they're coming from in front of us, we won't see them until they're on us."

She settled further back against the rock cliff and checked her ammunition. "Sounded like it came from behind to me. I didn't hear any bullet go by me, though." She gave him a curious look. "You expected this, didn't you?"

"I was prepared for it, yes." Sloan kept a grim eye on the trail ahead. He thought he saw movement in the evergreens just beyond the bend they had passed not too many minutes before.

"That's the second time someone's shot at you since we've been here. I suppose the fire was a different attempt? Or was that one an accident?"

She was entirely too sharp for her own good. Sloan scowled. "It wasn't any accident. Somebody set kindling and kerosene-soaked rags on fire in the room over my office, probably figuring I'd asphyxiate if nothing else."

Asphyxiate. That was a good word. It wasn't the kind of word uneducated men would use, however. Schools in Boston must teach fancy things, Sam surmised. "You've either got the luck of the Irish or an extremely incompetent enemy."

"I'm not Irish."

She hadn't thought he was. She checked the trail and caught the flash of something silver up above. She kept her rifle aimed in that direction.

"Don't shoot unless you see who it is. Joe's up there somewhere."

Well, that explained one or two things. Sam gave him a disgruntled look. "You could have told me you were baiting a trap."

"I could have been baiting it for you."

He didn't even turn and look at her when he said that. Damn, but he was a cool character. He was planning on bedding her even when he thought she might be trying to kill him. There ought to be names for men like him. Bastard was the only one that came to mind.

A minute later Joe came loping down the trail, signaling with his thumb for Sloan to follow him. Sloan holstered his Colt, picked up his rifle, and started out of the shelter. Sam came after him.

He turned and pointed back to the rocks. "Stay there."

"Says who?" Sam skirted around him, checking on her high-strung horse before mounting.

"Damn it, Sam, there could be more of them out there. Get back where it's safe." Sloan caught her reins and glared up at her.

"Unless Joe is out to kill you, I doubt that. I'm not some helpless female you have to feel obligated to protect, Talbott. I take care of myself." She shifted her weight and sent the stallion rearing at his reins, forcing Sloan to drop them.

Why argue with the fool female? It wasn't his concern if she got herself killed. But he kept his rifle carefully in hand as he rode behind her, his gaze searching every possible hiding place.

Joe waited in the road they had just come down. Off to one side sprawled a dark object which didn't fit the surrounding landscape. Sloan knew what it was. He wasn't fully certain Samantha understood. Again, he tried to cut her off, keeping her to the road and away from the gruesome sight.

This time, she didn't try to get ahead of him. She stayed on her horse, keeping it prancing restlessly on the path rather than dismounting to get a better look. From her expression, Sloan gathered she had already figured out what she was looking at and wasn't any too happy about it.

"He was aiming between those two rocks," Joe said, gesturing toward the broken chunks of granite lining the cliff's edge. "You can see the trail below from there. In another minute you and the girl would have been in his sights."

Sloan got off and walked over to examine the body. The man was dead. There wasn't a thing he could do for him now. He gave Joe a hard look. "You didn't have to kill him. I would have liked to ask a few questions."

The wiry gunslinger bristled visibly. "He turned a gun on me. I make a habit of shooting anyone who turns a gun on me."

Sloan didn't question that. When he wasn't drunk, Joe was good at what he did. He hadn't survived this long by playing the rules of civilization back East. Sloan knelt beside the body and searched his clothes. "He's one of the millworkers, isn't he? What in hell did he have against me?"

His search turned up a few coins and bills, a lint-covered horehound, a packet of tobacco, and a small leather folder containing a faded daguerreotype of a

woman and a wanted poster. He unfolded the poster while
Joe answered.

"Not a thing that I know of. We just hired him back in
December. He wasn't much of a worker."

Sam dismounted and Sloan wandered in her direction.
He had to give her credit for keeping her mouth shut
when it mattered. He handed her the poster. Joe couldn't
read.

"Wanted for stagecoach robbery." Sam raised her ex-
pressive eyebrows as she scanned the description, then
glanced over to the body on the ground. "Five-nine,
weight one-eighty, sparse brown hair, mustache, tattoo on
right hand." She looked expectantly at Joe.

He lifted the corpse's cold right hand and showed it to
her. "Tattoo. It fits."

Sloan gave a grimace of disgust. "A two-bit thief.
That's too easy. You're telling me that this mongrel
wanted to kill me just to rob me? He'd have done better
to wait until I went to bed and just taken the blasted
safe."

Still staying a distance from the body, Sam patted her
horse's neck. Softly, she said, "He could have been paid."

Both men turned to look at her. She shrugged. "Back
where I come from, we've got men like that. For a price,
they'll gun down whoever you want dead. When the law
gets too close, they move on, but they're usually pretty
careful."

Joe frowned. "He didn't spend money like he had a lot.
Suppose whoever might have hired him wouldn't pay until the job was done."

Sloan made a gesture of disgust. "I don't want to hear
about it. Haul him back to town, ask questions, and get
him buried. If you hear anything important, you know
where to find me."

Joe didn't look particularly happy about those orders.
"There could be more where this one came from." He
glanced in Sam's direction. "You're risking more than
your own neck this time."

"I can handle myself," Sam insisted quietly.

At Joe's doubtful look, Sloan said, "I'll look after her.

I don't think there'll be any others down here, though. I think we've got the one we wanted."

"You'll be at the Regis, then?" Joe still didn't look satisfied.

Sloan held back his grin, though he knew his lips twitched from the effort. He'd be at the Regis all right, with a woman in his bed for twenty-four pleasurable hours. They'd be even more pleasurable now that he knew he wouldn't have to constantly look over his shoulder. He gave Sam a glance. Her sour look said she had gathered the drift of his thoughts. His mouth twitched a little more. This just might be the best time he'd had in a long time.

"The Regis," he confirmed, swinging back on his horse. He couldn't get there soon enough.

As Sam mounted, Sloan pushed back his hat and offered, "Thanks, Joe. I owe you one."

"You owe me a hell of a lot more than that," the older man muttered gruffly.

That was probably so, but he didn't mean to stand around and argue it. It was a little difficult to put a price on saving someone's life. Sloan nudged his horse toward the trail and Samantha.

He'd spent the morning trying not to look at her, but he felt like indulging himself right now. Her hair had grown longer these last few months, and it sprang from beneath her hat brim with a life all of its own. He wondered what it would feel like when he crushed it between his fingers. She set her horse into step beside him, so it was a little difficult to admire thick dark lashes and baby blue eyes, but he could appreciate the pert tilt of her nose.

But it wasn't precisely her face that held Sloan's interest at the moment. It was the contents of that figure-hugging blue cotton shirt beneath the open coat. He could barely keep his horse on the path for glancing over there to see if he was seeing correctly or if his imagination had taken over.

She didn't wear a corset. He'd known that for some time. None of the Neely women wore corsets. It had been the topic of numerous late-night drunken conversations at the saloon. He'd heard men debating whether or not the women wore some fancy new garment that pushed their breasts up but left them looking natural or if all that resplendent roundness was just nature's gift. Sloan pretty well sided with the nature's gift explanation. Those high, soft curves bounced much too easily for there to be anything hampering them.

The male part of him hardened predictably, and he shifted in his saddle. He needed some distraction before he was in no condition to ride. Instead, as they rode past their earlier hiding place, he found himself following the path of his thoughts and asking crudely, "How many men have you known?"

She didn't even deign to turn and look at him when she gave her reply. "More than I wanted. That's a stupid question if I ever heard one."

As an answer, it wasn't particularly precise, but it told him enough. She had some experience, and it probably hadn't been pleasant. That was why she dressed and behaved as she did. She didn't want to attract men's favors. Maybe she'd been raped. The war had been brutal on women as well as men. That might make this encounter unpleasant for both of them, but she was the one who had agreed to it. Maybe he could teach her that sex could be good.

He liked that idea. If he could teach her to like what he did, she might be available more often. He didn't want a clinging vine like the widow, but if they could slip off down the hill occasionally like this, he'd be satisfied. It was a hell of a lot more than he had now—providing he let the Neelys stay.

Scowling at the ramifications of that notion, Sloan pushed on ahead. By now, he ought to have learned better. Women were insidious. Once a man let them into his life, they took over. He had fared much better these last years by keeping women out and visiting them only when necessary. It wouldn't do to start contemplating keeping one handy. That would open a whole can of worms he didn't want to have to deal with.

Sam kept quiet this time, he noted. She was probably searching every clump of trees for a rifle barrel aimed at her. That's what he should have been doing when she'd been talking his ear off earlier. But he'd let her distract him and almost got his head blown off as a result. He would have to start concentrating on the important things and keep his lust where it belonged.

They ate a hasty lunch on a hillside overlooking an open meadow. Sloan could almost hear the little cogs in Sam's brain whirl as she examined the scrub trees and coarse, dead grass. He suspected she was just itching to dig her hands into the dirt to test its quality, but oddly enough, she refrained. He had difficulty seeing past his lust, but he was aware that he dealt with a woman of complicated character. Lord only knew, just her manner of dress would tell him that.

The level of the land flattened as they rode into the early winter sunset. Sloan felt his companion's restlessness, but refrained from commenting on it.

"Are we going to camp out before we get to town?" she finally asked. "It's getting dark, and I don't see any sign of civilization."

"We've got a way to go yet. If you're tired, we can stop here." He began scanning the horizon for a suitable stopping place. He was eager to reach the hotel, but he wasn't an uncontrollable adolescent any longer. He could wait.

"I'm not tired," she answered defensively, "but the horses need resting." Reluctantly, she added, "And I promised Mama I would put on a dress before going into town."

He turned and looked at her with interest. "A dress? Were you planning on pulling it on over your trousers?"

She gave him a steely look. "That's none of your damned business. Just give me some warning of your plans so I can prepare."

At this point, he didn't care one way or another if she wore dresses, pants, or nothing at all. He was hot and hard just thinking about her without contemplating what she was or was not wearing. He'd damned well waited entirely too long for a woman this time. The images he conjured right now would scare her halfway till tomorrow if she could see them.

"We'll camp then, hit town tomorrow. We won't accomplish much there by the time we ride in tonight anyway." Sloan found the place he was looking for and guided his horse in that direction. He wondered if he could talk her into sharing a bedroll. From her prickly attitude, he suspected he'd have to talk mighty fast.

She knew how to make camp. She had her horse hobbled, fed, and brushed down before he had their gear unloaded. She had a fire started and coffee cooking while he took care of his horse. He bagged a rabbit while she made pan bread and beans. They worked easily together, without either one having to say much.

As he sat and savored the evening meal under the stars, Sloan contemplated the women he knew back East doing what Sam had just done. His mouth curved maliciously at the thought. He'd only have to mention scorpions and snakes and they wouldn't even get off their horses. Sam had already killed one of the insects without a second thought. He'd wager she'd offer to cook the snake if he caught one.

It was almost like camping with another man. Almost. The firelight gleamed in copper tresses and accented the shadows of hills and valley revealed by the open neck of her shirt. When she spoke, that sultry voice of hers went straight from his ears to his loins. She was slender and soft in all the right places, and he couldn't keep his eyes away, so he kept his hat pulled down to hide them.

"I didn't think you cooked," he said, just to hear her answer. The bread was delicious, light and sweet, unlike anything he'd cooked for himself over a campfire.

"Not like my mother," Sam admitted, sipping her coffee. "But everyone ought to know how to cook. Once I have my farm, I'll have to cook for myself. I'd rather know how to do it right."

"Your family must have had land back in Tennessee. Why didn't you stay there while your father explored California?"

She cocked an eyebrow at his unusual interest, but she answered calmly enough. "We lost family in the war. We lost people who had worked with us for as long as I could remember. We lost friends and neighbors. And the ones who lived or stayed behind are consumed with hatred. We were Union supporters, and everyone knew that. Even though we've been friends and neighbors all our lives, we were suddenly the enemy. It wasn't so bad during the war when everyone helped everyone else, but once the South lost . . ." She shrugged.

Sloan had left Boston before the war started. He had never considered joining. He couldn't bear to go back there, even to fight. Three thousand miles had scarcely been far enough away from home. When he'd first left, he had considered taking a ship for the Far East, but he hadn't had a dime at the time. So he'd buried himself out here. The war inside himself had been vicious enough without hearing of the war back there.

He was just realizing how much he had locked himself away from, but it was too late to matter now.

Sloan sat up and unrolled his bedding. With only a glance to the woman still nursing her mug of coffee on the other side of the campfire, he said without inflection, "It's warmer if we share. We can start our twenty-four hours now if you like."

Chapter Twenty

Samantha reached for her own bedroll. "Dream on, Talbott. We look for my father first."

"We'll look for him. I don't make promises I can't keep. I just figure we can get home sooner if we start now."

Impatience was his middle name. The sound of it in his voice now shouldn't send a shiver down her spine. Sam cast a surreptitious glance to the man sprawled—fully clothed—on top of his blankets, his hands propped behind his head as he watched her. She could go over there and lie down beside him now and get this over with. He would use those big, competent hands to undress her and then himself. Then he would straddle her body, and she would feel the weight of him pushing her into the blankets and the cold, hard ground. She couldn't fantasize any further than that.

That was quite far enough. Her hands were shaking as she shook out her bedroll. "I want sheets and a decent bed," she informed him calmly, as if she said these kind of things every day.

He grunted disapproval, then sat up to pull off his boots. "Bring your blankets over here," he ordered.

Sam continued spreading them out where she was—on the opposite side of the fire from him.

When she didn't move, he growled under his breath, picked up his own bedroll, and came around the fire. Then he went back to fetch his boots and rifle.

She stared at him as if he were a serpent. When she wouldn't even sit down and remove her boots, Sloan's expression revealed his irritation. "We're likely to shoot each other in the cross-fire if something wakes us in the night. Lie down. I'm not going to get up in the middle of the night to rape you. I could do that no matter where I put my bedroll."

Sam reluctantly lowered herself to the blankets. Sloan was little more than two feet away and pulling off his shirt. Her insides clenched and froze. She couldn't even bend over to remove her boots. Firelight gleamed over taut muscles and bronzed skin. She tried to tell herself she'd seen all this before, but that didn't work. Knowing she could reach out and touch him, and knowing what he wanted her to do made his presence much too real. She tried not to stare at the soft, dark fur on his chest, but her breasts tingled at the thought.

When Sloan leaned over and jerked at her boot, Sam nearly toppled over. He held her leg with one powerful hand and pulled with the other. His touch shot straight up her leg, and she thought she would be paralyzed for certain. She closed her eyes and tried to ignore the sensation when he reached for the other boot. The feeling only intensified. She could feel him right in the center of her, and it made her pretty damned uncomfortable.

She heard amusement in his voice when he spoke. "You can open your eyes now. I'm getting between the blankets."

"Why can't you wear underwear like everybody else?" she grumbled as she turned her back on him and pulled her blankets up. She wasn't about to sleep undressed, but she unbuttoned her pants for comfort.

"I could ask you the same thing," he said with the same amusement. "I know you're not wearing a corset under those things. Are you wearing long johns or one of those frilly lace things? Does a lady who wears pants wear drawers?"

"My father refuses to let us wear corsets. He says they're unhealthy. And for the rest, you'll just have to guess, won't you?"

"Not for long," he replied with satisfaction. "By tomorrow night I'll know all your little secrets." He hesitated, then continued, "And for once, I'm in agreement with your father. All that whalebone and steel is crippling. They ought to shoot whoever invented it."

Sam snuggled down inside her blankets, then pulled her rabbit coat over the top. It was getting damned chilly out here. "I figure a man who hates women invented corsets. It couldn't have been a woman. Women aren't allowed to invent anything."

"Women don't have minds of their own. They like being told what to do. That's why they don't invent anything."

Sam laughed out loud. "And women wear corsets because that's what they've been told to do. I guess men are going to have to tell them to stop wearing them."

"That's what your father did," he said, suspicious of her good humor.

She giggled. "So he did. And we obeyed."

"It's good to know that you obey someone, at least." Instead of sounding satisfied, he sounded mystified.

"When we feel like it," she admitted.

"Are you telling me you wouldn't obey him if you didn't feel like it?"

He was getting closer. Sam adjusted the saddle she used as pillow. "I'm telling you I wouldn't wear a corset if you paid me."

"So by telling you not to wear a corset, your father only told you to do what you were already doing."

"Very good," she said softly. "You'll catch on one of these days."

"The hell I will," he answered irritably, turning his back on her. "Any woman of mine will do what I tell her or pay the consequences."

She giggled again. "Good luck, Mr. Talbott."

Disgruntled, he ignored her taunt.

The shoe was on the other foot when they finally rode into town the next day. Ariposa was a run-down mining town, barely more than a shanty town, but Sam still felt self-conscious and uncomfortable riding in wearing a long gabardine skirt that hiked up over her boots to show her stockings while she sat astride. Sloan's interested looks didn't help any. A person would think he'd never seen legs before.

It was nearly impossible to get down from her horse gracefully in this getup, and she was forced to accept

Sloan's assistance. He grasped her waist as if he had every right to do so and swung her down so easily it left her breathless. She was left standing nose to chest with him, and she grimaced. He was taller than any man had any right to be. She liked it when she could look a man in the eye.

She stepped backward hastily as soon as he released her waist. "Where do we begin?" she asked, filling in the awkwardness. She was scarcely aware of where they were or who was watching. Sloan seemed to encompass her entire world at the moment.

He chuckled. "I know where I'd like to begin. I like that little frilly thing you're wearing behind that gawd-awful bodice. Where do you get your clothes anyway? They never fit."

The man had more nerve than a pride of lions. Sam tugged at her bodice, trying to pull it up, but the dress had belonged to her mother, and she hadn't tucked it in enough when she'd altered it. She pulled her coat around her. "This was my mother's," she answered defiantly.

His eyebrows raised slightly. "I get it. All those rags you've been wearing belonged to your sisters or your mother. Don't you own any gowns of your own?"

"I outgrew them and I don't wear them much and I don't sew. Let's just get on with this, shall we? My wardrobe isn't any business of yours." Hastily, before he got the wrong idea about her poorly worded demand, she said, "Where's the first place to ask about my father?"

"The livery. He rode a horse as hot-blooded as that one you're riding. They're not much use in the mountains, but there's a few people down here who want to raise them. Someone will remember the horse."

Sam wondered if he was being deliberately insulting by assuming people were more likely to remember a horse than her father, but she wouldn't antagonize him by challenging him just yet. She followed him to the livery, trailing Gallant behind her.

He was right. The men at the livery remembered the horse. They thought it had been through sometime early last summer, but they couldn't remember when. They didn't know where the owner was going when he left, either.

Sam pulled out the miniature daguerreotype she kept in her pocket. "Is this the man?" she asked.

The men passed the photograph around, frowned, nodded, and studied it some more. "Looks like it. Been a while, but he seems familiar."

She wanted to stamp her feet and rage and demand that they be certain, but she merely returned the miniature to her pocket. If these men knew what they were talking about, then her father had actually left the mountain alive. She glanced hesitantly at Sloan's stony expression. Maybe she had been falsely accusing him of murder in her mind.

She hadn't believed it of him for a long time, but it was a relief to have it confirmed. She was as bad as he was, each thinking the other capable of murder, but still making this insane agreement. She didn't like realizing they had more in common than she would admit.

"Where now?" she murmured as they stabled the horses and walked back through town.

"The hotel."

Alarmed, Sam halted where she was. Her skirt dragged in the dust, and she knew her brimmed felt hat scarcely resembled a lady's bonnet, but she disregarded the stares she drew. "One question is scarcely sufficient, Sloan Talbott. If that's what you consider your end of the agreement, then this whole thing is off."

He came back and looked down at her, and she felt like the half-pint he called her. He might stand only a head taller, but he was twice as broad where it counted. She was acutely aware of the way his muscles bunched beneath his coat when he reached for her.

He caught her arm and dragged her forward. "Your father would have stayed at the hotel," he growled. "If I have to explain everything to you, you can stay in the damned room until I'm done."

Of course. She was too nervous to be reasonable. She would have to get a grip on herself. She hurried after him.

The hotel clerk remembered her father from the photograph well enough. "He tried to tell the Chinamen working on the railroad that they were being exploited. He wanted them to organize and file a complaint. Never heard the like. He was lucky to escape without tar and feathers. We need that railroad."

"Did he say where he was going?" Sloan asked without looking at Sam.

" 'Frisco or Sacramento, I imagine. He was pretty hot under the collar about it. He got the names of the railroad board and lit out in their direction."

Sloan laid a bill on the desk. "Give us a room. We'll be staying the night. Does Hawkins still hang around the Emporium?"

The clerk didn't even question his command. He offered the register and let Sloan sign them in as Mr. and Mrs. "Far as I know. He's not a man whose path I mean to cross."

Sloan slammed the pen down. "Have someone bring up a hot bath." He shouldered their saddlebags and started for the stairs.

Sam gathered up her skirts and hurried after him. She wasn't ready to call it quits yet. She wanted to go on to San Francisco. People always remembered her father, so he shouldn't be hard to trace. They'd just seen an example of that.

"How far is it to Sacramento?" she asked breathlessly, hurrying after Sloan's long strides as he took the stairs.

"Your father would have figured on catching the board meeting in 'Frisco, and that's a day's ride, at least." He turned down the hall, found the door he wanted, and inserted the key.

"Couldn't we go? It's still early morning. We could almost be there by nightfall." She was too interested in pleading her case to hesitate on the threshold. She followed Sloan in and didn't even quiver until he slammed the door behind her.

She quivered then. Sloan stopped in front of her, and the look in his eyes was totally masculine. She could almost feel him touch her, though he hadn't lifted a hand. Her breast tingled, and she clutched her coat closed again.

"The agreement was for Ariposa only. I'll hire Hawkins to go into 'Frisco." He dropped the saddlebags.

She jumped an inch and continued to clutch her coat. "Maybe we could extend the agreement?" she asked tentatively, uncertain exactly as to what she meant, but hoping he'd put it into words.

The question raised a spark of interest. Sloan removed her hat and ran a hand through her tangled hair, squeezing it between his fingers, then massaging her scalp. Sam tried to hold still, but she was quaking in her shoes. Her insides felt incredibly odd, and she wondered if she was coming down with something.

"Forty-eight hours?" he asked speculatively.

Her eyes widened. She'd thought she'd understood what men did to women when they got them in bed, but even horses couldn't do it for forty-eight hours. She gulped and nodded. "After we go to 'Frisco."

She could see he didn't like that notion. He frowned and ran his hand through her hair some more. She still had the coat wrapped around her, but she could tell where he was looking. He wasn't content with looking. He dropped his hand to the front of the coat and pushed her hands aside. The coat fell open, and he pushed it back. Her bodice didn't fit tightly as it should—it hung like an old sack—but he could apparently see something that she couldn't in it. He nodded slowly.

"All right, but we're going to ride like hell. You'd better not complain you're too sore when we get there."

She hadn't thought about that. She'd continue not thinking about it. When he bent to pick up the saddlebags, she hurried to help him. "What about that bath you ordered?"

"They can give it to somebody else." He threw open the door and started down the stairs at a pace Sam could barely match.

She was going to regret this, she knew. She already regretted it. As Sloan threw the key and some money on the desk in front of the astonished clerk, she hurried out the door, hiding the color in her cheeks. She wondered what the clerk thought they'd done up there in that brief amount of time. It didn't pay to wonder.

She had just agreed to give Sloan Talbott forty-eight hours with her behind the closed doors of a room just like

that one. She hadn't paid much attention to the bed while
in there, but it rose before her mind's eye now. It hadn't
been a very big bed. It had just enough room for two people to lie side by side. With someone the size of Sloan,
they wouldn't even have space between them. He would
see to it that they wouldn't have space between them.
They would be naked and on top of each other.

Maybe she would die before this was all over. Maybe
she'd just keel over dead before she had to share that bed
with him. It had all seemed rather abstract before, but
now that they'd spent twenty-four hours in each other's
company, it was becoming a little too real.

She heard Sloan's boots on the walk behind her. He
was beside her within seconds. He didn't say anything as
he let her set the pace. She knew he was there, every masculine inch of him. She just might break out in hives any
minute now. She could still feel it where he'd brushed her
coat aside.

"You see to getting the horses saddled. I'm going to
find Hawkins." He finally broke the silence as they
reached the livery.

Only then did she realize she hadn't even changed out
of her dress. She gazed down at the skirt in dismay, then
nodded dismally. It was going to be a hell of a long ride.

Sloan lifted her chin with the side of his hand. His eyes
were almost warm as they met hers. "I like the skirt. It
will give me something to think about while we ride."

Then he was gone, leaving her hot all up and down as
she stared after him.

Chapter Twenty-one

Sam had the horses saddled and ready to go by the time Sloan returned. He checked the fastenings, nodded in approval, and threw her up on her horse. He could feel her stiffen at his touch, but he didn't have time to waste on proprieties. He knew he'd just committed himself to another day and night of torment, but the price was worth it. He would simply have to make certain she didn't try this little gambit again until he'd had a taste of what she'd promised.

He could almost look forward to chasing her damned father around the state if he knew every night he would have this redheaded witch in his bed. It was winter. Business was slow. The men wouldn't miss him for a while. He could afford a week, maybe even two, of total self-indulgence. Wasn't that what he'd worked toward—enough money to enjoy himself?

Riding out of town behind her, watching her rear end sway in the saddle, he almost convinced himself. It didn't matter that she wasn't like any other woman he knew. It just mattered that she was a woman and willing. That's all he wanted.

But as they rode at a steady pace across the valley, Sloan found himself pointing things out to Sam, knowing how quickly she would grasp their significance, looking forward to her eager questions. She knew considerably more about farming than he did, and more than once he had to keep her from veering off their course to ask questions at some nearby household. It had been a long time since he'd been able to converse with anyone of equal intelligence. It rather dismayed him to discover that a woman could be his match.

Oh, Emmanuel Neely had made a pleasant conversationalist the first few nights he'd spent in town. Sloan could respect his mind if not his far-fetched beliefs. But talking with Emmanuel wasn't the same as talking with Sam. Emmanuel knew everything and wasn't much interested in anyone else's opinion. Sam's mind was wide open, willing to snatch up every piece of information and work it through the incredible store of knowledge she already possessed. She dismissed popular beliefs with incisive logic, and granted careful thought to notions Sloan considered little more than superstitions.

They still argued over the right of the railroads to lay down tracks at the cost of lives versus the necessity of growth and expedient communication when it came time to stop for the night. Sam still naively defended the argument that the end never justified the means when Sloan pulled her down from the horse.

"I'm going to kiss you," he warned her. "You tell me if the end justifies the means when I stop."

She opened her mouth to protest, but he merely took advantage of the situation. He closed his lips across hers and dipped his tongue inside.

She nearly bolted from his arms. When she settled down, she responded with a surge of electricity that jolted Sloan right down to his boot heels. She'd finally learned to wrap her arms around his neck, and he lifted her to fit more exactly against him. It was like toasting himself against a hot furnace. He couldn't get enough.

He'd only meant to shock her into shutting up, but he was having difficulty letting her go. Her unbound breasts pressed against him, and her hips wriggled for a better placement right where he ached the most. If he didn't peel her away soon, they would be rolling on the ground without benefit of even a bedroll, and certainly not bed and sheets.

She tilted her head back to gasp for air, and he moved in on her throat. She had a lovely throat, long and slender and smelling faintly of lavender. She tasted delicious, and she made no move to stop him. Already he had his sights on a more luscious part of her anatomy—but the unwieldy bodice sagged in his way.

It apparently buttoned up the back. He didn't have a chance of getting up beneath her heavy coat to release those buttons without raising her hackles. Sighing, Sloan finally admitted surrender. He kissed her cheek and her brow, and taking a deep breath, he lifted his head to look down at her.

"Maybe we should keep on riding tonight. The steamboat has already left so we can't take the river, but if we ride hard across country, we could be in bed by midnight."

She was staring at him again. Amusement rose up in him as it never did with any other woman. She didn't blush prettily or look away shyly or smile at him boldly. She just stared at him, as if he were something new and amazing and altogether wonderful. Sloan knew he wasn't that, but he still liked the feeling it gave him. He rubbed a finger along her lips. "Sam?"

She shook her head and pushed away. "You said you didn't want me sore," was all she said before turning back to unsaddle the horses.

Hell, right now, he'd take her any way he could get her, but it wouldn't be much fun for her. He still had this wild idea of teaching her to enjoy sex. Sloan knew he'd offered her a crude bargain, but he thought she might get a little bit more out of it than the terms specified. If she ever did decide to marry, she could go to her husband with more confidence than she had now. He didn't think himself particularly conceited in the matter. He just had reason to know more than the average man.

"What do you think those railroad men would do to my father if that's where he went?" she asked carefully as they prepared camp.

"Put him on a slow boat to China." That's sure as hell what he would have done, given the opportunity.

She frowned, uncertain of his seriousness. "They wouldn't hurt him, would they?"

Sloan shrugged and threw coffee grounds into the pot. "The men building the railroad aren't exactly patient, understanding types. You can't blow up mountains and drive hundreds of workers to their deaths and be kind and understanding, too." He caught a glimpse of her face and re-

gretted his harshness. "But your father wouldn't mean
much more to them than a buzzing gnat, unless he's inclined to bellow his views in newspapers to foment public
outrage. He wouldn't go buying a newspaper, would he?"

"He never has before." Samantha stirred the corn mush
she was making. "Mostly, he just invents things. He sees
something needing to be done, and he works on it until he
figures out how to do it. It's just he always has an opinion
on everything and isn't afraid to voice it."

"Yeah, I noticed." He gave her a curious look. "He's
not going to appreciate it if you show up in my company."

Sam shrugged. "What matters is knowing he's all right.
I don't think we'll find him in San Francisco. He always
writes, and he's never been gone this long. Something's
happened. I want to know what it is."

"I went ahead and hired Hawkins. He'll follow behind
us. You'll have to give him that picture you're carrying
before we leave."

She nodded, and the sadness of her expression tugged
at the heart he no longer had. Grimacing, Sloan turned
away and occupied himself elsewhere. He didn't have
time for sympathizing with a wildcat.

Later, when they had settled themselves down in their
bedrolls, he lay awake listening to her breathing and cre-
ating pretty fantasies of what he would do to her once
they got to that hotel. If he could just concentrate on the
real reason he had her out here, he wouldn't have to think
about how it must feel to have a father disappear off the
face of the earth. She was holding up pretty well. The
Neelys were a self-reliant lot. They didn't need that
rabble-rousing maniac they called father and husband. He
shouldn't feel the least bit ashamed of what he was doing.

But some small piece of the man he used to be lived inside him, and that piece nagged at his conscience every
time he thought about the sadness on Samantha's face. He
couldn't drive it away, so he finally gave up his fantasies
and fell asleep.

The next day dawned bright and unusually warm for
the time of year. They both tied their coats up in their
bedrolls and set out to enjoy the sunshine. After inquiring

if they would reach town today, Sam had donned her gray gabardine dress again. He still hadn't gotten a good glimpse of what she wore under it, but today she had covered the top with some kind of foolish pink jacket that came to her waist and tied at the neck. The wide sleeves gave her ample room for movement, and the flowing material covered too much of her figure for Sloan's taste. He scowled at it, but said nothing as they set out.

He decided to avoid the civilized areas along the river where they could catch the steamboat into 'Frisco. Uncertain of his reasoning, he preferred thinking he was saving Sam's reputation. In truth, it was more likely that he preferred to keep her to himself a while longer.

But by noon he knew they came near the bay area. Samantha seemed to sense it, too. She asked constant questions about the sights around her and practically bounced in her seat with eagerness.

"Are we near the coast yet? Will we see the ocean?"

It hadn't occurred to him, but she probably had never seen the ocean. Sloan knew this area, and he scanned their location briefly. "We're just south of the bay. The ocean is a bit out of the way, but I can take you there if you want."

"Really?" She turned those brilliant wide eyes to him, and Sloan couldn't have refused her anything.

He led her off the main trail and through waist-high acres of wild oats. She should get her first sight of the water from a natural viewpoint and not that of the homely wharves of San Francisco with their rickety warehouses and derelict boats. Even he relaxed and felt more at home when buffeted by the ocean breezes and surrounded by nothing but the natural splendor of this wild coast.

Sloan found a protected spot behind a dune out of the wind. While he hobbled the horses, Sam took off running through the sand, lifting her skirt so high he could see not only her ankles, but glimpses of her legs. It was a hell of a thing when a man with his background was straining for a glimpse of leg, but with Sam it seemed the thing to do. She wasn't a child to be indulged, he'd seen ample evidence of that. Yet she wasn't the stiffly proper lady of his former acquaintance either. And whatever else she might be, she wasn't one of the loose females of his more recent acquaintance. She wasn't any of the things he thought a woman might be, so he felt free to act with her as he wished. She didn't seem to object.

By the time Sloan strolled over the dune and into sight of the breakers, Sam had already reached the water's edge. She'd managed to dispose of her shoes and stockings as well as her dainty jacket, but she seemed to have forgotten her skirt as she stood where the waves could splash around her, damping the heavy material to her knees. Sloan shoved his hands into his pockets, resisting the urge to join her.

Gulls screeched overhead, and the winter sun gleamed against the rich red of her hair as she stood, entranced, her arms wrapped around her waist. The wind caught her loosely pinned curls and sent them streaming behind her. The waves splashed and puddled and seeped away around her feet. The gown clung to her like seaweed, and Sloan had the instant vision of some sea goddess arisen from the deep. She was so much a part of the nature around her that he couldn't separate one from the other, and his longing for something he could not see intensified.

Only then did he note the massive swell rolling in from beyond the line of breakers. Sam had never seen the ocean and knew nothing of its power, but he did. He'd grown up in Boston, sailed the Atlantic, and knew the Pacific to be even more treacherous. He didn't know the slope of the ground beneath those deceptively innocent waves. And Sam knew nothing at all.

Sloan took off at a long lope across the shifting sand. Sam didn't even hear him coming. Her eyes were wide and as blue as the sea beyond her as she watched the wave build and foam and crest. With a shout of triumph, Sloan caught her just as the breaker crashed, dragging the sand out from beneath their feet and soaking them from top to bottom.

They stumbled and fell in retreat, hitting the sand hard, and Sam's delighted laughter filled his ears. They were soaked and shivering and coated in sand, and she laughed as if this were the highlight of her life. Her arms had instinctively clung to his neck when he grabbed her, and they remained there now. Breathless from the fall, Sloan kept his eyes closed and absorbed the feel of her beneath him.

It wasn't enough. Somehow, their salt-crusted lips found each other. He kept his eyes closed, savoring the moment of this untarnished surrender. Waves crashed not inches from their feet, but the heat of Samantha's proximity was all that mattered. Sloan slid his tongue between her teeth, felt the furnace of their desire, and quit thinking of anything at all.

Her gown was drenched, and so was he. But instead of feeling the cold, he felt the hardened points of Sam's breasts pressing through the cloth, begging to be touched. He obliged, taking one between his fingers and rolling it lightly. She groaned beneath him, arching eagerly into his palm. Shattered by a surge of lust so great he could barely control it, he ground his mouth against hers and filled his hands with the mounds of both breasts.

She was making weak cries—whether of protest or desire, he couldn't discern. It didn't matter. The wind swept over them, but he kept her covered with his body. The air smelled of salt and Sam. Sloan would recognize her distinctive scent anywhere: sweet and rich and all his. Her hands roamed his back, clinging to his waist when he pulled at her skirt, sliding upward to clench his arms when his fingers brushed her bare leg. He didn't have to force his mind to quit functioning. His body had already taken over. That happened so seldom he made no effort to regain control.

She writhed beneath him, making him frantic. Sloan blessed the looseness of her bodice when he discovered he could slide his hand beneath the waistband through the gathered folds of the skirt he'd shoved up to her waist. His fingers discovered the satin of her flesh when he pushed aside the frail covering of her chemise. She moaned, and this time he knew it was in pleasure as his hand captured her bare breast.

Her kisses were nearly as frantic as his passion. He didn't dare meet the clarity of Sam's eyes just yet. The moment was still too innocent, too spontaneous to be broken by lies or truths. Their bodies responded of their own accord, as naturally as the waves breaking against the sand and rocks. He didn't want anything to interfere.

Sloan untied her drawers and pushed aside the flaps so he could touch her there. Sam gave a high, keening cry as his fingers found the place he meant to violate, but she was wet and moved eagerly with the motion of his hand. It was still right. He wasn't doing anything wrong. She wanted this as much as he did.

He wanted to suckle her breasts, but the hampering bodice stood in his way. That, too, didn't matter. There would be time for that later, when they lay between the sheets he'd promised her. She was sculpted beautifully, of delicate lines and slender curves. He cherished her breast, slid his hand downward to the slope of her waist, then around to the fullness of her buttock. She whimpered and lifted herself, and Sloan finally opened his eyes to look at her there, where her hair was a darker red and her unblemished skin shone like fine porcelain in the noon sun. He touched her again, and her thighs parted for him, and he knew he couldn't wait any longer. He had the whole world around him, and this was all he could see. He was obsessed. He knew it and didn't care.

He moaned a sigh of relief as he unfastened the buttons of his pants and released his hardened flesh. If the wind still whipped around them, he didn't mind. He had found the harbor he needed.

Sloan covered Sam with his body, seeking her mouth as well as reassurance, teasing the crests of her breasts beneath the hampering cloth. Her fingers dug into his back through the dampness of his shirt, but they didn't push him away. He shifted his hips to slide between the warmth of her thighs, and she gasped at the sudden abrasion of something thicker and harder than his finger, but still, she returned his kisses.

It was right. The ocean crashed against the shore behind them. They were wet inside and out and all over. The heat of their bodies chased away the chill of the wind. There could only be one more perfect moment than this.

He needed to be inside her.

Gently, Sloan pushed her legs apart. Concentration

came naturally to him, but he was on the verge of losing it when he felt Sam quiver and resist slightly. He touched her again, searching out the swollen place that made her quake and moan while his own body roared in protest. He couldn't hold off a great deal longer. It had been much too long already.

She was moaning and writhing again, her hips rising in a natural rhythm that made him breathe easier with relief. He caught her in his hands, sliding her drawers further downward, lifting her until she was free. Her skirt fell upward, and he no longer had to wait.

He plunged deep and sure and true—and heard her scream as tissues tore.

Sloan cursed. He cried. But his body couldn't halt its plunge any more than it could halt its bucking motion afterward. He'd waited too long, held himself back too hard. He couldn't stop.

And to his surprise, she joined him. She rose to meet his thrust, gasped in wonder as he filled her, and clung to him when he withdrew. He repeated the motion and so did she, until he knew he couldn't withhold his response any longer.

With a groan of regret, Sloan jerked himself from the welcoming warmth of Samantha's body and spilled his seed in the sand.

Chapter Twenty-two

Samantha kept her eyes closed and felt the sea breeze cool her heated face as well as other unmentionable parts of her. She ached with a pain so intense that she wasn't certain it was physical. For a moment she had come so close to bliss that she could almost touch it, and Sloan Talbott had been the man who had taken her there. It defied belief. Somehow, he had entered her and done something to her soul, and she would never be the same again.

So she lay here listening to the gulls squawking overhead, the ocean crashing gently against the shore, and pretending she was alone. She didn't want to imagine how she looked with her skirt hiked to her waist and the rest of her sprawled in wanton abandon. Sloan had left her. She would just lie here and die peacefully.

A cold wet cloth slapped between her thighs where she still burned, and she squawked as loudly as the gulls. Her eyes flew open, and she tried to sit up, but Sloan's palm flattened over her stomach as he used his handkerchief to cleanse her tender flesh. She would no doubt have died of embarrassment if he wasn't so clinically efficient. The tight-lipped scowl on his face kept her silent.

She could see anger burning beneath the dark flush of his jaw, and she wondered idly why he should be angry. He had practically raped her out here in the middle of nowhere, with gritty sand for a bed and their clothes wet and plastered to their bodies. It wasn't exactly the romantic moment she had quaintly envisioned. Yet oddly enough, she wasn't sorry for it. She was quite content to lie here and listen to the waves—if Sloan would just leave her alone.

The wet linen of his shirt clung to his torso like a second skin. She could practically see through it to the ridges and bulges of his shoulders and chest. It would have been nice if she could have seen him without his shirt, perhaps touched him. A lot of things would have been nice, but it had all happened too swiftly.

Well, she was no longer a virgin. She now knew what it was like to be with a man. Did that make her more of a woman? She didn't think so. She sat up and pulled her skirt over her legs as soon as Sloan released her. Her body felt different, open and vulnerable and aching, but it was still her body and not his. She gazed out at the ocean rather than meet his glare.

"Why in damnation didn't you tell me you were a virgin?" he shouted against the wind, as if she weren't sitting just two feet away.

"I can't remember your asking," she answered politely, trying not to let his anger get under her skin. She was shivering now, and she didn't think it was entirely from the cold. She had to fight back tears, and she never cried.

"You told me you knew more men than you wanted!" He jumped to his feet and finished fastening the buttons of his soaked denims.

Sam watched with undisguised curiosity as he covered the black swirl of hair arrowing down over his taut abdomen. She hadn't even seen him naked, but she could still feel him inside her. Their forty-eight hours had only just begun. She wondered if her inexperience had put an end to it.

"I hadn't realized you were using the biblical definition." She tried to keep her thoughts around her, but it was increasingly difficult while watching him pace like a panther. "Actually, if I'd known, I would have been insulted and probably shot you. I probably ought to shoot you now, but I can't decide whether you're insulting women in general or me in particular by assuming we've all known more than one man."

He gave her a look of controlled fury. "What in hell was I supposed to expect when you agreed to this damned bargain?"

Sam sighed and stood up, brushing ineffectually at her

sandy skirt. If it was a fight he wanted, she certainly could give him one. "I expected you to think I desperately wish to find my father, but I don't suppose a self-centered pig like yourself would understand that. Is it time to go yet, or do you want another roll in the sand to prove your manly prowess before we leave?"

He looked as if he would strike her, and she took a step backward. She caught her heel in her skirt and stumbled, and he grabbed her elbow and jerked her upright.

He was practically standing on her toes. Without her boots she had to force her head backward to look up at him. Her breasts burned where they rubbed against him, and she now had some knowledge of what the tingling between her legs meant at this sudden proximity to his hips. She took a hasty step backward, but he didn't loose his grip on her arm.

"Don't pretend I was the only one who wanted what happened. You were there with me every step of the way." His eyes narrowed as his gaze fell to her bodice, finding the jut of her nipples pressing against the clinging cloth. "You're as ready as I am to have another go at it."

She took a deep gulp at the sudden twinge of excitement in the lower part of her body at his words. Amazed, she looked down between them, at the way her breasts swelled. She was already swaying instinctively toward him, and she couldn't help but look at the place concealing his masculine secrets. She gulped and looked away again. The old cloth was too tight and too worn to disguise his desire.

She jerked from his grasp and lifting her skirt, started over the sand dune. "First, we look for my father."

Sloan was beside her in a few long strides, catching her by the waist and lifting her from her feet. Samantha found herself plastered against him as his mouth caught and tormented hers once more. Damn, but he needed only to touch her lips with his and she turned into liquid pudding. She took his tongue and met it with her own as she slid down his front, and he lowered her feet to the sand.

"Then we'll find a bed," he growled against her mouth, pushing her slightly away. His head came up so that their eyes met. "And I'm not marrying anybody."

Sam set her lips and glared back. "I wouldn't marry you if you were the last man on earth."

"Good. Then that's settled. Let's get going."

He spun on his heel and set out across the dune, ungallantly letting her make her own way through the shifting sand. She stopped to gather her shoes and stockings and put them on at the crest of the hill. Sloan was already checking their gear and unhobbling the horses.

It was a damned good thing she wasn't a romantic or Sloan Talbott would get under her skin real quick, like a tick on a dog. He was rude and uncouth, but he unrolled her coat and threw it to her to stop her shivering and offered to ride slowly if she wanted to sit sideways on the saddle. She supposed that was all the concession she would get for what they had just done together.

She didn't need any concession. She got up in the saddle by herself, wincing only slightly as she threw her leg over the broad back of her horse. The pain served to remind her how thick he'd been when he'd shoved into her. She refused to complain. He was right. She had wanted what they'd done as much as he had, and it had felt as natural and right as the clouds floating in the sky above them. She just hadn't wanted him to stop.

But he'd taken precautions as he'd promised. There wouldn't be any unwanted results from their coupling. That gave her some feeling of relief and security to carry with her to the next time. Knowing it was probably the wrong time of the month for conception wasn't enough. Mistakes happened, and she couldn't afford mistakes with a man like Sloan. And there would very definitely be a next time and quite possibly a time after that for mistakes to occur.

Samantha gave herself into her daydreams as she watched the sway of Sloan's broad shoulders and narrow hips on the horse in front of her. Next time, maybe they wouldn't be wearing so many clothes. She flushed heatedly as she tried to imagine him without anything on. The image came to her easily if she thought of him covering her body with his as he had done earlier. She wanted to see him like that, not just imagine him.

She didn't know why it had to be Sloan Talbott who

drove her to these wild thoughts. He didn't care for her in any way except for what she offered him between her legs. He'd already proved that. The difference in their ages and experience loomed suddenly immense between them. She was little more than a fool girl in his eyes, although she knew she was mature beyond her age, and she was no spring chicken. But he had the advantage over her in the one area where they shared an interest—sex. She couldn't do much to change that.

She turned her attention to her surroundings as they rode out of the wilderness into the civilized countryside around San Francisco. On the busy highway, a stagecoach raced by, forcing a wagon to the road's edge. The wagon driver cursed and shook his fist. In the distance Sam could see the sparkle of sun on water and the bobbing of ships in the harbor. The low line of buildings spewing brown smoke rose in front of her, cutting off any further sight of the bay.

Sam held her tongue as they rode through town, and her senses were bombarded by more exotic scents and sounds and sights than she'd ever encountered in her life. Chinamen scurried down side streets and hauled two-wheeled carts as if they were beasts of burden. The stench of rotting fish carried in on the breeze, mixing with the aromas of incense coming from a nearby building with foreign writing on the outside. Sam craned her head to see more, but Sloan's pace didn't allow for lingering. She hurried her mount to keep up with him.

Brick buildings surrounded them. Her father had written of the fires of earlier decades, but she could see no sign of them in these substantial businesses. Men in frock coats and top hats walked the streets in company with women in respectable mantles and bustled gowns. No one paid heed to a rough mountain man and a woman wearing a skirt while riding astride.

She should have changed into her other gown, Samantha decided the moment Sloan stopped in front of an imposing edifice labeled HOTEL. The men going in and out the large double front doors wore respectable business suits. She didn't see any women entering those portals.

When Sam didn't get down herself, Sloan came around

and lifted her from her horse. The clasp of his hands around her waist didn't help the situation any. She was reminded of what he would expect her to do once they were in private. She shuddered and tried to keep her attention on her bedraggled state of dress.

"I look a mess," she whispered before he could walk off.

"When did that ever concern you?" he asked rudely. "We won't know anyone here. Who's to care how you look?"

She would, but she knew better than to explain that to a man. Resigned, she tucked her coat around her so the disgrace of her wrinkled bodice couldn't be seen. Then, to his surprise, she took Sloan's elbow and let him lead her into the lobby.

It was even more grand than she feared. She tried not to look at the glittering gas chandelier overhead. The mirror behind the desk made her grimace, and she instantly stood behind Sloan so she didn't have to look at herself. She heard him order a bath just as he had before, but this time she didn't make the mistake of protesting. She could look for her father after she made herself presentable.

There was even a porter to carry their saddlebags upstairs. Dazed at this amount of luxury, Samantha simply kept her grip on Sloan's arm and tried to pretend she was accustomed to carpeted lobbies and mahogany staircases.

When they were finally alone in a room with a massive brass bed and blue velvet draperies and a wardrobe that must have sailed around the Cape, Sam took a deep breath and tried to gather her failing courage. The fact that this room was twice the size of the one he'd taken her to before was of no relevance. Sloan Talbott seemed to fill any room he entered, and he was all she could see now.

She watched as he casually threw his sheepskin coat on the bed and rummaged through his bags. She eyed her grand surroundings and doubted that they were for her benefit. Somehow, Sloan Talbott belonged in a room like this.

When a knock at the door indicated the bath had arrived, Sloan gathered up the collection of clean clothing he'd pulled from his bags. Glancing at Samantha as if just discovering she was still there, he announced, "I'm going to the bathhouse to get cleaned up. I'm going to have to send around a few messages before we can get started asking questions here. I'll have them send up some food until I can get back."

She was relieved to know that he didn't intend to take his bath right here and with her, but she didn't like the idea of being left behind either. "How long do you mean to be gone?"

He shrugged dismissively and opened the door. "Long enough to get done what needs to be done. I'll come back before dinner." He gave her bedraggled gown a stoic look. "Is that the only dress you brought?"

A porter carried in a large copper tub, and two maids carried buckets of water. Samantha regarded them nervously. "I've got my linsey-woolsey. There's not too many gowns can be worn without hoops and whatnot."

He nodded curtly. "All right, I'll have someone send around something decent then. I mean to meet with the railroad board, and it's probably best if you go with me."

He was gone before she could fully register what he said. She stared at the door closing behind him, trying to convince herself she hadn't heard him right. She might possibly imagine Sloan calling on the powerful railroad board. If she really worked at it, she could possibly see him dragging her along for the slaughter. But the first part of his statement, the one about sending something around decent—that part she must have misunderstood. Surely he couldn't mean clothes.

He must have been talking about the food he'd said he'd send up. She certainly hoped it was decent. She was about to starve to death. But first she wanted that bath. She watched impatiently as the servants filled the tub and finally departed. Her family was respectably wealthy, but they'd never really had servants. Her mother had always done the cooking, and Sam and the twins had helped with the housework. They had someone out to do the laundry once a week, and men to work in the stables and so forth, but not house servants. She wasn't certain what to say to them, but they didn't seem to expect anything. She watched them go and began to strip off her soiled clothing.

When she was almost naked, she felt suddenly nervous about Sloan walking back in on her, but the desire for a bath was greater than her fear of Sloan. She ached. She felt grubby. And she had a need to smell like roses and lavender.

The food arrived after she'd soaked away the soreness and two days' worth of dust. Her hair was wet and tangled in a towel, and she had to wrap a blanket around her to open the door, but the maid didn't seem to find her attire unusual. She'd apparently seen stranger things in this city where anything could happen.

Samantha gave her the wrinkled gown from her saddlebag and asked if it could be pressed. The maid assured her she would return it immediately, and satisfied she had done all she could for her limited wardrobe, Sam sat down to enjoy her food. She didn't know if it was the ocean air or the unaccustomed exercise, but she was starving.

She kept listening for the sound of Sloan's footsteps in the hall. Now that she was clean and feeling better, she wondered what it would be like to really share a bed with him, with both of them naked and prepared for it. She sizzled inside just thinking of it. If she was going to get only forty-eight hours of experience in a man's arms, she didn't want to waste a minute of those hours.

But she finished her repast without any interruption. She found clean linen in her bags and donned it, delaying as long as she could. She really didn't want to rumple another gown if Sloan decided to return once she got all dressed again. She wrapped the blanket around her and gazed out the window to the street below. She didn't see any sign of him.

A knock indicated the maid had returned with her newly pressed gown. Grimacing at her faint reflection in the glass, Sam turned and opened the door.

A line of red-capped porters bearing armloads of boxes entered in single file, covered the bed with their burdens, and filed back out again.

Chapter Twenty-three

Samantha paced up and down the carpeted hotel-room floor. Her new crinoline swung in an irritable arc, bouncing off the bed and the wardrobe and just missing the washstand when she made a hasty turn. The green silk whispered as it swished over the modified hoops of the crinoline to trail on the floor behind her. Lace spilled over the bodice front and adorned the wide sleeves of her gown, lace that matched the undergarments concealed beneath the acres of skirt.

The stockings she wore were fine silk and the shoes were barely slippers. The only thing the dratted man hadn't provided was a corset, but the gown had obviously been adapted to accommodate that unfashionable lack. Samantha didn't even want to think about how Sloan had managed to have all these clothes put together in the short length of time he'd been gone. It spoke volumes of his relationship with some dressmaker.

She wasn't certain which irritated her the most, that he didn't consider her wardrobe adequate to be seen with him, or that he considered her the kind of woman he must reward with clothes. She alternately considered scratching his eyes out or flinging the wretched gown at him, but she was bound by one major restraint—he'd promised to help find her father and this was his way of doing it.

By the time Sloan finally put in an appearance, Sam was barely able to speak. She flung the astronomically expensive cashmere shawl at him as he walked through the door and was reaching for the box of gloves when he grabbed her wrist.

"What in hell's the matter with you?" He caught her other wrist when she swung her fist at him.

"You! Who do you think you are? What do you think I am? Where did you get all this fancy gear? And why in *hell* did you think I ought to wear it?" Sam practically screamed the questions at him, ineffectually swinging her arms in an attempt to strike him.

Sloan caught her flailing arms more securely and held them at her waist with one of his own. Pressed back against his hard body, she scarcely noticed as her hoop went sailing out to the side. His other hand rested right below her breast, rubbing at the underside, and he wasn't pretending he didn't notice. One finger reached to tentatively stroke higher.

"I should have known a damned little hellcat wouldn't appreciate my efforts. You were the one worried about your appearance. I suppose you'd be happier if I dragged you in front of some of the most influential men in the state while you're wearing your mother's made-over Sunday gown?"

"There's nothing wrong with my made-over gowns," Sam said with a sniff, but she knew she was lying. The linsey-woolsey without petticoats hung on her like a sack. It might be adequate for watering horses, but not for meeting important men who might know her father. She tried to elbow Sloan and distract him from her breast.

"Fine. You can wear your made-over gown when we go out to dinner tonight. We haven't got time for you to change right now. The board is having a meeting this afternoon. We're invited to join them."

He released her, and Samantha swung around to stare at him. He had actually gotten them in to see the railroad board! How had he done that?

Sloan was wearing his newly pressed frock coat and the shirt with the ruffle down the front. His cravat was neatly tied, and his embroidered silk vest was buttoned. He had shaved, and even had his hair trimmed. Samantha stared at the handsome stranger staring back at her and muttered a curse. She had agreed to go to bed with this man who could have any woman he crooked a finger at? No wonder he'd found her disappointing.

Sloan's eyes narrowed at her silence. "What's wrong? Do I look that bad?"

Startled by this admission of unease, Sam blinked, then shook her head. "No, of course not. You look fine. I just . . . You . . ." She closed her eyes and sighed. There was no way of explaining it. He was more than she knew, and she was still peeling off layers. She would never know the real Sloan Talbott.

He cupped her chin and gave her a swift kiss. His fingers were hard and possessive as they caressed her throat. When he lifted his head again, he murmured, "We'll have this discussion later, when all our finery is on the floor."

Lord, but the way he said that made her shiver and want to strip off all her clothes right now. Her desire must have been blatant in her eyes because the look Sloan gave her practically smoldered. He almost looked regretful when he stepped away.

"It's a damn good thing this coat is long," he muttered obscurely as he picked up the shawl and threw it at her.

Sam tried to pretend she didn't know what he meant as she sailed out the door ahead of him, but she couldn't help glancing swiftly at his hips. The frock coat covered everything interesting.

The railroad board met in a long, elegantly furnished room in one of the banks. As Sam and Sloan were ushered into the presence of these men who meant to transform the continent, Sam tried to be properly appreciative of the honor. Instead, she couldn't help noticing that they were just men, and not particularly distinguished ones at that.

"Good to see you again, Talbott," one of the men with dark side-whiskers said as they entered. "Understand your mining ventures are doing well these days."

Sam tried to look politely disinterested, but catching Sloan in another lie didn't sit easily. He'd told her family he owned just a small quicksilver mine. She should have known he didn't need a town full of miners for that.

"I reckon timber will be worth more than mining in the long run," Sloan replied laconically. "I'd like you gentlemen to meet Miss Samantha Neely, a family friend."

Sam nodded a greeting and tried to smile pleasantly at this circle of avaricious men staring at her as if she were a stake ready for claiming. The one at the far corner of the table frowned slightly as Sloan rattled off their names. That man recognized her name, she was sure of it.

"Miss Neely's father disappeared some time after leaving my territory. We've tracked him here. His opinions sometimes run counter to prevailing thought, but he's a talented inventor. We thought one of you might have availed yourself of his talents. He expressed interest in seeking you out."

That was a diplomatic way of putting it. Sam watched the angry tic at the corner of the mouth of the man at the end of the table. She'd wager he was carrying around a whole lot more anger than Sloan, and that was saying something.

Sloan gave her father's name and described him. Sam knew she ought to tell these men how wonderful her father was, but she could sense they not only wouldn't listen, but also that they'd already made up their minds. They didn't mean to tell her anything.

The whiskered man spoke up when Sloan stopped speaking. "Your father sounds like the kind of man we could use out here, Miss Neely." He effectively dismissed her by directing his gaze toward Sloan. "He might have been able to figure out how to get those rails through the pass without those damned expensive snowsheds, pardon my language. But I can't say that I've met him, I'm sorry."

She couldn't tell if he lied, but she judged some of the others guilty of lies of omission. They merely nodded their heads in agreement with the speaker, but the undercurrent in the room made her uneasy.

Sloan caught her elbow to take her out, but Sam spoke softly before he could lead her away. "My father is a gentle, generous man. He might have opinions that people don't like, but he's never harmed a soul. My mother and my sisters are devastated by his disappearance. My uncle died while bringing us out here to locate him. He left a son who needs a man's hand to guide him. If there is anything you can do, any word you might have heard, I beg you to let us know. I will never be able to just let the matter drop."

Sloan's hand pinched her arm, but she ignored him while she met the gaze of each man in that room. One looked away. One looked sympathetic, but essentially uninterested. Another glanced at his watch. Furious, she spun on her heel and marched out without need of Sloan's support.

"Dammit, Sam, you shouldn't have said that," he muttered as she marched through the building and out into the street. "Now they're going to have to keep an eye on us."

"Good. Maybe they'll try to disappear us as they did my father, and we'll find out where he is." She stalked down the walk without any idea of where she was going.

"We don't have any evidence that they know anything about your father." Sloan grabbed her arm and held her pace to a stroll.

She would have bruises where his fingers held her. She glared at the manacle of Sloan's hand, then up at his stubbornly set jaw. "They know him all right. I could see the guilt in their eyes. I have half a mind to go back there right now and listen through the walls."

"You'd be looking for trouble then. Those men didn't get where they are by being polite."

She scowled at him. "You should know."

Sloan squeezed her elbow tighter and drew her to his side. "Much as I might have liked to, I didn't murder your father."

She knew that. She wouldn't have done what she had with him if she thought that. What she was going to do again. She flushed and looked away as they approached the hotel.

"That's better," Sloan grunted as they entered the building. "You keep thinking those kind of thoughts, and we'll get along just fine."

"I've contemplated murdering you since I first rode into town, Sloan Talbott," she muttered beneath her breath as they crossed the lobby. "And that's all I'm contemplating now."

He gave her a swift look that reminded her someone had been trying to murder him, but she dismissed the notion immediately. They'd caught that man.

"You're a lousy liar, Miss Neely. You might want to

murder me, but that isn't what you're contemplating now. You're wondering how long it will take me to get up under your skirts again."

Sam turned to smack him, but he caught her wrist before she knocked them both down the stairs they climbed. They had almost reached the room, and her head spun giddily with the knowledge. It wasn't completely dark yet. They couldn't do *that* now.

"We need to ask questions at the livery," she reminded him. "And all the hotels."

Sloan took the key from his pocket and unlocked the bedroom door. "There are dozens of liveries and hundreds of hotels. That's what I'm paying Hawkins to do." He pushed her through the open door.

"It's not night! There are plenty of things we could do." She wheeled and tried to get past him.

Sloan shut the door and locked it, dropping the key in his pocket. "There are plenty of things we can do, all right, and we can do them right here." He stripped off his coat and threw it across a chair, his gaze never leaving Sam.

She was melting, and he wasn't even touching her. Why had she ever thought those eyes of his were icy? They were like white-hot coals right now. Her gaze dropped anxiously to his hands. He was unfastening his vest.

"Sloan, you promised." She was startled that the words came out as just a whisper. She couldn't seem to manage any more as his vest joined his coat and she could see the hard planes of his chest outlined against his shirt.

"I promised to help you find your father, and I am. I called in a lot of favors to get that meeting with the board today. I've got queries out all over town with men who are in a position to have met your father. I hired Hawk. There isn't anything else we can do but wait."

His expression said there was something they very well could do while they waited. Samantha swallowed hard. It had been one thing to be overwhelmed by the moment back at the ocean, but it was quite another to discard her clothes cold-bloodedly as he did now. As curious as she might be about what he could do to her in that bed, she couldn't bring herself to assist in her own seduction.

"It's almost dinnertime," she pointed out nervously. "You promised to take me to dinner."

"I changed my mind." Sloan took the chair and began pulling off his shoes. "Do you need help with that gown?"

"No. Yes. I . . ." She couldn't say it. He was across the room before she had to.

She gasped as he swung her around and quickly unfastened the row of buttons at her back. The beautiful satin bow went tumbling next. When she didn't move swiftly enough, Sloan shoved the sleeves of her gown off her shoulders and down her arms and located the tapes that held her skirt and crinolines together. The whole concoction drifted to the floor, leaving her standing in nothing but drawers, chemise, and stockings.

Sloan stood behind her, but Sam knew he was looking at her. She could feel the heat of his gaze on the bare expanse of flesh revealed above the top of her chemise. He'd bought this damned revealing silk for just that reason, she realized. She covered herself with her hands, but that was a mistake. His hands immediately followed, wrapping themselves around her fingers, pulling them apart. She could feel the brush of his knuckles against her breasts, and she shuddered.

"This time will be much better, Samantha. When I enter you, you won't want me to stop."

She hadn't wanted him to stop last time. She was shameless. She didn't want him to stop what he was doing right now. He had shoved her hands away and was massaging her breasts, lifting them, caressing them, making them swell and tingle and ache for a more intimate touch. When he finally untied the chemise ribbons and reached beneath the fabric to touch her, she nearly collapsed in his arms.

"That's it, Samantha. Don't fight me. Just let it happen. It's a perfectly natural reaction between a man and a woman."

His voice was soothing, but she scarcely heard the words. His fingers had found the bare crests of her breasts and played them shamelessly. She was a quivering mass of raw nerve endings, and she knew he hadn't even begun.

He nibbled her ear. While one hand bared her breast and caressed it, his other hand slid downward, stroking her abdomen, reaching lower. When he finally touched her between her legs, she threw her head back and a low groan escaped her throat.

"That's it, my love, just let it happen." Sloan bent his head and kissed her exposed throat, then lifted her with one arm around her waist.

When his mouth closed around her nipple, Samantha gave a scream of pleasure.

A moment later, she lay flat on her back across the bed, watching Sloan rip off his shirt.

Chapter Twenty-four

Sloan had a beautiful chest, all angles and planes and rippling muscles beneath a skin of golden bronze. But Sam already knew that. She had bandaged that shoulder bearing the rough white scar. This was different though. She couldn't keep her gaze away from the silky pattern of dark hairs spreading from nipple to nipple and dipping lower.

Her stomach clenched when she realized he unfastened the buttons to his trousers. She lay here sprawled across the bed, wearing nothing but her underwear, inviting what he was about to do now. And she wasn't doing a thing to stop it.

This was Sloan Talbott, she reminded herself. This was the man who had driven her father out of town, who had made her wear dresses, who had cursed her and chased her and driven her mad with his demands.

But still she lay there, watching. The last button came undone, and his trousers fell to the floor. Had she been drinking wine, she would think she was drunk. The languorous haze she was in registered nothing more than the beauty of the man standing naked before her and the ache in her insides where she wanted him to be.

He lifted her as if she were dandelion fluff, pulling back the covers and laying her against the sheets. The sheets were cold, but once he came down beside her, she didn't notice. She was suddenly warm all over.

He leaned over and kissed her. She closed her eyes, absorbing the myriad sensations his touch engendered. His lips were gentle, prying at hers until she gave him what he wanted. The invasion of his tongue was hot and sweet.

The grasp of his hand around her breast was possessive, making her gasp with the sudden pressure of it.

That was her last coherent thought. His kisses melted her inhibitions into nothingness. She scarcely recognized the moment when he removed her chemise, but she knew the precise moment when his mouth covered her nipple. She nearly wept from the pleasure of it and eagerly offered the other breast when he lifted his head.

His kisses wandered, and her drawers disappeared. She still wore her stockings, but they offered no obstruction. His hands caressed her legs. His mouth laid claim to every inch of skin available. When he moved lower, she clutched his hair, certain she would burst from her skin at any moment. Undeterred, he bent to kiss her between her legs, and she was lost.

She twisted and arched and called his name until he finally rose up to cover her. She didn't realize she had her eyes closed until he told her to open them. She looked up, startled, and found Sloan's angular jaw hovering just above her. She raised her eyes to his, found the smoldering desire there, and didn't look for anything else.

Her gaze dropped to the breadth of his shoulders. He was braced above her. She could feel him pressing between her legs. She didn't know when she had opened them as she had, but he was on the threshold, and she was asking him in. She shuddered and looked lower. From this angle, he looked like the stallion she had imagined.

"Look at me, Samantha. I want you to know it's me and not someone you fancy." His voice was harsh, and she forced her gaze back to his face.

She'd never fancied anyone but Sloan Talbott. She couldn't disguise that fact any more than he could disguise his arousal. From the satisfied look on his face, she knew he could see that. But then his mouth found hers again, his hands made demands she had only recently learned, and her body arched upward into his.

She cried out when he came into her, and her cry only caused him to push deeper. He filled her, stretched her beyond all the limits of her comprehension, and then he began to move inside her until she danced to his rhythm.

It was like nothing she could ever dream of. He took

possession of her so that she wasn't herself anymore. She was somebody else, somebody lovely and desirable, and Sloan Talbott wanted her. He was part of her. He was inside her and part of her and there was something ... something just beyond her reach.

And then she exploded with it, burst like a giant balloon and collapsed in waves of splendor. She heard Sloan groan, felt his spasming jerk within her, and wouldn't let go. Not this time. She wanted all of him.

She felt the hot flood of his seed with satisfaction. So much for the master of conception and control. Drowsily, she slid into a half sleep, knowing only that Sloan was still beside her, inside her, and all around her. The weight of him made her whole.

They woke some while later and made more gentle love. This time he used some contraption to cover himself before he entered her so he didn't have to pull out. It didn't satisfy either of them, and they forgot to use it the next time. It didn't matter. They'd already made the error once. Another time couldn't hurt.

Somewhere along the way they sent for dinner to be brought up. They sat wrapped in sheets and nothing else and drank thirstily, but the chicken went cold before they got around to finishing it.

It was like a compulsion they couldn't control. Sam had only to look at Sloan, and he knew what she was thinking. She could touch the stubble on his jaw, and he would kiss her. She could rub her lips gently against the roundness of his shoulder, and he would have her flat on her back within minutes. She didn't object. She did it on purpose. She wanted as much of him as she was allowed in these forty-eight hours.

And she took him until she was sore and aching and not a particle on her hadn't been rubbed raw by his beard. She felt like liquid, lying on the sheets beside him, feeling the even breathing of his sleep. He was a big man, and he filled even this wide bed. She didn't mind. His leg covered hers, and his hand entwined in her hair, holding her against his chest. For the first time in her life, she felt sheltered.

If she slept, she wouldn't have to remember that this

was Sloan Talbott and this was all there would ever be
between them. So she slept.

When they woke, it was nearly noon. The room
smelled of sex and lavender and the wine they'd left the
prior night. Sloan propped himself on one arm, lifting his
big body over her, and Sam felt small and feminine beside him. She felt even more so when he cupped her
breast.

"We're supposed to meet Hawk. I don't suppose you'd
be interested in putting him off for a day or two?"

The sheets had slid away. She could see his magnificent male body already awakening, getting ready to perform again. She shook her head in disbelief. She hadn't
thought it possible, but he made it so. She met his eyes
and was fascinated by the odd assortment of emotions
flitting across them. She hadn't thought Sloan had any
feelings at all, but she thought she could see regret and
desire and something else, something a little less harsh
than before.

"I might be interested, but I'm not certain I'm capable," she murmured apologetically. Once they got up from
here, they might never get another chance. She owed him
one more night, she knew, but experience had taught her
that good things seldom came around twice.

A purely masculine look of satisfaction settled on
Sloan's features. He caressed her cheek with his finger.
"I'm sorry. I forgot you were new to this. You're very
good, you know." He pressed a kiss to her lips before she
could reply.

"Maybe just once more," she murmured when he lifted
his head. She wrapped her arms around his neck and
arched upward, feeling feminine satisfaction when he instantly glanced down to her breasts.

"I'm going to regret this, but for your own good, we're
getting up. I don't want you too sore for tonight." He
rolled away and climbed out of bed.

Samantha felt voluptuous and satiated lying there naked across rumpled sheets, knowing he was looking at
her. Just his gaze made her tingle. She squirmed her hips
a little and watched the heat fire Sloan's eyes. She liked

having this power over him. She could come to like this game very much.

But it was one where anticipation was almost as much pleasure as the culmination, so she sat up with her back to him and pulled a sheet around her.

"We could come back here as soon as we're done talking to Hawk," he said.

He sounded like Jack when he wanted to wheedle something out of her. She would be triumphant if it weren't that she wanted it as much as he did.

Sam's stomach sank to her toes as she had a sudden thought, and she glanced warily over her shoulder. What if this feeling didn't go away? What would they do when they got back to the mountain?

She didn't dare think about it. Surely they ought to be thoroughly sick and tired of each other before another night was out. How much of this could one person take, anyway? Animals only came into heat a couple of times a year. That must be what had happened to her. She had just gone without a man too long and had a lot of catching up to do. It would be over shortly in the natural order of things.

She went behind the dressing screen and scrubbed all over. Sloan threw her garments over the screen as he found them. They felt as alien to her now as her naked skin had yesterday. She ought to feel shame, but she felt only eagerness for what the day would bring.

Sloan actually gave her a genuine smile when she came out from behind the screen. Her hand instantly went to check her hair, but he caught her hand and ran his fingers through the thick curls.

"If all redheaded women are as passionate as you are, I think I'll restrict myself to redheads from now on."

She wanted to kick him. Instead, she smacked his hand away and marched to the door. "Save it, Talbott. I'm ready to eat."

He caught her by the bow at her back, untied it, and began tying it properly. "I'll not quarrel if you want to be the only redhead for me, but it would be a trifle difficult to keep it from the rest of the town."

"Dream on, Talbott. We have a bargain, that's all. We'll

go out and complete your end of it today, and tonight we'll finish it."

His hand caressed the back of her neck as she threw open the door. "It won't be quite that easy," he murmured tauntingly near her ear as they moved out into the hall.

Sam ignored him. It would be that easy. She'd lived all her life without Sloan Talbott, and she could live without him again. She'd just been curious, that was all. Well, her curiosity was satisfied. She could go back up the mountain right now if she didn't owe him one more night.

They ate lunch with the man Sloan called Hawk. He never introduced him by any other name. Samantha thought the tracker rather looked like a hawk. He had a hatchet nose and high, sharp cheekbones that spoke of some Indian heritage. She supposed there could be some Spanish there, too. He was dark from the sun, but from nature also, she suspected.

He watched her warily, through eyes so dark as to be almost black. He seemed content to talk only to Sloan, but Samantha wasn't used to being ignored. When she asked a question and he answered it by speaking to Sloan, she rapped her spoon against his glass. Startled, he looked back to her.

"You can't find my father if you can't acknowledge his daughter exists. A blind man is useless."

Hawk regarded her without expression. "A blind man can see what a sighted one cannot, but I am not blind. If you are much like your father, I will pick him out of a crowd."

"She's too damned much like her father, but you'd better keep your eyes out for him and not for Samantha. I'll take you down to the livery and show you her horse. Her father has one just like it. It attracts a lot of attention." Sloan shoved his chair back and stood up, holding out his hand to Sam. "I'll take you back to the room first."

"I'll take myself where I want to go, and I want to go to the livery." Ignoring his hand, Sam maneuvered her hoop from beneath the table and stood up. Hawk was already on his feet and watching her as if trying to decide if she were cat or mouse.

Apparently deciding squabbling in public wasn't politic, Sloan didn't argue, but took her arm to escort her to the street.

When they reached the livery, Sam raced through the stable to Gallant's stall. The horse stuck his head out to be petted and nudged her hand expectantly. Samantha's smile crumpled. "I should have brought him an apple!"

Sloan was frowning at her proximity to the spirited stallion. Horses like that were prone to taking fingers and ears off. He caught her arm to pull her back to safety.

Hawk stood near the door, watching Sam's unbridled exuberance with curiosity. At her fearless handling of the magnificent stallion, he wandered forward. The hand previously in his pocket appeared now, bearing chunks of raw sugar.

Gallant snickered and eagerly accepted the offering.

"I have never seen his like," Hawk said, running his hand down the animal's graceful neck. "Your father breeds these?"

Sam shrugged. "He used to. I've been in charge since before the war, while he was more interested in munitions. My father's horse is full-blooded brother to this one."

Hawk stroked the horse and looked tentatively from Sam to Sloan. Sloan still held a possessive hand on the lady's back, keeping her a safe distance from animal and any man but himself. Hawk almost smiled at this dead giveaway, but their relationship wasn't any business of his own. He smacked the horse's neck appreciatively.

"The animal is as much a clue as the portrait you gave me. I will track your father much faster if the horse is in my possession."

Samantha jerked as if shot, then looked from Hawk to Sloan with distress. Sloan shook his head in dismissal. "The lady prizes her horse. She wouldn't care to lose it."

"I will not lose it." Hawk looked to Sam. "I will give you my own horse. He is much better for the mountains, as this one is meant for the valleys. I will treat him as my own kin and bring him back to you when I am done."

She didn't want to give up Gallant. She had surrendered her virginity for her father's sake, but she had done that because she wanted to. It hadn't been a sacrifice. To give up Gallant would be a sacrifice.

Taking a controlling breath, she dipped her head in agreement. "I would see your horse first, to be certain Gallant will be treated well."

Sloan shook his head in disapproval, but Hawk looked satisfied. It wasn't for either man to say what was right. She followed Hawk to examine his mountain pony.

By the time they retraced their tracks to the hotel, the afternoon was waning. Samantha was unusually silent, but she had approved the exchange of horses. Hawk's horse was well-bred, sturdy, and carefully tended. As horse deals went, it was fair enough, if she had some hope of finding her father as part of the bargain.

In these last few months she had wagered and bargained away a good deal of the life she had once known. She didn't think she was the same person she had been when she had left Tennessee. A good deal of that was due to the man beside her.

She glanced up at Sloan. He, too, was unusually silent. She didn't think he understood how much she wanted her father back. Perhaps he didn't know what it was to love someone so much that you would do anything for them. Perhaps he ought to be grateful he didn't.

Sloan Talbott was a handsome, intelligent man. It seemed odd to think that he might never have known love in his life, but it was possible. He certainly didn't make it easy for anyone to get close to him. She rubbed her fingers along the fine wool of his coat where she held his arm, drawing his gaze down to her.

"Thank you for helping me," she said softly. It was something that needed saying. She hadn't expected him to do as much as he had, and she was forfeiting very little in return. She would more than likely have done what she had for nothing, but she wouldn't tell him that.

"Don't thank me. I've got what I wanted. I just hope your damned father is worth what you've given up." His response was gruff. He didn't look at her when he said it.

She didn't expect anything more of him. Sloan Talbott had lived too much on his own. He didn't know how to respond to genuine emotion.

He pushed open the hotel door and helped her in. When she straightened her hoop and gown and looked up, Sloan was standing stiffly at her side, his hand crushing hers as he stared at something or someone rising from a chair near the wall. She could feel the fury emanating from him without even seeing his expression. She looked to see what he saw, and uttered a low groan of dismay.

Doc Ramsey was coming toward them, holding out his hand and grinning with malicious delight.

Chapter Twenty-five

"**W**ell, imagine running into you here, Talbott."
Ramsey made a mocking bow when Sloan refused to take his hand. He turned to admire Samantha.
"And you, Miss Neely. I don't believe I've seen that gown before. It's quite becoming. I'm sure your good mother will approve."

Sam seemed too stunned to comment, and Sloan was grateful for that much. He had never expected to run into anyone she knew down here. He'd known traveling with her was compromising, but without proof, no one could accuse either of them of anything. But if he took her up those stairs with him right now, Ramsey would have all the proof he needed.

Sloan was tempted. It would be a cruel thing to do, but it would label Sam as his. Other men might try to trespass, but no one would fault him if he defended his property. Only, Samantha wasn't likely to cooperate with that kind of male notion of property rights. She and her mother would raise one hell of a stink. He'd rather not be put through that.

He definitely didn't want to be put through the only alternative that came immediately to mind, but it was the one he offered.

"Ramsey, if you don't quit looking at Miss Neely like she's a side of beef, I'll take it as an insult in her father's place and break your nose." He turned to Sam. "Why don't you go up to Jeanne's room and freshen up? I told my brother we'd meet them down at the dock." He slid the key to their chamber into her hand as he released her fingers from his arm.

She blinked and stared at him as if he were crazed, but

she grasped the opportunity he offered. With the key tightly wrapped in her fist, she made a brief curtsy to Ramsey, said a few words, and soon disappeared up the stairs.

Momentarily distracted by the plethora of information dumped on him all at once, Ramsey quickly recovered. Cynical amusement twisted the corners of his dissolute mouth. "Find her father, did you?"

"Not that it's any of your business, but no, not yet. We've been talking to several people who know him, however. Now, if you have nothing else to say to me, I need to arrange our transportation." Sloan turned as if to walk off. Maybe he'd confused the good doctor to the point he wouldn't inquire further. Maybe there were back stairs he could sneak up. He sure as hell didn't want to have to give up his last night of ecstasy.

God wasn't on his side. Ramsey stuck with him.

"The clerk said you're registered here for the night. Why do you need to get to the docks at this hour?"

Sloan gritted his teeth and summoned a porter. "Because Miss Neely is staying with my brother and sister-in-law. Are you quite satisfied now, Ramsey?" He gave the porter instructions for hiring a carriage and fetching the horses from the livery.

Ramsey shrugged. "Whatever you say. Didn't know you had a brother out here."

"There's a lot of things you don't know, and I don't intend to tell you." Sloan nodded and strode off as if he were a man in a hurry rather than one who had contemplated spending the next twelve hours in bed with a beautiful woman. Ramsey was damned lucky he hadn't killed him on the spot.

When Sloan got to the corner, he hurried around the side of the building, looking for another entrance. Ramsey was more than capable of sitting in that lobby, waiting for the next stage of the play. Sloan didn't have to wonder how the doctor had found him. He was a creature of habit and always stayed in this hotel. He did wonder *why* Ramsey had found him, though. He didn't think it was coincidental. Ramsey seldom ever left the mountain, and when he did, it was generally to visit the cribs of Ariposa, not 'Frisco.

Finding a back set of stairs, Sloan breathed a sigh of relief. Maybe they wouldn't have to leave after all. Ramsey had seen him leave by the front door. He'd seen Sam go up the stairs in the opposite direction. He couldn't make anything of the fact that Sam never came back down again, not unless he waited there all night. That didn't seem likely.

Sloan took the stairs two at a time. If he was really lucky, Sam would have rid herself of that hideous contraption and would be down to her underwear by now. He would have to buy her some more of that silky lace, this time with an even lower cut to the chemise. Sam would look damned good in an evening gown. She had young, full breasts that filled a gown just right. She had freckles where she left her shirt collar open in the summer, but the rest of her was a creamy white. Just the thought of those white, upthrust breasts beckoning him made him randy as hell.

He knocked at the bedroom door and Sam cautiously peeked out. Seeing him, she hastily stood out of sight behind the door to open it.

She had changed back into her gabardine traveling dress. Disappointment clogged Sloan's throat as she darted out of his way and went to the window. He wished he'd thrown out that gown. Maybe he could persuade her they were safe here.

"I saw them bringing our horses around. I thought maybe you were ready to leave." Her voice sounded far away and a little sad.

Sloan came up behind her and wrapped his arms around her waist. She was slender. She scarcely filled his hold, but she was tall enough for him to rest his chin on her hair. "Maybe we've fooled him. I could send someone to take the horses back to the livery."

She didn't move away, and for that, he was grateful. She nodded at the street below. "Aren't those some of your miners coming from the saloon?"

They were crossing the street and yelling at each other as they recognized his horse. At least Samantha's horse wasn't there for them to recognize. Sloan gave a sigh of resignation. "They'll be at the desk, asking for me. We'd better get out of here before they decide a shivaree is in order."

When he released her and went to gather their saddle-bags, she turned and followed him with her eyes—those damned big blue eyes that followed him even in his sleep.

"Why are they here in the middle of the week?"

"The hell if I know. I expect Ramsey just got nosy. He's been rubbing my face in it ever since I let the bunch of you move in. He just rounded up a few drinking buddies to make certain he staggered home in one piece."

That sounded plausible. The tension between Sloan and Ramsey had been obvious from the first day they rode into town. And Ramsey had taken an oddly protective interest in the ladies of the household ever since Sloan had shown his antagonism. Sam didn't like to think that Ramsey was down here to protect her reputation, but she had this niggling feeling that in the back of the doctor's drunken mind, that was just what he was doing.

She held up the lovely gown Sloan had bought for her and shook her head in regret. She couldn't possibly get it into her saddlebags. She looked up to find him watching her with an odd expression.

"I'll have the maid pack it up and send it on to my brother's if you want to keep it. Otherwise, just leave it there." Sloan's tone was dismissive as he walked toward the door.

Sam's eyes widened as she recognized the same defensive tactics Jack used when he was trying to be manly. Sloan Talbott was hiding his real feelings behind that care-nothing attitude! She clutched the gown to her as he reached for the knob. "I want to keep it," she whispered, unable to say more.

He turned, noted the way she held the gown, and nodded, but still nothing reached his eyes. "I'll have it sent on."

He walked out without looking back. Sam felt a queasiness in her stomach, but she couldn't place its origins. He had spent a lot of money on this gown. Of course he'd be insulted if she'd wanted to leave it behind. That's all there was to it. She shouldn't look for shadows where none existed.

But they existed, all right. A maid came to take care of her gown, and a porter arrived to carry their saddlebags. Sam followed them downstairs and through the lobby, pretending she didn't see Ramsey hiding behind a newspaper and a drink. She didn't know where the miners had gone. Sloan must have gotten rid of them.

Sloan waited outside beside a doddering carriage he'd hired from somewhere. Sam wished she'd kept her elegant gown on as he handed her up as if she were a grand lady on the way to the ball. The Neelys had never owned a carriage. The country roads back home were too rough for visiting in carriages when a wagon would do. She settled back in the seat, pretending this wasn't all new to her.

Sloan checked the security of the horses tied on behind, watched their gear loaded, and climbed up beside her. As he signaled the driver to depart, Sam noticed Doc Ramsey wandering to the door to see them off. It would have been better if she could be seen traveling with the mysterious Jeanne, but they couldn't do anything about it now. Her mother knew she was down here with Sloan. She didn't have anything to conceal—except a night of raw passion.

"Where are we going now?" she whispered as the carriage maneuvered the narrow, hilly streets to the bay.

"To my brother's," Sloan answered in a tone of resignation. "There's not that many decent hotels in the city, and I wouldn't put it past Ramsey to check every one of them to make sure we're not there."

Trapped by too many conflicting emotions, Sam set her lips and pursued the more obvious question. "I thought you made up that stuff about your brother."

"Unfortunately, no. My brother, Matthew, and his wife, Jeanne, have a ranch over in the valley. We'll stay there tonight to confirm our story."

"Unfortunately?" Sam raised her eyebrows questioningly.

Sloan scowled. "They tend to be rather proper. We'll sleep apart tonight."

She'd rather surmised that. Sitting back against the seat, Sam gazed out over city streets and tried to make some order out of the chaos of her emotions. She should be glad that their bargain had come to an abrupt end. Instead, she felt as if someone had called a halt to an idyll. She hadn't had time to explore all the ways Sloan's hard masculine body fit into hers. She would have to stop thinking about that.

When they reached the dock, Sloan led the saddled horses onto the steamboat. The smokestack was already belching fumes, and Sam hurried to join him. She had hoped they could stay in the city longer, ask further questions, maybe discover some new lead, but she could tell from the grim determination in Sloan's eyes that it wasn't going to happen.

He kept a safe distance from her as the boat slipped from land. He offered to take her inside, out of the wind, but Sam had never been on a steamboat before. She'd seen them. She knew this was a rather disreputable packet. But it was sailing into the middle of the bay, and she didn't want to miss a minute of it.

Sloan leaned against the cabin wall, hands in pockets, glaring out over the water. She supposed he was angry about getting cheated of his end of the bargain. She could tell him she would willingly go back to the hotel in Ariposa if he wanted, but she thought he ought to suffer a little longer. It would do him good.

He caught her by surprise when he came to prop his hands on the railing beside her. "Ramsey isn't going to keep his mouth shut," he said flatly. "I registered at that hotel as Mr. and Mrs. Every damned man in town is going to believe the worst."

Sam shrugged. "And they'll be right." She didn't feel as insouciant as she appeared, but she really didn't see where she had any other choice. She'd made her decision. Now she had to live with it.

"I don't think you understand." Sloan leaned his hip against the railing and crossed his arms as he turned to look at her. "They're going to think you're available for the taking unless I make them see otherwise. The only way I can do that is if you move in with me."

That got her attention. Forgetting the magnificent view, Sam turned to stare up at him. Sloan's angular face was as grim and expressionless as always. A person would think he was made out of granite if they didn't know better. She knew better. She'd seen desire in those icy eyes. She'd seen those hard lips go soft with her kisses. He was a man like any other, just an exceedingly aggravating one.

"I wasn't born yesterday, Sloan Talbott. I'm nearly twenty-five years old and more than capable of taking care of myself. I don't intend to become any man's mistress for such a feeble reason."

He muttered a curse, but didn't cease his relentless stare. "The reason isn't feeble. The only thing that has prevented rape these last months is the very obvious respectability of your family. Once that respect is gone, you're free game for every horny man in town."

Sam gave him her raised-eyebrow look. "And living with you would return my respectability?"

"My guns would offer you protection. The men keep away from anything that is mine."

She almost felt affection for his obvious obtuseness. Men were so very thick-headed. She almost believed that he meant well. It couldn't be easy for Sloan Talbott to force himself to allow a woman into his precious all-male quarters. But he was guaranteeing himself a free woman in his bed at the same time, so she didn't feel real sorry for him.

"I'm certain your offer is most kind, but I have guns of my own. I'm more concerned about the way my family thinks about me than how a bunch of randy-minded men think. I'll decline your offer."

He gritted his teeth and turned to grip the railing again. "I knew you would say that. We can pretend we got married when we came down here then. Tell your family I did the honorable thing by you. I'm not the marrying kind, so you don't need to think I'll go looking for any other woman. We're damned good in bed together. We can work it out."

Sam was so astonished that she didn't have an immediate reply. When she was younger, she had imagined many ways of men proposing to her, but she had never dreamed of a proposal like this. It was a good thing she'd given up those dreams years ago or she'd be devastated now. "I don't know how I can refuse such a generous offer," she finally answered dryly, "but I will. I'll not be your . . ." She forced herself to say a word that had never crossed her lips before, "Whore."

Sloan jerked as if she had shot him, then turned a baleful glare on her. "You do have a way with words, don't you?" He looked out over the bay again. The sun was setting, and the wind was cold, but they were closing in on land. "You weren't planning on marrying anymore than I am, were you? You want your damned valley and gardens and horses. I can get you that. What we've got in bed doesn't come around too often. We won't be able to discard it as easily as you're assuming. If we weren't surrounded by people, I'd have you on the floor right now with your skirts up."

Sam considered shoving him overboard. If he hadn't hit so close to her own worries, she might have. But she had to be honest with herself. She was standing here hoping he would find some way for them to share a bed together before they had to go to his brother's. She wanted to feel his arms around her right now. She also wanted to beat him with a gun butt.

"I'm not the only one with a way with words." The sarcasm was as much for herself as for him, but she was glad to see him wince. "You don't know where to find my valley any more than I do."

"I know how to find it, which is more than you can say. I've also got the money to build there when we find it." His fingers gripped the rail tighter as the boat maneuvered into shore. They were running out of time for this argument.

Sam sighed as they bumped against the dock. "I'm ashamed to say, you almost tempt me. If I hadn't been raised to know better . . ." She shrugged. "But it won't work. I won't shame my family. I won't shame any children we might have. I'll just have to fight this battle on my own."

"Your family won't have to know, and we won't have

any children," he said grimly, standing upright as the plank was unloaded. "I sure the hell don't want children."

"You sure the hell know how to make a woman feel wanted, don't you?" Gathering up her skirt, Samantha stalked away.

Chapter Twenty-six

Cursing Sam's stubbornness, cursing the sinking feeling in his stomach, Sloan unloaded their horses while keeping an eye on his wandering mistress—"whore," as she had so politely put it. "Lover" had little to do with anything. She was his woman, and he meant to keep it that way. Neither of them really had a choice, much as she might like to believe otherwise.

It was nearly dusk, and Sam blithely wandered the docks as if half a dozen men weren't watching her as closely as he was. Did she really think she looked so much like a man that they wouldn't notice she wasn't? She wasn't even wearing her damned denims. Some men out here would jump anything in skirts. One as attractive as Sam was a sure target.

One as attractive as Sam. Damn, but he better start listening to himself think. She was a she-cat in petticoats. Just because she looked deceptively innocent ... Hell, she had been innocent.

Groaning at that memory, knowing he only dug the hole deeper, Sloan checked the saddle straps and set out after Sam. He wouldn't make the mistake of trying to label her again. She was just Sam, a female who was so damned good in bed that she made him forget why he didn't want a woman there on a regular basis.

Sam wasn't speaking to him, and that was a relief. He would have to change her mind before they went back up the mountain, but her silence gave him time to think. The sight of the little adobe church on the plaza gave him a different direction of thought.

Sloan looked at Sam. He looked at the church. And wheels began to spin.

It would be a dirty thing to do, but his experience with women had taught him that they fought dirty. This would just be a way of protecting himself while protecting her. He'd tried being honest with her. He'd meant every word he'd said. He thought he could manage having Sam around on a permanent basis. She wasn't like most women. She'd go her own way most of the time and keep out of his hair. She wouldn't pry into his private life. And he hadn't lied about what they had between the covers. He'd never had it so good.

In his opinion, the end justified the means. Sam wouldn't agree, but Sam wouldn't know.

Of course, he had one major hurdle to overcome before he could perpetrate the dirty deed—persuading Sam. He'd find a way. He was almost whistling by the time they rode up the lane to his brother's ranch.

A maid answered the door when they knocked. Sam shifted nervously from foot to foot and gave him sidelong glances as they waited. Good. Keep her off balance and maybe he had a chance of pulling this off.

Jeanne rushed out with a breeze of expensive perfume and a rustle of skirts as she reached to hug Sloan. "You didn't tell us you were coming! It's been ages. Come in. Come in." She glanced curiously at Sam, waiting for an introduction.

"Jeanne, this is Samantha Neely. Her family moved into town a few months back. Sam, Jeanne Montgomery, my brother's wife."

Sloan didn't have to look at Sam to see the curiosity in her eyes about the difference in names. He was getting to know her too well. That's why he'd sprung it on her without warning. He knew she'd be too polite to question him in front of others.

"Welcome, Miss Neely. Won't you please come in? Knowing Sloan's abominable habits, you are probably quite worn out from your journey. Let me fetch you some coffee." Jeanne didn't actually go for the coffee herself; she signaled a maid to do it. Her dark eyes followed Sam and Sloan with even more curiosity than Sam was showing.

"Where's Matt?" Sloan asked without sitting down. He

had no desire to get involved in a hen party where he would be the one pecked to death.

Jeanne gestured vaguely. "He's out in the stable with one of the mares. One would think animals couldn't give birth without help the way he carries on."

Sloan groaned as he saw Sam's head instantly raise with interest at this news. Already he knew better than to interfere.

"Do you think he'd mind if I went to watch? We had to sell our mares when we came out here."

Sloan hid his grin as his very proper sister-in-law's mouth almost flopped open. She recovered admirably and threw him a questioning look. He shrugged. "I'll go out with her, show the way." He didn't even try to apologize for Sam's unladylike request. He'd rather be in the stable, too.

"I didn't offend her, did I?" Sam whispered as they walked through the dark to the barn.

Sloan stuck his hands in his pockets and shrugged. "Most likely she's just dying because we didn't tell her anything. I don't often show up with a woman on my heels."

"I can understand that."

He was learning to appreciate her dry understatements. He almost grinned at that one. She really was pissed at him, but she wasn't throwing tantrums or anything else. He racked up a point in her favor.

The barn was cold and dark except for the corner stall where someone had hung a lantern and stoked a wood stove. More interested in seeing Sam in action than watching a horse, Sloan let Sam stay one step ahead all the way down the aisle. Coming out here had just been an excuse to get out of the house.

Two men struggled with the mare lying in the bloody straw of the last stall. Neither looked up as their visitors appeared. Their attention was focused entirely on the sweat-covered animal straining to give birth.

They looked up when Sam knelt down in the straw with them, though. The light-haired one glanced over his shoulder, gave Sloan a surprised look, then looked astonished as the woman kneeling beside him asked, "Breech?"

"Leg caught," Matthew replied curtly. He turned away when the mare struggled again. Sloan rested his arms on the stall gate.

"She owns a stallion that can beat any of these plow horses you've got, Squirt. Says she raised him herself."

Both Matthew and Sam gave him a look of disgust. Sloan couldn't help it. He cracked a smile.

"If you're not going to help, get your ass out of here, mama's boy," Matthew grunted, turning back to his work.

"My hand is smaller. Let me help." Sam threw her coat in Sloan's general direction.

Matthew looked at her as if she were crazed and ignored her offer.

Sloan caught the coat and laid it over the rail. "You might as well listen to her. She's a royal pain in the ass when you don't."

"Just like someone else I know." The mare snorted and kicked and tried to roll, and Matthew grabbed her legs. He glanced at the other man holding the mare's head and received a hesitant nod in return. With that silent exchange, he moved over. "You're going to ruin your gown," he warned, "But then, Sloan can always buy you another. That's all he's good for anyway."

Sloan could almost swear he heard Sam mutter "I wouldn't say that," but no one else seemed to notice. Maybe he was just imagining things—or reading her mind. It sounded just exactly like something she would say.

He watched as she inserted her hand as gently as if she dealt with a newborn babe, and Sloan felt his stomach do another double clench. He'd brought her out here to tease his brother. He hadn't expected to be reminded of what he was and could have been and wasn't any longer. His hands ached with the need to feel what she felt. It was all he could do to restrain himself from giving her directions.

Horses weren't people, he reminded himself. It didn't matter if one animal lived or died. But he couldn't keep himself from watching avidly as Samantha struggled to guide the bloody newcomer into the cold world. The mare whinnied and kicked in pain. Matthew and his stable hand held her down hard. And the sticky, slimy new colt slid into Samantha's arms.

"You did it! You did it! Bless you a thousand times whoever you are." Ecstatic, Matthew knelt beside her, hugging and kissing her, admiring the perfectly formed colt struggling to return to his mother's warmth.

"She's mine, and I'd thank you to remember that," Sloan commented as he joined the rest of the crowd in the stall.

Holding the wiggling colt in her arms, Sam looked up at him with stars in her eyes. "Isn't he beautiful? Isn't he the most gorgeous thing you've ever seen?"

She was covered in blood and slime and sweat. Her gown was ruined. And she was holding a bloody awful long-legged creature too weak to stand. Sloan nearly staggered beneath the painful memories suddenly engulfing him.

He'd said those very words himself once, but they hadn't been said over a horse. And they hadn't been met with that starry-eyed look Sam gave him now. They'd been met with the same look that he was probably giving her at the moment.

Relenting as Sam's happiness began to fade at the disapproval she probably perceived in his face, Sloan crouched down beside her. He stroked the tiny creature before Matthew returned it to the mare's side. "He's beautiful, all right, but there's someone else here even more beautiful right now."

Sam's wide-eyed astonishment at his whispered words made Sloan smile again. She was so damned easy to please, it tickled him. He leaned over and kissed her nose. "Gotcha. I meant the mare. You're a mess."

She slammed her fist into his shoulder, sending him stumbling backward. "And you're a liar and a scoundrel, Sloan Talbott. I'd never speak to you again, but I know that would only make you happy, so I won't."

Sloan's laughter practically knocked the grin off his brother's face. Standing up and wiping his hands off on clean straw, Matthew looked from one of them to the other as they pulled themselves out of the straw. "I don't know who you are, ma'am, but I'd pay you to stick like a burr to Pretty Boy's side here for a week or two. I'd charge admission to watch."

Sam cleaned her hands on the rag he gave her. "You'd have to pay me more money than the government could print, I'd wager."

Sloan kept chuckling as the two of them skirmished around each other. "Meet Samantha Neely, comedian extraordinaire. Sam, this is my brother, Blowhard, and that's his faithful sidekick, Pedro, down in the straw."

Sam nodded. "It's a pleasure to meet you. You'll forgive me for not shaking hands right now." She exchanged nods with the small man still working with the horse, gave the new colt a critical look, then turned her gaze up to the blond version of Sloan beside her. "I take it you're Matthew. Sloan hasn't told me a blamed thing about you."

Sloan made a "tsking" noise. "Your language, Miss Neely. We wouldn't want to reveal that we're from the hills, would we?"

She continued looking at his brother. "Why haven't you killed him by now?" she asked with a perfectly straight face.

Matthew grinned. He grinned so wide that Sloan thought he might crack his face. Sloan crossed his arms and leaned against a post. He might as well let them get it out of their systems. He'd known it would be a mistake to bring her here.

"He's bigger than I am," Matthew replied, shrugging. "And he was never around much when I got old enough to kick him where it hurts. What's an intelligent woman like yourself doing in his company, I'm afraid to ask?"

"Suffering," she said succinctly. Then turning to Sloan, she finally conceded his presence. "I need to go in and wash now. I don't need your assistance if you'd prefer to continue this charming reunion."

"Jeanne will no doubt faint when she sees you. I'll come along to pick her up off the floor." Sloan raised his shoulder from the post and looked his brother squarely in the eye. "And I meant what I said earlier. Hands off."

Sam gave him a look of disgust. "Only someone as

filthy as I am would put their hands on me. Just keep yours at your side, Pretty Boy."

Matthew's roar of laughter followed them outside. Sloan contemplated meeting her challenge and taking her in his arms right here and now, but he had a feeling all he'd get out of it was a bruised shin and a ruined suit. He was learning caution where Sam was concerned. He could see that they were in for a rough-and-tumble time of it once he had her where he wanted her, but he certainly wouldn't be bored anymore. For the first time in ten years, he actually felt a tingle of anticipation.

"Are you going to want to catch those damned wild horses as your father did?" he demanded, denying any feelings at all. "If so, I might take back my promise about the valley."

"I'll find the valley myself. I was just waiting for spring."

She still wasn't happy with him. He would have to turn that around somehow. Sloan kept in step beside her. "I can buy you real horses to raise there."

She threw him one of those looks that told him she wouldn't buy that tale from a tinker. Sloan caught her shoulders and held her still. "I mean it, Sam. We'll be good together. Just wait and see."

He could see the moon reflected in the fathomless bottoms of blue she turned on him. He would drown in those eyes one of these days, if he didn't die of lust first. His body hardened at just the feel of her slender shoulders beneath his hands.

Quickly, before either of them could think twice about it, Sloan closed his mouth over hers.

She was so right in his arms. She swayed into them without a word of protest. Her lips melted into his. They parted and gave him full access to the sweetness beyond. Her tongue responded to his thrusts, and he felt it clear down to his loins. He couldn't remember it ever being this way with any other woman. There was too much trust, too much innocence.

He didn't think he would make it all night without taking her. She damned well belonged in his bed. There was no question about it anymore.

Sloan set Sam back from him, completely unconscious of the mess she'd made of his suit. Her face was pale in the moonlight, but her hair was a glorious fire against the chilly wind. He stroked her cheek gently and wished he could offer her what had been taken from him so long ago.

Instead, he whispered, "Marry me, Sam."

Chapter Twenty-seven

Marry him? Sam pulled away and searched Sloan's face for laughter or cynicism or whatever other idiocy had made him say those words. She was quite certain she had heard him right. Perhaps she just hadn't translated his meaning correctly.

"I've always admired the way you hold your tongue until you have something intelligent to say, but this is carrying it a little too far, Miss Neely. I've got a lot riding on the outcome of this question," Sloan reminded her.

She actually thought she saw a trace of uncertainty in his hardened face, but perhaps it was a trick of moonlight. Sloan Talbott was never uncertain. Actually, he hadn't even asked her a question. His words had been more of a command. Realizing that made her feel a trifle better—for what reason, Sam didn't know.

"I'll say you've got a lot riding on that question, so let me release you from your error at once. I told you from the first that there's no need to marry me. That's not part of the bargain. Now you may breathe a sigh of relief, and we can go in and get some sleep."

She would have started toward the house, but Sloan didn't release her shoulders.

"It's not relief I'm feeling, Sam. It's frustration. I've thought about this all afternoon, and it's the only solution. Give me credit for having a little more experience than you. What we're feeling now won't go away anytime soon. It's some kind of spontaneous chemical reaction that's going to keep on burning unless we do something about it. I don't relish sneaking into your bedroom window under your mother's nose every night to get at you. I'm too old for that kind of foolishness. I want you in my bed every night. I offered you every other alternative I could think of, but you turned me down. This is the only one left. Think about it, Sam."

Utterly flabbergasted, Sam stared at Sloan through the moonlit darkness. His newly trimmed hair no longer fell in his face as before, but it still curled about his ears and neck, tempting her fingers to touch it. She couldn't read the shadows of his eyes, but she saw signs of strain in the muscles along his cheekbones. His fingers were digging almost painfully into her shoulders. He wasn't teasing. He really meant it.

"It won't go away, ever?" she whispered in disbelief. Neither one of them had to question what "it" was. "It" was burning through their clothing right now, surging up and down their veins, pumping their hearts so loud it sounded like thunder in her ears. She was almost ready to beg him to move his hands a little lower, to touch her as he had last night. And she was perfectly aware where that would get her.

"I don't know about 'ever,'" he admitted. "I've not had any woman that long. But I can't imagine either one of us deciding we don't want what the other's got to offer. It's a pretty basic instinct, and I'm damned tired of ignoring it myself."

Sam managed a weak smile. She supposed it was something to have a man actually admit that he wanted her. She shouldn't expect anything more. Maybe Sloan was right. Maybe they could be good for each other. It would certainly be the solution to a number of trifling problems.

"How long do I have to think about it?" she asked wearily. The day really had been a long one, and she hadn't slept much the night before.

"There's a priest in the village. There's not one on the mountain. We'll have to decide before we leave." Sloan released her shoulders and looked down on her quietly. The red of her hair shimmered in the moonlight, but her face was turned away from him.

"Let me think about it. I'm still not convinced you aren't crazy." Sam started for the house again.

He caught her again, pulling her back against him, nuzzling her ear and brushing her breast softly. "A man would have to be crazy not to want you, Samantha. I don't know how you've escaped the others, but I don't mean to let you go."

She was stupid enough to want to believe him. She leaned her head back against his shoulder, felt his kisses trail down her throat, and reveled in the intimacy and security of Sloan's embrace. Whatever moon madness had seized them, she loved every minute of it. She'd sell her soul for more.

In the morning she would see things as they were, but for right now, she allowed herself to believe that she was a desirable woman and he was a man who wanted her for no other reason than that.

The sound of low voices and footsteps leaving the barn drove them apart. Sam hurried down the path to the house, her head spinning too dizzily to answer questions.

Fortunately, few were asked. She could see dozens of them dancing in the face of her hostess when they entered the house, but Jeanne Montgomery had sense enough to whisk her away to a bath and a bed and a good night's sleep. Sam followed her orders like a little lamb and found herself clean and warm and in a soft bed in rapid time.

She didn't find sleep quite so easily. She could hear the murmur of voices in the other room for some time after. She could imagine the inquisition to which his prim and proper family subjected Sloan, but he had the ability to deal with that without her help.

It seemed to her that he could deal with almost anything without her help. The Sloan Talbott she knew didn't need anyone. He certainly didn't need a wife, particularly one as unsuitable as she was. Maybe that was why he'd chosen her—because she wouldn't be much of a wife.

At that hour of the night, with her mind fuzzy with sleep, that seemed a perfectly reasonable possibility. Sam drifted to sleep, comforted by the thought.

Sloan wasn't so easily deceived by his wayward emotions. He'd lived with himself long enough to know he was walking right into disaster, but he sure as hell couldn't see any other way around it.

Matt and Jeanne had done their damndest to draw him out, but he wasn't about to tell them his plans. They knew too much and too little, and they would only scare Sam to death. No, he would wait until it was a *fait accompli* before he let them know.

But as he tossed and turned in the comfort of his feather bed and cursed the lack of Samantha's body beside him, he had a good idea what he was doing to himself. He was again placing himself within reach of a woman's claws.

He could console himself that Samantha was different. Sam wasn't likely to seek lovers when she grew bored or irritated with him. She didn't have enough confidence in her feminine attractions to seek other men. He liked that thought. She was so completely different from Melinda in this way, that fact alone more than likely drew him to her.

He could work around Sam. They had no emotional entanglements to complicate living. She would go her way, and he would go his just as always. They'd most likely try to kill each other a few times before they worked out all the rules, but he could kiss her into bed when that happened. He could handle it. He had experience on his side this time.

He would just have to prepare for the day when she grew beyond what he had to offer. Sam was a passionate woman. Sooner or later she would demand more of him than he had to give. And when she discovered it wasn't there, she would leave.

He would cover himself against that time. He refused to live through that horror again. There would be no children, no legal ties that bind, no financial disasters. She could walk away anytime she liked, empty-handed.

She just wouldn't know that until the time came. It would be his parting gift to her.

A cool breeze blew across her pillow, and Sam buried herself deeper beneath the comforter, chasing after the sleep so rudely interrupted by the cold.

The wind lifted her blankets, sending a chill down her

spine. She muttered beneath her breath and turned to snatch the covers back down. Her hand encountered something hard and warm and distinctly masculine.

She nearly shouted until she opened her eyes to find Sloan beneath the covers with her, his eyes dancing with amusement. The son-of-a-witch had on his black shirt and denims, but she knew how fast that could change.

She quickly moved to the other side of the bed. The gap between them wasn't comfortably large. "What are you doing here?" she demanded, all trace of sleep having fled.

"I thought you'd like to go into the village before everyone gets up and starts berating us with questions. You must realize Jeanne is about to shrivel up with curiosity. I'm not generally in the habit of bringing women here."

"You're not generally in the habit of coming here at all from what I can tell. And they won't have any questions at all if they find you in here. Now get out, Talbott. Let me get dressed before we go adventuring again."

"It would be much faster if I helped you." Grinning, Sloan caught her nightdress and began tugging it upward. Since she was lying on it, it didn't go much farther than her hips, but that was a start. He threw back the covers to admire his handiwork.

Sam brought her knee up to shove him out of bed, but Sloan was too quick. He dropped to his feet on the far side of the bed and leaned over to catch the hem of her dress when she struggled to escape.

Her only choice was to hastily divest herself of the linen before he tumbled down beside her again, and she knew how disastrous that could be. With a jerk, she pulled the nightdress upward. His grip on the hem succeeded in removing it completely.

He whistled as the soft morning light caught on the vibrant colors of her hair where it fell over her bare shoulders. Sam grabbed for the sheet, but she was aware of the picture she presented, even with her back turned to him.

Sloan threw himself across the sheet, preventing that source of cover. He wrapped his arm around her waist and pulled her backward, until he could curl around her and fasten his mouth to her bare breast.

Sam gave a squeal of delight and fury as the heat of his mouth warmed her clear to her toes and familiar sensations started their wild siege of her insides. He pressed her back against the blanket and suckled the other breast, and she was writhing beneath him before she could offer any objections.

"I'm hungry," he murmured against her skin, licking a nipple before moving upward with slow, seductive kisses.

"Breakfast is in the kitchen," she managed to answer, but she couldn't do anything to show him the way. In fact, her fingers were already entangling in the thick black curls she had wanted to touch last night.

"It isn't food I want. What I want is right here." His hand slid between her thighs to make his meaning clear, and Sam nearly jumped from the bed with the suddenness of his invasion. And then she melted around him.

"That's good," he whispered against her ear. "That's just how I feel." He moved his hand gently, pressing and rubbing and using his finger in the most amazing ways. "I can make you come like this, you know," he murmured, almost idly. "I can make you come in any number of different ways. And then there's the usual way in any number of different places. I want to take you under this waterfall I know about. We'll wait until it's hot summer. The air will be steaming. We'll be steaming. And the water will be icy cold."

She was already steaming, and he damned well knew it. He propped himself over her, grinning. Then in the next minute he climbed off her and left her lying there in the cold draft from the window he'd opened to get in here.

He held his hand out. "Come on, slugabed. We're going to town."

There wasn't much point in hiding her nudity after that. With resignation Sam took his hand and allowed him to pull her to her feet. The ache between her thighs throbbed, but she suspected Sloan already knew that. She knew her nipples puckered in the chilly air, and he showed no shyness at looking at her there. In fact, his stare was so warm that she forgot to be cold. She wanted him so much that she was willing to climb right back into that bed and damn the consequences. She looked at him with amazement. She wanted him inside her, and she could tell perfectly well from the bulge in his pants that he was ready to take her. Why wasn't he?

Instead, he reached inside the wardrobe to find her clothes and discovered someone else's clothes in there, too. With a thoughtful whistle he pawed through the selection.

"Sloan, stop that and give me my gown. I'm about to freeze." Sam grabbed the blanket off the bed and wrapped it around her, deciding damning him to hell was redundant.

He gave the blanket a frown and tossed a piece of white cotton at her. "You look like Chief Coyote. Put this on. It must be the maid's. I doubt if she'll mind if I leave her a coin to replace it."

Sam dropped the edge of the blanket and shook out the white cotton. It looked more like some strange form of underwear to her, but she pulled it over her head. The sleeves were full and didn't come down to her wrists but gathered about her elbows. The neckline gathered low and dipped a little too daringly over her breasts. Before she could protest, Sloan threw another garment at her.

"That ought to do it. Those silks and satins are fine for the city, but these will be better out here, unless you want to wear your trousers." He turned and lifted a questioning eyebrow.

She hastily covered the bottom half of her with the colorful skirt as his gaze fell to her revealing neckline. "These will do if I put my coat on."

"They'll do all right, as long as there isn't another man in sight." Sloan jerked the cotton shirt up to cover her breasts, then watched it fall off her shoulder. He whistled and walked around her as she struggled to pull the skirt up without revealing much more.

"That looks good on you. I particularly like knowing you haven't got anything on underneath." Sloan gave her a wolfish grin when she glared at him. "And it's too warm outside to wear that ghastly coat. Get your shawl. I'll buy you a piece of jewelry to keep it fastened, or I'll end up fighting every damned man in town."

He was bossing her around like one of his hired hands, but he had her head spinning so fast that she couldn't think for herself. The shawl sounded like an excellent idea. She grabbed it and covered her nearly bare shoulders.

"I need to put on my stockings," she said in what she hoped was a dignified manner. "Turn around."

Sloan grinned again, and Sam considered belting him one in the jaw. If the only time he knew how to laugh was at her, he deserved to be punched out.

But she ended up sitting on the edge of the bed while he pulled the stockings up her legs. He took every conceivable kind of liberty while he was at it, except the ultimate one. By the time he was done, Sam was ready for that, too.

The smoky look Sloan gave her as he helped her to her feet said he wasn't completely unaffected. His fingers traced the ruffled edge of her blouse, touching not her flesh but the cotton covering it. He found her aroused nipple and stroked that through the material. Sam shivered and waited for whatever came next, for she knew he had something planned to put an end to this burning inside them.

"To the village, then," he murmured, releasing her from his spell by removing his hand. "There's someone there we're going to meet, and then we're going to find the nearest bed or haystack and I'm going to lift that flimsy skirt . . ."

The words he whispered in her ear after that made permanent stains on her cheeks and warmed her all over.

Sam followed him out gladly.

Chapter Twenty-eight

The day burned as bright and beautiful as the previous one. As they rode the dusty trail into the village, Samantha stopped to admire the way the sun's rays struck the crumbling adobe and turned it gold. In the rear of one house, someone had spread a bright blanket of reds and blues over a bush to dry. A bird chirruped in a nearby piñon tree. It was an altogether delightful day, and when she turned to watch Sloan Talbott's broad-shouldered figure riding ahead of her, the thrill of living coursed through her.

She understood what he meant when he called her his woman. She felt the same pride of ownership. He was her man. He came to her bed, not anyone else's, even though he was the kind of man other women would covet.

She could see that in the eyes of one saucy female when the woman appeared in an open doorway to sweep away the night's dust. She was young with a full head of black hair and bright dark eyes and a voluptuous figure that Sam couldn't match. She smiled at Sloan as he rode by, tossed her skirt flirtatiously, but he didn't even seem to notice. Sam gave the woman a triumphant smile as she rode up behind him.

"You're looking smug this morning," he said suspiciously when she caught up with him.

"I was just indulging in a little pride of ownership. I know it's a fleeting thing, but it's a day for indulgence," she said lightly.

His eyes narrowed knowingly as he glanced back at the woman still sweeping her stoop, then to Sam. "She-cat," he muttered. "I'm sure as hell gonna regret this, but ownership works both ways. The possessor is also the possessed."

She widened her eyes. "My, but aren't we philosophical this morning."

"Under the circumstances, I have reason to be." Sloan stopped his horse in front of the derelict church. "Wait here. I'll be back in a few minutes."

"With breakfast, I hope," she called after him as he got down from his horse and started down an alley.

He turned and gave her an enigmatic look. "We'll get to that." Then he disappeared into the shadows between the church and the walled garden next to it.

He was wearing his ruffled shirt and frock coat without his vest and cravat this morning. Sam wondered idly if she'd ruined the others last night. He probably had more where those came from.

She tried to adjust her shawl more comfortably. She wasn't much used to managing one of these things. She needed the pin Sloan had promised her. With more practicality than style, she knotted the ends in front of her.

Deciding that sitting on a horse, waiting for Sloan to return was foolish, she swung down and examined her surroundings. She thought those might be orange trees in the garden beyond that wall. She'd like to see what else they managed to grow there.

The shutters of a shop across the street were being thrown open. A sign in Spanish hung above the door, but from the glitter in the small window, she thought it might be a silversmith's. She didn't wear much jewelry, but maybe he had a brooch.

She tied her horse to a rail and wandered across the street to examine the contents of the window. A man no bigger than herself came to the doorway and said a few words in Spanish. She could see right now she would have to find someone to teach her the language. She didn't like not being able to communicate.

"I can't leave you alone for two minutes, can I?"

Sloan appeared by her side, throwing a few words to the man in the doorway. The man nodded and disappeared inside.

Sam didn't even bother looking at him. A lovely

brooch in silver and black lay in the window. The design was so intricate that she could probably look at it for days and never follow it. "I didn't go anywhere," she murmured in response to his accusation. "Was that the man who makes these things?"

Sloan glanced over her shoulder. "Some of them. Some look Indian. I imagine he trades. Come on, there's someone I want you to meet."

She could hear the sound of the steamboat whistle blowing as it came into the dock. She turned and held her hand over her eyes to see it against the sun's glare. "I didn't know it was so late. I hope this person has breakfast. I'm about to starve to death."

Sloan caught her waist and impatiently led her back across the street. "I can see I'm going to have to feed you before I bed you, but that can be arranged."

Samantha turned him an expectant grin. "You really are a versatile man, aren't you? You could probably find a bed in the desert."

Sloan relaxed slightly and smiled down at her. "If you had any idea how long I've gone without a woman, you'd understand. On second thought"—he squeezed her waist as they stopped in front of the church doors—"maybe you do understand. You've waited a good deal longer than I have."

The way he looked at her made Sam's heart do flip-flops. He wasn't just looking at her breasts or frowning at her attire or any of those things he was prone to do. He was actually looking at *her,* and seeing her. It made her slightly nervous, just as his words did. She wasn't certain she wanted to be understood by Sloan Talbott. He could be entirely too perceptive when he put his mind to it.

Sam licked her lips nervously. "Well, I didn't know what I was missing, did I?"

Sloan's smile grew warmer as his finger caressed her cheek. "No, I suppose not. I'm glad I was your first."

Oh, Lord, but he was making her warm all over, and they were standing outside a church. It wasn't much of a church. It had seen better days. But there was a steeple if not a bell. And probably pews and an altar inside. She hadn't been to church since they'd arrived in California. Maybe that was why he was sending her soul to the devil.

Sloan's hand brushed the side of Sam's breast, then returned to her waist. That was all it took to make her feel all shivery inside. She could see hell staring her in the face if they returned to the mountain while she felt like this. She wouldn't be able to keep away from him.

That thought must have kept her moving when Sloan opened the church door and led her inside. She didn't know why he was taking her into a church, but she had a need for its sanctuary. Maybe if she prayed, she could grasp what was happening to her. She only knew right now she was capable of following Sloan Talbott anywhere he wanted to lead her.

He led her up the aisle.

A priest waited at the end of the aisle.

Samantha blinked, thinking perhaps she was seeing ghosts in the dim light of the chapel. The only windows were slits high up on the walls. The timbered ceiling soared far above them. She could hear sparrows chirping from their nests in the old rafters. The place was otherwise deserted.

If she was seeing things, she was hearing them, too. The ghostly shape in a priest's robes greeted them in Latin.

Sloan kneeled at the railing near the altar. He tugged Sam's hand until she kneeled beside him. She had a scary feeling inside, but it was an oddly wonderful feeling, too. Everything felt light and fluttery inside her as she found her leg pressed against Sloan's, her hand gripped tightly in his.

A band of sunshine came through the partially opened church door, glittering between them. Sam watched the dust motes dancing in the beam as the priest rattled above them in words she couldn't understand. The scary feeling went away, replaced by a blissful sense of peace. She smiled up at Sloan and found him looking down at her with an oddly unfocused expression on his face. At her smile he kissed her forehead.

At some command from the priest, Sloan stood and

pulled her to her feet. Samantha tried to follow some of the words, but they were all foreign to her. The tone was not. She wasn't the least surprised when Sloan followed a particularly long command with the words "I do."

Sam caught the sound of her own name in the next command. When he stopped speaking, the priest looked at her expectantly. She could feel Sloan's fingers close tightly around hers, felt his tension. She ought to be angry that he had tricked her this way, but he had been right to do so. She would never have agreed otherwise. She would never refuse now. To do so would be to reject Sloan and everything he wished to offer her, and she couldn't do that. And she couldn't give up this sense of rightness that suddenly filled her.

Her smile beamed brighter than the sun's when she turned it up to his worried frown. She felt lighter than air when she murmured, "I do."

Incredulity and wonder filled him as Sloan read the trust and sincerity on Samantha's upturned face. She had actually agreed to this farce. He hadn't dared let himself believe it would work. But it was working. He could see it in the moisture of happiness clouding her eyes. He could see it in the incandescent joy surrounding her.

He could see it, and for the first time in ten years, he felt the perfect cad that he was. He'd thought he'd come to live with the feeling, but what had gone before scarcely compared to what he did now as he slipped the ring from his pocket onto her finger. What had come before had been accidental, but this was deliberate. His actions ten years ago had condemned him to hell. He sealed the lock on the gates now. He felt truly rotten about the deception, but that wouldn't stop him.

As the fake priest finished his oratory and Sloan reached to pull Sam into his arms, he became aware that they had an audience. The beam of sunlight that had just been a sliver moments before had grown to a wide band, and long shadows extended down the aisle in front of it. Sloan's guilty conscience made him shove Sam behind him as he faced the intruders.

When he recognized them, he didn't feel happiness or

anger, just resignation. He hadn't wanted witnesses. He'd wanted to keep complete control of this story for Sam's sake and to prevent future repercussions. But he certainly had plenty of experience in rolling with the wheels of fate.

Sloan pulled Sam back to his side, keeping his arm firmly around her waist as she took in the sight of their unexpected guests. He could feel her face turned expectantly to him. He had to take things in stride, as if everything were perfectly normal.

"We weren't prepared for guests, but as long as you're here, you can be the first to wish us happy. May I present my wife, gentlemen?"

A cheer rippled and grew louder and echoed off the old rafters as the miners behind Doc Ramsey threw their hats in the air and rushed up the aisle to buss the bride. Sloan noted with disgust that Joe had joined them. He meant to demand an explanation the first minute he had the gunman alone, but he couldn't do a thing now. Joe gave him an inscrutable look, elbowed a miner aside, and pressed a kiss to Sam's cheek.

"Can't say as I approve of your choice in grooms, Mrs. Talbott, but if anyone can keep him in line, it's you."

Mrs. Talbott. Sam turned and gave Sloan a look that struck a knife through his heart. He didn't find much comfort in knowing she would be the only Mrs. Talbott. He couldn't have said the same for the Montgomery name. He ought to feel comfort in knowing he did this for her own good. But the radiant look on Sam's face told him she was thrilled, and Sloan already knew that marriage wasn't anything to be thrilled about.

With some persuasion he got the men out of the church and over to the café, where they drank toasts in wine and chowed down on eggs at the same time. When the chance offered, Sloan jerked Joe aside. "What in hell are you doing here? How did that sorry lot find us?"

Joe took a swig from his mug and wiped his mustache clean with the back of his arm. He looked at his employer speculatively. "I followed Ramsey when I heard he'd left after the two of you did. I caught up with him after he'd seen you. The turd had already talked your men into finding your brother so they could visit Sam." His eyebrows lifted in cynical question. "You never told me about a brother, especially one with a different name. Ramsey knew where to ask though. We caught the first steamer out this morning. You're the shit who left your horse standing outside the church."

Sloan grimaced. He'd been so certain no one would follow that he'd grown careless. More likely, he'd been so engrossed in finding a way to get Sam back in his bed, he hadn't given precautions a second thought. He'd better get her out of his system real soon. Once he got himself back to normal and had a woman in his bed on a regular basis, he'd think clearly again.

When the party grew so rowdy they even made Sam blush with their increasingly drunken jests, Sloan decided it was time to get the hell out. He wanted to be back on the mountain right now, where he could have Sam to himself.

But they still had to take their leave of his brother and his wife. That would be a sticky tangle, but he'd worry about that when he got there.

"Come on," he whispered in Sam's ear. "I want to do a little private celebrating, if you don't mind. These plug uglies will be here the rest of the day drinking themselves under the table."

Satiated with ranch eggs and big rounds of bread, Samantha gave him a glittering smile of acceptance and took his hand. Sloan remembered her earlier comment about ownership, and he had to smile back. Only Sam would have the courage to think she'd put her brand on him. He wouldn't do anything to discourage that notion. He liked having her a little brazen.

The knot she'd made in her shawl was starting to slip, reminding Sloan of the promise he'd made. His promises tended to be ambiguous at best, but this one was simple enough to keep. Outside the café, he led her back to the silversmith's.

She'd scarcely even noticed the ring he'd given her, so he figured he wouldn't impress her much with a brooch, but it would relieve some of the strain of guilt. He knew he'd get over the guilty feeling eventually, but it was a simple enough matter to ease the pressure now.

When he took her inside the shop, she grew suddenly quiet, so he had to look down at her to make sure he hadn't done something wrong. She had an odd look in her eyes that he couldn't interpret, so he shrugged and spoke to the shopkeeper.

When the man brought out the selection of brooches and he didn't see anything that suited him, Sloan almost bought one just to say he'd kept his promise. But something in Samantha's gaze made him turn around and remember the window display. After a few words, the shopkeeper emptied the contents before him.

The silver and onyx brooch jumped out at him immediately. When Sloan picked it out and carefully fastened it to her shawl, he could almost see her eyes light up. It was a simple thing, really. The price was three times anything else he'd looked at, but the money didn't matter. He had more than enough of that now. It was the look in Sam's eyes when he chose the one she wanted that counted. It made him feel damned good.

He hadn't felt good about himself in a very long time. He had no reason to feel good about himself now. Still, Sloan scarcely knew how much he paid the clerk before he ushered his bride out the door.

"I'm not going to make it back to the ranch," he whispered against her ear as they approached their horses.

He knew she would understand what he was saying, even if he said it crudely. A certain amount of shyness softened her eyes at his words, but there wasn't anything shy about the way she rubbed the knuckles of their entwined hands against his trousers. He nearly went up in flames at her boldness.

"I suppose we're too far from the ocean," she murmured before he set her on her saddle.

"Will a river do?"

He could tell by the way she smiled that a mud puddle would suffice if he asked it of her.

Damn, but it would feel good having his own woman again. It would be even better than the last time, because this one was innocent enough to think she found something worth keeping in him.

She was wrong, but he'd try not to let her discover that too soon.

Chapter Twenty-nine

The spot Sloan found beside the river was as peaceful as the church had been. He spread a blanket from the horse over the coarse grass in the full sun. Except for the chilly wind, the day almost felt like spring instead of January, and Samantha drank in this aspect of her new home. She was a Californian now. She would embrace this new setting fully, as she would embrace her new husband and make him a part of her.

She lay down on the blanket and watched the clouds float by in the sky above. She'd had entirely too much wine on an empty stomach, and even the breakfast she'd finally managed to consume hadn't absorbed all of its effects. She felt as pleasantly floaty as those clouds up there when Sloan finally kneeled down beside her.

"I don't think I love you," she told him honestly as he bent to kiss her and take her breast in his hand.

"I don't think it matters," Sloan answered without inflection as he brushed aside the loose blouse and reached inside.

Sam felt his touch so deep inside her that he might as well have opened her chest and caressed her heart. She looked up and saw the angular profile of her husband's face silhouetted against the sky. Lines from his chronic frowns creased his forehead, but crinkles from long-ago laughter marked the corners of his eyes. He was a man, not a boy, with all the experience and prejudices of someone set in his ways. But she thought perhaps there were a few things he had just forgotten how to do. Maybe she could remind him.

"You tricked me," she murmured languorously, lifting her arm to stroke his thick curls. The breeze off the river blew over her bare breasts, but she wasn't cold, not while Sloan looked at her. She was hot inside, and wet where he wanted her, but she wasn't fully aroused yet. She was still feeling the wine.

"I know I did. But you could have said no. You didn't have to go through with it." He kissed the upper curve of her breast while his thumb thrummed over the crest. He pushed her legs apart with his knees and lay between them, fully clothed, keeping his weight off her with his elbows.

"Yes, I did. I couldn't leave you standing at the altar." When Sloan bent to suckle her breast at this admission, she sucked in a deep breath before she could continue. "I didn't think anyone would ever like me enough to bring me to the altar."

Sloan stopped what he was doing long enough to meet her eyes. "There might be times when you're going to hate me, Samantha. I'm not your easygoing father. I'm an ogre to live with. But no matter what I do, remember that I like you one hell of a lot better than anyone else I've ever met."

Sam didn't think she could even do him the favor of returning the sentiment. She liked a whole lot of people more than she liked Sloan Talbott. But she'd never wanted any man as she wanted him, either. It seemed fair trade.

She opened the buttons of his shirt and slid her hands over the powerful chest beneath. His muscles rippled beneath her caress, and the silken hair curled around her fingers. "I have no idea what I promised back there in that church, but I can promise I'll always be there when you need me. If you ever need me," she amended.

"I need you now, Sam. Tell me you're ready." He rubbed his hips against hers to show his meaning.

She was ready. She'd been ready all morning. With a smile of joy, she pulled his head down to hers and told him with her kiss.

They made love beneath the winter sun, drank part of the bottle of wine Sloan had brought with them for lunch, and made love again. Time didn't seem to have any particular meaning when they were naked in each other's arms.

Sloan kept her covered with his warmth, but as the afternoon waned, Sam could feel the gooseflesh rise up on him as she ran her fingers over the lean muscles of his buttocks. She found his man's body quite fascinating, but he would turn blue with the cold if they dallied much longer.

Regretfully, she returned her hand to the powerful ridges of his chest and circled his flat brown nipples. "The wine's all gone," she told him sorrowfully, with a little hiccup.

He grinned down at her and kissed the corner of her mouth. "I think I'll keep you drunk these next few weeks. You're mighty inventive when you're not trying to be proper."

Her eyes opened wide as she regarded his face hovering over her. "I am? What did I invent?"

"Nothing any skilled courtesan doesn't already know, but you seemed to have discovered for yourself." He sat up and pulled her up with him so that she was nearly sitting in his lap. He reached to pull the wrinkled blouse over her head.

Sam squiggled her arms into the proper places and squirmed her back end against his thighs. She felt his instant response to the maneuver and giggled. She liked making Sloan Talbott respond to her.

"Damn, Sam, you're going to make me feel old if you keep that up. I can't remember the last time I was with a woman who giggled."

Sloan caressed her breast as he pulled the blouse down, and she arched into his hand. "Maybe you should have drunk more of the wine," she answered saucily.

"That's more wine than I've drunk these last ten years, so don't go pushing it. I'm a mean drunk."

"You're a lot of things, Sloan Talbott, most of which I know nothing about. But I do know you're my husband, and if you're mean to me, I'll shoot your toes off." She leaned her head back against his shoulder and let him pull her stockings on. Her hair spilled in red curls across his chest.

"Just as long as it's not the important parts of my anatomy you go shooting off." He smoothed the stockings over her knees and ran his hand the rest of the way up her thigh. "Or we'll both be mean." He touched her where she would feel it most.

Sam pressed instinctively into his hand. "I'll be most careful about my target then," she whispered huskily, her heart quickening with anticipation.

She felt a moment's disappointment when Sloan set her aside and returned to his feet, but he was right. The time had come to return to the real world. The sun was dropping fast, and the wind had turned cold. They should continue this conversation in a warm bed.

They rode to the ranch in relative silence. The giddiness of the wine had worn off, reminding them that they were not alone in this world. They had lives and responsibilities to return to. Sam looked at the ranch house sprawling across the horizon in front of them and wondered what Sloan's family would think of their marrying without asking them to attend the ceremony. Somehow, now that the glory had worn off a little, it seemed a strange thing to do.

Matthew was in the yard when they rode up. He lifted a hand in greeting as they dismounted, but went about his chores without questioning their activities. Sam glanced hesitantly at her husband. Sloan's expression had grown taut and unreadable again.

"You'd better leave me to explain this to Matt and Jeanne," he said as he lifted her from the horse.

At any other time, Sam would have objected to him hauling her down like a helpless infant, but right now she needed the reassurance of Sloan's hands around her. While Sloan touched her, the scariness of what they had done faded to the background. She gave him a brief nod to indicate she understood.

He made no effort to kiss her or reassure her in any other way. He merely released her and sent her into the house while he took the horses to the stable. Sam followed him with her eyes, wishing she could follow him in reality. Maybe she could use the excuse of seeing how the foal was doing?

But Jeanne was already calling to her from the doorway. Resolutely, Sam plastered a smile on her face and went in to help with supper. This was Sloan's family, and he would know best how to deal with them. After all, she knew very little about him and his relationship with these people. Keeping her eyes and ears open and her mouth shut seemed the best policy.

Matthew and Jeanne remained genial and accepting throughout the meal, making no mention of Sam and Sloan's new status. They asked about their day, questioned Sam about her family, and showed an interest in her father's theories about horse-breeding. No mention of marriage came up. They didn't even question why she traveled unescorted with Sloan.

Deciding Sloan was waiting until after the meal to break the news, Sam did her best to act as if everything were normal. Still, the thought that they would soon share a bed under this roof made her glance toward the bedrooms uneasily. It suddenly seemed a trifle embarrassing that these people would know what she and Sloan were doing when they retired to that bed together.

After the meal they started a fire in the front parlor fireplace and took seats to continue their earlier conversation. The men sipped brandy, and the women had tea. Sloan still made no mention of what they had done. Sam imagined that her hosts watched her with curiosity. She had changed into the dress Sloan had bought for her. She played nervously with the brooch she had pinned to it, then remembering the ring on her finger, she pushed it around for a while. It was old and heavy and well-worn. She'd have to ask Sloan if it was a family heirloom.

When Sloan spoke directly to her, her mind had drifted elsewhere, and he had to repeat himself before she heard. She blinked without comprehension when she finally understood what he was saying. He wanted her to go to bed now, without him?

"You're so exhausted you're not even hearing what we're saying," he said, holding out his hand to help her up. "You don't have to stay up to be polite."

Sam glanced uncertainly at the two people sitting by the fire. They were trying very hard to conceal their interest. They seemed more sympathetic than nosy, and Sam made her excuses to avoid their eyes. Maybe once she left the parlor, Sloan would explain. She didn't want to have to spend another night alone in that bedroom, not when her husband was so close by.

She heard the rumbling of Sloan's voice as she drifted down the hallway. She remembered how he'd climbed in her window just that morning, and she smiled to herself. She could count on Sloan to do the unexpected. She fully expected their marriage would be one noisy argument after another, but it would never be boring. And they would always have the bedroom for reconciliations.

It was a little worrisome knowing Sloan didn't want children. He might have all the experience in the world, but children sometimes happened. They had time enough in the future to worry about that. They were safe for a few more days. If Sloan used his precautions the rest of the time, then they could probably hold off quite a while before the question of children came up. Maybe by that time he'd welcome the idea.

Sam heard Matthew's voice rise angrily as she entered the bedroom she'd used the night before. The bed in here was small. Maybe Sloan had meant for her to go to his bed, but she didn't have enough nerve to do that until he'd told his family that they were married. Maybe if she just washed and waited, he'd come get her and take her to his room.

As she waited, she heard Sloan shouting at his brother and Jeanne's voice attempting to placate the two. A moment later, even Jeanne's voice sounded sharp and unhappy. Sam twisted her hands together and looked at her new wedding band. She hadn't thought Sloan's family had disliked her that much.

She knew she wasn't pretty. She certainly didn't behave like a proper lady. But she wasn't ignorant or stupid. She would make a good wife for Sloan. Even if she knew more about hunting than cooking, she could still take care of him—as much as he would let her. She didn't think that would be very much, but they would work it out eventually. There was no call for this kind of screaming argument over her.

The more she thought about it, the angrier she became. They were in there fighting over her as if she was too young and tin-headed to stand up for herself.

Shoving her hair back off her face, Sam stalked back down the hallway to the parlor. Sloan would have to learn that she fought her own fights. He must have sent her away knowing his announcement would instigate a family argument. He should have confided in her. She could have told him she would stand by his side.

"Dammit, Sloan, I've stood behind you and supported your decisions every minute of the way, but I can't condone this! God only knows, I understand what you've gone through, but you have no right—"

"*You* have no right, Matt! This is my life; I'll live it as I want. I'm not asking for your approval. We'll go back up the mountain and not come down again, if that's what you want. I just wanted you to know that I've found a woman I mean to live with. I'd hoped you would accept her since she's the innocent party, but if you can't—"

Sam started to step out of the shadows to lend her support to Sloan, but Jeanne's next words pinned her to the floor.

"You are already married, Sloan! Even knowing she is innocent, you would ruin her with this charade?"

Frozen, Sam swung her gaze to Sloan. Surely she had misunderstood. He would explain away this accusation. This was what she got for eavesdropping. She ought to just walk out there right now and make herself known so they could tell her what the argument was really about. But instead of moving, she fastened her gaze on Sloan.

He had his back to the fire, and his features fell in shadow, but she could tell by the tension in his stance that he was furious. He'd have no expression except that icy look she knew so well. Her heart pounded as she waited for his declaration of innocence.

"Melinda is not my wife!" he finally spat out. "She has my name, my fortune, and everything I ever was. She stole my life. I came out here to start a new one, and I've succeeded. I thought you would be happy that I've found someone to share it with. I can see I was wrong."

"You want us to be happy that you've started your new life as a bigamist?" Matt asked incredulously.

"Rodriguez was defrocked years ago," Sloan answered wearily. "The marriage isn't legal. That's the whole point, isn't it? I'm not going to live through that hell again."

Samantha felt as if every ounce of blood in her body had drained to her feet. The shock had numbed her beyond that, but a twinge of pain formed in her belly as the words gradually sank in.

She didn't want to believe what she was hearing. She wanted to believe she misunderstood everything. She knew very little about Sloan Talbott. She knew him as a difficult, irascible man who hid himself from the world. She knew he alone was responsible for saving dozens of lives during the smallpox epidemic. She knew he'd risked his life to save Jack during the fire. She knew he would never admit responsibility for either of those acts. And she didn't know why, not any more than she knew why he stood there saying these things now. She had to be dreaming this, or misunderstanding something.

Matthew gulped the dregs of his brandy glass and stood up to face his brother. "I don't believe for a minute that little girl in there is another Melinda, not any more than I believe that you killed your own son. You're a blockheaded idiot, Sloan, and I'm not going to let you ruin that girl's life as you're so intent on ruining your own."

When Sloan's fist lashed out to catch his brother on the jaw, sending him crashing into the furniture, Sam couldn't stay where she was any longer. She stepped out into the flickering light of the fire just as Matthew hit the floor.

Standing furiously over his prostrate brother, Sloan saw her at once. Without a word he casually returned to the mantel and refilled his brandy glass. Lifting it in salute, he threw back the contents in a single swallow.

Chapter Thirty

Matt picked himself up off the floor, rubbing his jaw. He glanced from the slender woman in delicate silk to the stone-faced man at the fire. The woman wasn't weeping hysterically or screaming epithets. The firelight played on a cascade of red hair and flickered across her porcelain features, making her cheeks paler than usual, but her expression was as inscrutable as Sloan's. For a moment Matt had an image of her holding a rifle and aiming it at his brother's heart, but he shook his head and the vision went away. The woman standing here was young and vulnerable and in need of sympathy and understanding.

Jeanne tried to offer it to her, but Samantha shook her off and stepped away. Her gaze remained fixed on Sloan. Catching his wife's arm, Matthew tried to see what Samantha saw in his brother's face. Sloan was so tense that it seemed he would shatter if touched, but he maintained his insouciant pose, leaning one elbow against the mantel and dangling the glass from his fingers.

"I'd appreciate an explanation." Samantha finally broke the silence. Her voice sounded quiet and reasonable, but Matthew could see her fingers trembling where she clenched them in the gathers of her skirt.

"There isn't any," Sloan replied, reaching for the brandy again.

The two of them acted as if they were alone in the room. Glancing at Jeanne, Matt met her eyes and nodded agreement with her unspoken words. This wasn't their argument. Silently, they slipped away.

Sloan scarcely noticed. He refilled his glass, but didn't drink. When he'd been younger, he'd used drinking as a crutch to get through this kind of emotional hurricane. He knew the tragic results. He'd hoped this time around he would be able to avoid hysterical scenes. There shouldn't be any emotions involved, just sex. He should have known women were anathema to him. They couldn't leave well enough alone. They had to play out every drama to its bitter end. Well, this time, he wasn't cooperating.

He watched as Sam paled a little more at his reply. She bit her bottom lip, turning it as pale as her cheeks. He remembered kissing that wide mouth of hers. He remembered the lush responsiveness of her kisses. He regretted losing the opportunity to kiss her again, but he didn't regret what he had done.

"Don't lie to me, Talbott, if that's really your name. You may be the meanest man this side of the Sierras, but I don't think you've ever deliberately lied to me. Let's keep it that way. Tell me you don't want to explain, but don't tell me there isn't any explanation. I'm not a total fool. Obviously, I'm not as smart as I thought was, but I'm not an idiot either."

"No, you're not an idiot." He swung the glass in his hands, watching her face for expression. She wasn't even crying. She hadn't lifted her voice once. Maybe he'd been right after all. Maybe it was just sex between them. He'd liked the way she'd looked at him as if he really were a man she admired, but maybe that had just been one of her woman's ploys. "I don't know how much you heard. What part needs explaining? It seemed rather clear to me."

This time she looked as if she would like to drive a timber piling through his middle, but she kept her fists clenched at her sides. "You told me from the first that you didn't want to be married. We had an agreement, and I was willing to abide by it. So why did you make a fool of me at that church? Do you despise me that much?"

That was an interesting approach. She didn't mind that they weren't really married. She just didn't like being made a fool of. He could understand that. But he couldn't answer it. He wasn't exactly certain of the answer himself.

Sloan set the glass aside and ran his hand over the back of his neck, trying to work out the tension. "I don't despise you, Sam. I didn't lie to you about that. For some insane reason I like you better than anyone else I know. I guess I was trying to make things easier for you." He shoved his hands into his pockets and leaned his shoulders against the mantel. He tried to follow her expression, but she had stepped back into the shadows again. He felt like an idiot trying to explain himself, but maybe he'd feel less like a cad if he tried.

"Your effort is not appreciated." Sarcasm laced her reply. "Why on earth would you think a fake priest and a fake marriage would make things easier for me? It sounds like they make things easier for you."

She was definitely not stupid. Sloan grimaced. "It made things easier for both of us. When you got tired of me, you could pack up and leave without any of the ties that bind, and I could let you go, knowing you weren't walking away with anything that belonged to me. But that wasn't the real reason I did it. I did it because I wanted to take you back to town and keep you by my side. I knew you would never go to bed with me unless your family accepted it as respectable. And I knew it would be impossible for the two of us to live in the same town without ending up in the same bed. So I took the easiest path."

He waited for the screams, but they didn't come. He couldn't tell how much he'd hurt her. She just stood there like a stone statue, watching him with a kind of silent wariness, making him feel as if he were a mallet poised to smash her to splinters.

"When did you mean to tell me that you were already married?"

So, she'd heard it all. Sloan sighed and wished for the brandy glass again. He kept his hands in his pockets and shrugged. "It isn't something that normally comes up in conversation." He could tell her that woman back there was no longer his wife, but it wouldn't change things. No one knew, not even Matthew. Allowing her to keep his name and social standing had given him his freedom, and he meant to abide by that agreement. He saw no reason to break it now. He'd have done the same whether he was free or not. He had no intention of ever marrying again.

"Well, that's honest." She turned as if to go, then looked back over her shoulder. "Is your name really Talbott?"

"I left the name Montgomery with her. Talbott was the name of the town when I bought it."

She nodded and walked out, back to the bedroom she had slept in last night, the one with the single bed. Sloan watched her go with a twinge of unhappiness.

He hadn't wanted it this way, but he'd known the time would come sooner or later. Maybe it was better that it had come now, before she really knew what a bastard he was.

At least, she hadn't asked him how he'd killed his son.

"Harriet, I really don't think it's wise to encourage Mr. ... er ... Riding Eagle." Alice Neely shook out the wet linen and pinned one corner neatly to the line the men had strung across the back lot.

"I'm not encouraging him, Mama," Harriet said calmly, pinning the other end of the sheet. "He wishes to learn to read, and I am teaching him. He's a quick student."

Alice sighed and tried to think of the words to explain. She wished Samantha were here. Her eldest daughter had a way of driving right to the point without being overly crude. "You might think you're teaching him to read, but he's likely having other ideas," she said cautiously. "And the other men are definitely having other ideas, especially since you started throwing them out when they hung around the store without buying anything."

"They were rude and insulting. If Samantha was here, she would have done the same." Indignation began to replace Harriet's earlier serenity. "Mr. Eagle grasps the letters of the alphabet much easier when he can associate them with words he knows. He knows what a bag of feed and a can of hominy are. It's not the same as teaching a child. A picture book won't suffice."

Alice removed the clothespin from her mouth and jabbed it over the linen pillowcase. "Then I suggest you ask Chief Coyote or that Miss Whitaker to attend while you are teaching him. It ought to be Miss Whitaker's place to teach him anyway. She's the teacher in this town, not you. And he's the chief's grandson. I can't chaperone you all day, but someone ought to."

"Miss Whitaker thinks Indians smell. And I don't believe she's much of a teacher. She tried to tell Jack that Nebraska is still a territory, and she didn't know Ulysses Grant has been elected president. She's more interested in flirting with Mr. Bradshaw than teaching anybody."

Lord only knew, but Harriet was right. Clara Whitaker was a disappointment as a teacher. Jack would grow up as wild as Riding Eagle if someone didn't take him in hand soon. Alice glared at the clothesline. "Well then, Chief Coyote will have to sit with you. He doesn't seem to have much else to do around here anyway."

Harriet looked dubious. "I'll ask him, but I don't think he'll properly understand. Indians don't seem to know much about chaperoning." She brightened. "Maybe I could get Bernadette to sit with me."

"You know I need her in the kitchen, and she would be worse than Chief Coyote, in any account. She'd no doubt start hanging curtains on the window and get distracted by a butterfly outside and forget you were even there. I have to keep an eye on that girl every minute."

Harriet smiled at this accurate description of her twin's vagaries. They might look identical, but they had certainly never been identical in character. Harriet was practical. Bernadette was . . . well, Bernadette was just Bernadette. There was no explaining her.

"I'll talk to Chief Coyote. I wish Dr. Ramsey would come back. He used to sit in on our sessions and come up with some helpful suggestions. Isn't it odd that he got called out of town just when Mr. Talbott and Sam left?"

Odd wasn't precisely the word for it. Alice alternated between grateful and worried at the doctor's behavior. He seemed a reasonable man when he wasn't drinking, and he'd done his best to welcome them to this town—unlike Sloan Talbott. Sometimes she thought Ramsey meant to court one of them but hadn't decided which. He was certainly old enough to be the twins' father, but Alice had made it very clear that she was married and wouldn't believe herself otherwise unless they found Emmanuel's body. And knowing Emmanuel as she did, she didn't expect his body to be found in anything less than a walking state.

"Dr. Ramsey's business isn't ours," she reprimanded her daughter gently. "I'm sure Samantha will be back directly, and perhaps she can come up with some other ideas about Mr. Eagle. In the meantime, I don't want you alone with him again."

Harriet looked the tiniest bit sulky. "You let Sam go off with Mr. Talbott alone. I don't understand the difference."

Alice didn't think she could explain the difference. She couldn't tell her younger daughter that Sam would do whatever she thought best regardless of what her mother thought. Harriet was rebellious enough. She didn't think she could explain that Sam thought like a man and could take care of herself like a man, and if Sloan Talbott tried anything untoward, he would likely wake up a eunuch. Alice wasn't entirely certain that was true, but the notion made it easier to accept what she'd allowed Sam to do. It wasn't any more palatable to explain that Sam was getting too old to go unmarried, and she hoped this trip would wake those two up to what they felt for each other. Harriet would never understand that in a million years. Everyone still thought Sloan and Sam hated each other. Alice had seen too much of human nature to believe that. Those two were like iron and lodestone. Keeping them apart would be impossible.

So Alice merely shrugged and replied, "Finding your father is a shade more important than teaching Mr. Eagle to read."

Harriet wisely accepted that reply.

Jack raced around the corner, his boot heels skidding in the dirt and throwing dust up on the newly washed clothes as he came to a halt.

"They're coming! I saw them coming! Can I ride down and meet them?"

Shaking out the now dust-coated wet sheet with exasperation, Alice Neely frowned down at her nephew. "Who's coming?"

Jack beamed and cleaned off his spectacles on his shirt.

"Everybody who went down to Ariposa, I reckon. I can't tell until I get there."

Sam. And Talbott. Alice sent Harriet a look of relief. They were home. She looked back to Jack, making certain he had his good boots on and his shirt tucked in. "You be careful now. If they tell me you galloped that pony down the hill, you won't be allowed to ride it again for a month."

Jack whooped and took off running for the stable.

The noise brought a few onlookers into the street. A few more got the word and wandered out to join them.

By the time Ramsey and the miners with him entered town, they had a welcoming party to greet them.

Sam and Sloan were nowhere in sight. Ramsey grinned in satisfaction at that discovery. Instead of heading for the saloon, he went straight to the hacienda. The miners were the first to inform the occupants of the saloon that one of the Neely women was no longer in circulation.

Sam patted the Indian pony's neck as they rode up the final stretch of mountainside. Sloan had scarcely spoken two words since they left the ranch, and the silence between them had grown so tense that she found the pony's company preferable.

There wasn't much she could say to end the silence. She had given him his forty-eight hours. He had set someone to find her father. They'd both upheld their ends of the bargain. It was easier to pretend the other hadn't happened. They'd both kept to their separate ways as much as possible since the revelation of Sloan's marriage.

The strain of keeping to herself was getting to Sam though. She wanted to demand better explanations. She wanted to know what Sloan's wife had done to him to make him think all women were scheming creatures not to be trusted. Or if he really thought he was so detestable that no woman would ever stay with him for long. Or just precisely what in hell made him think marriage was a state to devoutly be avoided to the extent that he would tolerate the outer confines but not the legal ones.

But she didn't say anything. They had known each other in the most intimate manner imaginable, but they didn't know each other at all. She realized what a mistake that had been now, when she could do nothing about it. He had used physical intimacy to manipulate her, and she had allowed it. She had only herself to blame. She'd stopped thinking with her head the moment she'd started thinking with her heart. That was a hard lesson to learn.

At least she could console herself with the knowledge that there wouldn't be any results from her foolishness. Sloan had promised to talk to Ramsey and his men when the miners returned to town, before they could say anything to anyone else. She thought he might be planning on bribing them to keep their mouths shut, but she hadn't inquired into the details. Mostly, she'd been relieved that Sloan had said anything at all.

She still worried that he might try again to throw her and her family out of town, but he hadn't mentioned it once. He could probably hire lawyers and find a sheriff somewhere to evict them if his deed held stronger than theirs. But that would take years, she suspected. If anything, he'd find a more devious method.

Lost in these dismal thoughts, Sam scarcely paid attention to where they were until she heard the hiss of Sloan's sudden intake of breath. She looked up, and her eyes widened as she saw what he was already cursing.

Above a crowd of well-wishers cramming the plaza rose a banner that read CONGRATULATIONS MR. AND MRS. TALBOTT!

Ramsey and his men had beat them to town.

Chapter Thirty-one

Sam's tongue stuck in her mouth as the crowd surged around them. She could see her mother's smiling face and her sisters jumping up and down with excitement. Doc Ramsey was there, grinning broadly. Injun Joe looked a little sour, but he came forward to grab the reins of their horses. She quivered a little inside as she turned to see how Sloan would deal with this unpleasant development.

Stoically, he dismounted and reached up to haul her out of the saddle. She couldn't fight him in front of this crowd. They thought she was his wife. A husband had a right to manhandle his wife. They probably thought it romantic.

Terror took root in her soul. Her family thought she was married to Sloan. Doc Ramsey had told them he had seen her stand before the altar with Sloan Talbott. They'd been gone several nights since then. No one would believe nothing had happened. What had happened hadn't been nothing. They had very definitely indulged in marital activities. She couldn't lie to her mother about that.

Sam was almost grateful for the support of Sloan's arm around her waist. Without it, she might have sunk into the dust, her knees were that weak. She tried not to think about it when Injun Joe took off their saddlebags and threw them on the porch of the hotel—her possessions as well as Sloan's. A wife would be expected to live with her husband. Her fingernails dug into her palms.

The crowd made way for Alice Neely to come forward. Sam's mother was considerably shorter than Sloan, but when she held out her arms to him, he bent obediently to accept her hug and kiss.

"Welcome to the family, Mr. Talbott. I knew you would do the proper thing."

Sam felt her heart sink to her feet when Sloan didn't correct her mother. The twins raced to give him a hug, and a roar went up from the crowd. Before Sam knew what was happening, every man in town crushed around her, attempting to kiss her as if this were the wedding and they had the right to kiss the bride.

Sloan set the twins firmly aside and grabbed the collar of the man currently bussing Sam on the cheek. Sam breathed a sigh of relief when he tugged her back to his side and proceeded through the crowd at her mother's direction. She simply wasn't in any state to slap every man in town right now.

"We've prepared a wedding feast," Bernadette said breathlessly as she ran alongside of them. "It's so exciting! Mama's fixed the biggest, prettiest cake you've ever seen. Doc Ramsey brought up some candied fruits, so it's just as pretty on the inside. Oh, Sam, it's so wonderful! I wish I could have been there."

Sam knew her sister well enough to follow these meanderings, but Sloan looked a trifle dazed. She imagined he was wondering if her sister was wishing to be on the cake's inside, and she couldn't help smiling just a little. If Sloan didn't get them out of this one, he was going to be saddled with a ready-made family of eccentric propensities.

He didn't seem in any hurry to disabuse anyone about their "marriage." He even managed a grim smile when the crowd parted to reveal the magnificent wedding cake they were expected to cut. Sam sighed in pleasure at the delicate fantasy of white tiered icing. Her mother made the best wedding cakes in all Tennessee. She had never dreamed of having one of her own.

Someone handed them a knife, and Sam held it uncertainly, glancing up to Sloan for guidance. Without a word, he covered her hand with his and helped her guide the knife through the top tier of cake. Sam watched in somewhat abstract fascination as he handed her the first slice. A cheer rang out as she took a bite, then shared it with him. It was almost like a real wedding.

Of course, Sloan already had experience at getting married, Sam thought miserably some while later as everyone chatted and carried on. Someone rosined up a bow, and others pushed tables against the walls. Sloan had already gone through one wedding with someone else. Or more likely, he'd gone through an elegant, more fashionable version with his prim and proper wife in Boston.

Wife. Sam ground her teeth together and watched her so-called husband bend over to listen to her mother speak. She didn't know how he had the nerve to stand there and act as if this celebration were real. He knew as well as she did that it was a farce. She just couldn't figure how to get out of it.

But she knew damned good and well that whatever happened, Sloan Talbott was sleeping in his bed alone tonight. When he took her in his arms to lead off the dancing, she gave him a look that warned he'd better not push her much further.

"You have a better idea?" he asked dryly, glancing around at the crowd merrily celebrating what they considered a happy occasion.

"The truth usually works wonders."

"Oh, it will work wonders all right. There isn't a soul in this town that would believe we haven't shared a bed together. And half of them wouldn't believe that we aren't really married. Your mother will come after me with a butcher knife and then insist that all of you pack up and leave, even if you haven't any place to go. The men will raise an uproar, and a pack of them will follow you to town. Word will spread like wildfire. Not only your reputation, but your entire family's will be smeared in mud as gossip grows. Truth is a marvelous thing."

Sam gritted her teeth as she acknowledged the probability of his words. "I'll not sleep with you," she warned. "I'm not an adulteress."

Sloan pulled her closer and swept her in a wide circle to the cheers of the crowd. "Would it make a difference if I told you I wasn't married?"

She glared up at him. "I'm not a whore, either."

His lips straightened into a grim line. "Fine. Just keep

out of my way, and we'll manage to go on as before. The hotel's a big place."

She didn't like the sound of that at all, but she didn't have time to argue. The dance came to an end, and men pushed around her, clamoring for the next dance. Before she could protest, Doc Ramsey swung her off in his arms, and Sloan was talking to her mother.

Sam watched helplessly as men carried her trunk of clothes out the front door, presumably to her new home. Her saddle and rifle were already there. She wondered if Sloan were brash enough to take her bed and mattress, too. Surely he wouldn't have them paraded through this crowd like some sort of trophy.

The music scarcely stopped before another song began, and still another man carried her off. Even her mother was dancing now. Some of the men danced with other men. The widow and the teacher and the blacksmith's wife all had partners. She couldn't tell if it was Bernadette or Harriet swinging around in the arms of the mine foreman. She looked for the other twin, but couldn't see her in the crowd.

Sam was nearly faint with exhaustion and dry as a desert by the time Sloan elbowed his way to her side and rescued her from her latest partner. She took the lemonade he offered gratefully and welcomed the support of his arm around her waist as he disentangled them from the crowd and found a place along the wall.

"I didn't think it wise to have my bride fainting on the dance floor. It might lead to some wrongful conclusions," he offered in explanation as she sipped at the soothing drink.

"Your concern is overwhelming." Sam searched the dance floor, trying to account for all her family. She'd spent too many years protecting them to give up the urge now.

She could still find only one twin. Nervously, she glanced over her shoulder in the direction of the kitchen. "Have you seen Harriet recently?"

Sloan scanned the room. "Isn't she the one with Craycraft?"

"No, that's Bernadette. I'm going to go back to the

kitchen and look for her. There seems to be a lot of whiskey around in here."

The last seemingly irrelevant statement brought Sloan from the wall to follow her. They both knew that men and whiskey made a dangerous combination. Add women, and the potential for an explosive situation multiplied. Sam couldn't say she was grateful for his accompaniment, but these were his men. He had as much interest in keeping the peace as she did.

They heard the faint scream as soon as they escaped the noise in the parlor. Sloan took off at a run, leaving Sam one pace behind.

They slammed through the kitchen and out into the darkness now enveloping the backyard. The screams were louder out here. From behind them, Sam could hear more running footsteps. Someone must have been watching and followed them out.

Everyone would have been watching them. As Sloan dashed through the darkness in the direction of the screams, Sam heard shouts of alarm being raised in the house behind them. Sam easily followed in Sloan's path. She could see the white of his linen shirt directly ahead of her. Someone ran out the kitchen door with a lantern in hand, and a broad swathe of light cut across the yard.

Fear and fury took equal place in her heart as the scene ahead unfolded. She could see Harriet's golden hair splashed against the dark side of the shed. A heavy masculine silhouette cut off the sight of the rest of her, but Sam recognized Harriet's screams and the suddenly muffled moan that ensued when the man holding her covered her mouth. Screaming with rage, Sam ran to leap on the man's back, but Sloan was there before her.

Jerking the culprit backward by the collar, he plowed his fist into a hard jaw, slamming Harriet's attacker to the ground. Then he bent over and jerked the man to his feet so he could pound him again, this time with a vicious blow to the stomach. The man gagged and fell to his knees.

Harriet collapsed into Sam's arms, sobbing against her shoulder as they watched Sloan pull the man to his feet one more time. His next punch was as methodical and

murderous as the first two. Sam gave a gasp of sympathetic pain as a bone-crushing blow again sent Harriet's
assailant into a huddled heap at Sloan's feet.

By this time a crowd had formed around them. Injun
Joe stepped into the circle around Sloan, preventing him
from reaching for the fallen man again. He grabbed the
culprit's collar and hauled him upward, shoving him into
the arms of two husky miners. "What do you want us to
do with him?" he asked laconically, of no one in particular.

"Hang him," Sloan replied as he wiped his face on his
sleeve and glanced back to the two women huddled
against the wall. Harriet's dress was torn and tattered, and
her usually neatly rolled hair had been jerked down
around her bare shoulders. His jaw tightened grimly as
the terror in her eyes grew with his order of execution.
"Or tar and feather him. Which do you prefer, Miss
Neely?"

Sam tried to identify the man being held, but he was no
more than one of the nameless faces that came and went
through town. His jaw was already swelling from Sloan's
blows, but she felt no sympathy for him whatsoever. Only
the fact that his trousers were still fastened kept her from
taking a knife to his throat.

Beside her, Harriet whispered, "Tar and feather."

The crowd whooped. Someone ran to find rope.

"Where's Chief Coyote?" Sloan called. "Has he still
got those chicken feathers?"

"I'll heat the kettle," the blacksmith offered, pushing
his way toward his shop.

The swift change from merriment to violence was sobering. Samantha released Harriet into her mother's arms
and turned to glance at Sloan. His eyes when they met
hers were cold but somehow reassuring. He wasn't drunk.
He knew precisely what he was doing. He was making an
example of this man for all the town to see, while venting
the violence surging through the crowd in a manner that
would bring harm to no one but the man who deserved it.

She let them go without following. The men swept
through the yard in search of the necessary ingredients for

the assigned punishment. She turned back to the house, her emotions in chaos.

She had always been the one to protect her family. It hadn't been easy. Men didn't take her seriously until she aimed a weapon at them. She wasn't carrying any weapon now. She was actually wearing her traveling dress instead of her jeans. She would have been helpless against Harriet's attacker. Sloan had stepped in and done her job for her.

It was a little frightening giving up that right to a man she despised, but she was the only one to resent his interference. Everyone else considered it perfectly natural, not just because he was a man and she was a woman, but because he was part of their family now. Sloan would have the right to protect the Neely women in any way he saw fit.

That was even more sobering than the violence taking place outside.

Not wishing to think about it, Samantha went to help her mother calm Harriet. Maybe in the morning when everyone was rested things would be a little clearer.

By the time the noise in the street calmed, Harriet had dozed off under the effects of her mother's sedative tea. Samantha nervously worked at returning the front room to order, not knowing what else she was expected to do. The men would be over at the saloon now, celebrating with liquor. She couldn't very well go over to the hotel on her own and make herself at home. But she had a feeling Sloan wouldn't appreciate it if she retired to her own bed in her mother's house.

When Sloan walked into the house without knocking, his back tall and straight and his expression forbidding, she knew she had made the right assumption. His eyes sought her out immediately, and something in the way his jaw relaxed told her he would more than likely have come and hauled her out of bed if she'd been silly enough to go there. After ascertaining she was waiting for him, he looked for her mother.

Alice Neely appeared immediately. He nodded cautiously. "How is she?"

"Asleep. She's learned a harsh lesson, but you arrived

in time. It could have been much worse." She took a deep shuddering breath. "I thank you for being there, Mr. Talbott."

He nodded and looked warily to Sam before speaking again to her mother. "The man's been informed we'll hang him if he shows his face around here again. He's not been here for long, and I don't know him well. Do you know why your daughter was out there with him?"

Sloan's hand clasped Sam's when she came to stand beside him. She could feel the anger still coursing through him in the way he held her hand, but he was doing his very best to remain polite for her mother's sake. He really was an unfathomable man.

"She wasn't. She was out there with Chief Coyote's grandson. He came to tell her good-bye. Bernadette is the twin I would think more likely to act so foolishly. I'm afraid Harriet has developed some romantic notions. After Mr. Eagle left, she dawdled outside a while longer. That's when the other man found her."

"Chief Coyote doesn't have a grandson," Sloan said harshly. "Who the hell is this Mr. Eagle?"

Alice Neely shook her head. "He appeared a few days after you left. He seemed a nice enough young man. He spoke English very well, but he looked Indian to me. He is quite good-looking actually. I can understand why Harriet was a little incautious. She was teaching him to read."

Sloan ran his hand up the side of his face as if to rub away the weariness. "Eagle. Hawk. Tall, long black hair, dark coloring, a gold ring in his ear?"

Alice nodded. "You know him?"

Sloan glanced down at Sam. "Hawk's younger brother."

She crinkled her brow in puzzlement. "You hired Hawk the day we got down there. Why would he send his brother up here?"

Sloan looked back to Mrs. Neely. "Was he asking questions?"

"Now that I think about it, yes. He always seemed to have questions on his tongue. I just thought he was naturally curious, like Samantha and Jack."

Sloan curled his arm around Sam's shoulders. "We hired his brother to find your husband. Hawk's the best tracker west of the Rockies, not because he can read horse droppings, but because he asks the right questions of the right people. He probably sent his brother to see if he could find any leads up here in case the trail got cold down in the valley. His name's not Eagle, and he already reads. If I remember correctly, he's a Harvard graduate."

A small smile twitched at the corners of Alice Neely's mouth. "Well, I can see Harriet hasn't fallen as far from the family tree as I thought. Is he even Indian?"

Sloan shrugged. "Does it make a difference?"

"No." She held out her hand. "Thank you again, Mr. Talbott. And welcome to the family."

He took her hand in his. "Call me, Sloan, ma'am. And don't be too hasty about welcoming me anywhere yet. Sam might have an opinion or two on that subject."

If she did, she wasn't about to express it right now. Her mother looked at her with a curiosity Sam was too tired to face. With resignation, she disentangled herself from Sloan's hold and said, "I don't know about the rest of you, but I'm ready for bed."

And with quiet resolution, she started for the front door.

Chapter Thirty-two

"**Y**ou can have the bed. I'll take the sofa in the other room."

Sloan stood behind Sam as she surveyed the ruggedly masculine bedroom he had brought her to. The bedposts looked like small trees with the bark still on them. The mattress looked thick and comfortable, though, even covered in bear fur.

Samantha glanced hastily at the tall wardrobe in one corner, found her trunk beside it, and tried not to look deeply into the rest of the shadows of the room. She'd had only a brief glimpse of the adjoining room, and she didn't have enough courage to turn around and look past Sloan to study it closer. "We can have my bed brought over in the morning," she said quietly, accepting his offer.

"Only if you want to replace this one. I don't want word getting out that we sleep in separate beds." With that curt remark, he closed the door between them.

The gesture was symbolic of the days and weeks that followed. Sloan shut her out as completely as if she didn't exist. Sam would get up in the mornings to find he'd gone to the mines or the mill or that he was working on his books and didn't want to be disturbed. She wouldn't see him for the rest of the day, and for that she was grateful. The evenings, when he had to make a show of being around her, were worse.

Sam didn't possess the disposition to do nothing while Sloan disappeared all day. His bachelor household revolved around him, leaving her on the outside looking in. She could buy anything she wanted at the general store or have Harriet order it for her and charge it to Sloan, but she wasn't much inclined to indulge in fits of shopping or decorating or whatever the women he knew normally did. Her new "husband" had a seemingly endless supply of suits and shirts that he sent down the mountain for laundering. He apparently ate whatever the men were cooking wherever he happened to be that day. The two rooms upstairs and the study downstairs didn't require a great deal of cleaning, and Sam declined the opportunity to become the widow's full-time cook and housekeeper. Her mother might run a restaurant, but managing a hotel was more Sam's style than actually operating one. That left her with little choice of occupations.

She was neither wife nor old maid, fish nor fowl. She didn't need to hunt for food any longer. It was still too cold and dangerous to look for her valley and too early to start a garden. She had no horses or cattle to tend. She helped in the restaurant when required, tried to teach Jack what she could, but she didn't belong in her mother's house any more than she belonged in Sloan's.

Reaching the conclusion that she would have to make her own home, Sam approached the immense barren hotel kitchen with trepidation. A wife was supposed to cook. She knew that much. She had to have a kitchen to cook in. This place looked more like a barn than any kitchen she'd ever seen, but she would make the most of it. It would at least give her something to do.

Discovering a dirt floor and an ancient stove were all she had to work with, she almost gave up the task in despair—until she discovered the stacks of floor tiles in a cobwebbed pantry.

They were gorgeous tiles in a clay red with hand-painted designs of green leaves and yellow suns and blue seas. She fell in love with them immediately, and when she showed them to Bernadette, her sister's eyes lit with feverish delight.

"We'll need to level the floor and get sand or something to set them in," Sam warned her when Bernadette began to lay the tiles out to make a pattern.

"Paint. We'll need paint for the walls. Sunny yellow, don't you think?" Bernadette gazed dreamily around at the dismal kitchen.

Samantha looked at the darkened beams covered with

years of grease and cobwebs and grimaced. She couldn't tell for certain which held up the ceiling, the timbers or the grease and cobwebs. "Hot water and soap, first," she admonished.

"You can grow flowers on the windowsill!" Bernadette exclaimed, running to the windows displaying two-foot thick walls.

That was the first good thought she'd had all day. Sam smiled and went in search of pails and help.

Sloan came hunting for her when it got dark. He stood in the doorway, staring at a scene that could have come straight from Dante's hell. Dirt-blackened creatures scrubbed at ancient walls and crawled through scraped clay and rock. A lantern swaying from a hook in an overhead beam threw a yellow glare over an assortment of mops and hoes and a giant rusted stove only half blackened with stove polish. He couldn't have thought of a more adequate torture chamber if he'd tried.

As his eyes grew accustomed to the dim light, he made out the figures of Joe and some of his cohorts leveling the dirt floor. One of the filthy creatures swabbing down the walls appeared to be Harriet, who should have been working in the store. She refused to work there now without one of the other women beside her, and since all the women appeared to be in here, he understood her defection. What he didn't understand was what in hell was going on.

The one figure he had hoped to find didn't appear to be anywhere in this chaos, but Sloan didn't make the mistake of assuming that Sam had nothing to do with this. His patience was rewarded when the door leading into the kitchen garden swung open and his young "wife" appeared wearing denims and an old coat and carrying a tray of flowerpots. She had mud on her face and ground into the knees of her trousers, and her hands were caked with the stuff. And she was smiling ecstatically.

"I've got them all planted!" she announced to no one in particular. "We'll have enough fresh basil and thyme for the whole town, and a geranium for every window."

"I hope you planted soap trees in there, too. It looks to me like you'll need a ton of it before you get done." The whole room came to a standstill when Sloan walked into the lantern light. He wondered what gossip was going around to make them all grow silent like that when he approached Samantha. That they didn't act much like newlyweds probably kept people wondering, but he didn't figure either of them would ever behave much like expected in any case. Out of a sudden sense of mischief, Sloan leaned over and kissed Sam's dirty cheek. He almost felt a palpable sigh of relief going up around them.

"I wondered how long it would take you to find something to do," he murmured against her ear as he took the heavy tray of pots from her.

"As soon as I can get out to find my valley, there'll be plenty for me to do," she informed him without warmth. "But for now, I'll be happy to get this stove going in here. These seeds need heat."

He set the tray on the cold stove. "And here all these years I thought stoves were for cooking. Pardon my ignorance."

All around them people were getting up and cleaning themselves off and making polite excuses before they disappeared into the darkness beyond the kitchen. Sloan didn't much care whether they thought thunderclouds or feather beds were forming in here. This was his time with Samantha, and he wanted them out.

He knew better than to expect Sam to greet him at the door, wearing the fancy gown he'd given her, holding his favorite drink, and beckoning him to a table covered in his favorite dishes. He didn't expect it of her, and he doubted if such behavior would even occur to the little hoyden. He'd had a woman once who had done all those things, and she had been a lying, traitorous bitch. He was quite content with the honesty of a woman who greeted him in muddy denims and a tray full of flowerpots. He flashed a smile at her wary expression.

"I take it the restaurant will be closed tonight. What do you propose we eat?"

She took a step backward to widen the space between them. Sloan took a larger step forward. Another step, and she would have her back against the stove. He wasn't averse to getting a little closer. Now that she'd had time to settle in a little and they'd learned to work around each other without drawing weapons, he thought it might be time to pursue his next course of action. If Sam thought for one minute that he'd forgotten what she was like in bed and wouldn't want a repeat performance, she had more feathers for brains than he believed.

"The restaurant's open. Mama has stew ready. We've been taking turns keeping it stirred." She edged to the side, realizing he would soon trap her otherwise.

"Are you going over there looking like that, or would you like a bath?"

Her eyes widened slightly, but she took his words at face value. "I meant to wash up just as soon as I got those seeds planted. You can go on over and get a table. I'll be there shortly."

"That pot Joe keeps cooking out back won't have enough hot water in it for a bath. Do you figure this stove still works?" Sloan let her slip away as he regarded the iron monstrosity with a critical eye. It was old and the outer parts looked rusted, but it seemed solid enough. He began to roll up his sleeves.

"Mama says it will now that Joe's cleaned out the flue. But it will take a lot of wood."

He could tell she was getting suspicious now, but he ignored her cynical mind. "That's one way of getting rid of all that debris left from the fire. Help me haul some of it in here."

One thing he could say for Sam, she was always willing to lend a hand. She moved her tray of pots to a windowsill and hurried into the darkness after him.

They hauled an armload of charred and ruined timbers into the kitchen. While Sloan broke pieces into kindling, Samantha gathered old grape-vines and bits of broken trellis to use for fire-starters. She fed the wood into the fire slowly while Sloan pumped water to fill an enormous kettle he dragged from the pantry.

"There aren't any curtains in here. You'll have to go upstairs to bathe," he told her matter-of-factly once the fire was blazing and the water heating.

"You can't carry that thing upstairs," she protested.

"We're heating entirely too much water. I'll go get a bucket and just take up what I need."

"You'll go and get that bathtub hanging behind the stairs and take it to your room. Let me worry about getting the water up there."

Sloan watched her hesitate between rebellion at his peremptory orders and eagerness for a real bathtub. He derived a certain sense of satisfaction from knowing he was learning to read her thoughts from the way she widened her eyes or pursed her lips. Samantha Neely might be an unruly handful, but she didn't have a devious bone in her body. Another woman might have played his obvious sexual desire for her against him to obtain what she wanted. Samantha not only didn't recognize the weapon she wielded, she wouldn't know what to do with it if she did.

For that reason, Sloan had every intention of giving her what she wanted without her asking. He'd already gotten the description of her valley from the deed, and he had people searching for it. Once the snow cleared, he would take her up there, even though he was quite convinced he owned the land. All he wanted in return was access to her bed, but he didn't mean to tell her that. Samantha tended to be a trifle prickly on that subject.

With a feeling of accomplishment, he watched her dart off to the bedroom. He had no particular skills in the game of seduction, but he knew what he wanted and he meant to do whatever it took to get it. Sam's scruples on the matter were irrelevant. Everyone thought they were married. He would take care of her just as he would take care of a wife, for as long as she consented to be his wife. He couldn't see where a lot of legal mumbo-jumbo would make any difference, and for what it was worth, they'd already had the words said in church. He just needed to make her understand that what they felt for each other were perfectly healthy, normal desires.

When Sloan carried up the first few buckets, he found Sam standing beside the newly scrubbed bathtub, fully clothed. Her shirt was wet where she had obviously held the tin tub up to clean it out, and he tried not to stare at the shape of firm young breasts outlined by the wet material. That would only make her warier.

"You can't take a bath with your clothes on," he reminded her. "The water will get cold if you don't hurry. I'll go get some more."

She had towels and lavender-scented soaps laid out by the time he returned. Her dirty clothes were lying in a pile by the door. But she had wrapped herself from head to toe in a bulky cotton wrapper that concealed everything. Sloan dumped the buckets of warm water into the tub and stood back to measure the water level with a gauging eye.

"Two more buckets ought to do it. Hurry up and get in and I'll be back to help you with your hair."

"I can wash my own hair, and this is plenty, thank you. You go on over and get something to eat. I'll be right with you." She stood firmly in front of the tub, holding the wrapper closed.

Sloan smirked as he planted himself in front of her. She couldn't move without falling into the tub or into his arms. He caught the edges of the wrapper and began to pry them from her hands. "You don't seem to understand, Samantha. I want a reward for my efforts. I think I've been exceedingly patient, don't you? Now let's get you out of this thing and into the tub."

She shivered as his hand slid beneath the robe and brushed her breast. Sloan had difficulty resisting the temptation to search out the sensitive crest to see if she was as aroused as he was. He didn't mean to rush her though. They wouldn't go any further than she wanted. He didn't know if her earlier assurances that they coupled at the right time of the month meant just after or just before her monthly period, so he played with fire if it had been just after. But if it had been just before, he'd given her enough time to recover, and the time would be right. He prayed it was the latter.

"Don't touch me, Sloan," she muttered, pulling the wrapper closed. "If this is payment for the bath, you can have it. I'll go wash in the creek."

"The creek's frozen. All I want to do is help you wash your hair. It's not as if I haven't seen you naked before," he reminded her.

That didn't make her any happier, but she allowed him to push the robe from her shoulders. She kept her breasts covered, however, and he couldn't see more than if she'd been wearing a revealing evening gown. Still, that was more than before. He licked his finger and ran it along the inside of one breast, leaving a moist mark against her skin. He watched her eyes turn from blue to a smoldering gray and knew she burned just as he did.

"I'll be right back. Climb in before the water gets cold." He removed his hand before it reached her nipple. He knew once he touched her there, there wouldn't be any turning back. He'd see that she got her bath first.

He was so hard he could barely walk as he descended the back stairs to the kitchen to refill the buckets. He would have to see about installing water pumps inside the house, upstairs and down. Maybe he would even figure out how to install a bathing room. He could casily imagine Samantha coming in hot and dirty from her gardening and gratefully relaxing in a tub of nice sudsy water. And he would be right there to help her out afterward.

He was going to have to break into his limited supply of condoms. He didn't think he could make it through the next hour without burying himself inside of her, no matter what time of the month it was, and the chances that he would withdraw in time were slim. His control with Sam was nearly nonexistent. Just the memory of her standing there with her robe falling off her shoulders sent steam through his blood. He'd be lucky to get her out of the tub before joining her.

Engrossed in these thoughts, Sloan never knew what hit him. He didn't hear the shot fired as he hurtled down the stairs. He didn't feel the burning pain. He was only aware of Samantha's high-pitched scream of terror as he hit the ground below.

Chapter Thirty-three

The shot shattered the sensual warmth surrounding Sam as she stood in Sloan's bedroom, contemplating the lavender-scented bath. Actually, she had been contemplating the heat of Sloan's gaze, not the water. She forgot her tingling skin the instant gunfire echoed up the stairway.

The stairway. Sloan hadn't had time to get all the way down those stairs. He wasn't wearing his gun.

Grabbing her rifle, Sam raced barefoot into the covered hallway leading to the open back stairs. She had long ago decided a maniac had designed this building, but she could now see its advantages. She was guarded on three sides while anyone standing in the open below was completely exposed. She didn't see Sloan standing there.

The man she did see was raising his gun to fire again at someone or something just out of her line of sight. She lifted her rifle and took aim without a qualm. The man with the gun wasn't Sloan. That meant his target was.

The gunman must have heard her just as she pulled the trigger. He turned to fire in her direction a fraction too late. The shot meant to take his hand off ripped through his chest instead.

Sam blinked and swayed as the inner courtyard below seemed to erupt in activity. She watched Joe run in, guns drawn, just as the gunman crumpled to the ground. Other men from the saloon followed. She tried to force her feet down the stairs, knowing in the back of her mind that there was something down there she couldn't see, but she was numb, inside and out. She had just killed a man. She could tell by the way Joe and the others ignored his body.

Sloan. Sloan had to be down there. She closed her eyes

and tried to stop the dizziness. She clenched the railing and willed her feet to move. She heard Doc Ramsey's shouts. Sloan wouldn't like it if Ramsey tried to treat him. She had to get down there.

She hadn't known how terrified she was until she heard Sloan's furious roar rise up from the ground below. She went nearly faint with joy and grabbed the railing to keep from falling headfirst down the stairs.

Sloan raced up to grab her before she could lose her hold. Sam was so glad to see him up and mobile that she willingly fell into his arms, clutching his shirt and burrowing her face against his shoulder. Not until he hugged her awkwardly and murmured some silliness in her ear did she realize she was sobbing hysterically.

She rubbed her hand against her eyes and tried to stop, but the tears kept coming. The sobs turned into hiccups as she tried to control them, but the last few minutes kept replaying before her eyes, and her hands kept reaching for her gun. Instead, her fingers curled in Sloan's shirt.

"It's all right, Sam," he pleaded against her hair. "Everything's all right. It's just a little scratch. I'm fine. You saved my life, sugar. Don't cry."

He sounded so helpless, she almost managed a smile. If she could just forget . . . A little scratch?

Her head jerked up to see the blood streaming down the side of Sloan's head, and she screamed in horror. "You're wounded! Oh my God, Sloan Talbott, you get yourself up here right now." She leaned over the railing. "Joe, go fetch my mother and tell her to bring her bandages!"

The men below watched in astonishment as Sam suddenly transformed from hysterical woman to stern nursemaid, wrapping her arm around Sloan's back and supporting him up the rest of the stairs. One of them gave a whistle of approval as a shapely ankle and bare foot appeared beneath the cotton wrapper. Others just stared in covetous awe as Sloan's hand slipped from the narrow curve of her waist to ride possessively on a round derriere so neatly outlined by the cloth that it was obvious she wore nothing under it. No one hurried to send for help.

"Sit down in that chair and let me clean you up," Sam insisted as they entered the bedroom.

Sloan didn't protest as she nearly shoved him into the room's only chair. His head spun, but he didn't blame it entirely on the wound. The woman wringing a cloth out in the cooling bathwater was a stranger to him. She wore Sam's clothes. She had Sam's tumble of red curls. But he'd never seen that tender look of concern in Sam's eyes or felt gentleness in her hands. She was somehow warmer, rounder, softer than the sharp-eyed, sharp-tongued virago he'd "married." He was always on guard with the other Sam. With this one, he closed his eyes and let her clean the wound without a word of complaint.

"I think it's time you tell me what's going on," she murmured once she had the graze cleaned and bandaged to her satisfaction. She didn't seem to notice that no one had come to help her with dressing the wound. "If I'm going to live with a man everyone wants to kill, I'd like to know why."

"You tell me, and we'll both know," he answered wearily, leaning his head against the back of the chair. He didn't know what he wanted right now, but it certainly wasn't a return to matching wits with his all too perceptive "wife."

"I think Mama recommends that you stay awake for some time after a head wound."

Sloan could hear her moving around the room, cleaning up whatever utensils she had brought out. He could tell her that he wasn't likely to be suffering a concussion, but he wasn't in a humor to discuss medical diagnoses and treatments.

"I hate to let this bathwater go to waste," he heard her say, more to herself than him, he imagined. "It's not really cold yet." He had his eyes closed, so he couldn't see her turn to him, but somehow he could feel the focus of her eyes. "Would you like to try the bath?" she asked hesitantly.

Sloan let the shock of that question ripple through him. He'd expected her to ask him to keep his eyes shut so she could bathe. He'd expected her to ask him to leave. He hadn't expected her to think of him first. His eyes opened and he saw her standing in the lantern light, holding out a towel and soap.

A dozen images danced through his head. He saw her scrubbing his back while he sat naked in that tub. He saw them both naked in that tub. He saw himself lifting her from the water, dripping wet, and laying her across the bed. A surge of lust heated his loins as he imagined what he would do then.

And the throbbing in his head and the weariness in his bones told him not one of those things was possible right now. He wondered idly if he could persuade her to sit on his lap and take care of him that way. He didn't think she was quite that experienced yet.

"Why don't you go ahead and bathe," he answered quietly. "I'll just close my eyes and rest a bit. Maybe when you're done, I'll be ready to take you up on that offer."

Instead of accepting his generosity, her face instantly expressed concern. She returned to his side to feel his brow. "You're not feverish. Your head must be hurting. Why didn't Joe send for Mama?" she asked with frustration.

"There's some powders in that wooden box in the other room. Bring the box here and I'll show you which one. You can mix it in a little water and I'll be fine in a few minutes." Sooner or later she would learn about him if they continued to live together this way. She might as well start learning now. She was too bright to do otherwise.

She returned a few minutes later with his medical kit. Sloan forced his eyes open and pointed out the powder, told her how much to mix, and left her to it. He was just grateful that she wasn't asking questions yet.

"Here, if you rest your head on my arm, you won't have to lift it."

Sam slid her arm behind him and Sloan rested his head as he sipped at the drink she held out for him. He was more aware of the roundness of her breast hovering near him than of what he drank, however. She still didn't wear more than that wrapper, and it gaped enticingly. He knew the extent of his injury by his ability to resist that much temptation.

"I don't suppose you'd be willing to sit in my lap right

now," he murmured, leaning his head back against the chair when she started to move away.

Sloan didn't open his eyes, but he could feel her suspicious regard at his question. He knew the instant she discovered the reason for his request. The bulge in his pants was probably pretty noticeable by now. He'd always thought it unfair of nature to make a man's desire so blatantly obvious. He didn't expect the amusement in her reply.

"I might be willing, but I'm also wise. I don't think you need any extra exertion right now."

He sighed as she moved away. "I don't suppose you're going to take advantage of that bath, either."

"Are you going to keep your eyes closed?"

"If you're not going to sit in my lap, what choice do I have? I'm already suffering enough."

She giggled. She actually giggled. As if he weren't sitting here suffering the seven torments of the damned, she had to laugh. Life very definitely wasn't fair, but right now he would willingly forgive her anything. She'd killed a man tonight to save his life. For a brief few moments he had made her forget that. He wished he could.

Sloan kept his eyes closed while she splashed in the bath. Even though the water couldn't still be warm enough to send out fragrance, he imagined he smelled lavender anyway. Sam might occasionally look like a ragged gypsy or a filthy urchin, but she always smelled good. He squirmed in the chair, thinking about just how good she smelled when he held her in his arms. She had to be a witch to do this to him when no other woman had been able to these last ten years. He'd kept complete control over his sex life until this red-haired brat wandered into it. Not brat—young woman. Hot-headed, lovely young woman.

A knock at the door sent Sam squealing after her wrapper again. Sloan managed a frown, opened his eyes long enough to ascertain that she was fully covered, then growled at the intruder outside the door.

Accepting a growl as admittance, Joe walked in. His gaze took in his employer still sitting in the chair, a makeshift bandage around his head, then diffidently slid to the woman now adding a blanket to her attire. He made a brief nod of acknowledgment to Sam, then returned his attention to Sloan.

"I had a talk with some of the boys. Don't any of them know the perpetrator. Hank said he thought he'd seen him around Ariposa when they were down there. People there seemed to know him. I'll send someone down to find out more."

Sloan watched as Joe shifted from one foot to the other and glanced nervously at Sam. He had more to say, but not here. His bodyguard was trying desperately to impress Sam as it was. Joe couldn't read, but he collected words like gold nuggets. He pulled them out when he wanted to impress.

Sloan didn't look to where Sam hovered in the corner, hanging on to every word of their conversation. He addressed Joe as if she weren't there. "Give me the rest. Sam has a right to know. I'd be ready to push up daisies now if not for her."

Joe nodded, diverted his gaze briefly to Sam, then took off his hat to twist it in his hands. "One of the men that followed Ramsey down the mountain said a fancy fellow from back East stayed in the hotel down there. He was asking questions about you and the town, flashing a bank-roll while he was doing it."

Sloan didn't want to hear that. From back East. He'd left that life behind a decade ago. No one knew where he was. He'd even changed his name. They couldn't know who he was. He'd been very careful to hide his identity, although admittedly, he'd been getting a little careless lately. He'd even visited Matthew. Dumb. That had been dumb.

He closed his eyes again and nodded. "Send Bradshaw down. If Hawk's kid brother is still around, have him poke around a little, too. It's probably nothing but some idiot who thinks I've got the world's largest gold mine up here, but we might as well put a stop to it now."

After Joe left, Sloan waited. He didn't have long to wait. He could smell the lavender on her skin as she sat on the chair arm. Her cool hand felt his brow for fever, then returned to her lap.

"You're mining more than quicksilver up there, aren't you?"

He hadn't expected the attack to come from that angle, but then, Sam never did the expected. He grimaced. "It's not all mine, either. Each man owns a share in the profits. We just decided it was quicker and safer if we all worked together."

"Then how come you're the one with the money? Nobody else seems to have anything around here."

Sloan relaxed and propped his feet on the edge of a table. "Because the land is mine. Nobody thought there was anything up there. It had been prospected to death. I bought up all the shares for nothing. I just wanted the damned mountain, not the gold. There's timber out there, and quicksilver, and other ores that could make a profit once we get in some transportation. Mostly, there's privacy. I liked that. I was willing to wait to turn a profit. Then some idiot found a nugget, and all hell would have broke loose if I hadn't stepped in to control it. Bradshaw and some of the others were as tired as I was of the stink and the crime and the back-breaking labor of prying a few dollars' worth of gold out of these hills. So we kept it a secret. We work at it carefully, following the lode. There's no claim-jumping, no stealing tools, no working twenty-hour shifts. Every man gets paid for his share of the work. If he doesn't work, he doesn't get paid. Most of them drink up their share of the profits. I invest mine."

He liked the way her hand brushed the hair off his forehead. The headache was already starting to fade. In another minute he might be asleep. He was going to have to get himself out of here.

"So killing you would only give your men a bigger share of the profits?"

He was too tired to think about it. "It would mean they'd have to do their own books, do their own selling, and find someone to run the town and make the decisions. I doubt that there's one of them willing to take on that much responsibility."

"So much for that theory," she murmured. "Do you

think you've stayed awake long enough? You sound awfully sleepy."

"If I had a concussion, I'd know it. I'm just too lazy to get out of this chair." And too enthralled by the scent and touch of her to want to move unless it was into her bed, but he didn't tell her that.

"You'll be stiff if you stay there. Put your arm around my shoulder. I'll get you over to the bed."

He'd have gone out and got himself shot sooner if he'd known that's what it took to get into her bed. Feigning more weakness than he felt, Sloan wrapped his arm around her shoulder and let her help him up. His stumble was real as he reached his feet, and he shook his head to clear it. Maybe he'd lost a little more blood than he'd thought.

But he wasn't so far gone that he didn't know where he was when she pulled back the covers and helped him to the mattress. Quick, clever little hands pried open the buttons of his shirt and slid it back, then held him up to help him take it off. Eagerly, he waited to see what she would take off next. If he hadn't been feverish before, he most certainly was now, and the damned head wound had nothing to do with it.

She tugged off his boots and set them neatly next to the bed. Sloan could feel her hesitating, and he didn't dare open his eyes and let her see what was in them. He would have killed to have her reach for the buttons of his trousers right now, but they'd not had enough time to get to know each other that well. Sam might have her brazen moments, but this wasn't one of them.

Stifling a sigh of regret, Sloan held out his hand to her. "Lie down beside me. I'm not going to do anything but snore for the next twelve hours. You'll be safe enough."

He wasn't even trying to be persuasive, but she gave in without a single protest. She turned down the lantern and climbed in on the other side of the bed. From the way she snuggled against him a few minutes later, he figured she needed his company right now as much as he did hers.

Turning on his side, he scooped her against him. He didn't even try to take advantage of her gaping wrapper.

It was enough just to have her pressed against him from top to bottom. For now.

The morning would be time enough to explore the attractions of this captivating woman he fully intended to make his.

Chapter Thirty-four

"Samantha! Samantha! Open the door. My hands are full. Aunt Alice said I was to bring this to you."

Groggily, Sam opened one eye. Sunlight crawled across the floor, illuminating what had just been shadows a few hours before, or so it seemed. Recognizing Jack's shouts, she started to throw her legs over the side of the bed, then realized she was caught. Pushing aside the covers, she glanced down—and found a man's arm wrapped around her waist. The heat of him warmed her back.

That woke her fully. Her robe had fallen open during the night. What on earth had possessed her to go to bed, wearing just a robe? She watched in horror as Sloan's rough hand began to stir, seeking the warmth of her skin beneath the cotton, rising higher until he almost brushed her bare breast. Holding her breath wouldn't work. She had to get out of here.

When she tried to pull free, his hold tightened. He was awake, the bastard. She turned enough to look over her shoulder. He had his eyes closed, but he was smiling. She poked him with an elbow. "Let me up, Talbott. Jack's out there."

"He'll go away."

He pulled her against him so her buttocks tucked into the curve of his hips, and she swore under her breath. She might not know a whole lot about lovemaking, but she knew enough about Sloan Talbott by now to know the meaning of that hard ridge pressing against her. If she didn't get out of this bed in the next few minutes, he'd have her under him in the following few.

"Let go, Sloan, or I'll scream." She tried to wriggle away.

"That should create a little amusement around here. You don't think last night was enough?" His hand slid upward to encompass her breast.

He wasn't holding her trapped now. She could easily pull from his grasp. But he was doing horrifyingly lovely things to her nipple, and she was having difficulty separating right from wrong. He had only to touch her and she melted. She had the reckless urge to part her legs and press back against him so he could settle the tiny explosions he was producing in her belly.

That thought sent her rocketing out of the bed. It was the worst possible time of the month to do what he wanted to do. It was bad enough they played out this charade of being married. She refused to let him trap her with his children.

Sloan groaned and flung himself on his stomach when she got up. It was a damned good thing she'd left his pants on him last night, Sam decided. Tugging her robe tighter, she opened the door for Jack.

He looked at her curiously, glanced at the bare shoulders of the man in her bed, then set his tray down on the square oak table in the corner. "Aunt Alice said you might not be up to fixing breakfast this morning. She sent this over." He glanced toward Sloan again, then asked in a loud whisper, "Did someone really try to put a bullet through his heart?"

"They were fools if that's where they aimed," Sam said dryly, poking at the contents of the tray. "There's only one portion of Sloan's anatomy that would kill him, and they missed it by a mile."

She heard him choking against the pillow and figured the feathers would be flying in her direction shortly. She blocked the breakfast tray from possible artillery and nodded at the door. "Thank Mama for me, and tell her we're fine. We'll be over directly."

Jack left reluctantly, sneaking another peek at the wide shoulders of the man sprawled against the pillows. The bandage around Sloan's head made Sam's words even more puzzling, but girls were a little strange. He slammed the door after him.

Sloan groaned at the noise. "Remind me to send him down a mine shaft and forget about him until he's thirty."

"I suspect that's what someone should have done with you." She poured a cup of coffee and took it over to the bed. "How's your head? Do you need more powders?"

He rolled over carefully, trying not to lift his head from the pillow in the process. Sam winced when he did, then tried not to be distracted when she realized that sometime during the night he'd unfastened his trousers. It was a little difficult to ignore the dark swirl of hair descending from his navel and disappearing beneath the heavy cloth.

"You can't drink this lying down. Want me to help you sit up?"

She knew that was a mistake the moment she said it. There was a definite gleam in his eye now. Before he could get any ideas, she reminded him, "The coffee's hot enough to scald."

Sloan scowled and pushed himself to a sitting position. "Remind me sometime why I got mixed up with a termagant with more brains than she needs when there's bound to be dozens of featherheads out there waiting to grace my bed."

"Because you like a challenge." She set the cup carefully on the washstand beside the bed and moved out of his reach. It was time she got dressed and out of here.

"If it's a challenge I wanted, I could have tried digging a hole to China," he said grumpily, sipping at the scalding coffee and watching as she examined the clothes in her trunk. "You could order a wardrobe full of clothes if you wanted, you know. I'm the one who got you into this fix. I ought to be the one who pays the price."

Sam shrugged and pulled out one of her old work shirts and a pair of denims. "I'll earn my own way sooner or later. I'm not worried about that." She sent him a swift look over her shoulder. "And I don't mean in bed, either." She gathered up the clothes and started for the other room. "I ordered some material so I could make more pants. I can't order ready-made pants that fit."

"Samantha," he called after her. She stopped in the doorway to look at him questioningly. Sloan touched his hand to the bandage wrapping his head, and he looked

slightly embarrassed. "Thanks for last night. I thought I
was a goner." At the uneasy expression crossing her face,
he asked quietly. "You've never actually shot a man before, have you?"

Sam pulled her wrapper bodice tighter. "If I'm going to
carry a gun, I've got to be prepared to use it. I knew that
from the first time I picked one up for target practice."

"It's not the same as hitting a target or a deer." Sloan
closed his eyes as if struck by a debilitating pain. When
he opened them again, they were cold and glazed over. "I
know, believe me. I'm not worth what you're going
through. Next time, just let them shoot me."

Stunned, Samantha stared at him. In only twenty-four
hours his beard stubble had darkened his jaw. Combined
with the bloodstained bandage and thick tousled curls, he
looked the part of outlaw or worse. For all she knew of
him, he very well could be. She just didn't think too
many outlaws had a conscience, and it looked to her as
though Sloan Talbott suffered the effects of a guilty one
now.

"There are times I'd just as soon shoot Jack, but I'd
never let anyone else do it." Sam turned around and
walked out, closing the door behind her. Let him puzzle
out the sentiments behind that. She couldn't.

Sloan stayed close to the hotel for the next few days
while his minions went down the mountain to investigate
this latest attempt at murder. Sam found it a trifle disconcerting while in the middle of laying the kitchen tiles or
stirring soup on the stove, to look up and find him standing there, watching her. His expression had a brooding
quality that she found particularly disturbing.

She thought she knew what he wanted, but she
wouldn't let him have it. He'd tricked her, used her, and
driven her from her home. No matter how her insides
quivered when he came near, she wouldn't let Sloan
Talbott shame her.

"If you haven't anything better to do, you could finish
painting that wall Joe was working on." Sam nodded at
the half-yellow wall. Since Joe had gone down the mountain, Sloan had assigned other men the task of standing

guard around the hotel. None of them were much inclined to be helpful.

"There are enough layabouts in this town you could hire to do the work," he reminded her, drifting in to examine what had already been completed.

"They don't listen to orders real well. They want to lay tile before the walls are done or paint without preparing the walls. I'd rather do it myself and have it done right." She sat up in the middle of the newly tiled section of floor and watched as he checked her flowerpots for new growth. The twins had gone back to the house to help her mother serve the noon meal. She wished she had gone with them.

"You've been cooking soup all morning. Isn't it ready to eat yet?" He nodded at the pot simmering on the stove. The heat from the fire had warmed the kitchen until it felt like a spring day in here.

"It's ready if you are. There isn't much in the way of utensils around here, but what few I found are over in the cupboard. Help yourself."

Amusement almost curled Sloan's lips as she went back to what she was doing. "It's hard to remember that there was once a time when women went out of their way to impress me," he commented, checking the cupboard for a bowl and spoon.

"Well, I reckon there might be women out there desperate for the attention of a surly, inconsiderate wretch, but I'm not one of them."

Since there was no table, Sloan sat cross-legged on the tiles with his bowl of soup, watching as she laid out the pattern. "I'm not any more surly than you are, Samantha Neely, and we both know the reason for that. The urge to procreate is a natural one and not meant to be stifled unnecessarily."

"Hogwash," she answered succinctly.

"You'll run out of things to clean and scrub and build before you exhaust those urges," he said calmly, sipping at the soup.

"You're the one who can't keep his pants buttoned," she snapped. "You'll remember I was doing just fine until you came along."

That hit a mark. He winced, but the sound of Joe's voice floating through the window interrupted before he could retaliate. Sloan stood up and yelled for Joe to get himself in here.

Sam produced another bowl and spoon and handed them to Joe when he entered. Sloan glared at her for this defection, but she didn't care. She meant to hear what the gunman had to say, and he would more likely say it around her if he was feeling kindly toward her.

Joe leaned against the windowsill and took a spoonful of soup. He, too, ignored Sloan's angry glare. Rolling his eyes in defeat, Sloan refilled his bowl and returned to his earlier position.

"Just give me the news anytime you're ready," he said dryly. "I might die of old age between now and then, but it's better than the alternative."

Joe glanced at Sam innocuously sitting in a far corner, picking at her own bowl of soup.

Sloan grimaced. "She'll nag it out of me if you don't say it in front of her. Save me the trouble."

She'd never nagged in her life, and he darned well knew it. Sam glared at him, but he was impervious to glares. If it made him feel better to blame things on her, fine. She had a strong back. And as long as she was parading around as his wife, she had a right to know who was trying to kill him and why.

Joe swallowed the beef he'd been chewing. "The eastern fellow left as soon as he heard you were still alive. Word gets down that mountain mighty fast these days."

They both stared at him impatiently, waiting for more. He sipped some broth directly from the bowl. "Good soup, Miz Talbott. Kinda nice having real meals around here."

"You're welcome to have more, Joe," she answered sincerely, "But if you don't stop playing games, it's likely to be served over your head."

She heard Sloan choking over his bowl, but she didn't dare look at him. He thought her unwomanly and ill-mannered. She might as well prove it. She'd never seen Joe draw those deadly weapons he wore on his hips, but she'd seen him drunk and helpless. She wasn't afraid of him.

Joe shot her a straight look that could have been a glare, but it didn't equal one of Sloan's. She shrugged, and he continued with his story.

"The sorry bastard that tried to kill you was in over his head at the gambling tables in Ariposa. I ain't got proof, but there's two men down there swears the easterner offered to help them out with their debts if they'd put a permanent end to you. I reckon this one took him up on the offer."

Silence reigned. It didn't take Sam long to figure the other attempts on Sloan's life had been arranged in the same way. The first attempt might even have been the easterner himself. The men up here weren't trying to kill him. It was hired strangers. She looked to Sloan to see how he was taking this new knowledge.

He scraped his bowl clean and left it sitting on the floor since he had nowhere else to put it. "Did you find Hawk's kid brother?"

Joe nodded. "He's on the trail of the easterner now."

"I don't suppose the man had a name?"

"Clark. He called himself Harry Clark. Mean anything to you?"

Sloan shrugged. "I doubt it's his real name. Did you get a description?"

"Slender. Not quite six-foot. Brownish blond hair. Wore suits. Ladies like him."

Sloan's face went stone cold. "Anderson. My God." Without another word, he got up and walked out.

Sam and Joe were left to stare at each other. Sam broke the silence first. "Who's Anderson?"

Joe shrugged. "Hell if I know."

Sam looked out the window where a sparrow searched for a treat among the dried grapevines. "Well, I guess one of us had better find out," she said with more serenity than she felt.

"It ain't easy to get him drunk," Joe reminded her in an almost mournful tone. "I don't know how else you get a man to talk if he don't want to."

Sam did. She figured Joe did, too, but he was too polite

to say it. A woman could make a man talk. There were ways. She just didn't think she was woman enough to do it. She didn't have any business doing it. She wasn't his wife.

But she might as well be, she realized gloomily. She was in love with the damned man.

Chapter Thirty-five

Sloan swung his boots up on one sofa arm and rested his head against his hands on the other. The damned sofa was too short. Maybe he'd do better to stay in the mining camp. But it wasn't the shortness of the sofa that made him think that.

He glanced over at the closed door cutting him off from the bedroom. Sam was behind there. He'd heard her moving around earlier, carrying pails of hot water, opening and closing her trunk. He'd walked in on her when she was trying on the new trousers she'd sewed. They were made of some material lighter than denim and fit her tiny waist and rounded buttocks perfectly. They also emphasized the length of those marvelous legs of hers. She would have men crawling on their knees and panting if she wore them outside. She'd thrown a hairbrush at him when he'd tried to tell her that.

He probably hadn't phrased his objection in the smartest terms. He hadn't been in the best of humor at the time. Sloan sighed and tried to stretch his cramped legs. He knew perfectly well that he had insulted her when she'd been doing her innocent best to impress him. He also knew damned well why she'd been flaunting her derriere at him. Sam just wasn't cut out to be devious.

Two days ago he might have taken her up on the challenge. He'd give half a year of his life to have Samantha trying her wiles on him. He'd give more than that to be in her bed right now. But even if he wanted to—which he didn't, he reminded himself—he couldn't marry her with Anderson sneaking around. It was dangerous just pretending to be married to her. And Sam had already proved she wouldn't settle for anything less than the real thing.

For her own good, he needed to figure out how to get her out of here. If that really was Anderson down there, Sloan couldn't imagine what he wanted or how he'd found him, but it wasn't safe to keep Sam around while he found out. Anderson knew everything. He could probably drive Sam away just by telling her what he knew. But if for whatever insane reason Anderson had decided to take revenge on Sloan, he wouldn't hesitate on taking it out on Sam, too.

He had to tell Sam the truth, though he didn't like the idea. He would rather somebody had found her confounded valley so he could send her out there to farm. Then maybe someday he'd have the chance of talking her back into his bed again. There wouldn't be a snowball's chance in hell of that once he told her the truth.

Sloan still might have delayed the inevitable if Sam hadn't taken that moment to walk in on him. She was wearing a nightshift made of some kind of long, filmy material that made his staff rise to the occasion without need of any other stimulant. It was probably just good quality lawn—Sam wouldn't have any of that French stuff Melinda wore—but the lantern light behind her allowed Sloan to see clear through the material.

Her legs went on forever, he decided idly, staring at the shadows revealed through the gown. Her hips were long and narrow also, but they indented nicely at her waistline. He didn't need to raise his gaze any farther to know he was in trouble.

"We need to talk," she said bluntly, dispelling any illusion that she meant to seduce him.

"Talk isn't what comes immediately to mind when you're dressed like that." Sloan was amazed at how calmly he made that sound when his throat was nearly raw with desire and his blood pumped through his veins faster than a mountain stream in spring.

"I thought I might hold your attention a little longer this way." There was dry humor in her voice as she took the overstuffed chair nearest him.

A seated position put her breasts in direct line with his gaze. Sloan studied this new view with concentrated interest. She had all but the top ribbon of her bodice fastened, so he could see very little skin. Poor planning on her part, he decided. She probably didn't realize, though, that the tug of fabric outlined every curve when she sat down. The gown even had an innocently placed blue ribbon just below her breasts to emphasize the roundness above. He could almost imagine he saw the darker shadows of her nipples beneath the thin cloth.

"You've got my attention all right. I'm just not certain I'll hear a word you say. You're not even wearing drawers under that, are you?"

She pulled her legs up under her, probably attempting to hide her embarrassment. It only served to focus his attention more avidly on the juncture hidden behind them. Sloan wondered how he could persuade her to the sofa so he could pull her down on top of him. He almost groaned at the aching response that thought brought to his loins.

"It's the wrong time of month," she told him primly, "so you can just put those thoughts out of your head. Let's divert them to this fellow Clark or Anderson or whoever he is."

She was giving him the opening he needed to drive her away. Sloan screwed his eyes closed and tried to cooperate, but he'd buried the story for ten years. He didn't want to unearth it now. He wanted to bury himself inside her instead, cloak himself in her innocence, bask in her concern, revel in her intelligence. He didn't want to give her the final excuse she needed to leave.

"Let's go to bed first and talk about him later. I can protect you if that's all that's stopping you."

Sloan dared to look up at her face then. The almost naked desire in Sam's eyes would have knocked him over if he hadn't already been lying down. That look pierced him right through the hard shell he'd developed these last years, drove right into his gut and twisted with a vengeance that took his breath away. She wanted him. After all the hurt and pain he'd caused her—all the growling, frowning, surliness—she still wanted him. She was as mad as he was.

"That's not all that's stopping me, and you know it." As if they weren't both sitting here going up in flames, she turned the conversation back to him. "Does this

Anderson have anything to do with the wife you left back East?"

She may as well have slapped him. Sloan drew his gaze back to the ceiling. "Among other things, Harry Anderson is her stepbrother. But that doesn't mean it's Anderson down there."

He heard her sharp intake of breath. He'd just confirmed that he had a wife. That ought to drive her away fast enough without revealing the rest. Just because it was a half-truth at best didn't mean it wasn't effective.

He underestimated Sam's tenacity.

"You told me once that you might not really be married. Is that the reason he's here?"

Sloan scowled at the ceiling. He said entirely too many things to this tempting witch. He ought to just bed her and send her on her way. He couldn't figure out why he didn't. The Sloan Talbott he'd become these last years would have. Maybe he could throw a knife at her and she'd go away.

She hadn't the last time he'd done that. She was still here. That knowledge ground at his insides. He'd done his level best to keep her at a distance, but she'd somehow wiggled under his skin like some damned parasite that he couldn't live without any longer. Parasite wasn't the right word. That would mean she was living off him, and she wasn't. More likely, it was the other way around. She was keeping him alive. Maybe, if they ever had a chance, they could develop a mutually beneficial symbiosis, drawing on each other for strength.

They would never have the chance. Drawing a deep breath, Sloan gave Sam the answer she didn't want. "Harry probably just found out that I divorced Melinda, and she can't get anything else out of me. Of course, I just broke the terms of our divorce agreement by telling you that."

"Your name is really Sloan Montgomery. You've been married and divorced and your ex-wife still carries your name. I assume the secrecy about the divorce means she's pretending she's still your wife. Or widow, by now, I expect. What does her stepbrother have to do with all this?"

She must enjoy disappointment, Sloan thought glumly

as he considered what to tell her next. He'd just told her he was divorced and free to marry, but he still hadn't married her, and she hadn't blinked an eyelash.

"Harry's her lover, has been since she was old enough to know what a lover was." There, he'd said it. That part ought to be enough to scandalize her Southern Baptist morals.

When Sam said nothing, Sloan turned to catch a glimpse of her face. She managed to look horrified, disgusted, sympathetic, and curious all at the same time. He still wanted to pull her under him and lose himself in her. To hell with all the rest. He had to force himself to remember why he was stripping himself naked.

"It happens." Sloan shrugged, but he doubted if she could see it. "They grew up in an isolated area. They only had each other. Their parents were . . ." He couldn't use the word that most adequately described those brutally self-absorbed and abusive creatures. He substituted, "Not affectionate. Harry and Melinda learned about love from each other—or their rather warped version of the word."

She was nodding now, he could tell from the movement in the corner of his eye.

"At least they weren't related."

Sloan turned and watched her squirm under his regard. She gave him an unhappy look. "I knew a girl . . ." She hesitated, then forced herself to say it. "Her father was widowed. They lived out in the country. She had two babies but no husband. I heard it whispered about. It's not all that unusual, I suppose."

Sloan wanted to take her in his arms and tell her it was unusual and wrong, and she shouldn't know anything about any such things, but he kept his head firmly against his hands and returned to looking at the ceiling. It had grown a cobweb on it since it had been rebuilt and painted after the fire.

"In the case you're talking about, it's called incest, and it's perverted as all get-out. But there was no blood relation between Harry and Melinda. They could have married, but neither of them had any money. They couldn't support themselves. Harry would probably have inherited his stepfather's farm if he could have waited long enough, but he didn't consider himself a farmer. So he eventually ran off to the city and found himself a rich woman. Then he brought Melinda to the city and introduced her as his sister."

"And you were wealthy, and he married her off to you," she finished quietly. "You couldn't have been very old. How long were you married?"

"I was a young, idealistic fool. Melinda made me think I was her savior. I still had two years left to get my degree. I knew I wanted to get it in Scotland, and that was no place for a delicate lady. Damn, but I was dumb."

"Degree? You can't be completely dumb if you have a degree. Not even my father went to college. I don't think I know anybody who actually has a degree."

She stopped abruptly, and Sloan could almost hear the little wheels spinning around in her head. In less than a minute she had it worked out. She was a damned sight smarter than he was at that age.

"Medical degree. You bastard. You have a medical degree, don't you?"

Sam glared at him as if he'd just declared himself Lincoln's assassin. If there'd been anything on the table beside her to throw, she probably would have thrown it. Sloan didn't think it would have helped much.

"Dr. Montgomery, at your service, my lady, for all the good it does anybody," he answered cynically. "I never practiced. I got home from Scotland, discovered my father had died, leaving me a wealthy man, and my wife was having the time of her life with my inheritance. It took just about one year for me to discover that nothing I could say or do would make Melinda into a physician's wife, or even the loving wife of a rich man."

Sam was sitting frozen, hanging on to his every word. It wasn't as if it were an unusual story, or even a sad one. Not what he'd told her so far, anyway. But she was listening to things that weren't there, as usual. Sloan supposed that a woman who could talk to grapevines could hear things that weren't said, too.

"You blamed yourself for neglecting a young wife for two years," Sam surmised, quite accurately.

He grimaced. "That's what I told myself anyway. I was

a little older by then—a little more mature. I hadn't exactly been celibate those two years myself. I'd practically forgotten what she looked like. I wouldn't call what we had a love match, but I'd meant to make it work. There wasn't any reason we couldn't have."

"Except Harry," she filled in for him.

"Except Harry." Sloan thought his fingers must be numb by now from keeping his head pressed into them. "I don't want to tell you the rest. Go on to bed, Samantha. In the morning I'll find some way to send you down to stay with my brother. It will be easier for Hawk to get to you there when he has word of your father."

"I won't go. I'll move back with my mother if you want me out of here. You don't have to bend over backward to protect my reputation. I figured you'd get tired of me sooner or later. I think you've accomplished your purpose by now. Everyone will just think I'm your wife, but we can't get along." She stood up and started for the door.

That was half of what he wanted, but not enough. "Sam," he called to her.

She turned around, and Sloan saw that she was learning to keep her expression as closed as his. He didn't like that feeling. He wanted her to rage at him, to throw things, to go for her gun if nothing else. But she stood there calmly as if he hadn't ripped her insides out by telling her to get out of his life. She'd thought she was marrying him, for pity's sake. She'd actually agreed to marry him. Him, the bastard incarnate. Hell, he took it all back. She was even more naive than he'd been all those years ago.

"Sam, it isn't you. The only way I could persuade Melinda not to contest the divorce was by promising her she could have my name and everything that I owned so there wouldn't be a scandal. The divorce would become public if I married you legally. I'm a doctor, not a lawyer. I don't know the legal ramifications of marrying you under the name Sloan Talbott, or even what would happen if I broke the agreement and used Montgomery. Besides, it wouldn't be right to tie an innocent like you to a man like me. It couldn't ever last. I simply don't want you blaming yourself."

She gave him a watery smile, and he could see she was

near tears. He hated it when she cried. Tears made him feel helpless. Melinda had used tears quite effectively until he learned they were fake. Sloan had the gut-wrenching certainty that Samantha's weren't fake.

"I'm not exactly the wifely type, I know," she said quite clearly. "Once spring gets here, I'll probably forget to cook your meals, and the dust will be so thick I could use it for planting. I'm not pretty and delicate, and I don't need a man to protect me. So I guess I really don't need a husband. I'd never thought about having one anyway. It was kind of nice pretending for a while, even if you are as lousy a husband as I am a wife."

She closed the door between them.

If he was any kind of man at all, he'd get up from here and go to her and promise her heaven. He would make love to her until they were both giddy and then go look for a good lawyer. He'd left her thinking she wasn't the kind of wife he wanted, when she was everything he could ever hope to have and more. That thought grated on him worse than any other.

But he stayed where he was because he was the kind of man he was: the kind of man who fell for the wrong sort of women, the kind of man who would desert his profession, the kind of man who could kill his own son.

At least, if he drove Sam out of the hotel, he wouldn't be the kind of man who invited his past to endanger the future of anyone but himself.

Chapter Thirty-six

S am packed up and moved out the next day.

Alice Neely came over and tried to persuade Sloan to reason with her, but he had the art of noncommunication down to a fine science. He put his boots up on the desk, listened silently, shook his head when she was finished, and began throwing darts at a painting of George Washington on his wall. He left her nothing else to say or do. He rather admired the grace and dignity with which she departed.

Joe glared at him with hostility and retired to the saloon with a bottle of his best whiskey. Ramsey called Sloan every foul name in his vocabulary and pulled a few from his long-forgotten medical encyclopedia, then met Joe at the bar. Sloan rather wished he could join then, but he knew liquor would only compound the situation. He was a mean drunk. He was likely to drag Sam out by her hair and rape her before the effects wore off. And he couldn't afford to be without all his faculties if Harry and his hired killers were still around.

Chief Coyote chose that moment to steal Sloan's best horse and ride off to parts unknown. Sloan considered going after him, but he was reluctant to leave town with a snake like Anderson around. He found someone willing to go off on a wild-goose chase and sent him after the mad Indian. He didn't expect results, but it kept him from feeling helpless.

The first night without Sam, Sloan tried to retire to the bed she'd slept in these last weeks. He stripped off his clothes and collapsed against the linens as if she'd never been there, but the first thing that hit him was the scent of lavender. He hadn't changed the damned sheets. He grabbed a blanket and went to sleep on the sofa.

It wasn't the same. He couldn't pretend she still slept behind that closed door in next to nothing, available for the asking. He tossed and turned and woke up the next morning on the floor.

Cursing, he took to dismantling the bedroom as a relief from frustration. He ripped the sheets from the bed, only to find one of Sam's dainty undergarments caught beneath the mattress. He heaved the mattress out the hall door to air, and found one of her gardening gloves beneath the bed.

A book she had been reading rested open on a table in his parlor. A bonnet hung on a hook downstairs where she'd taken it off and left it. Her pots of plants had multiplied and spilled over to his study windows and the gallery railing. He couldn't walk through a single room of his own home without finding some reminder of Sam, and every single reminder cut into him like the sharp point of a knife.

He didn't know why it was so. Melinda could have dumped her entire wardrobe and all her perfume across his floor and he would have set fire to it gladly and without an ounce of remorse. But he left Sam's book where he found it, watered the pots of plants, and kept her damned lavender-scented undergarment in his trunk. The glove he placed with the bonnet downstairs, where she could find it if she came over to look at her plants. He was out of his mind.

He methodically worked over his bookkeeping until he found every misplaced penny, then strolled over to the store to check on Harriet's ledgers. He forgot the ledgers when he found Sam taking her sister's place while Harriet answered a call of nature. She asked after her plants and he told her she was welcome to check on them anytime. Then he walked out as if that was all he had come in to do.

Sloan knew he'd made a fatal mistake when he heard whistling later that afternoon and traced it to the kitchen. Copper hair tied up in a scarf, slender fingers caked in mud, long legs encased in tight gabardine, Sam sat happily, replanting seedlings in a sunny spot by the window. Her whistling faltered slightly when he wandered in, but she managed a bright smile that faded immediately as soon as he turned his back and walked out.

He'd made some giant mistakes in his life, but he didn't think any of them matched getting involved with one Samantha Neely. Deciding a single whiskey wouldn't be amiss, Sloan joined Joe and Ramsey at the bar.

Joe picked up his bottle and retreated to a table as soon as Sloan came to stand beside him. Sloan glared at this defection and poured his own.

"Kind of quiet around here," Ramsey said to no one in particular, before turning to acknowledge Sloan's presence. "Want me to shoot at you and liven it up a bit?"

"You couldn't hit the broad side of a barn when sober," Sloan answered acidly.

"And you don't know your ass from a hole in the ground." Ramsey replied in kind, then lifted his glass and swallowed the contents.

"You're the one who studied anatomy in butcher's school. What did you get your degree in? Bullshitting?"

Red-eyed, Ramsey gripped the bar rail and turned his glare on his nemesis. "I didn't get any highfalutin education like some fancy-pants easterners I know, but money can't buy common sense. If you had one ounce of brains, you'd know you threw away one of the finest creatures this side of paradise. Someone ought to shoot you just to put the world out of your misery."

Ramsey straightened drunkenly, pulled his disheveled frock coat into some semblance of order, and tried to tug at his nonexistent cravat. "As a matter of fact, being a man of common sense, I think I'll court Miss Samantha myself." He lurched toward the doorway.

Sloan grabbed him by the back of his coat, swung Ramsey around, and plowed his fist into his jaw, sending the drunken doctor flying across the polished floor. "Mrs. Talbott!" he shouted, standing over his adversary, daring him to return to his feet. "She's my wife, and you damned well can't court her."

But Ramsey had passed out cold and didn't offer the fight Sloan wanted.

Joe gave his employer a look of disgust and spat into a corner. "Looks like you'll have to go find your wife if it's a fight you're spoiling for. She's the only one who can stand up to you."

The truth of that spun him back on his heels. Sloan wished he was drunk enough to ignore it, but one whiskey didn't begin to desensitize him enough.

Walking over Ramsey, he left the saloon for the mining camp.

With Sloan gone, Sam felt free to finish her project of restoring the kitchen. She supposed it was a futile effort since Sloan would never use it for cooking, but this part of the winter always made her restless. She needed something to occupy her hands, if not her mind.

No one seemed to find it odd that she worked on a place that was not her own. The men still called her Mrs. Talbott. She suspected most of the town figured she and Sloan had had a little tiff that would blow over after a while. They all knew Sloan was a difficult man. Their misplaced sympathy was entirely with her.

She didn't see any point in correcting them. No one would believe her anyway. Accustomed to ignoring public opinion, she went her own way as usual.

Joe returned to painting the kitchen walls. Bernadette helped with the tiles when she wasn't with Harriet in the store or their mother in the restaurant. Jack mixed paint and ran errands when he wasn't digging for buried treasure in the garden or listening to tall tales in the saloon. Amos Donner offered to build a table and chairs, and he seemed to spend an inordinate amount of time discussing their dimensions with her whenever Bernadette was around. Sam smiled and blamed it on spring being around the corner, just as she blamed her own restlessness on the caprices of that season.

She couldn't sleep at night. More often than not, she found herself staring out over the moonlit mountains stretching across the horizon. She found dozens of ways to exercise her energies during the day—climbing ladders, scrubbing walls, digging the soft dirt of the hotel's kitchen garden. Just as Sloan had warned, nothing helped.

She not only couldn't scratch the itch that he had created, but she couldn't drive him out of her mind. When she heard the shouting of men in the street, she hoped it was Sloan returning. When she heard footsteps coming down the wooden back stairs, her heart skipped a beat. She found herself dusting and sweeping Sloan's rooms in his absence, something she had never bothered doing when he was there.

She ran her fingers over books he'd touched, and opened the humidor containing his cheroots, just to smell their aroma. She stole a shirt from his dirty laundry and wore it to bed because it still held a faintly masculine odor that conjured images of Sloan beside her.

She was quite certain she would recover from these hallucinations once spring arrived and she found her valley. She just didn't have enough to keep her mind occupied at this time of year. Sloan would become part of her past as much as the old hound dog she used to sleep with when she was a child. She'd loved countless animals in her lifetime. Sloan was simply one more.

At the end of February, Hawk's younger brother rode up the trail. It was late in the evening of a particularly stormy day when he rode his horse into the neglected livery everyone used as a stable. Sam saw him from the hotel kitchen window and slipped out to catch him before anyone else knew he had arrived.

He gave her a brief, dark-eyed look, then returned to unhitching his saddle. "Where's Talbott?"

"Still in the mining camp. What did you find out?" Sam hugged her shawl around her against the damp and moved as close to the warm horse as she dared.

"Hawk has gone to Mexico. There are reports of your father there not too many months ago."

He still wasn't looking at her. Sam frowned. He hadn't struck her as the particularly shy type. Perhaps he worried that Harriet had told her about his improper advances. That was scarcely what was on her mind now.

"Mexico." His words finally began to sink in. Her father had been seen alive not many months ago. Why hadn't he written? "Did those reports say if he was ill?"

"If all the other reports we've heard are true, I'd say he was. But Hawk told me not to report hearsay. I've come to talk to Talbott."

He was ostentatiously brushing down his wet horse ...d ignoring her. He was a young man, not as hard-bitten as Hawk, but his face was dark and uncommunicative as she watched him. It looked like she wasn't going to get another word out of him.

"What's your real name?" she asked, just to see if she could pry anything off his tongue.

"Riding Eagle will do," he answered curtly.

"Well, I'm sure it makes you feel more manly than Samuel or Henry, but it sounds perfectly silly when somebody tries to use it. If you'll leave that horse alone, I'll get you some coffee and soup. Those are two things I know how to cook without difficulty."

Sam swept out of the livery and ran through the grape arbor to the kitchen door, dodging raindrops. Riding Eagle followed her with some reluctance, but she knew about the empty stomachs of young men. She'd hit him where it would do the most good when she'd mentioned food.

She kept the huge stove burning to keep her seedlings warm. Her mother often used it for the overflow from the restaurant. Soup went fast on a day like this, and the stove at the hacienda couldn't hold enough. Sam had been tending this pot all afternoon. She scooped some in a bowl and offered it to the wet young man.

"You'd have to pay for this over at the restaurant, so don't tell the others I fed you," she warned.

He nodded and ate a few bites greedily, then sipped the coffee she handed him. He was beginning to notice she existed, Sam realized with some satisfaction. She intended to pry the rest of his information out of him before he left here.

"Donner is making a table and chairs, but they're not ready yet. I'm sorry I can't offer you a better seat than the floor. I think I'll make Sloan pay for the furniture. That would serve him right for calling Donner worthless and throwing him out." She pushed aside some flowerpots and took a seat on the windowsill.

Riding Eagle remained standing, setting his cup on the stove while he ate from the bowl. He watched her warily. "I thought Talbott was your husband. Why are you so angry with him?"

"I'm not angry with him. Or maybe I am. It doesn't make any difference. He thinks I'm a helpless female and that he's God. Apparently my position in life is to teach him differently."

A hint of a smile cracked his high-boned face. "Sloan Talbott is an arrogant man. I have his horse down in Ariposa. My adopted grandfather thought Talbott needed to be cut down a peg or two."

Sam grinned in delight. "The chief is an intelligent man. But that is getting us neither here nor there. What did you find out about this Harry Clark?"

Riding Eagle's face shuttered closed again. "I will tell Talbott when I see him."

Sam gave a sigh of exasperation. "Men are God's plague upon the world. I thought you might have a little more sense than most. I know all about Harry Clark or Anderson or whatever he's calling himself. I know more about Sloan Talbott than any man in this town. And I know your name isn't Riding Eagle and you're not an ignorant Indian, whatever you would like to pretend. Now, are you going to tell me what I want to know or shall I call Harriet over here and begin to give her explicit details?"

The look he gave her would have done Sloan credit. Sam returned it with an angelic smile.

"Do you know you're not really Mrs. Talbott?" he asked curtly.

"My, I did manage to make you angry, didn't I? I thought Indians were supposed to be as stoic as the ancient Greeks. But then, you're not all Indian, are you? The Spanish are supposed to be an emotional people." Sam waited to see if he would throw the bowl at her or leap at her with the wicked knife in his belt. When he merely gave her a thoroughly disgusted male look and reached to help himself to more soup without being asked, she nodded approval. "Very good. Harriet isn't nearly as meddlesome as I am, but she can be extremely irritating when she sets her mind on something. I know I'm not really Mrs. Talbott, but I'd appreciate it if you didn't spread the word around. Sloan is a mite sensitive on the subject. Why were you talking to the priest?"

"Drunken ex-priest," Riding Eagle clarified. "Because Clark was. He knows you're not really married now also. As does Sloan's brother and sister-in-law, of course. Clark sought them out, too, but I was ahead of him. Matthew Montgomery is an intelligent man. He expressed great surprise at seeing a man called Harry Anderson so far from Boston. He told him he'd shoot him if he ever set foot on his land again. And he escorted him out of town at gunpoint without telling Anderson anything he wanted to know. Am I going too fast for you?"

"No, you're doing just fine. Did Matthew have any idea what this Anderson-Clark person was after?"

Riding Eagle gave her a puzzled look. "You really don't mind that Talbott lied to you about the priest?"

"Of course I mind. I contemplated shooting off certain vulnerable parts of his anatomy, but Sloan and I understand each other. He didn't take anything I hadn't offered. The whole thing would have blown over if some of his cronies hadn't got nosy and spread the word faster than we could shut them up. When I learned we weren't married, I told him to back off and he did. Not that any of this is any of your business, of course."

"Of course." He sipped his coffee and eyed her contemplatively. "I suppose you would go after the vulnerable part of any man's anatomy who would try to do the same to one of your sisters, wouldn't you?"

"Of course," she answered complacently. "My sisters are more gently bred than I am. They couldn't do it for themselves."

He gave a snort of disbelief. "Your sister Harriet is the stubbornest female I've ever met in my life. She might not wield knives and firearms, but I wouldn't put a hot poker in her reach when she's angry."

Sam shrugged. "I wouldn't put one in reach of any woman when she's angry. Or any man, for all that matters. Did you learn anything else besides our personal secrets while you were out there? Where's Anderson now?"

"He's in San Francisco, talking to a lawyer. A paleface like Talbott is more likely to get information out of a lawyer than a 'breed like me. As far as I can tell, Anderson hasn't tried to hire any more killers. He does seem to know a great deal about the mine and everything else Talbott owns."

"Not good." The heavy clouds outside seemed to thicken and throw a pall over the room as Sam crossed her hands in her lap and looked out over the garden. "I don't suppose you know anyone who would kill Anderson, do you?"

"I'll thank you to remember I'm a Harvard graduate and not a savage, ma'am," he answered dryly.

"That's a lot of bull," she said without inflection, not looking at him. "But you've answered the question. Why don't you go say hello to Harriet? She's at the store, but I'll warn you she won't be quite as amenable as before. Some man attacked her after you left last time. She thinks men are lower than chicken droppings right now."

Giving a violent curse, the man calling himself Riding Eagle strode rapidly out of the kitchen.

Sam remained where she was, replaying everything she'd learned.

Her father was alive and ill.

Sloan was in big trouble.

What should she do now? Track Hawk and her father into Mexico or stand by Sloan's side?

It was difficult turning her back on the man she'd adored all her life for a man who had turned his back on her. But sometimes a woman had to make the decision to leave her home and family for the man she loved, regardless of whether she loved rightly or wrongly.

Sam knew that. Now she had to make herself act upon it.

Chapter Thirty-seven

Sam assumed Riding Eagle went up the mountain to find Sloan after Harriet wouldn't give him the time of day. All she knew for certain was that Sloan came riding down out of the hills the next day, and Harriet wouldn't even mention Riding Eagle's existence.

Sam made no effort to hunt Sloan down when he returned. She saw men coming and going from his office. She saw men leave town to go down the mountain. She saw Joe bringing him food from her mother's restaurant. She didn't see Sloan.

Her pots of herbs in the kitchen were growing very nicely. The geraniums hadn't come up yet. She watered them both, then began papering the shelves in the cupboard. The place really could use a china cabinet and some china. She wondered what Sloan would do if she ordered them.

On the first sunny day after Sloan's return, Sam went outside to work on the kitchen garden. She kept her rifle on hand at all times these days, but when her hands were occupied with a hoe, she wore her father's gun belt. She wasn't much of an expert with the Colts, but Joe taught her when he had time.

"That doesn't look like more than rocky sand. How are you going to grow anything in it?"

The voice didn't catch Sam entirely by surprise. She'd known the instant Sloan had ventured out. She just hadn't expected him to speak to her. She continued her hoeing.

"Compost. Manure. This is good sandy soil, not like the clay back home. Once I add a few nutrients and some water, it will grow anything. The main problem is the number of growing days. I don't know when the first and last frosts come out here."

"It varies. We're not so far up the mountain that it snows in June, but it doesn't necessarily get real warm either."

Sam could tell from his voice that he was keeping his distance. It didn't matter. Just knowing he was here and talking to her made her sing silent hallelujahs. She wanted to keep him talking forever.

Who was she fooling? She wanted Sloan to come over and haul her into his arms and make mad, passionate love to her. Talking was a poor substitute. Her knees went weak at just the thought.

She continued hoeing, keeping her back to him. "That's all right. I can grow a lot of things in cool weather. I'm thinking of putting out the lettuce and pea seeds now. I wish I had a better source of water than the town pump."

"I've been thinking of having plumbing installed in the hotel. I could have a pump put out here if you like."

Sam couldn't stand it any longer. She rested the hoe on the ground and turned to look at him.

It was a good thing she had the hoe handle for support. He looked marvelous. He looked awful. He wore his fanciest frock coat and frilled shirt and embroidered vest. The dark color of the coat suited his dark coloring. The white of his shirt emphasized the bronze of his sun- and wind-burned face. But he looked leaner, his cheeks more hollow, his features sterner. There was a fading bruise on one cheek, and when he stepped forward, he limped. She didn't know what he'd been doing to himself these last weeks, but he hadn't been enjoying them.

He couldn't disguise the fire in his eyes though. It helped some to know he was burning up inside just as much as she was. Gone were the days of the icy Sloan Talbott. He looked as if he'd gone to hell and back.

"I bet the men at the mines are glad to see the last of you," Sam commented casually.

"I like to spread myself around, keep everyone on their toes. I'm considering going down to 'Frisco. Want to come with me?"

She'd always thought his eyes were gray. They seemed

nearly black right now as they burned through her. She knew what he asked, but it wasn't the question she wanted to hear. Sloan Talbott could keep right on burning in his own hell if he thought she was that easy.

"Planning on making it simple for Anderson? You never have told me why he wants to kill you."

He didn't come any closer. "I've got a couple of theories but no proof. I don't like leaving you so far away. The camp is only a few hours' ride. 'Frisco is more than a day. I'd feel safer if you were where I could see you."

"That works both ways. You're the one Anderson is gunning for. But the only way I'm going down that mountain with you is if you promise to stay away from me. I'm not Melinda. I don't sleep with men who aren't my husband."

His features hardened. "I don't have anything left to give, Sam. I've given up my name, my reputation, my profession, my home, and everything I ever owned to my wife. My bed is all I have left to offer. Take it or leave it."

She shrugged. "I already left it. You made your decision. I made mine. Take Joe with you to 'Frisco."

He looked as if he wanted to say something else. His hands gripped into fists and his jaw muscles perceptibly tightened. He looked as if he'd like to shake her. Instead, he just turned around and left her alone with her garden and her hoe. She hadn't expected anything more.

But it hurt. It hurt to know that all she would ever be to him was a woman in his bed. She could understand that his first wife had destroyed everything he'd ever thought of himself. She didn't know why or completely understand how that could be, but she knew that's how it was. Still, he'd made a new life for himself. Why was he so reluctant to share it?

Sam didn't believe for an instant that it was the ramifications of the divorce. That was just an excuse. The Sloan Talbott she knew would consult a good lawyer and get himself out of any legal bind that he was in once he put his mind to it. He just preferred holding that agreement between them like a wall that would keep them apart forever. Except in bed.

He should have found someone younger and sillier,

Sam thought vengefully as she attacked the stony ground. Or maybe it would have been better if she could just be as naive as he thought her. Whichever the case, neither of them would get much sleep while the other was around. He'd certainly been right about that part. She was so aware of him that her skin felt electrified every time he came near.

She waited for Sloan to leave town, but he didn't. He found plumbers willing to come all the way up the mountain to pipe water from the stream into the hotel. He had carpenters in to enclose the back stairs and add on rooms. Men in fancy suits started arriving in wagons hired from Sacramento, indicating they had come up the river by steamboat. Carriers bearing official-looking packages of documents came and went on a regular basis. The spider improved his web daily rather than moving it.

Sam was impressed by the amount of activity one man could generate, but she'd apparently buried her usual curiosity along with her heart. The only room of the hotel she entered was the kitchen. The only things she spoke about to Sloan or any of the other men were the weather and the plants starting to poke their heads through the soil. When the first pea leaves showed through their rocky bed, she held a christening party, and after that, men stopped by regularly to check the growth of her garden.

A March snow covered the ground, but Sam buried her tender lettuce beneath straw, and the courtyard walls prevented the wind from burning the other plants. Those same walls held the sun's warmth when it came out again, and the snow melted rapidly.

Sloan came out to inspect the damage when she did. He knelt in the garden and gingerly pushed his fingers into the dirt around a seedling, tucking it more firmly into the bed. The young green shoots pushing joyously through previously barren ground struck him as strangely symbolic. He knew his literature. He knew about the symbolism of breathing new life into the old, of the earth's annual rejuvenation bringing hope where all had been bleak before. He just feared it came too late for him.

He glanced at Samantha as she gently removed some of

the straw from around her lettuce. Her wide mouth was set in a serene smile. Her copper hair glowed in the sunlight as she kneeled in the dirt. She hadn't worn a dress again since she'd left him, but he didn't mind. He knew by now that she would drive him crazy whatever she wore or didn't wear. From the first moment he'd tried to look down her shirt he'd been drawn to her. It had taken him this long to realize, however, that the attraction wasn't entirely sexual.

He couldn't bring himself to think about that, though. He focused his attention on the gun belt she wore around her hips. "Why in hell are you wearing those things?" he demanded.

She had to follow his gaze to figure out what he was talking about, then she only shrugged. "Varmints are everywhere this time of year."

"Like hell, they are. Has someone been bothering you?" Sloan heard the fury in his voice, but couldn't control it. The idea of anyone else laying a hand on Samantha unleashed some irrational part of his brain. She was his, whatever anyone else thought about it.

She sent him one of her blasted lifted-eyebrow looks. "You're the only man in the country who has the audacity to bother me. I think I'll make it a rule that only happy people can come out here to the garden. Plants can hear, you know. Anger makes them unhappy."

"I don't know any such thing. That's the silliest statement you've ever made. Plants don't have ears. They don't even have brains to identify sounds. Plants are just plants. You step on them, and they die. They don't scream for help."

She smiled forgivingly at him. Standing up, she sang softly to herself as she examined the remaining vines on the arbor. No sign of life showed in the blighted wood, only Sloan couldn't help but entertain the notion that some of the tiny tendrils leaned toward the sound of that damned sultry voice.

"I've got a man who says he's found your valley," he said abruptly. He hadn't meant to say anything at all until he'd had time to go out and inspect the place himself, but he had to say something to drive these other crazy notions out of his head.

She swung around in midnote and stared at him eagerly. "Really? Could we go out today? The ground really needs to be broke early so it has time to settle before I plant. It's almost too late already."

"There's still snow back in some of those pockets, and I haven't been able to go out and look for myself. He may be wrong. There's no point in getting all excited yet."

"Who found it? Could I talk to him? Maybe he could take me out there since you're so busy. I have lots of time. The kitchen is about finished, and there isn't much more I can do here until the weather turns warmer. Let me go, Sloan. I need to see it."

He couldn't tell her no. He had only to look into the depths of those eager blue eyes to lose himself. He wanted that day at the beach back. His soul ached for just a touch, just a reminder of what was between them. Hell, he hadn't even known he possessed a soul. He'd thought it lost long ago. She was destroying something inside him with those eyes. They were like lanterns of truth, lighting the dark passageways of his existence, revealing the cracks and deteriorating walls in their clarity.

"We'll go together when the snow clears." Sloan turned and walked away abruptly, before she had him groveling at her feet.

It had been nearly a month, and Anderson was still in San Francisco from all reports. Sloan's men hadn't been able to get a word out of him. His inquiries in Boston hadn't received any answers yet. He didn't know why Harry wanted him dead at this late date, but he was too far away to cause a great deal of harm right now. It should be safe enough to take Sam to her valley. He would take an army with them to make sure it was safe.

It would take an army to keep them separated once they were together again.

It was nearly the end of March before Sloan deemed it safe enough to venture out to seek the valley. It hadn't rained or snowed in days, and the weather had grown warm enough to turn mountain streams into rivers. The sound of water crashing over boulders and gurgling down mountainsides accompanied them as they set out.

Sam thrilled at the enchantment of clear air, warm sun, and bird song as the horses swayed slowly around the side of the mountain. Towering evergreens exuded the thick scent of pine beneath the sun's warmth. New green leaves added a misty quality to frail branches, and the tender shoots of wildflowers sprang out of every crack and crevice. The air practically vibrated with spring, and she couldn't wipe the smile from her face—not even if she had to ride in the company of half a dozen men bristling with guns and rifles. They strung their horses out in front and back of her, keeping watchful guard as if expecting a troop of mounted bandits to appear any minute. Sam ignored their silliness. She was too happy to allow them to drag her down with their oppressive outlook.

She pointed out a squirrel scolding them from the branches overhead, a robin wrestling with a piece of straw for its nest, and the first opening buds of a wildflower she couldn't identify. Neither could any of the men around her. Sam turned around and found Sloan riding close behind her.

"You should have brought Chief Coyote along. I bet he could tell me the names of those flowers."

"Either that, or he could make them up for you. The chief's not exactly right in the head, you realize," he answered amicably.

"Just because he sees things you don't doesn't make you right and him wrong. He's been around a lot longer than any of us. He's seen more than we'll ever see. He simply doesn't choose to communicate in the same way as we do."

"He doesn't sing to plants either," Sloan said with amusement. "I haven't got anything against Coyote. I didn't even bring charges against him for horse stealing. I just wouldn't exactly rely on anything he says without further proof."

There wasn't much use in arguing with him. Samantha smiled and watched a deer stop on a nearby rise. She shouted at a man who raised his rifle to bring the animal down. There had been a time when she would have been the one raising that rifle, but they didn't need the food now. She felt harmony with all living things at the moment. She watched in satisfaction as the deer crashed through the shrubbery and disappeared.

Sloan offered no seductive innuendoes as they rode. They'd packed blankets and saddlebags for the sake of caution, but this was merely an exploratory expedition. They weren't planning to spend the night in close proximity. Still, he rode as near to her as the trail allowed, and she was aware of his presence every minute.

Sam had a number of reasons to be aware of him, but she was too happy at the moment to worry about them. Sloan pointed out the high ridge leading to his mining operation, showed her where an eagle built its nest, and generally made himself pleasant for a change. It pleased her that he made the effort to at least show the world they were settling their differences, even if it was just that—a show.

The men relaxed their guard gradually when nothing threatened their journey, except the occasional screech of a squirrel or crackle of a falling branch weakened by the winter's snow. Joe rode up to say he'd found a bear's den, and they made a wide berth around it since there would be cubs at this time of year, and mama bears didn't like being disturbed. Sloan strictly forbade Samantha to sneak a peek.

She didn't argue, but started to sing as their guide warned they were getting close to the valley. The song was slightly bawdy and familiar to most of the men, and they gargled out the words if not exactly the tune as they rode. Sloan grinned and sent her a dancing look, but didn't attempt to make the same joyful noise as his men.

Just the fact that the man she loved was smiling and riding alongside of her was sufficient for Sam, for now. She wanted a great deal more, but for this moment what she had was enough. The sun was warm, the scenery was beautiful, her valley was straight ahead, and Sloan Talbott was at her side.

When their guide brought the line to a halt, she eagerly rode ahead of the others to see where he pointed.

There it was, an evergreen crevasse between two walls

of gray rock. Sam sat back and admired the simplicity of it. Whatever tumult had created these mountains had split that wall of rock right down the middle, and the centuries since had seen a forest of trees eat away at the crumbling stone of the split until the narrow passage had become a wider one hidden in forest growth.

It was obvious from this viewpoint, although probably not so obvious when riding alongside of the wall of rock. Sam wondered how her father had ever found it, but she didn't sit there wondering long. With a whoop of joy she sent Hawk's Indian pony racing down the trail toward the opening.

She heard Sloan shouting behind her, but he could scold her later. Right now she wanted to be the first one through that narrow aperture, the first one to view the valley beyond.

She was aware that the men scattered across the field behind her, playing their war games. But they didn't have to worry about what was up ahead. The gray walls of stone were impenetrable except at that one point.

Whooping as she entered the belt of trees spilling through the only opening in the wall, Sam slowed her mount and approached with a cautious eagerness that had her gaze seeking out every nook and cranny of her new abode. This was where she would live when she had her house built and her fields planted. This was hers.

Sloan came to ride beside her. He had his hand on his rifle, but he, too, seemed absorbed by the forest's silent stillness.

The trees followed a slight incline. The bed of rocks that had produced them over these last centuries was obvious through the thin layer of soil and matted evergreen needles. Gravel rolled away beneath the hooves of their horses as they drew closer to the walls.

As they broke through the evergreens, it became clear that the walls were more shattered at this aperture than had been noticeable earlier. Boulders and loose rocks and gravel that had fallen over the millennia made sloping hills on either side of the opening. Sam sensed Sloan's uneasiness, but the ground beneath their feet seemed firm enough. She plunged onward.

The ring of trees ended abruptly at the walls. They walked their horses up into the rock opening, side by side. Sam settled back in her saddle with satisfaction as the view beyond opened before them.

The slope down into the valley from this point was gentle. A few trees had found their way across the rocky walls towering high along the valley's boundaries, but mostly unbroken meadow filled the interior. Water crashed down a cascade of rocks along a side wall, spilling into a well-worn bed in the valley floor. From here they couldn't see where the stream exited, but it was enough for Sam to know there was water. As if of one accord, they both dismounted.

Sam knelt to crumble the rocky soil between her fingers. When she stood upright again, joy illuminated her face as she turned to Sloan. "It's everything I ever dreamed it would be. Thank you for finding it."

He reached to brush a straying curl from her face. Their horses moved forward into the canyon a few feet, searching for the winter dry grass. Sloan's fingers brushed the smooth skin of Sam's cheek just as the earth moved beneath them.

In the next moment a cascade of giant boulders erupted around them as the air shattered with an explosion equal to a ton of ignited gunpowder.

Chapter Thirty-eight

The ground rumbled, and the air exploded in a confusion of flying rocks and debris. Sloan heard Sam scream, and his blood froze in his veins as she went tumbling down the slope without him. Instinctively, he threw himself after her, wrapping his fingers in her shirt and using his body to break her fall.

Their horses bolted. He refused to let go of Sam as they continued rolling down the incline. He wasn't letting her out of his hands. When they stopped tumbling, he covered her body with his, sheltering her from the flying debris.

Rocks still tumbled from the walls behind them, but the noise lessened. The dust-filled air obscured his vision. He didn't need sight to know that Sam still lay safely in his arms.

The fall had knocked the breath from his lungs, and Sloan lay still a moment. He'd be bruised from head to foot by morning, but all his bones seemed intact. He could feel the press of rocks at his hips, but the rest of his uneasy bed seemed to be firm dirt and weeds. He tucked Sam more securely against his chest and brushed her hair away.

"Sam? Are you all right?"

At first, he thought the fall had stolen her breath as it had his. He waited for her to shake her head or gasp for air. When she did neither, something made of steel constricted his ribs.

He brushed his hand through the tumble of curls on his shoulder until he found her cheek. It was warm. His fingers sought and found a pulse at her temple. "Sam," he whispered in terror. "Sam, say something."

The silence following the violent storm of explosion continued unbroken.

The air slowly cleared. Carefully, Sloan rolled over enough to ease his precious burden from his arms. Red curls spilled across the dry brown grass. Sam's wool-trimmed jacket fell open to reveal the slight rise and fall of her blue gingham-covered breasts. A thick fringe of dark lashes lay closed over her eyes, contrasting starkly with the pale skin of her cheeks.

Holding his breath, not realizing he did so, Sloan slid his fingers beneath the gingham. Her heart beat softly, but steadily. Her breathing was still a little erratic, but so was his.

Not even considering the implications of his hand brushing against the soft mounds of her breasts, he fastened the shirt again and reached to pull back one eyelid. The pupil was dilated, and she remained completely unconscious of his touch.

Terror multiplying with every passing moment, Sloan ran his hand through the thick mass of her hair again. The familiar stickiness of flowing blood brought a wail of despair from his throat.

"Boss! Boss, are you all right?" Joe's voice echoed from distance somewhere above them.

The prosaic sounds of the real world jarred him back to practicality and away from the volcanic jungles of his emotions. Sloan glanced up, searching for any sign of the men they had brought with them.

All he saw was the fallen barricade of rocks where they had stood scarce minutes before.

The realization that they were trapped renewed a flicker of his earlier panic, but Sloan squelched it with the aid of his powerful concentration. The loose rocks would be dangerously impassable. He didn't dare move Samantha any more than necessary. They were safer here right now than trying to climb that hill.

With a strength he wasn't certain he felt, Sloan shouted, "I'm all right. Sam's hurt. You're going to have to get the men to dig us out. I can't get her over those rocks without hurting her. Is everyone all right out there?"

"We've got a horse down and one man with a sore rump, but we can make it back all right. We might have to blow our way through this, though. Can you get Sam far enough away?"

"I'll wait awhile before I try to move her. It's going to be nightfall before you can get back here with picks and powder. If I can catch the horses, we'll have some blankets and supplies for now. You'd better bring up extra when you come back. Have Mrs. Neely pack up some bandages, headache powders, and alcohol. Tell her it's just a small knock on the head. Don't scare her any, Joe."

Joe's voice was faint and a little scared when he asked, "Is she going to be okay, Talbott? Tell it straight."

"So far, all I've found is a knock on the head, just like I said. Get going, Joe. I don't want to spend the rest of my life back here."

The reassurance Sloan forced for the sake of the outside world disappeared the minute he heard Joe scrambling back down the rocks, and he turned to see the faint blue coloring of Sam's lips. That wasn't a good sign at all.

Very gently, he raised her enough to slide his coat under her. Then, with the professional care he had learned a lifetime ago, he examined her from head to toe, searching for signs of broken bones and internal injuries. He double-checked everything, his fingers shaking nervously as forgotten routines were remembered, and he applied them to this woman who had given his life back to him.

As he searched for injuries, other oddities registered in the back of his mind. Sam stirred, and he lost his concentration, forgetting all else as hope rose, but she didn't open her eyes. Sloan cursed. He couldn't find anything wrong except the bloody knot on her head. The shock of the explosion and the fall might explain her continuing unconsciousness, but he couldn't place his hopes on that.

He pulled her coat around her and fastened it to keep her warm. He wished she'd worn that rabbit fur of hers, it would have been warmer, but the day hadn't been cold when they started out. It probably wasn't cold now. He just felt that way.

Sloan stood up and examined their surroundings. They

had little in the way of cover out here other than the natural undulations of the earth. He could see the horses drinking from the icy stream. They shouldn't be hard to catch. He scanned the rocky walls enclosing them, but they were stark and unlikely to conceal dangerous predators.

His gaze drifted back to the tumble of rocks blocking the valley's entrance. The ground had shook. It could have been an earthquake that sent those walls sliding downward. He'd been through similar tremors before. Sometimes a loud noise accompanied them. He just found it difficult to believe that God would have waited until they stood right there between those two fragile walls before churning up the earth and tumbling rocks that had lain there for centuries.

If it was an earthquake, there would be an aftershock. He'd have to get Sam farther away, out in the middle of the valley where they would be safe. Moving an accident victim was always dangerous, particularly if it involved any injury to the spine or head. But staying here was the height of folly.

He didn't have time to catch the horses and rig a travois. Another quake could come at any minute. Bracing himself, Sloan slid his arms beneath Samantha, supporting her head as best as he could in the jacket he'd used for her bed, then propping her against his shoulder as he walked slowly away from the unstable wall of stones.

Sam wasn't a small woman, but Sloan carried her effortlessly, with a strength born of sheer terror. She didn't make a sound when he picked her up. She was a bundle of limp limbs as he held her. Sam wasn't supposed to be that way. She was supposed to stride joyously across this land of hers, bristling with boundless energy, laughing and singing as she pointed out the advantages of this barren plain of mud and straw.

Sloan would have given his right arm at this moment if she would do just that. The very real terror that she would never laugh and sing again held him in a grip so powerful that he feared it would squeeze the breath from his lungs.

He couldn't lose her. He'd thought it possible to gradually put her out of his mind as time went on, but he'd only been making the usual ass of himself. He'd thought because he lost everything ten years ago and still managed to live that he could do it again. He was wrong. He'd lost only material things and a little pride last time. This time, he would lose his soul. Sloan could feel that knowledge seep deep into his heart and take root there as he grasped Sam's still body in his arms. The joy that was Sam was all that kept him alive. He would die in truth if he lost her.

He wouldn't lose her. He was a doctor, a damned good doctor. He would use every power at his command, including prayer if necessary, but he would bring Sam back. She might curse him for a fool, take a knife to his belly, but she would wake and live again.

He found a run-down shack hidden in a stand of cottonwoods near the stream. The cottonwoods had to have been planted as surely as the shed had been built by human hands. He didn't question either anomaly. He merely kicked the door open, examined the interior for intruders, and laid Sam carefully in the square of sunlight pouring through the open door.

She didn't stir, but satisfied she was as protected as possible there, Sloan went out to catch the horses. They didn't exactly come when called, but they didn't raise any objections when he walked up to them. He fed them a handful of oats from one of the saddle pouches and led them back toward the shack.

It took time, but he got the saddles and blankets unloaded and a bed of grass and dry leaves made in one corner of the floor. He covered this crude mattress with a blanket and gently moved Sam to its relative comfort. He removed her coat and used it to cover her chest, then threw his own coat over her legs. The coats were thicker than any blanket he possessed.

He used the icy water of the stream to cleanse her wound. By this time, the knot had swollen to twice its earlier size, but the blood had clotted. He kept her head slightly elevated, praying that the blood wasn't coagulating behind that knot, applying pressure to her brain.

The cold water made her stir again. Sloan thought he

saw her lashes flutter, but it could have been wishful thinking. He tried to appease himself with the knowledge that everything seemed in working order: Her toes responded when he stroked them, her fingers moved, and there weren't any of the danger signs of internal injuries. She just wouldn't wake up.

He started a fire and set on a pot of water to boil. He examined their small store of supplies and figured he could stretch them for forty-eight hours at best. He wouldn't likely find much game in this abandoned hole.

Close to sunset Sloan returned to the rock dam blocking the valley entrance. He called to see if anyone was there and got an answer from one of the men who had stayed behind. Joe hadn't returned.

He made a brief attempt to find his footing over the wall, but rocks slid from every place he touched. They would have to dig their way through or blow it up. The latter sounded a trifle dangerous.

The guard on the other side yelled that he could see Joe coming. Sloan tried to be patient while he waited, but his gaze as well as his attention kept drifting back to that cabin hidden behind the trees. He didn't want Sam waking up and finding herself alone.

His impatience grew as the men tried to figure a way to lower the supplies over the rocky wall. He didn't care about the food, but he wanted the medical kit. Someone finally got the idea of climbing an evergreen and lowering the kit by rope from one of the branches.

Sloan jumped up and pulled it down, waving to the shadowy figure on the distant limb. "Got it. Is Bradshaw out there? He's the best man to figure the way through here."

Joe's voice called down from whatever perch he'd discovered on the other side. "He's here. We've got every piece of equipment from the mine. I told Miz Neely we'd have you both back safe and sound by tomorrow sundown."

"You do that, and I'll give you the saloon," Sloan answered dryly. He'd worked with rock before. He knew better than to expect miracles.

"Well, it made her feel better," Joe said defensively. "I

told her the medical supplies were for one of the men. It's a good thing that woman can't ride a horse or she'd be up here now."

"Is Ramsey sober enough to keep an eye on her and the twins?"

"He and Donner are there." There was a brief hesitation before Joe continued. "You know that guide that found this place?"

Sloan's heart stilled. "Yeah. Said he used to work these mountains back in '49."

"He's gone."

The wind blew through the following silence.

"Look for where he planted the explosives when it's light," Sloan finally ordered. "There may still be some left. Don't let anyone set any fires anywhere near these rocks."

"Aye, we'll be careful. How's Sam?"

"Sleeping," he lied. "We've found a cabin down by the stream. I've got to get back there."

He didn't know why he was lying to make everyone else feel better, Sloan thought as he made his way back through the twilight shadows of the meadow. Maybe he was trying to fool himself. He knew what a concussion was. He knew how dangerous it could be. He was too worried right now to even curse the dirty bastard who had planted those explosives. He'd wring Anderson's neck when he got out of here, but that wouldn't be until Sam was well enough to go.

The aroma of the coffee he'd made filled the air as he approached the cabin. He hadn't even taken time to be hungry, but he had to eat. He was half afraid to enter the cabin, but hope was an insatiable thing. He felt it lodge in his throat as he walked through the open door.

The evening shadows fell deeper in here. Sloan knelt beside the makeshift pallet and laid his hand against Sam's forehead. It felt cool to the touch. He laid open the medical kit and blessed Alice Neely's foresight. She had included everything he might possibly need, even if things like headache powders were useless unless Sam woke up.

He cleaned the wound more thoroughly with the alcohol and poured icy water into the bag Mrs. Neely had supplied. He applied it to the swelling and watched with anxious eyes as Sam stirred at the touch.

Her fingers twitched, and her head rolled back and forth, dislodging the bag. Sloan caught her hand and held it between his own. "Sam? Samantha," he pleaded, then added more forcefully, "Samantha! Wake up."

She lay still for a moment, but he squeezed her hand. "It's me, Sam. Everything's all right. You're going to scare me to death if you don't wake up."

Her eyes fluttered open, and she stared right at him. Sloan tried to rein in his wildly galloping hopes. "Sam? Don't just look at me like that. Say something."

A small frown lined her brow. Her gaze drifted vacantly from him to their crude surroundings. Her fingers clutched his hand in a frightened spasm, then pulled away.

Eyes wild, she looked back to him again. "Who are you?"

Chapter Thirty-nine

Sloan tried not to panic. She was awake. She was conscious. She could speak coherently. He tried to smile reassuringly, although smiling was still a rusty accomplishment for him. "I'm your husband. Remember me?" he asked teasingly as he tested Sam's pulse and watched the pupils of her eyes.

She looked bewildered as she glanced around. He could tell her head hurt from the way she winced and closed her eyes when she turned her neck. He knew that feeling well enough.

"I've got some headache powders here. I don't want to give you too much, or they might make you sleepy. I think you need to stay awake a while longer."

When she made a feeble nod of acquiescence, Sloan emptied the coffee out of his cup, filled it with water from his canteen, and mixed in the powder. He lifted her head slightly from the pillow of clothing he'd made for her, and helped her sip the drink. She gulped it thirstily, then lay back with a small murmur of relief.

"I've got to keep you awake, Sam. I'm sorry. Can you tell me what year it is?"

She kept her eyes closed, and her frown deepened as she seemed to struggle for this detail. Sloan's mouth went dry in fright until she finally answered, "1868." This was only March of the new year. Technically, she was only a few months off.

He tried again. "Tell me your name."

She opened her eyes sufficiently to glare at him for this stupidity. "Samantha Susan Neely."

He smiled at this return of the Sam he knew. "Susan. I

like that. I'll never understand why your father could name three beautiful girls by men's names."

She closed her eyes again. "Because he wanted boys. Because family tradition called for him to name his off-spring after his relations, and all his relations were men."

Sloan allowed himself a modicum of relief. Her first words after waking had terrified him, but she was slowly returning to normal. She was obviously in pain, and he hated keeping her awake, but he refused to lose her to that black unconsciousness again. The niggling of doubt at the back of his mind made him ask, "All right, Samantha Susan, tell me my name."

He saw a brief flutter of fear when she looked at him, then she threw up that stony wall of defensiveness she could do so well. "How should I know? I don't know you from Adam."

Sloan bent with the blow, but didn't break. She was alive. She seemed in control of most of her faculties. This was just a temporary aberration that would correct itself shortly. Carefully, calmly, he asked, "What is the last thing you remember, Sam?"

She lay still, as if gathering her thoughts. Then she tilted her head in his direction, and in a very soft, slightly fearful voice, she answered, "The wagon train. I remember the wagon train. It's sort of fuzzy though. I can't remember exactly . . ." She stared at him through the growing darkness. "What happened? Where is my family? Are they all right?"

He squeezed her hand to reassure her against growing panic. "It's all right, Sam. I told you everything is all right. They're fine and happy and waiting for us to get back to town. You got hit on the head after we found your valley, and you seem to have lost a few months. I'm sure it will all come back in a little while, after you've rested."

She clung to his hand and watched his every move as if he were all the world she knew. "My valley? We found my valley? Is that where we are now?"

Sloan nodded and grinned. The real Sam was still with him. She was just short a few months. "Right smack dab in the middle of it, sugar. You've got some cottonwoods and this tumbledown shack and a stream that probably won't dry up until August. I don't know a blamed thing about dirt, but you seemed happy with it when we got here."

She pushed up on her elbows, wincing slightly, but trying to look through the open door of the cabin. "I want to see it. How big is it? Will it hold horses as well as grain?" She looked at him worriedly, "If there are only cottonwoods, am I going to be able to get timber in here?"

"Whoa, sugar, one thing at a time. I don't want you moving at all just yet. It's too dark out there to see anything in any case. Let me bring you a bite to eat. You haven't had anything all day."

With no small amount of trepidation, Sam watched the stranger go outside. She felt as if she had fallen through a hole and come out on the other side without any idea of where she was or how she got there. She could be in China for all she knew. The stranger was the only concrete thing between her and reality. He seemed so calm and reassuring—as if everything was perfectly ordinary—that he made her feel better just by his presence. She didn't want him to leave her alone.

That he claimed to be her husband didn't terrify her as it ought to. Maybe that meant her mind accepted the truth even if she didn't recognize it. That made some sort of weird sense. She leaned back against her makeshift pillow and watched as he returned with their saddlebags and a bowl of something he'd apparently been brewing over the fire.

"Can you sit up?" he asked with concern as he threw the bags down in a corner and settled on the floor beside her.

If she had managed to catch a husband like this one, she must be the luckiest woman in the world. Aside from the fact that he was ruggedly handsome, he seemed to genuinely care for her. His eyes reflected his concern, his touch was gentle, and he spoke to her with all the sympathy and respect of someone who truly had affection for her. It seemed incredible that a man like this could have an interest in the Samantha Neely she knew, but maybe she had changed over these missing months.

She managed to sit up with his help. Her head hurt ter-

ribly, making it difficult to swallow the scrambled saw-
dust that passed for food, but she chewed obediently on
the hunk of bread he gave her and sipped at her water. His
nod of approval stirred an interesting warmth in her middle.

"You're going to have to tell me your name," she finally said in embarrassment. "I don't remember you on
the wagon train, so we must have just recently met."

He seemed to retreat slightly into the shadows as he
sipped his coffee. "We met the day after you arrived in
town. We've known each other six months now. You
saved my life that day. We were married three months
later."

She'd been married for three months. She knew this
man intimately. And she couldn't remember his name. He
must be horrified. How could her wayward mind play
such a terrible trick on her?

"Are we happy together?" she asked as a way to break
the silence that threatened to separate them. "I should
imagine I must make a horrible wife. I'm not very domestic."

She could sense more than see the stranger's half-
smile.

"That's all right. I'm not very domestic either. We've
been known to yell at each other upon occasion. We have
our differences of opinion. But somehow, we manage to
get along. My men are even beginning to think you might
tame me."

That was good to know. Sam set her bowl aside and
curled against the wall. She smiled sleepily. "I've been
known to train a wild animal or two. Do you fit in that
category?"

"Probably. How's your head?"

"It's still there," she said wryly.

"I think I've kept you awake long enough. You'll probably want to go outside before you go back to sleep,
though."

Before Sam knew what he meant to do, he was lifting
her from the pallet and carrying her out the door. She
couldn't imagine any man lifting her, but it felt right. She
wrapped her arms around his neck and released him only

when he lowered her to the ground on the far side of the cottonwoods.

"I'll be right over there. Call me when you're done, and I'll carry you back." He walked off into the darkness of the trees.

She hadn't forgotten what it was to use the ground as her privy. The fact that this stranger knew what she needed should have embarrassed her, but his straightforward practicality made the intimacy seem natural. When she was done, she washed her hands in the stream, but she didn't seem to be strong enough to dare broaching the stand of trees. Still, she didn't know what to call the stranger and had to settle for saying, "I'm ready."

He was there in an instant, his strong arms swinging her from the ground and holding her safely against his chest. Samantha rested her head against his shoulder and thought she could lie here for the rest of her days. She ought to be terrified. Instead, she felt safe and protected. It was a rewarding change after months and years of being the protector.

When he returned her to her pallet and began to arrange a blanket on the other side of the room for himself, she frowned slightly. "Are we in the habit of sleeping apart?" she asked with a trace of suspicion.

He hesitated before turning to look at her. She could see little of his stark features, but sensed the caution in his reply.

"You don't even remember who I am, Sam," he answered gently. "I don't know what the etiquette books say, but I think you'd be a trifle uncomfortable sleeping with a stranger. I'd best wait until you recover."

"What if I don't recover?" she murmured sleepily into her pillow. It was a question that ought to make her fearful, but she was too tired to confront it in its entirety.

She heard the amusement lacing his reply. "Then I'll just have to court you and marry you all over again. Everybody in town got such a kick out of it last time, I'm sure they'd be delighted if we repeated the performance."

She laughed softly because it sounded as if the memory pleased him. She'd chosen the right man, and it seemed as if he had chosen her, too. It made her feel good knowing someone outside her immediate family could want her. She fell asleep instantly.

Sloan wasn't so fortunate. He lay awake far into the wee hours of the night, contemplating the implications of what was happening.

It was almost as if he'd been given a second chance to do what was right. He didn't want to muff it, but he had a terrible aching dread that was just what he was going to do.

Sam woke up before the stranger. Her husband, she had to remember. It seemed odd to have a husband she didn't remember, but then, it seemed odd to be in this shack with nothing familiar anywhere around her.

The ache in her head had faded to a dull throb. She managed to get herself up without falling flat on her face, but her stomach roiled at the motion. She got to the stream before she heaved up last night's supper.

Feeling slightly better at ridding herself of that burden, she answered nature's call, washed, and went in search of coffee. Men liked coffee in the mornings. She remembered that much, even if she didn't remember her husband's preferences.

He was already up and starting the fire when she returned to the cabin. Sam felt him studying her as she approached, and she wished she could look beautiful and alluring for his benefit, but she felt more like something the cat had left.

She shoved her hair out of her face and realized how much longer it was than she remembered it. She'd chopped the blamed stuff off before they crossed the Missouri. It was down to her shoulders now. That thought made her stomach roil uneasily again.

"Is there a coffeepot? I can start breakfast."

The stranger relaxed slightly, but wariness still lingered about his eyes as he handed the pot to her. "We've got some cornmeal and bacon. Once the men figure out how to get supplies over the wall, we'll have a better selection."

She had been so wrapped up in the worries of her relationship to this man, that she had forgotten another world

existed out there. She looked around her with interest.
The cottonwoods formed a shelter around the cabin, but
beyond them, she could see acres of fallow land. Acres.
Hers. That felt good to know.

Her mind finally focused on what he was saying, and
she tried to comprehend it. "What wall? Didn't we bring
enough supplies to stay?"

"Fill the pot, please, Sam. It may take all day to answer
your questions, and I'm a starving man."

Of course. Feeling foolish, Sam went to the stream and
filled the pot and returned to set it over the fire. She
wasn't used to having a husband. She wasn't used to
doing her own cooking. Her mother and the twins had always handled that task more than adequately. Surely she
must have learned to change her ways these last months.

While she cooked their breakfast, her husband explained the rock slide cutting them off from his men.
While he talked and sipped his coffee, she noticed that he
moved with some degree of pain. Evidently he hadn't
come through the disaster without injury either.

"You'd better take your shirt off and let me look at
those bruises," she said as casually as she dared when she
handed him his breakfast. "You might have broken a rib
or two."

He shrugged. "I've checked. Far as I can tell, they're
just bruises. They'll go away after a while."

She sat back on her heels and frowned at him. "How
can you tell? You're barely able to move. I'm not much
of a nurse, but I know how to wrap ribs and bandage
holes in your carcass."

He gave a sudden, fleeting smile. "I know. Your healing touch took care of me that first day we met. Sit back
and eat, Sam. I'm a doctor. I'd know if I'd broken a rib
or tore a ligament. And I know your head aches like hell
right now. You shouldn't be doing anything but resting."
An uncertain frown replaced the smile. "Do you hurt anywhere else? Are there any other pains bothering you? No
bleeding?"

Sam shrugged and sat cross-legged on the ground, taking her plate in her lap. "I'm not much used to having my
head hurt, and I think I bruised my tailbone, but that's

about it." She gave him a quick, darting look. "Seems to me you took the worst of it."

"I've got a strong back and a thick head. Maybe I'd better examine you again when you're done. You took a pretty nasty fall."

Sam squirmed uncomfortably. He was a physician, he'd said. She'd married a physician. That was hard to imagine. He was looking at her with questions in his eyes, and that same grave concern she had noticed the night before. But the idea of undressing and letting him examine her gave her butterflies in her stomach. She didn't think that was the way a patient felt toward a doctor.

She shook her head. "I'm fine," she said nervously.

He gave her another one of those tentative smiles. "Not something a courting couple would do, is it?"

She felt her cheeks redden. "Probably not." She forced herself to meet his eyes again. Just looking at him made her insides all fluttery. She tried to imagine a man like that touching her as a husband would, and she had nervous palpitations. She controlled them by saying, "I still don't know your name."

He gave her an odd look, stretched out his legs, and stood up. "I go by Sloan Talbott out here."

Sloan Talbott. The man who had driven her father out of town. The man she thought she might have to kill.

Lord Almighty, what had she done to herself?

Chapter Forty

"Don't look at me that way, Samantha," he warned. "You and I have covered a lot of territory these last months. Whatever you're remembering is only half the story. Don't make us relive it all over again."

She took a deep breath and nodded. She desperately wanted to believe him. Right now, he looked like a hero to her, a man she could trust, a man who cared for her. She didn't want to give all that up, not now, when she felt like a part of her was missing, and the whole world looked vaguely out of kilter.

"All right, but what if my memory never returns? What do I do then? It's all gone—everything that brought us together." She gave him a look of hope. "Is my father back? Was everything between the two of you settled?"

She didn't like the brief flash of guilt in his eyes. He was hiding something. But his answer—while worrisome—seemed honest enough.

"We'll settle it when he comes back. I have men out looking for him. They think he may be in Mexico. They should be back from there any day now."

"All right. I suppose if I'm your wife, I have to trust you. I don't think I'm much good at trusting anybody. Has that been one of the things we've argued about?"

"Not particularly. Upon occasion, you've been too damned trusting. I'm the ornery one. But that's going to change. You gave me one hell of a scare yesterday. I'm not going to risk losing you again." He held out his hand to her. "Come on. I think you'd better lie down and rest a while. I'd rather not have to explain these last six months if it can be avoided. I'd rather you just woke up and remembered it all so I could promise to change my ways. So let's see if we can get you feeling better."

She took his hand, liking the solid grip and strength of it as he hauled her to her feet. Her head only came to his chin, and she liked that, too. Daringly, she touched the bristling whiskers on his chin. "Forget our shaving gear, did we?"

Sloan froze for just half a second, then grinned a wicked grin. Bending slightly, he rubbed his whiskers against her cheek, then caught her mouth with his in a movement so swift she couldn't have stopped him if she wanted to. She didn't want to.

The kiss was intoxicating. She swore she'd never been kissed like this before. His lips were hot and hard, and his tongue traced her lips until she dared to part them. She tasted the coffee on his breath, felt the rough brush of his tongue, smelled the masculine aroma of his skin as he wrapped his arms around her and held her tighter. She flung her arms around his neck and pressed herself against him, surrendering totally into his embrace.

"Damn, Sam, you haven't forgotten how to do that," he muttered against her cheek when he came up for breath. "If we don't stop this now, I'm going to have you in there on that bed so fast we'll have both our heads spinning."

Her breasts were pushed so close against him that she feared he would feel the wild beat of her heart. But she didn't want to stop. She knew there was more, that he had been the man to show her what followed a kiss like that. Her breasts tingled in anticipation already. She rubbed them temptingly against his chest, easing some of their ache.

"Is that so wrong?" she asked innocently. "If we're married, we can do whatever we want, can't we?"

His expression was that of pure male frustration as he looked down at her. His hand roved upward to cup her breast through the thin gingham, and she arched eagerly into it. He groaned and returned his hand to her buttocks, where he pressed her more tightly against him.

"You don't even know who I am, Sam! I told you, you're too damned trusting. I don't want to make love to you just to relieve a simple itch. I want you to know who you're making love to. Do you understand?"

She pressed gently into his arousal, knowing what that hard ridge against her abdomen was. She felt the desire spiraling through her, the desire no other man had ever stirred in her. She didn't need her memory to know he told the truth. She'd made love to this man before and enjoyed every minute of it. Her body could tell her that without need of her mind.

"I don't want to understand," she pouted. She held up her left hand with the band on the ring finger. "That says I'm married. The rest of me feels married. Even if I can't remember what it's like to make love, I know you're the man who taught me."

He laughed dryly. "Maybe I ought to take you up on the offer. A man seldom has the chance to take the innocence of the same woman twice. I could teach you all over again, without the pain of that first time."

She heard the rough hunger in his voice, and it stirred strong desires deep inside her. Some primitive claim had been made between them, a primeval instinct of possession that branded her forever as his. She accepted this feeling more readily than any ring or words. She was his as surely as this land was hers.

"I'm ready to be taught whenever you're ready to teach me," she murmured near his ear, clinging to his broad shoulders. His hard body holding hers felt totally right. She wouldn't willingly be parted.

"Sam, you make an offer that would tempt the devil. It's only because I know you're still hurting that I'm going to resist this time. Don't tempt me a second time unless you really mean it." Sloan wrapped his hands around her waist and set her away from him. Desire mixed with concern as he studied her expression. "You haven't got any idea how much I regret telling you no. Maybe when your memory returns, you'll chalk this up as a point in my favor."

Sam wrinkled her nose and crossed her arms protectively across her chest. "You'd better hope it returns then, 'cause it's a point against you at the moment." Looking away to distract herself from the temptation of his proximity, she gazed out over the land that he said was hers. "I want to explore. I don't want to sleep."

"Well, so much for the theory that amnesia victims are a clean slate," Sloan muttered grumpily. "You're Sam through and through. Just once, couldn't you listen to orders?"

She gave him a happy smile. "Nope. You've already turned me down once today. It's my turn now."

Running his hand through his hair to keep from touching her, Sloan managed a matching smile. "Damn, but I should have taken my chances and told you I was a complete stranger. I must be some kind of fool. I've got to go see what they're doing over at the wall. Will you grant that going all the way across the valley is a little too strenuous for you at the moment and agree to stay right around here?"

She would grant that. She wasn't even certain she could manage a horse at the moment. She'd just wanted to exert her wishes for a change. She liked knowing he would listen. She nodded. "I may be stubborn, but I'm not dumb. I won't wander far."

He didn't look particularly relieved, but he accepted her promise. He rode off after issuing only half a dozen more warnings.

The blockade of rocks wasn't easily removed, even with carefully placed blasting powder. The loose wall still left at the end of the day was too dangerous to try to get Sam over it. Sloan gritted his teeth in frustration, but privately, he thought it might be better that they had this extra time. He would prefer to have Sam in complete charge of all her mental faculties by the time they returned to town.

He wasn't granted that wish either. She had supper ready for him when he returned to camp, but she still remembered nothing of their time together. Resignedly, he admitted that it might take a return to town to jog her memory.

"I think I can raise grain and horses," she said complacently as they ate their meal. "It looks like there's the remnants of an old paddock on the other side of the stream, and the foundation for a barn or stable. My father said it was once part of an old Mexican land grant. Apparently, the previous owner hasn't used it in a generation or two."

Sloan wanted to tell her that it appeared to him that he actually owned the land according to the deeds he possessed, but it was a moot point at best. He meant to make her his wife. What was his would be hers. He couldn't believe he was thinking this, not after Melinda, but material possessions no longer held the same attraction for him. Without Sam, the land was worthless to him. The blow to Sam's head had either restored his senses or made him crazy.

"You're about a two-hour ride from town out here. Are you going to like living so far from people?" Not that Sloan intended her to live that far from him, but he played along with the Sam of six months ago.

She shrugged. "I get along with animals and plants better than I do people. Once my father comes back to look after my mother and the twins, I'll be able to move out on my own." She looked startled at her own words and glanced up at him with shock in her eyes. "What about you? I mean, I must be living with you in town. Were you going to move out here? Isn't this a little far for a physician?"

Sloan allowed himself a small smile at this sudden concern for him. "I'm not a practicing physician. I'm the town bully. They'll be glad to see the back of me if I settle out here with you. I just don't promise to be much of a farmer. This isn't too far from my mining operation and the lumber mill. I've got some cattle I could move in here if they don't interfere. Will you let me live out here with you?"

Her eyes widened. "A wife's place is with her husband. Of course we'll live together. I was just a little worried . . ." Her voice trailed off as she tried to explain all the things she didn't know and didn't understand.

"Don't Sam. Don't worry. I mean to make everything work out for us. If your memory doesn't return, I'll take you down the mountain to a real priest and a real church, and we'll stand up in front of the whole congregation and say our vows together and start all over. And if your memory does return, remember what I've just said, because I mean it. That damned explosion may have closed your mind, but it sure as hell opened mine. I'm going to do things right when we get out of here."

She looked pleased, a little startled, and a little frightened. "Are you saying things weren't right for us before we came here?"

"I blamed you for things that weren't your fault, and blamed myself for things beyond my control. I'm not a very good person, Samantha. I haven't been for a long time. I mean to change all that now that I have you."

"A cat can't change its stripes," she said doubtfully.

"He can if they were painted on. I'm going to change, Sam, but the world out there isn't. They're going to still think of me as I was, still believe what they knew before. I'm going to have to unravel some things that have been knotted for a long time. It may take me a while, but I hope you'll trust me."

"You're not an outlaw or anything, are you?" she asked, puzzled.

"No, just a fool and the town bully, as I told you. But you've taught me a few good lessons these last months. They didn't all sink in until yesterday, but I'm not likely to forget again."

She offered a sleepy smile. "Well, I'm glad I'm good for something. There's been times I had my doubts. Have you taught me any lessons I should remember?"

"That's a loaded question if I've ever heard one," he said with amusement, unable to hold back a grin at the flicker of mischief in her eyes. "I'll teach you plenty after we stand in front of that priest. You'd better get on to bed now."

Sloan sat beside the fire until he was certain she slept. It took a while to wash painted stripes out of a cat, he figured. There was no point in pushing temptation too far.

He was scared—damned scared. He hadn't ever meant to take another human being into his protection again. He didn't want the responsibility. He didn't want the pain. He'd fought it with every ounce of his strength for six months. Hell, he'd been fighting it in one manner or another for ten years. By all rights, he should keep on fighting. If Sam's memory returned, she might throw all his tentative plans in his face, and he'd be free again.

He didn't want to be free again. He didn't want to return to that lonely existence. He'd rather be scared half out of his wits than return to what he had been these last years.

They had a safe opening into the valley by noon of the next day. Sam's memory hadn't returned, and Sloan could tell she still suffered some pain, but she insisted on mounting her horse and riding out with him. The men waiting outside cheered as she appeared, and she looked disconcerted and a trifle frightened, but Sloan caught her reins, leaned over, and kissed her cheek. Then she relaxed. He didn't want to think how it must feel surrounded by a sea of strangers who knew more about her than she did. It was easier for the moment if they didn't explain. He led her horse down the trail and let the men pack up and follow behind them as they would.

"They all know me," she whispered when the path widened enough for Sloan to ride beside her.

"It won't take you long to remember them. I'll tell you who they are now, and remind you when they come around, and pretty soon you'll have their names down just fine."

She nodded uncertainly and squeezed his hand when he reached over and took hers. Holding hands seemed to be one of those fundamental elements cementing a relationship, Sloan decided as they rode that way until the trail separated them. He was going to remember to hold her hand more often.

The town poured out to greet them as they rode in. Sloan watched worriedly as Sam slid from her horse and ran to her mother, but she seemed to have no problem recognizing her family. As he dismounted, he watched them hug and kiss and exclaim excitedly on three different topics at once. Amusement curled his lips. If Sam could manage a conversation like that, she didn't need her memory of these last months. Her mind was quite capable of filling in the blanks without it.

He felt a tug of warmth when she turned around to search for him, going so far as to reach out and hug his waist while she chattered about an adventure she didn't really remember. Sloan sensed her need for reassurance and hugged her back, filling in the details of her story as if accustomed to this kind of family gathering. Alice Neely looked at him oddly, but Sloan didn't care. He wasn't a stranger to uphill battles.

He claimed his ground and took up his battle stance at the first opening in the conversation. With his arm still sheltering Sam, Sloan announced, "I better get Sam into bed. She took an ugly blow to the head and ought to rest. We . . ."

Whatever he meant to say trailed off as a horse came galloping up the mountain full speed, its rider shouting incoherent warnings.

Behind them Joe shouted to a few of the men still sitting their horses, "Get down there now! Don't let any strangers in here without a full guard. We'll let them know we're not going to take any more of this."

Sloan felt the questioning looks of the townspeople surrounding them. Joe obviously hadn't spread the news that the rockfall hadn't been accidental, but had taken it upon himself to post guards on the road. After what happened to Sam, Sloan couldn't blame him. He wanted to know every damned man who came into this town from now on.

It didn't take long to discover who the intruders were. Sloan groaned mentally as he recognized the tall man sitting stiffly on the spirited stallion, obviously harboring a load of resentment at the guns bristling around him. But it was the second figure who gave him the worst palpitations. He wasn't riding the beautiful horse he had last ridden through here. His lanky frame was even lankier, and his formerly erect posture seemed to sag with illness or weariness now, but Sloan didn't have any doubt as to whom he was seeing.

The twins' shrill cry of "Daddy!" notified everybody else.

Emmanuel Neely rode into town under Sloan's armed

escort, and the fury in his eyes belied the weakness of his posture.

Sloan clasped Samantha closer to his chest and waited for the axe to fall.

Chapter Forty-one

"**G**et your filthy hands off my daughter, you dirty, lying, conniving ..." The tirade halted briefly as Neely dismounted and shoved his way through the armed guards to push Sam aside and grab Sloan by his shirt front.

Samantha screamed and grabbed her father's arm, pulling him away from Sloan. It was all coming back to her now in horrifyingly incomprehensible chunks, but she knew one thing of a certainty: Sloan was her husband. She placed herself firmly between the two men.

"Daddy, stop that! If it weren't for Sloan, you wouldn't be here right this minute."

Alice Neely came to stand beside her husband, and Emmanuel caught his wife's shoulders, as much for support as in greeting. He continued to glare at Sloan over Sam's shoulder. "Hawkins is the one brought me, not that damned monster of depravity. Get away from him, Samantha. He's shamed you. He's shamed this family. And I'm going to tear him limb from limb."

Sam glanced nervously over her shoulder at Sloan. She wasn't precisely certain to what her father referred, but the expression on Sloan's face told her he knew. She knew uneasiness, as if the memory was right there. He had told her he'd made mistakes and that he'd meant to correct them. And she was remembering things now. She was remembering the fire and how he'd saved Jack at the risk of his own life. She remembered the epidemic and his distraught reaction to the loss of the infant. And she remembered other things, too. Her cheeks blazed with those memories, and he gave her a slightly rueful look now as he noted the color.

"It's all right, Sam," he murmured near her ear. "I don't know what you're remembering, but I like the way you're looking at me. I'll fix this. You just go on over to the hotel and get some rest. I'll be there in a little while."

She shook her head firmly as her father tried to reach around her to grab Sloan again. "I'm not going anywhere until Daddy does. He looks like he needs a good deal more rest than I do."

Emmanuel Neely gave a roar of rage when, at a nod from Sloan, one of Sloan's men caught Neely's arm to escort him to the house and away from Sam. Impatient, Sam stomped her foot and glared at both men. "Stop it, both of you! This isn't a game of tug-of-war." She turned to her mother for help. "Mama, can we go in the house?" She didn't want to say out loud that she didn't care to be made a public spectacle. Her mother would understand that. It was the people crowding around them that she didn't want to offend. She was having difficulty remembering who all of them were, but the memories were coming back fast and furious. She clung to Sloan's arm as the one sure ground in the swamp of her current existence.

She felt his worried look and gave him a faint smile she hoped would reassure. She didn't think it worked, but he followed her toward the hacienda, gesturing for his men to keep back, and that was all she wanted right now. Although once inside, she thought a glass of water and a seat would be very nice. Her head was beginning to spin dizzily.

Sloan seemed to understand without being told. He grabbed one of the velvet chairs and pulled it out from the wall, pushing her down into it before she could fall flat on her face. Her mother worriedly sent the twins after the required refreshment while she helped her husband onto the couch. Emmanuel seemed reluctant to sit, but she whispered some words in his ear that made him relinquish the floor, if not his furious glare.

With a gesture from Sloan, Joe kept everyone but the immediate family outside. Grateful for the sudden privacy, Sam leaned her head back against the chair and momentarily closed her eyes. Memories spun crazily inside her head, but she didn't have time to sort through them.

She clung to Sloan's reassuring hand and tried to concentrate on the relief of having her father home again.

"Get your hands off my daughter, you dagblasted double-dealer!" Emmanuel roared from his position across the room.

Sam jerked her eyes open again. "You can't talk to my husband that way, Daddy. I'll get up and leave the room if you do."

"He's not your husband!" Emmanuel shouted. "He's a lying son-of-a-gun! I'm going to kill him with my bare hands." He lurched from his seat and started forward.

Sending Sam a worried look, Alice Neely stood in front of her husband and caught his shoulders, holding him back. Sloan grabbed a glass of lemonade from one of the twins and gave it to Sam, then pressed her into the seat while he spoke. She was grateful for his interference. She didn't have any idea what to say.

"We'll send someone for a preacher right now if that's what you want," Sloan said calmly. "We'll be married in front of the whole damned town so there are a dozen witnesses. You can pick the preacher. But you aren't going to change anything. Sam is my wife, and that's the way it's going to be."

Neely shoved aside the offered drink. His eyes blazed fire as he watched Sloan rest his hands on Sam's shoulders. "You'd better ask my daughter about that, mister. Let me tell her what a crime you've perpetrated, and see if she doesn't take a whip to your hide."

Sam knew this was where she stepped in. She could feel the hesitancy in Sloan's hold. He didn't know how much she remembered. He was afraid of what she would do when she heard what her father had to say. She had memory enough to know they hadn't been living together, but she could also guess why. Sloan's emphasis on saying he would marry her all over again, and her father's charges now held enough clues. They'd lived together as man and wife, but they hadn't been married. She ought to make him suffer for that, but she had no difficulty remembering her feelings for this man. The anger she may once have felt was no longer there to cloak the depth of her love.

Sam wrapped her hands around Sloan's where they rested on her shoulders. "I already know, Daddy," she said confidently, even if she fudged the truth. "It doesn't matter. I love Sloan. If he wants me to be his wife, I accept."

The room erupted in an uproar of questions and excitement. Sam watched dizzily as her father leapt from his seat and lunged for Sloan again. Sloan came out from behind the chair to defend himself. Jack threw himself between them and the twins began screaming. Sam wondered idly where Hawk was. He could probably put an end to this battle. She was going to have to do it herself, she guessed. Her mother seemed on the brink of tears.

With a sigh Sam pulled herself upright, took two tottering steps into the room, and making a small noise of exasperation, started falling to the floor.

Sloan got there first. Dodging Neely's weak blow, he dived to catch Sam before she could hit the floor. With a curse of concern he gathered her up in his arms and started for the door.

Over his shoulder he flung the challenge, "I told you she's suffered a blow to the head. She needs rest and I'm going to see that she gets it!"

"You're not taking her anywhere until you stand before a preacher!" Neely yelled after him.

"Then you'd damned well better get one because she's going with me," Sloan yelled back, slamming the door after him.

All in all, Sam decided as Sloan stalked through the crowd still milling outside, it was an exceedingly embarrassing way to learn that the notorious bully, Sloan Talbott, really wanted her for his wife. He could have saved a lot of people a lot of trouble if he'd just done it right the first time.

She meant to tell him that just as soon as her head stopped spinning.

Sloan paced back and forth between the bedroom and his parlor, keeping an eye on Sam as she slept and watching the activity in the road below. He ached in every bone and muscle of his body, but it wasn't the physical aches bothering him. Guilt crawled at his insides. Sam had just loyally declared her love for a despicable cad in front of her entire family, and he wasn't at all sure that she remembered half of what he had done to her.

Hawk came up to make his report, but Sloan told him to get some food and take a rest in one of the hotel rooms until Sam awoke. He saw no point in telling the story twice, and he wasn't in any state to hear it now.

He watched as one of the twins came out to greet Hawk and lead him back to the restaurant. Sloan went back to the bedroom and watched Sam sleep for a while. She seemed to be resting peacefully. He couldn't disturb her, but she sure as hell disturbed him, lying there like that. She disturbed too many memories. Lust didn't even drive him now, although that always hovered there, beneath everything else. Fear was his greatest emotion of the moment: fear that he would fail Sam, fear that he had irreparably damaged the future, fear that he would never explain himself well enough to make her understand.

Lord help him, but he'd operated these last ten years on fear. He recognized that now. He hadn't kept women out of his life all these years because he hated the gender. He'd kept them out because he was terrified of what they could do to him. He had been running for ten solid years. He wanted to stop running. He wanted to face the horrors that had driven him out here and lay them to rest once and for all. Then maybe he would feel free to offer Sam the kind of life she deserved, if not the kind of man she deserved.

It was dark before she finally stirred. Sloan tore his gaze away from the lithe figure sprawled comfortably across his bed and went in search of something practical to do.

He had the boiler stoked and hot water running for her bath by the time Sam rubbed her eyes and sat up in the bed. She stared at him in confusion when Sloan led her to the newly added room behind the bedroom, but her eyes widened with delight as she gazed upon the huge claw-footed tub and the water pouring into it from the pipes the plumber had installed.

"Running hot water," she marveled, testing its heat with her fingers. "A real bath!"

Before Sloan knew what she intended to do, she began stripping off her shirt. He froze in longing as the dirty gingham fell to the floor, revealing the soft lace of her dainty chemise and the white curves of her breasts beneath.

When her trousers dropped around her feet, his gaze was diverted to long legs garbed in ruffled drawers and stockings. Sloan tried to force himself to look away, but she didn't even seem aware of his presence. Before he could move one foot backward, she propped her toes on the tub's edge and peeled off one stocking, then the next. Her calves were smooth and long, and he distinctly remembered how they felt when they wrapped around his hips. Blood surged instantly to his groin, and he nearly bent double with the exquisite pain of sudden arousal.

"Sam . . ." He tried to warn her, still unable to move. She merely turned and looked at him impatiently. "I don't suppose you have any bath salts, do you?"

He was going to be crippled for life. He was going to ignite in a spire of flame and go up in smoke right here and now. He was going to strangle one Samantha Susan Neely as soon as he recovered the use of his muscles. Sloan shook his head, having forgotten the question already as she peeled off her chemise and added it to the pile of discarded clothing.

That was it. He couldn't take anymore. His gaze came unfocused as he watched the full globes of her breasts bob and dive while she divested herself of her drawers. As far as he could tell, she was all breasts and legs that went on forever until he caught sight of that red thatch of hair before she climbed into the tub. He nearly erupted right there and then. With more dignity than control, Sloan turned his back and walked out, hobbling.

By the time she returned to the parlor—wearing the robe he kept on the bathing room door—Sloan had poured himself a drink and settled his throbbing loins into the room's most comfortable chair. God was punishing him for past sins, he knew. He would take the punishment like a man, even if it meant watching the enticing display revealed when his overlarge robe gaped as Sam sat down across from him.

"You don't look too good," she said worriedly, eyeing his tense and battered face.

"I don't feel much better," he agreed. "I've sent for some supper. Are you hungry?"

She shrugged. "I'll eat. Why are you staring at me like that?"

"I can't decide what to do with you first," he said slowly, "Bed you, murder you, or give you back to your father."

For one brief moment he managed to make her look slightly uncertain. Sloan gloried in that moment. It might be the last one he would ever have. He'd bullied, intimidated, and threatened her for six solid months. If she hadn't learned by now, she never would. He was ready to give up the attempt.

He watched the uncertainty disappear behind a satisfied smile when Joe knocked at the door with their dinners. Sloan kept his hand near his gun as he let him in. They still hadn't settled the problem of Harry Anderson and his hired killers, but right now that seemed a minor cause of concern compared to the one sitting right there in that chair. Joe gave them both anxious looks, but left without asking questions. For that Sloan gave a prayer of gratitude.

"Is this my last supper?" she asked mischievously as she cut a piece of steak.

Sloan kept a strict rein on the relief welling inside him. He wasn't off the hook yet. Sam was perfectly capable of shooting him down while she grinned. He took another drink rather than face the dinner tray.

"Maybe mine. How much of your memory has returned?"

She sat back and considered as she chewed her meat. He wanted to heave the food out the window to speed the process, but he waited patiently without saying a word until she swallowed.

"Most of it, I think," she answered with a frown. "Some things are still a little hazy. I haven't tried to piece it all together in order. There may be gaps." She turned a frank look to him. "I remember enough. What I don't understand is why you want to marry me now if you didn't when you had the opportunity."

Well, that got right to the crux of the matter. Sloan shoved his tray aside and walked to the window overlooking the street. There seemed more than the usual number of idlers leaning against porch posts and strolling through the plaza.

He turned back to face Samantha. She had made some attempt to brush her curls into order, but they made a silky nimbus around her face in the lamplight. He tried to imagine her sitting there like that every night for the rest of his life, and his heart yearned for that image of tranquility. He had to do this right, but he didn't see how he possibly could.

"I don't know if I can explain it," he told her honestly. "I told you once I was protecting you. You told me I was protecting myself. Maybe we were both right. You didn't know anything about me then. You didn't love me. You told me so yourself. I taught you the secrets of your body, and you were enamored with the mystery. I just wanted to keep you to myself and protect you from gossip until you woke up and realized what I was."

Samantha sipped her water. "Thank you for that high opinion of me," she said wryly. "I'd throw something at you, only I know you think even lower of yourself. What I can't understand is why. Having a two-timing wife isn't any reason to destroy yourself."

Sloan shoved his hands into his pockets and leaned against the wall. "That's because I didn't tell you the whole story. Harry Anderson is out there somewhere, probably eager to correct that lack. I'd rather you heard it from me, even if it means I'll lose you forever. At least this time I know you have your father nearby to look after you."

Sam pushed her food aside, curled up her legs in the chair, and folded her hands in her lap. "You'd better tell me you're a bank robber and a murderer if you think you're going to get rid of me that easily."

Sloan's jaw tightened painfully. "Worse. I didn't murder a stranger. I murdered my own son."

He saw the shock in her eyes and turned to look out the window. He didn't have the courage to watch his future smolder into ashes after all.

Chapter Forty-two

"You had a son?" Samantha choked the question out somehow. She could see the pain tensing the shoulder muscles of the man standing at the window. He was as rigid as any statue, and she thought he might fall just as hard with a good shove. She didn't want to shove him. She wanted to love him. Contrary of her, she knew, but she never had been one to do what was expected.

Sloan took a minute to answer. She could hear the degree of control he exerted by the stilted calmness of his reply.

"I thought if we had a baby, Melinda would settle down. Melinda thought if she gave me an heir, I'd leave her alone. As soon as she knew she was carrying a child, she moved out of my bed. Matters between us went from bad to worse after that. I'm not a particularly patient or understanding man."

Samantha made a crude noise in agreement with that. Sloan didn't turn around to acknowledge it. He merely hunched his shoulders tighter and continued staring out the window.

"We argued constantly. I thought Harry the cause of her discontent, and I ordered him to stay away from her. They sneaked around behind my back instead. I couldn't threaten to throw her out, and they both knew it. I wanted the child she carried. I started drinking to hide my frustration and anger.

"After the baby was born, things settled down for a while. Melinda was confined to bed, and I had my son to myself. I even contemplated buying the practice of a doctor considering retiring. I was still drinking, but not as much."

He finally turned around and faced the room. The light outside had grown dim, but neither of them lit a lamp. Samantha stayed where she was, knotting her fingers in her lap. She didn't know how to reach him, if she could ever reach him. But he'd already told her all she needed to know. He loved his son. He hadn't killed him in cold blood. Sloan Talbott had been capable of love once. He could love again.

When Sam said nothing, Sloan grunted and threw himself into a chair. His long legs sprawled out in front of him as he contemplated his boots. "Melinda recovered remarkably when Harry returned from wherever he'd been. The arguments began again. She wouldn't let me back in her bed. She was out running around town every night. We had nursemaids to care for Aaron. She never looked at him. I started drinking more. We were probably the two lousiest parents this side of hell. Then I came home early one night and found Melinda half dressed and in Harry's arms in the front parlor."

Shock and disgust rippled through Sam even though she remembered the night he'd told her about his wife and her stepbrother. Put this way, it seemed even uglier. She wanted to go to Sloan, hug him and tell him she would never be another Melinda, but he wasn't even looking at her. He was rejecting her with every part of his body: the nonchalant sprawl, the avoidance of her eyes, his hands curled around the chair arms. He didn't want her near him. So she stayed where she was.

"I learned to carry a gun while I was in Edinburgh. I was helping a doctor whose practice included some of the meanest streets in the city. I don't know why I continued carrying it in Boston. I shouldn't have. I was carrying a load of rage and violence around. I didn't need the burden of that gun, too."

He shrugged and reached for his wineglass. "The first thing I did when I saw the two of them together was pull the gun. Harry saw me in time and lunged for it. That was a stupid thing to do, but considering how drunk I was at the time, I suppose he thought he could stop me. He almost did. He shoved my arm up and away from Melinda before I fired. The bullet went through the ceiling."

Sloan threw down the contents of his glass in a single swallow and didn't even choke. His voice remained dead of all emotions as he finished. "Aaron slept in a cradle just above the parlor. The bullet was already blunted by the time it went into him. It tore a hole right thought his tiny lung. I heard him . . ."

For the first time, Sloan's voice choked and caught, as the mental images of that night returned. He'd picked Aaron up and held him, vainly attempting to stanch the flow of blood. He had screamed in anguish as the infant face slowly turned blue, and the tiny gasps for air became a rattle. He'd screamed and cried for hours afterward. Nothing would ever heal that pain. Nothing would ever return that tiny life.

Sam's eyes blurred with tears. She might be imagining the wetness on Sloan's cheeks. It was certainly the Sloan she knew who finally slapped his hand back to the chair arm to end the story. The Sloan she knew didn't cry, but slapped things around.

This time he glared at her. "I couldn't save him. All my years of education that had cost me my wife couldn't save my son. He died in my arms."

Tears poured down Sam's cheeks, and her hands shook by the time he finished. She didn't know if she could save him from the enormous load of guilt and bitterness he'd carried around all these years. She wasn't a soft, cuddly kind of woman like her mother and the twins. She couldn't go into his arms and make him forget Melinda and the past. She was terrified of the responsibility she needed to assume if she meant to make him understand she still wanted to be his wife. She didn't know how to heal with words or hands. She could start a fire and hunt a deer and ride a horse. She couldn't heal gaping emotional wounds.

But she knew how to be Sloan's woman. No other man had ever made her feel feminine and desirable. She knew how to distract him, even if she couldn't heal him. Maybe, in time, if she could make him forget about the wound long enough, it would heal itself.

She didn't have the words to comfort him, but from somewhere, she had to find the courage to reach out to him. He'd lived alone with this torment for too long. It was time he shared the burden. If she loved him, she could do it.

Awkwardly, not knowing how to go to a man and make him see her as a woman, Sam rose from her curled position in the chair. Seeing her movement, Sloan immediately came to his feet and started for the door.

"You'll want to get dressed and see your father. I'll give you some time alone."

She wanted to slap him. She knew how to handle this kind of blind insensitivity. Sam stepped in front of the door and crossed her arms over her chest.

"I'm not Melinda," she told him slowly and succinctly. "You don't turn your back on me, Sloan Talbott-Montgomery or whoever you are. If you've got a problem with me, you'll tell me right here and now and to my face, and we'll fight it out until it's settled. But don't you dare walk out as if I don't exist."

Sloan stared down at her as though she were crazed. She felt the moment when he was suddenly distracted by the gaping neckline of the robe. It made her feel warm and afraid at the same time, but she refused to back down.

"I know you exist, Sam. You've made yourself very visible for six months now. And if you don't get out of my way right now, you're going to be even more visible. I've only got so much restraint, and you've worn right through it."

That was an easy one to counter. He laid himself open for that one. Grinning maliciously, Sam pulled the belt on the robe and let it fall open. "Is this visible enough, or do you want more?" she inquired.

His look seemed stunned, but his hands knew how to respond. Callused fingers reached out to circle her breasts, lifting them with a gentle rasp of his rough skin against her smooth flesh.

Sam drew in a breath at this sudden intimate contact, but she didn't regret what she was doing at all. Heat flared between them, and that cold, detached look in Sloan's eyes became something else entirely, something hot and hungry and filled with longing. She could feel that look as surely as she could feel his hands on her.

With a brazenness she didn't know she possessed, Sam reached her arms around Sloan's shoulders and pressed her mouth to his. His shirt studs dug into her bare breasts, and the buttons of his pants pressed against her abdomen, but the slight pain of those pressures sent increased spirals of desire through her.

In the next moment her feet were off the floor, and Sloan was carrying her through the parlor and into the bedroom.

Sam clung to his neck without protest, pressing kisses anywhere she could reach. Sloan growled and dropped her against the sheets, but she rose instantly to her knees to help him strip off his shirt.

She didn't stop to study the powerful, hair-roughened chest emerging from the linen, but immediately attacked the row of buttons on his trousers. He ripped the remaining buttons open when the pressure of his arousal made the fabric too taut to manipulate easily. He was actually wearing drawers for a change, but with only a drawstring to hold them closed, they concealed and held back nothing. Sam stared in fascination at that male part of him looming before her as he dropped the last of his clothes, and then vaguely remembering one lesson he'd taught her on her own body, she leaned forward and kissed him there.

Sloan roared like a wild man. He shoved her back against the bed and covered her in a single bound. He tore at her mouth with his tongue and teeth and lips and tormented her breasts with his hands.

Sam opened her mouth for his possession, wrapped her hands around his shoulders to lift herself more readily to his touch, and spread her legs to feel him against her softness. She wanted him inside her. She wanted him now and forever and in every way possible. She would never let go if he would just give her that right.

When he drove into her, she was more than ready. He filled her until she thought she couldn't take any more, then proved her wrong and took her even deeper. She gasped and clung and tried to keep up with his frenzied thrusts until she lost herself in him and just let go.

He howled in ecstasy and carried them into that shattering space where they were neither one nor the other but both. The explosions of their bodies left them drifting weightless for long moments, healing moments, when all outer surfaces fell away to reveal the vulnerability beneath.

Gradually, as she recovered her senses, Sam felt the hard muscles of Sloan's bare arms wrapped around her. He had rolled his weight off her, but their legs were still entwined, and she luxuriated in the sensation of his hair-roughened skin rubbing her own. He was all hard male strength as he held her, but she had learned a few lessons of her own these last months. She had power over that strength, one she must wield wisely.

"Satisfied?" he murmured tauntingly against her hair when she stirred against him.

"Pig," she whispered without insult when his hand moved to cup her breast again. She thought she felt him shake with laughter, and satisfied, she curled closer into his embrace.

"Does that mean you'll marry me and punish me the rest of my days for my sins?"

"I don't doubt it," she answered calmly, exploring his chest with her fingertips.

Sloan didn't respond to that challenge immediately, but tested the weight of her breasts with his hand, then moved it intently down her abdomen. With studied deliberateness, he pushed and prodded until she shoved him away, glaring at him.

"I am not a prime candidate for your return to physicking."

Warm gray eyes watched her expression carefully. "No, you're not. You're pregnant."

Shock hit her like a cold wave. Sam stared back at him, letting coldness seep through her when she saw no emotion one way or another in him. She had a vague recollection of his saying he didn't want children. She glanced nervously down at herself. She couldn't see anything. Maybe her breasts were a little larger. She couldn't tell. "I can't be," she finally murmured in perplexity, returning her gaze to his.

"When was your last monthly?" His voice was calm, without any hint of expression.

She searched her erratic memory and shook her head. "I'd have to look at my calendar. I don't remember." Nervously, she searched his face again. "We took precautions. I remember that. It was a safe time."

Amusement began to kink the corners of his mouth. "What exactly do you consider a safe time?"

Her eyes lit with remembrance. "That's it! It was the end of January when we went to San Francisco. My monthly was nearly two weeks before that. So I couldn't possibly be pregnant. You're dreaming." But she had a sudden guilty feeling that wasn't right, that she had known differently for some time now. Biting her lip, she looked uncertainly to Sloan for confirmation of her words and not her feeling.

The laughter that had leapt to his eyes at her erroneous declaration died when he saw her uncertainty. Tilting her chin upward with his fingers, he said, "You're breeding, Sam. I don't know what you think your father told you about the right times of the month, but you got it all wrong. That was the worst possible time of the month. And if you haven't had any bleeding since then, there's no doubt about it. You carry our child. Does that make you unhappy?"

"Frightened," she admitted. "And I'm getting more scared by the minute. Are you going to hate me now?"

Sloan was startled by the question. Then his gaze softened to tenderness. "I love you, Sam. Anything you want to do is all right by me, but if you're brave enough to carry my child, I think I'll love you into eternity. You'll make a good mother even if I'm a terrible father."

Relief swept over her, relief so heady and overwhelming that she couldn't speak for a minute. She closed her eyes and let his words sink in, basking in them, letting them fill her soul with sunlight. Sloan Montgomery was a force to be reckoned with, a man of strength and intelligence and courage, a man any woman would be lucky to have. And he was hers.

It was scarcely credible. Plain Samantha Neely—loved

by a man like Sloan Montgomery. Her eyes flew wide again, and she stared up into his square-boned face.

"You're not just saying that, are you? Because of the baby?"

The worried look that lingered in his eyes a moment before turned to amusement again. "Of course, I am. Do I look like a fool? What man wouldn't tie himself up for life in return for a squalling, red-faced, shitting piece of himself rocking in a cradle? I can't imagine any other reason for loving and marrying the most beautiful redhead this side of the Atlantic, even if she is smarter than a brand new penny and twice as nice."

She swatted his chest and shoved him backward. "You're a hateful, despicable man, Sloan Montgomery. And just to get even, I'm going to love you until the hair falls off you head and you go wrinkled and blind. And I think I'll have a dozen children simply to keep you in line."

Roaring with laughter, Sloan let her climb on top of him, but it wasn't her pummeling punches he sought. Catching her wrists, he pulled her down until her mouth met his, and he could show her what she wouldn't believe otherwise.

Chapter Forty-three

"Why didn't he write?" Sam cried with as much pain as anger when her mother tried to explain Emmanuel's prolonged absence.

Sloan wrapped his arm reassuringly around Sam's waist and was rewarded by the slightest tilt of her weight in his direction.

They spoke in whispers in the empty restaurant/parlor of the hacienda while Emmanuel napped on the parlor couch.

"He did." Frustration wrinkled Alice's eyes as she glanced at her sleeping husband. "He wrote right after he left here, telling us not to come yet, to wait until he got back. He's been writing back home ever since. I don't know what happened to the letter telling us not to come, but the post office must not have known what to do with the others. They're probably sitting back there waiting for someone to pick them up."

Samantha groaned in despair. That was just typical Neely luck. She felt Sloan snuggle her a little closer under the guise of being helpful and let her frustration slip away. If they hadn't come to California, she wouldn't have met Sloan. She wouldn't be carrying his baby now. She gave a secretive smile at that thought. Her father was going to die when he found out.

She wore the gown Sloan had given her, and while he seemed appreciative of the honor, she wasn't particularly impressed. The skirt and petticoats kept her distanced from the man behind her. She wasn't ready to be separated from him for any length of time, not after a night like last night.

"You'll need to keep a supply of quinine on hand for

the malaria." Sloan's gravelly tones rumbled over her head. "It's the only thing that has proved effective. He's lucky to be alive."

Alice sent another anxious look over her shoulder. "I know. He pretends it wasn't anything, but I don't think he'll wander so far from home anymore." She turned a speculative look to Sloan. "If he really was shanghaied in San Francisco by those railroad people, is there any way we can prevent it from happening again? Do you think we ought to go back to Tennessee?"

That was an opportunity Sloan would have paid money for not so long ago. Sam leaned against his chest and waited with curiosity for his reply.

"No, ma'am, I don't want you doing any such thing. This town needs a good restaurant, I need someone running that store, and your grandchild is going to need more civilized influences than Sam and me. I think we can find some way to smack a few hands, and if your husband is anything like Sam, I figure he'll have a few ideas of his own on the subject. He'll be safe enough."

Before the words were entirely out of Sloan's mouth, the figure on the couch stirred, stretched, sat up, and growled like a grumpy bear. "What's that you're saying? You plotting behind my back already? Sam, where the hell have you been? I'll not have any child of mine living in sin. You get yourself away from that two-bit no-good until we can get the preacher up here."

"There aren't any two-bit no-goods in here, Daddy. There's just Sloan, and if he's going to be your son-in-law, he's got to be worth a whole lot more than two bits. I've got good taste." Her voice was at its sultry sweetest as she went to hug her father.

He hugged her, then glanced down at the gown she wore. "I'll be damned, girl, I'd almost forgotten you were female." He sent Sloan a black look. "But it's obvious he hasn't."

Sloan grinned. "Not by a country mile was I going to miss that fact, even when she was beating me at target shooting."

The front door burst open, and Jack came bounding in, scraping to a halt at a glare from his uncle. Still bouncing, he announced, "The preacher's coming! There's a whole gang coming up the hill!"

Sam glanced nervously at Sloan, but her father's sudden stride toward the door diverted her attention. Emmanuel looked immensely satisfied with himself, and she had just one more reason for nervousness.

As Sloan made his apologies and hurried out after Neely, Sam turned to her mother. "What's he planning now?"

Alice made no pretense of not understanding the question. His family knew Emmanuel too well not to recognize his expression. She glanced toward the window and the crowd of people forming in the plaza. "I don't know. He and that Hawk fellow seemed to be getting along pretty close. They were gone half the night doing something, but I don't have a clue."

She turned and gave her eldest daughter a swift look. "And if we're talking grandchildren already, I expect whatever he's planning comes none too soon. At least this time it involves a real preacher. That's Reverend Hayes out there."

Sloan wished he had a cheroot to chew on as he stood with the preacher at the end of the kitchen overlooking Sam's garden. The green shoots of her early vegetables could be seen clearly through the windows from here, but his attention was more on the crowd of people filing into this impromptu church. He hadn't thought the town had this many inhabitants.

The whole setup reeked of something fishy, but he couldn't put a finger on it. Neely had taken charge of the arrangements, sending Sloan off to get himself appropriately dressed. Donner's new kitchen table had been pressed into service as an altar. The new kitchen chairs as well as every other form of seating available in the entire town had been lined up in disorderly rows as pews, with what could pass for an aisle down the middle of them. But from the looks of it, a body couldn't pass down those rows of chairs without bending at the knees and everywhere else, they were set so close together. He supposed the arrangement worked, whatever it might lack in aesthetics. Sloan just couldn't see the purpose. It took only two minutes, three at best, to say a few words and tie the knot. Why in hell did they all have to have seats?

He was just getting itchy, he decided, twitching uncomfortably at his tie. Samantha ought to be here by now. Every crowded, cramped seat had filled. Joe and Hawk and a few of his more trusted men had chosen to stand and act as ushers, making certain everyone in the audience had chairs. They glanced over their shoulders now, waiting for Sam and her father. The few ladies present had been gallantly given front row seats, and they were sniffling into their lace hankies already. Sloan looked away from them impatiently. What in hell was that contraption on the ceiling?

Momentarily distracted by the phenomenon, Sloan almost missed Sam's entrance. Only the solemn chords of what sounded like a funeral march coming from a harmonica brought him back to the moment. He couldn't see the musician, but he could see Sam.

She was gorgeous. There weren't any other words for her. The women had pulled her hair up in fancy curls and sprinkled tiny silk flowers through it. They'd found white lace to cover the shoulders of the blue taffeta gown he'd bought for her and made up a bouquet of evergreens and silk flowers torn from every fancy gown in town, he surmised. The uncertainty wavering around the corners of her full lips disappeared when her eyes met his, and a smile brighter than a summer's day lit her entire face until even the blue of her eyes shimmered. Sloan felt the impact of that smile clear to his toes, and he couldn't look away.

She moved slowly, in time to the music. Impatiently, Sloan wanted to grab her hand and pull her up here beside him. Only the presence of Emmanuel Neely at her side kept him stranded where he was. Neely obviously meant to make a full production of this. That was fine with him. Let the whole damned town know she was his from this day forward.

Sloan held his patience by remembering Sam's whispered words of love during the morning hours while they lay entwined in his bed. He thought of the child she carried, the burden that would tie her to him forever, and which she accepted joyously if he read her smile right. He'd never known it could be like this. His heart hammered so hard as she approached, he was surprised no one could hear it.

That's when Sloan saw a movement behind her, the sudden rise of a shadow in the back row, the scraping of a chair as someone shoved out of the cramped seats to the aisle. His gaze jerked instantly to the disturbance. Scarcely another person in the audience noticed, but his nerves had been stretched beyond watchful to wary for months now. He saw a flicker of silver in sunlight, a shadowy arm lifting as Sam came to stand beside him. Sloan roared in fury and threw her to the floor, rolling so he took the brunt of the fall.

The explosion of gunfire in the high-ceilinged kitchen rattled the rafters. Sloan felt the jolt of noise, fully expecting the jolt of pain to follow. Instead, shrieks shattered his eardrums as a ghostly shape whizzed over his head down the haphazard aisle and careened into the shadow silhouetted by the open doorway.

A hundred-pound bag of flour now dangled where an arm pointing a gun had raised just seconds before. Propping himself on his elbows, Sloan blinked and looked again. He shook his head as Samantha wrapped her arms around his waist and buried her face against his chest. He looked again at the ceiling contraption, then back to the dangling flour sack and the recumbent body beneath it, and a noise began to choke his throat.

He didn't have to look for his prospective father-in-law. Emmanuel Neely was striding down the narrow aisle between the chairs with a gloating look of satisfaction. In the back of the room Jack triumphantly took his hands from what appeared to be a giant latch. From the back of the room Sloan's men converged on the gunman lying flat on his back in the aisle.

When Hawk reached beneath the dangling flour sack to haul the body up, Sloan gave a sigh of defeat. Anderson. Somehow, someway, his insane father-in-law in cahoots with every damned man in town had managed to do what

Sloan hadn't these last six months. They'd caught Anderson in the act. He just didn't know how.

And didn't care. With a grim look of determination Sloan stood up and pulled Samantha to his side, turning her to face the preacher. She looked at him in starry-eyed wonder, as if he hadn't been made an idiot of in front of the whole damned town. He supposed he had it coming, but he'd be damned if he would acknowledge their triumph until he'd got what he came for.

"Marry us, Hayes," he commanded.

The preacher looked nervously from the bridegroom to the father of the bride and the small riot in the rear. Sloan glared. Hayes opened his book and began to read.

The room gradually grew quiet as the crowd realized the service had begun again. Emmanuel Neely gave the prisoner a frown as Hawk and Joe hauled him out, then he hurried to take his place beside Samantha, giving her away with stiff pride and a glaring look at Sloan.

Hayes blessed the wedding ring again. Instead of the Latin of the mock ceremony they had shared the first time, he spoke the vows in words Samantha could understand. She repeated them solemnly, watching Sloan's face every minute. He felt he'd grown a foot in her eyes, and he swelled with pride. This was the woman he'd waited for all his life. This woman was his equal. She would stand by his side through thick and thin, but stand up to him when he was wrong. They would fight, he had no doubt about that, but they both would win when it came down to it, because every fight would be made with love. He personally meant to see to that.

Despite the tears in the front row, the rest of the room erupted in cheers when the final words echoed through the room and Sloan kissed his bride. Chairs clattered to the floor in the excitement as men pushed and shoved to the front of the room to stand in line for their share of kisses.

Sloan pushed Samantha behind him and glared at their audience. "I'll have Neely turn that damned thing loose again if you don't back out of here you bunch of layabouts! You don't really think I'm going to let my wife be mauled by the likes of you?"

With the widow on his arm, Doc Ramsey looked from Sloan to the still swinging bag of flour dangling from its precariously erected pulley on the ceiling, and shook his head. "I'm getting out of here before the roof comes down," he said to no one in particular, although his voice carried loudly enough to send a number of nervous glances upward.

That warning sufficed to start the musician playing a lively tune that quickly opened a path down the aisle. The twins grabbed the chance and, carrying baskets of colored confetti, spread a paper trail for the bride and groom to follow. More cheers erupted, and half the crowd followed the twins, forgetting the newlyweds and leaving them behind. Beside Sloan, Sam began to snicker.

If he looked down at her, he would do the same. Clutching her fingers around his arm, Sloan tried to keep the moment solemn as he elbowed his way out of the makeshift church, but when he stumbled over the flour bag at the entrance, he couldn't help himself. He cursed, and the laughter tumbled out of him.

Gunmen, miners, Indians, mad inventors, and flying sacks of flour marked this wedding day instead of the formal pomp of his previous marriage. He preferred the laughter to the polite phrases he remembered mouthing that day. He caught the amusement and questions dancing in Sam's eyes as they stepped over the flour, and he shook his head. He couldn't explain if he tried.

Grinning like fools, they walked into the hacienda, where the wedding party gathered.

Only then did he realize a silent circle had formed around the man bound and tied in the center of the room.

Sloan took one look and with a roar of "Anderson!" slammed his fist unerringly into the other man's jaw.

Chapter Forty-four

"So, what is going to happen to Harry Anderson now?" Sam asked as she sunned herself on the little balcony overlooking the hotel courtyard. The late June sun made her drowsy as she watched two figures wandering in and out of the leafy shadows of the vine-draped grape arbor.

Sitting on the lounge chair beside her with his back to the courtyard, Sloan was more interested in measuring the kicks of his child as he cupped his palm around his wife's rounded abdomen. "They can't hang him. He never managed to murder anybody. Until they find one of his hired killers, we can't even prove anything else against him but the one attempt. He had to have been half crazy to have tried that. They've locked him away for a while."

Sam turned a worried gaze to her husband's face. "That means he can get out and try again. Surely, they can do something more?"

Sloan leaned back against the railing and grinned mischievously. "We could have your father rig up some of those weird contraptions all over town and disarm all strangers."

"Daddy likes to invent strange weapons. I don't know how you dare let him near the mines. That doesn't solve the problem. What are you going to do about Anderson?"

Sloan was still grinning as he watched her. He grinned a lot these days, even when she frowned at him as she did now. "I could hand Harry over to your father. It was your father's damned letter to that friend of his in Boston that gave Harry a clue of where to find me. But I'm afraid your father would forget what to do with him. I've contemplated wiring Melinda and telling her where to find him. That would be sufficient vengeance in my book. She'd probably murder him single-handedly."

"But you said she'd run through all your money already. She couldn't come get him."

Sloan's expression grew a little more serious as he leaned over and brushed a straying curl from her face. "Sam, don't fret. Before your father even insisted on the wedding, I'd wired my lawyers in Boston and hired some in San Francisco. The ones in Boston say Melinda has already found herself another rich fool. Harry didn't realize he'd been replaced. She was as eager as I was to get that divorce agreement straightened out. She's no longer a Montgomery. I very officially gave you that name on our wedding day. Melinda is wealthy enough to do whatever she wants again."

"But you didn't wire her about Harry," she prodded. Her gaze drifted back to the figures in the arbor. She couldn't see them anymore. She frowned, but her attention turned back to Sloan when he spoke.

"After I told Harry about the divorce, he wasn't much interested in going back East. He had thought he would make Melinda a wealthy widow by knocking me off, and then they could finally marry. But he hasn't been slow about making female acquaintances out here. Harry and Melinda never did know the meaning of fidelity. There's always going to be someone to fall for good looks, fancy clothes, and a few sweet words."

Sam looked outraged. "You mean he spent six months trying to kill you, and pretty soon he'll be free to marry some poor innocent woman and steal her money?"

Sloan leaned forward and began circling an exploring finger higher than the rounded hill of her belly. "Do you really think I'd let him off that easy? You must think you've turned me into a real pussycat, sugar. What do I have to do to show you I'm not?"

She slapped uselessly at his hand. "Tell me Harry Anderson will never bother us again."

"Harry Anderson will never bother us again," he said in his most reassuring voice, moving his finger inexorably upward. "I've scared off the few decent women he courted. The only choice he'll have when he gets out is

Marvelous Mary. She made her money in the mining camps. A woman does not make her money lying flat on her back in the camps unless she's one tough female. She knows precisely what she's buying in Harry. He won't be able to touch a cent that she doesn't give him. Now don't you think you've had enough sun, Sam? Isn't it time to go inside for a nice siesta?"

Sam closed her eyes and enjoyed the sensations disturbed by his wandering hand. She could never get enough of Sloan's loving, and she knew she would give in to him time and again, but that didn't mean she always had to make it easy for him.

As his fingers eased open the fastening of her gown, she murmured, "Harriet is down in that arbor with Hawk's kid brother. You'd better go see what they're doing."

Sloan chuckled. "I know what they're doing. The same thing Bernadette and Donner are probably doing over in the wagon shed. Let Jack watch them. His head's been practically spinning for weeks now. Remind me to order some new anatomy books. Nap time."

Without waiting to ask her again, Sloan lifted Sam from the lounge and carried her through the open door to their bedroom. Sam gave a gasp of surprise and clung to his neck, but she made no other protest as he laid her across the bed. When he began unfastening his shirt as he stood over her, she merely watched him with her usual fascination.

"I wanted to get out to the valley to see how they're progressing with the house," she reminded him lazily.

"They're progressing very nicely without you. Joe threatened to turn it into a saloon if you didn't leave them alone. The field's planted, and Hawk's looking for a few good mares to bring up for breeding stock." He dropped his shirt and started on his trousers. "Are you going to get that gown off, or make me do it?"

Sam lifted one long leg and wiggled her bare toes at him. A portion of the skirt slipped backward, revealing a limb uncovered by stocking, or possibly anything else. "You do it. You're the one who wants to make me take naps. I don't suppose you can talk Hawk into staying this time? The way this town's growing, it's going to need a sheriff."

Sitting on the side of the bed to remove his boots, Sloan leaned over and slid his hand beneath her skirt, pushing one side of her gown up. No drawers. "Damn, Sam," he muttered under his breath and hastily started pulling at his boots. "He owes you one for letting him keep that damned stallion," he said out loud, more to distract himself than anything else. He couldn't keep losing control like this around his wife. He'd officially been married for three solid months already.

"He's promised to bring Gallant back when I need him for breeding. It wouldn't have been fair to leave a horse like that idle, especially since you won't let me ride anything faster than a mule. You're a stubborn man, Sloan Montgomery."

Finally undressed, he sprawled on the bed beside her and resumed unfastening the buttons of her bodice. "And you're an ornery woman, Samantha Montgomery, but I love you anyway. You didn't really think I was going to let you have our baby in the middle of a mountain trail while you scampered back and forth between the valley and town, did you?"

"I'm only five months along, you monster. What are you going to do, tie me to the bed at six?" Her fingers raked the unruly curls back from her husband's forehead as she spoke.

"Tying you to the bed sounds like an excellent idea." Sloan leaned over and applied his tongue to the portion of skin uncovered. "I'm going to remember that when you get too fractious."

She arched eagerly into his embrace for more, letting the flaps of her bodice fall open to reveal the scantiness of the chemise beneath. "No matter how much I love you, there are some things I won't forgive," she murmured, before his teeth took her breath away.

"Oh, you'll forgive that," he promised between nibbles, "especially when you see the bed I'm having delivered as soon as our house is finished."

"Bed?" was the last thing she remembered saying before he pulled her skirt up.

Later, when they were entwined in each other's arms and too lethargic from the aftereffects of lovemaking, they didn't even bother moving when a fusillade of what sounded like gunfire went off.

Sam opened one eye and scanned her husband's tranquil expression questioningly.

Sloan didn't bother opening his eyes. He just adjusted her more comfortably and murmured, "Chinese firecrackers. I gave them to Jack to use when he thought appropriate."

Sam closed her eye again. "I hope you warned him not to use them when Riding Eagle was wearing his gun."

Sloan chuckled softly. "Hell, no. The man ought to be given an even chance. Let Horace deal with the monster for a while."

"Horace?" Incredulity laced her sleepy voice.

"Riding Eagle."

She snickered.

He smiled.

And the town of Talbott slept comfortably in the golden California sun.

Except for Horace Riding Eagle and Jack, who were engaged in a mad footrace down the side of the mountain.

And perhaps for a few miners farther up the hill who were learning about a powerful new explosive called dynamite that would blast the gold right out of the ground. They'd already learned to distrust some of Emmanuel Neely's wilder ideas and currently edged backward toward their horses before he lit the fuse.

When the rumble of the explosion shook the whole side of the mountain sometime later, Neely was the only one left to watch the tower of dirt rise into the sky. Shrugging at this lack of a receptive audience, he pocketed a gold nugget to show Sam and started back down the trail on foot, the horses having all mysteriously disappeared.

He glanced up as a golden ray of sun shot through an opening in the canopy of evergreens overhead. California gold. He'd struck treasure here.

Let Sloan Montgomery think he owned this land. God and Chief Coyote knew better. But Sloan would take care of the mountain. Sam would see to that.

COMING IN AUGUST

Lord Satterwaite was stunned. He looked from Miss Hedgeworth's resolute, steady gaze down at the tearful, cringing girl. He said explosively, "You cannot possibly go down in that neighborhood by yourself."

"I can and I shall. Betsy needs the sort of help that Mrs. Savage can provide to her." Fredericka regarded the viscount with a sparkling of anger. "Come, my lord! You have already seen how disgracefully this poor female has been used. Shall I throw her into the gutter as well?"

Lord Satterwaite found that unanswerable. He had as much compassion as the next man, he thought, throwing another look at the fearful maid. From between clenched teeth, he said, "No, of course not. Nothing could be more monstrous. She shall go to Mrs. Savage. But I shall take her there."

This pronouncement threw Betsy into a fresh paroxysm of terror. She clung tighter to Fredericka, crying piteously, "No miss! 'e'll abandon me for certain. I'm a'begging you, miss, don't send me away wif'im!"

"I shan't abandon you, girl. I give you my word," said Lord Satterwaite in a hard voice. He wanted only to be done with this matter. There were still passersby and they were getting too curious.

But his assurance seemed to fuel Betsy's terror. "It were breach of promise. It were just what the other toff said, miss!" she cried. "Oh, don't send me off wif'im!"

"I do not think that I could, even if I wished to, such a hold you have of me," said Fredericka with a streak of humor.

The girl's screeching was beginning to attract fresh stares. "We must get out of here, Miss Hedgeworth. We'll have every nosy body in town upon us in another minute. Come, Miss Hedgeworth! Here is a hackney. I shall escort both you and the girl to Mrs. Savage's house." The words were bitten off with a good deal of exasperation.

Fredericka thanked the viscount gratefully. If the truth

was to be known, she was not perfectly comfortable with the notion of being driven down into the winding, narrow backstreets with only the helpless Betsy as her companion. She caught up her skirts and ascended into the hackney, urging the maid inside with her. As Lord Satterwaite made to latch the door, she stopped him. "Are you not getting inside, my lord?"

"I shall ride on top with the driver. I shall be better able to see trouble coming if there should be any," said Lord Satterwaite.

"Thank you, my lord."

"Have I a choice, Miss Hedgeworth?" There was an edge of temper in his voice, but nonetheless she detected a softening of his expression. Fredericka smiled at him.

Lord Satterwaite abruptly slammed shut the carriage door with unnecessary force.

During the jolting ride, Fredericka did her best to soothe and reassure the maid, but with indifferent success. The girl seemed to understand nothing beyond the fact that Miss Hedgeworth was the one person in the world at that moment who was disposed to treat her with kindness. The thought of leaving Miss Hedgeworth's protection kept her sniffling morosely.

By the time that the hackney reached its destination, Fredericka was exhausted by her efforts. She was never more glad of anything in her life than when the carriage door was opened and she saw Lord Satterwaite's silhouette. "We have arrived?" she asked hopefully.

Lord Satterwaite handed her out, and Fredericka saw that she was indeed in the dusty yard of the old coaching inn. "Thank God," she breathed, turning then to help the maid out of the carriage, the girl having refused the viscount's hand.

Lord Satterwaite obligingly stepped back. "She is still watering everything in sight, I see."

Fredericka threw him a look that was easily read, and he cracked a laugh. In impatient accents, Fredericka asked the viscount to escort them to the entrance. He politely offered his elbow.

A lantern was burning beside the door. The door was already opened to them and the same dour individual that Fredericka had noticed before motioned for the trio to come inside.

They did so and Mrs. Savage met them in the hall. The lady cast one comprehensive glance over the trio and ushered them into the parlor. "Miss Hedgeworth, this is an unexpected surprise. Pray make known to me your companions."

Fredericka introduced Lord Satterwaite and then drew forth the maid. "And this is Betsy. She is in the family way. It was discovered today and as a result she has lost her post."

Mrs. Savage lifted a hand. "You have no need to say more, Miss Hedgeworth. It is not an uncommon story, unfortunately." She glanced at the viscount. Her voice turned markedly arctic. "Had you aught to do with this, my lord?"

Lord Satterwaite looked at the woman, his teeth snapping together. Quite coldly, he said, "I am not certain what you mean, ma'am. If you are referring to the fact that I have provided escort to Miss Hedgeworth and this female to your door, then yes."

Fredericka realized of a sudden what Mrs. Savage was inferring. She intervened hastily. "It was not Lord Satterwaite who gave her a slip on the shoulder, ma'am. Betsy was an undermaid in Lord Comberley's household. His lordship has a son—"

"It were breach of promise, mum," interjected Betsy tearfully.

Mrs. Savage glanced down at the maid and her countenance softened. "Yes, my dear child. I see just how it was."

Some minutes before Mrs. Savage had pulled a bellrope and now the door to the parlor was opened to admit a portly dame. "Yes, Mrs. Savage?"

"Mrs. Stoueffer, this young woman is called Betsy. She is a former undermaid. Betsy would like some supper and a place to wash up," said Mrs. Savage.

"Of course, she would. Come along, chick. I'll see that you have nice cup of broth and some buttered bread," said Mrs. Stoueffer, coming forward to take the maid's hand and gently draw her away.

Betsy looked back uncertainly. Fredericka nodded reassurance. "You may trust these good ladies, Betsy. They shall see that you are cared for properly."

"Thank you, miss," said Betsy, dropping an instinctive curtsy. Then still teary, she went away with Mrs. Stoueffer.

When the door was closed, Mrs. Savage shook her head.

"That is a good girl. It is a pity that she was gotten into this predicament through blandishments and false promises," she said, sighing. Mrs. Savage turned once more to Fredericka and took her hands. "You have shown true compassion and kindness, Miss Hedgeworth. May the Lord bless you for it."

As though realizing that she had stepped out of her usual austere role, Mrs. Savage smoothed away her expression of sentimentality. "I shall not keep you, for I know that it grows late. You will not wish to be caught out in these streets too long after dark."

Mrs. Savage did not encourage them to linger, but neither Fredericka nor Lord Satterwaite would have wanted to in any event. Fredericka got back into the hackney. Lord Satterwaite climbed up on the box again with the driver. He rode topside until the carriage had left the worse neighborhoods behind. Then he had the hackney stop and he climbed inside.

As Lord Satterwaite settled against the musty seat squabs and the carriage set forth again, he commented, "There is scarcely a dull moment to be found when you are anywhere in the vicinity, Miss Hedgeworth."

Fredericka eyed the viscount askance. "I am not sure what you mean by that, my lord. It does not sound to be particularly complimentary."

"On the contrary. I never knew a Season to be so fraught with novel difficulties," said Lord Satterwaite. "I am becoming quite inured to it, I assure you."

Fredericka was amused by his air of resignation. "Why, my lord, surely you are not implying that I am the cause of upset in your untrammeled existence?"

Lord Satterwaite uttered a short bark of laughter. "Implying, Miss Hedgeworth? I rather thought I was quite clear on the matter."

"What a horridly boring time of it you have had, then," said Fredericka. "You should be grateful to me, my lord, for enlivening your life."

"I foresee that I shall end by wringing your neck, Miss Hedgeworth," said Lord Satterwaite thoughtfully. "How dare you tell that woman that I was not the one who had given that wretched female a slip on the shoulder?"

"Well, you were not," said Fredericka calmly. "Oh, you are thinking that I should not have used such warm language."

"That thought did cross my mind," admitted Lord Satterwaite with considerable restraint. "You should not even know such a phrase, but undoubtedly you have a perfectly good explanation for it."

Fredericka let that last comment pass, feeling it to be unnecessary to explain that the daughter of one of the tenants at Luting had found herself in just the same predicament and that the girl's father had been too distraught to watch his language.

"Well, I shan't do so again. It is just that the circumstances seemed to warrant a rapid and unequivocal disclaimer." Fredericka's glance was brimful of amusement, but she said meekly, "I was so concerned for your reputation, you see."

After a stunned instant, Lord Satterwaite said appreciatively, "You little wretch."

Fredericka laughed then. "I'm sorry! But you must see the exquisite irony."

"I do. Believe me, I do!" There was a peculiar glint in Lord Satterwaite's eyes, compounded of humor, frustration, and something else. Before Fredericka guessed what he had in mind, he had tilted up her chin with his long fingers and kissed her thoroughly.

"Oh!" She drew back, blushing hotly.

In the passing lamplight, he observed this phenomenon with satisfaction.

The carriage was slowing. They were nearing their destination, it seemed. "Let that be a lesson to you, Miss Hedgeworth. Playing with fire has its inevitable consequences," he said.

Before Fredericka had sufficiently recovered possession of herself, his lordship had opened the door of the carriage and leaped down. Lord Satterwaite held up his hand to aid her descent. Very much on her dignity, Fredericka refused to look into his face.

Astonishment was giving way to anger that he should have treated her so freely, but she could not speak to him as she had in mind to do. There was such a confusing riot of emotions inside her that she recognized the sheer impossibility of addressing the viscount in any very coherent manner.

Lord Satterwaite escorted Fredericka up the front steps, but he declined to enter at the butler's invitation. Instead he took punctilious leave of Miss Hedgeworth. Taking her gloved hand and raising her fingers to his lips, he said, "I have rarely spent such an interesting evening at the opera, ma'am."

Her color considerably heightened, Fredericka swept into the town house.

LOVE AND DANGER . . .

☐ **STOLEN HEARTS by Melinda McRae.** Death was his enemy, and Stephen Ashworth fought it with all his skill as a surgeon, though his methods made some call him a devil. Lady Linette Gregory felt the young doctor must be stopped, and she was the woman to do it. Linette and Stephen were rivals—yet when they were thrust together to save a young girl's life, a tenderness blossomed . . .   (406117—$5.50)

☐ **PRINCE OF THIEVES by Melinda McRae.** "Gentleman Jack" and Honoria are playing a hazardous game of deception, but together they are dis-covering the desire between them is no game.   (404890—$4.99)

☐ **DARLING ANNIE by Raine Cantrell.** When the likes of Kell York, leanly built, lazily handsome with a dangerous streak, meets up with the beautiful barefoot girl Annie Muldoon, she is not what he expected. Neither was the gun she pointed between his eyes when he insisted he and his "soiled doves" be allowed to move into Annie's boarding house. But both of them soon learn that true love changes everything.
                                              (405145—$4.99)

☐ **DAWN SHADOWS by Susannah Leigh.** Maria McClintock is as beautiful and free-spirited as the windswept Hawaiian island of Maui where she was born and raised. And soon she catches the eye and wakes the lust of powerful planter Royall Perralt, who traps her in a web of lies and manipulations to get what he wants.   (405102—$4.99)

*Prices slightly higher in Canada

WE NEED YOUR HELP

To continue to bring you quality romance
that meets your personal expectations,
we at TOPAZ books want to hear from you.
Help us by filling out this questionnaire, and in exchange
we will give you a **free gift** as a token of our gratitude.

- Is this the first TOPAZ book you've purchased? (circle one)

    YES   NO

    The title and author of this book is: _____

- If this was not the first TOPAZ book you've purchased, how many have you bought in the past year?

    a: 0 - 5   b 6 - 10   c: more than 10   d: more than 20

- How many romances in total did you buy in the past year?

    a: 0 - 5   b: 6 - 10   c: more than 10   d: more than 20 ____

- How would you rate your overall satisfaction with this book?

    a: Excellent   b: Good   c: Fair   d: Poor

- What was the main reason you bought this book?

    a: It is a TOPAZ novel, and I know that TOPAZ stands
        for quality romance fiction
    b: I liked the cover
    c: The story-line intrigued me
    d: I love this author
    e: I really liked the setting
    f: I love the cover models
    g: Other: _____

- Where did you buy this TOPAZ novel?

    a: Bookstore   b: Airport   c: Warehouse Club
    d: Department Store   e: Supermarket   f: Drugstore
    g: Other: _____

- Did you pay the full cover price for this TOPAZ novel? (circle one)

    YES   NO

    If you did not, what price did you pay? _____

- Who are your favorite TOPAZ authors? (Please list)

- How did you first hear about TOPAZ books?

    a: I saw the books in a bookstore
    b: I saw the TOPAZ Man on TV or at a signing
    c: A friend told me about TOPAZ
    d: I saw an advertisement in_____magazine
    e: Other: _____

- What type of romance do you generally prefer?

    a: Historical   b: Contemporary
    c: Romantic Suspense   d: Paranormal (time travel,
        futuristic, vampires, ghosts, warlocks, etc.)
    d: Regency   e: Other: _____

- What historical settings do you prefer?

    a: England   b: Regency England   c: Scotland
    e: Ireland   f: America   g: Western Americana
    h: American Indian   i: Other: _____

- What type of story do you prefer?

  a: Very sexy
  b: Sweet, less explicit
  c: Light and humorous
  d: More emotionally intense
  e: Dealing with darker issues
  f: Other

- What kind of covers do you prefer?

  a: Illustrating both hero and heroine
  b: Hero alone
  c: No people (art only)
  d: Other_____

- What other genres do you like to read (circle all that apply)

  Mystery   Medical Thrillers   Science Fiction
  Suspense   Fantasy   Self-help
  Classics   General Fiction   Legal Thrillers
  Historical Fiction

- Who is your favorite author, and why?_____
  _____

- What magazines do you like to read? (circle all that apply)

  a: *People*
  b: *Time/Newsweek*
  c: *Entertainment Weekly*
  d: *Romantic Times*
  e: *Star*
  f: *National Enquirer*
  g: *Cosmopolitan*
  h: *Woman's Day*
  i: *Ladies' Home Journal*
  j: *Redbook*
  k: Other:_____

- In which region of the United States do you reside?

  a: Northeast   b: Midatlantic   c: South
  d: Midwest   e: Mountain   f: Southwest
  g: Pacific Coast

- What is your age group/sex?   a: Female   b: Male

  a: under 18   b: 19-25   c: 26-30   d: 31-35   e: 36-40
  f: 41-45   g: 46-50   h: 51-55   i: 56-60   j: Over 60

- What is your marital status?

  a: Married   b: Single   c: No longer married

- What is your current level of education?

  a: High school   b: College Degree
  c: Graduate Degree   d: Other:_____

- Do you receive the TOPAZ *Romantic Liaisons* newsletter, a quarterly newsletter with the latest information on Topaz books and authors?

  YES   NO

  If not, would you like to?   YES   NO

  Fill in the address where you would like your free gift to be sent:

  Name: _____
  Address: _____
  City:_____Zip Code: _____

  You should receive your free gift in 6 to 8 weeks.
  Please send the completed survey to:

Penguin USA•Mass Market
Dept. TS
375 Hudson St.
New York, NY 10014